BLITZ

Volume 3

Original creation: **Cédric BISCAY**
Illustrator: **Daitaro NISHIHARA**
Written by **Cédric BISCAY** & **Tsukasa MORI**

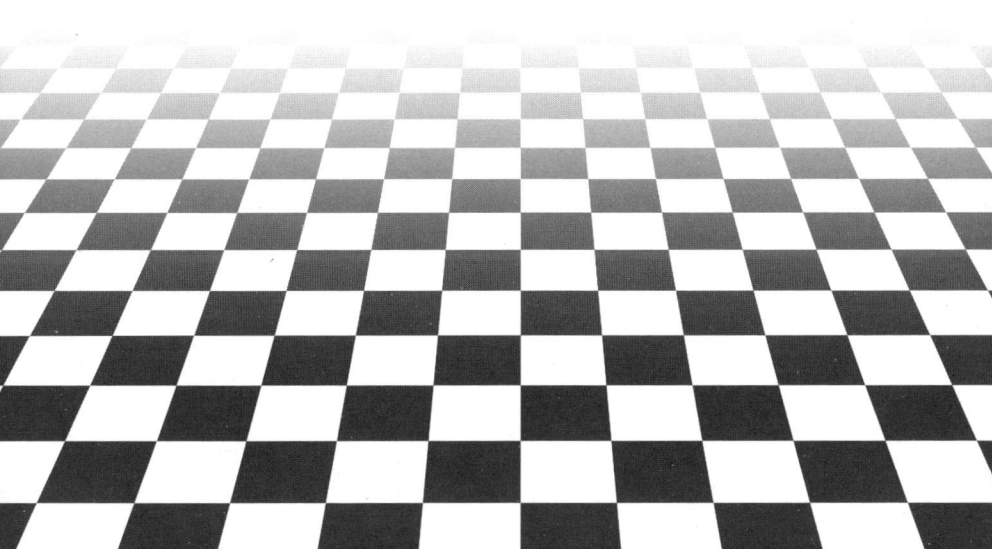

SUMMARY

Tom is a middle school student and a bit of a troublemaker. The young man decided to join the chess club at his school, the International School of Shibuya, in an attempt to get close to Harmony, the chess champion he is secretly in love with.

In the meantime, Garry Kasparov decided to start his international tournament for young players, which will take place in the Monte-Carlo Casino.

Tom's astounding progress allows him to take part in the qualifying Kantou tournament, along with his teammates. He ends up stumbling into Kou, the boy he fought with and who caused him to lose the good luck charm Harmony had lent him. Tom sees Kou as his nemesis, and wants to crush him. However, he will need to get to the finals in order to accomplish that.

While playing under the watchful eye of Karl, the junior chess champion who came incognito, Tom manages to pull off an incredible move…

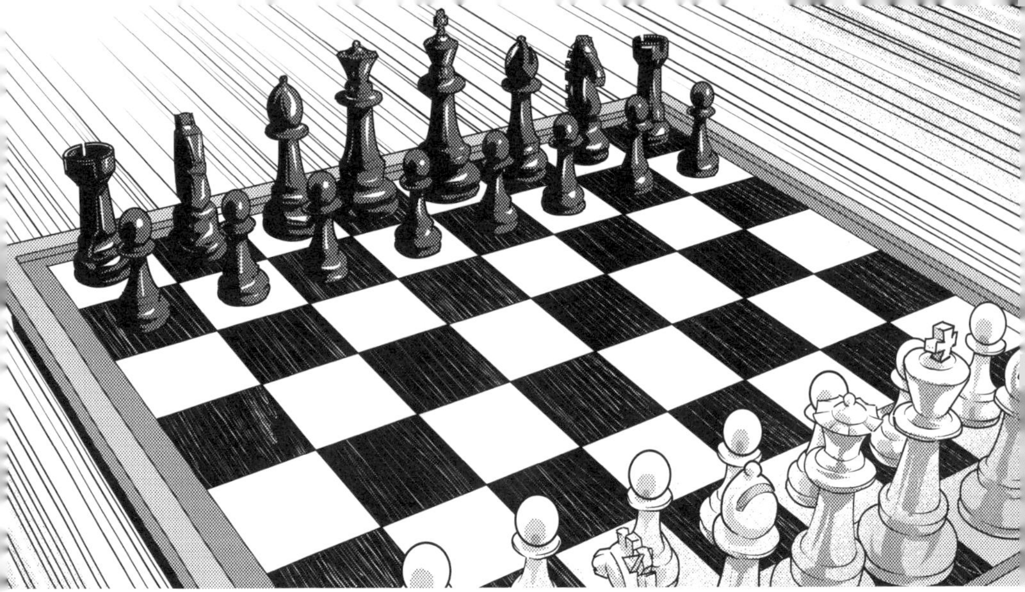

CHARACTERS

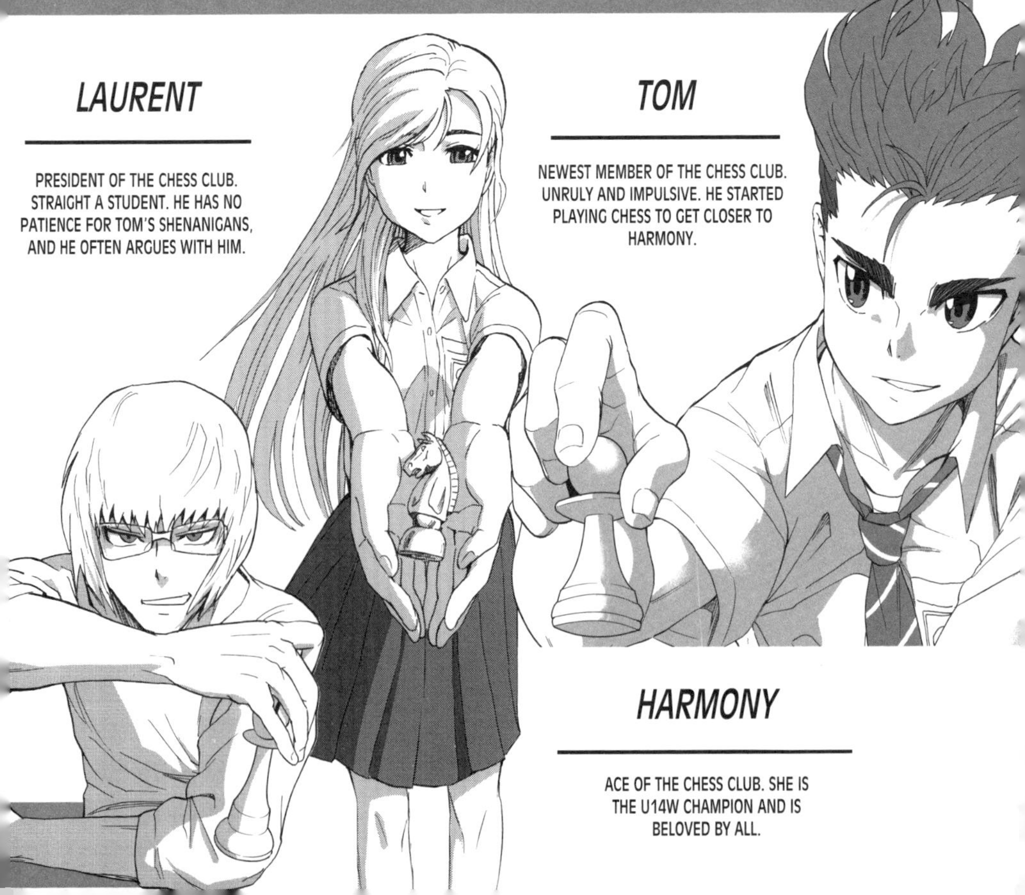

LAURENT

PRESIDENT OF THE CHESS CLUB. STRAIGHT A STUDENT. HE HAS NO PATIENCE FOR TOM'S SHENANIGANS, AND HE OFTEN ARGUES WITH HIM.

TOM

NEWEST MEMBER OF THE CHESS CLUB. UNRULY AND IMPULSIVE. HE STARTED PLAYING CHESS TO GET CLOSER TO HARMONY.

HARMONY

ACE OF THE CHESS CLUB. SHE IS THE U14W CHAMPION AND IS BELOVED BY ALL.

RIKO

PRESIDENT OF THE NISHIMATSU MIDDLE SCHOOL CHESS CLUB. SHE IS ALSO A RENOWNED PLAYER ON THE INTERNET.

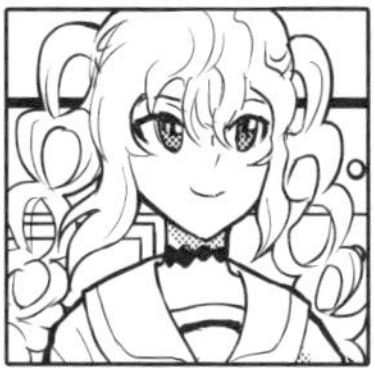

KOU

MEMBER OF THE TOUTO MIDDLE SCHOOL CHESS CLUB. HE HAD AN ALTERCATION WITH TOM BEFORE THE START OF THE TOURNAMENT.

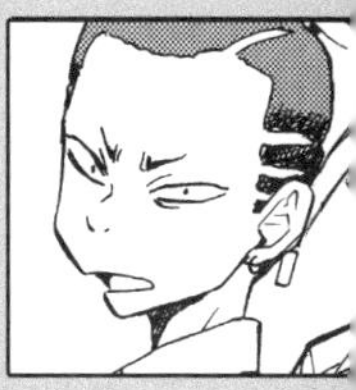

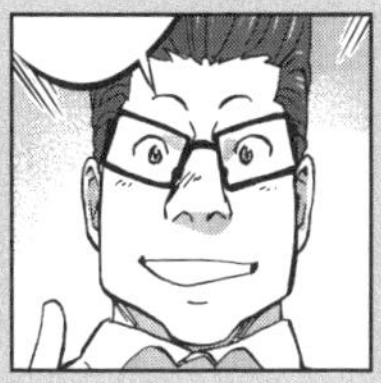

MISTER DOYLE

CHESS CLUB ADVISER. FRIEND OF JEAN-MARC. CHEMISTRY PROFESSOR AND TOM'S HOMEROOM TEACHER.

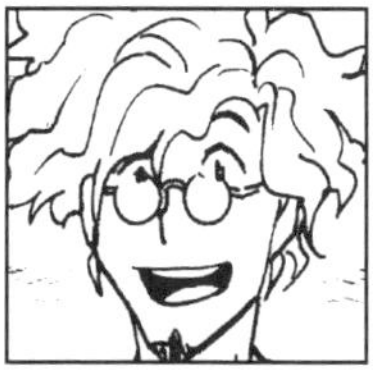

MISTER SOUMILLON

ASSISTANT ADVISER OF THE CHESS CLUB. COMPUTER SCIENCE TEACHER.

KARL

14-YEAR OLD JUNIOR CHESS CHAMPION. HIS COMPOSED PLAYSTYLE EARNED HIM THE NICKNAME OF AICE (ACE + ICE).

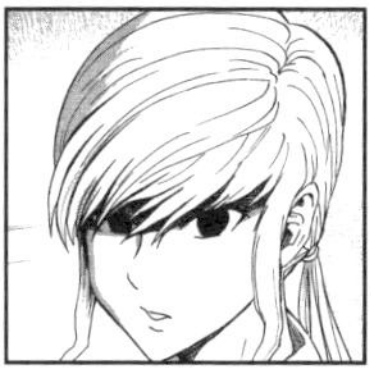

GARRY KASPAROV

FAMOUS CHESS CHAMPION. HE LAUNCHED "PROJECT T" FOR THE FUTURE OF CHESS.

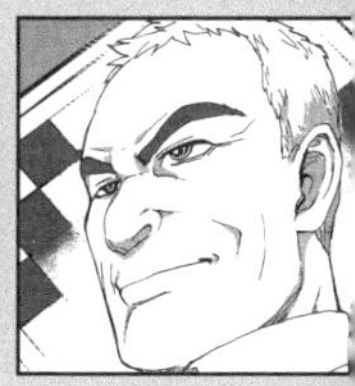

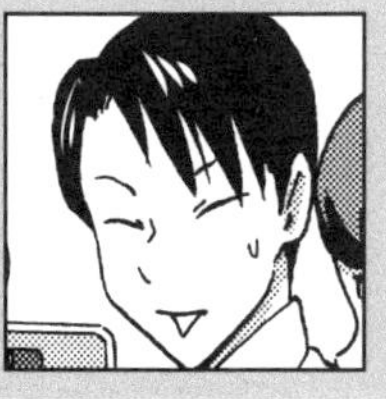

ZHANG

CHESS CLUB MEMBER. VERY GOOD AT GETTING INFORMATION.

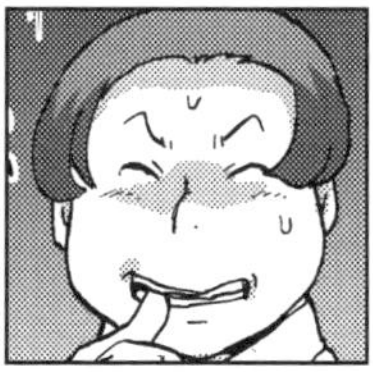

MARIUS

CHESS CLUB MEMBER. EXPERT IN SWEETS.

THE OWNER OF YORUZUDO

OWNER OF AN ANTIQUE SHOP. HE LENT CAÏSSA TO TOM.

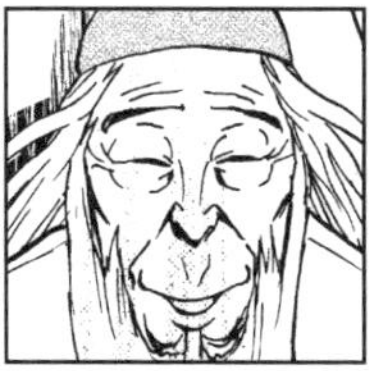

JEAN-MARC

OWNER OF A PANCAKE SHOP. TOM'S BEST FRIEND. HE HAS ALWAYS BEEN INTERESTED IN CHESS.

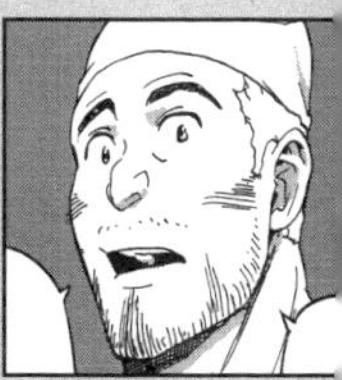

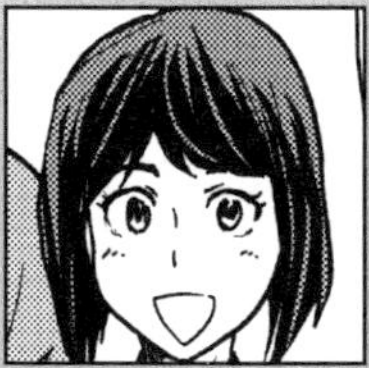

SAORI

NEW MEMBER OF THE CHESS CLUB. SHE HAS RECENTLY STARTED PLAYING CHESS.

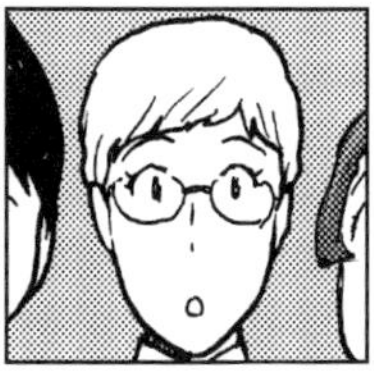

ANNE

CHESS CLUB MEMBER. SHE USES A COIN AS A GOOD-LUCK CHARM.

BLiTZ

TABLE OF CONTENTS

Chapter 18: One second 7
Chapter 19: Princess 33
Chapter 20: A bitter victory 55
Chapter 21: Here comes Touto middle school! 75
Chapter 22: All-out battle 99
Chapter 23: Fatal blow 125
Chapter 24: Onwards to the training camp! 151
Chapter 25: Tom v. Kaoru 177

BONUS PAGES

Afterword: intuition 208
Alexis Champion 212
Garry Kasparov 213
How to use the Zazen meditation technique 214
The Monte-Carlo Casino 218
Chess glossary 220
Basic annotations for a chess game 223
Analysis of the Riko v. Harmony game 224
Game references 232
Acknowledgments 234

This is a work of fiction.
Aside from Garry Kasparov and Shôshô Yamada, any resemblance to real people is purely coincidental.
The situations are totally fictitious.

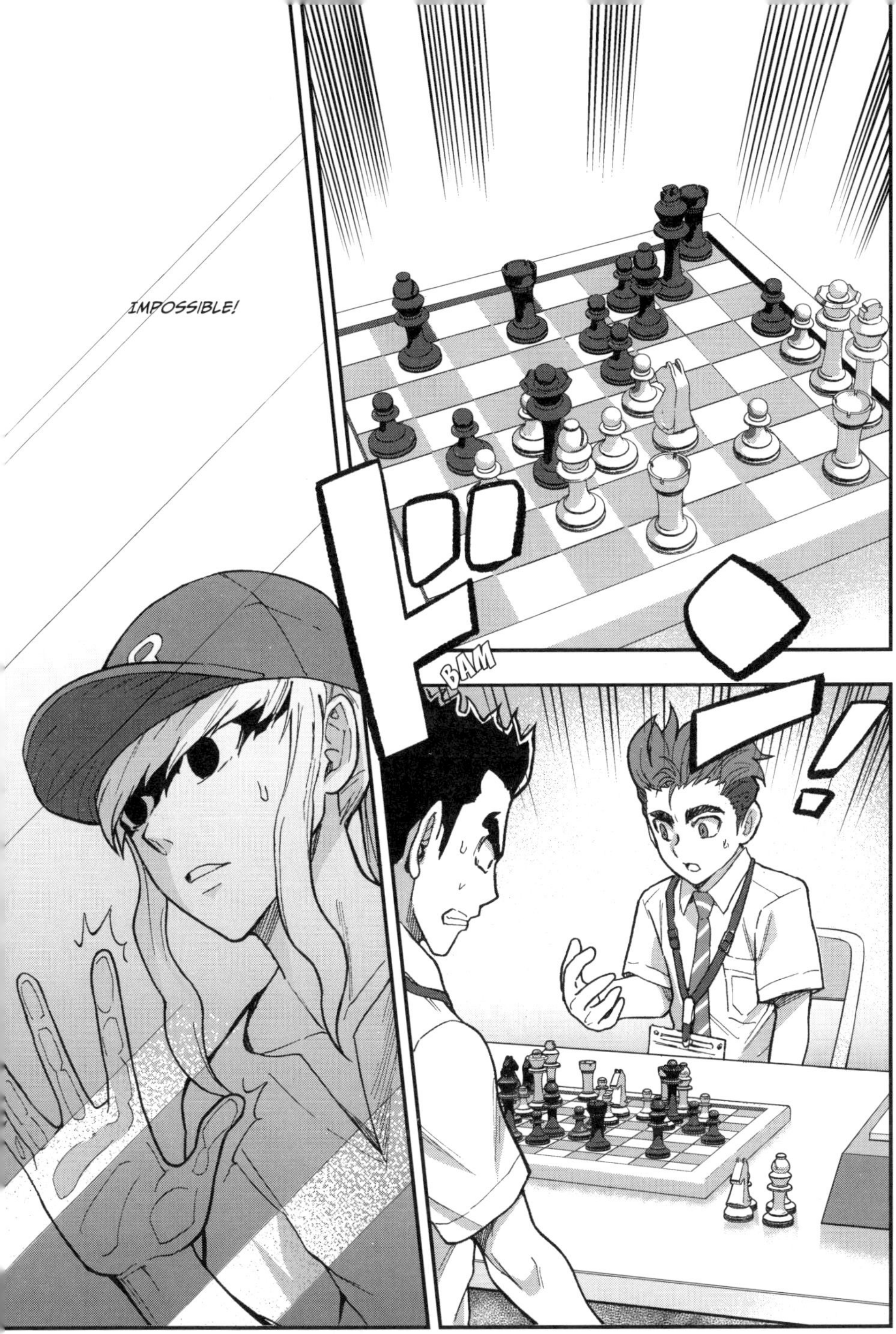
BAM
IMPOSSIBLE!

Chapter 18: One second

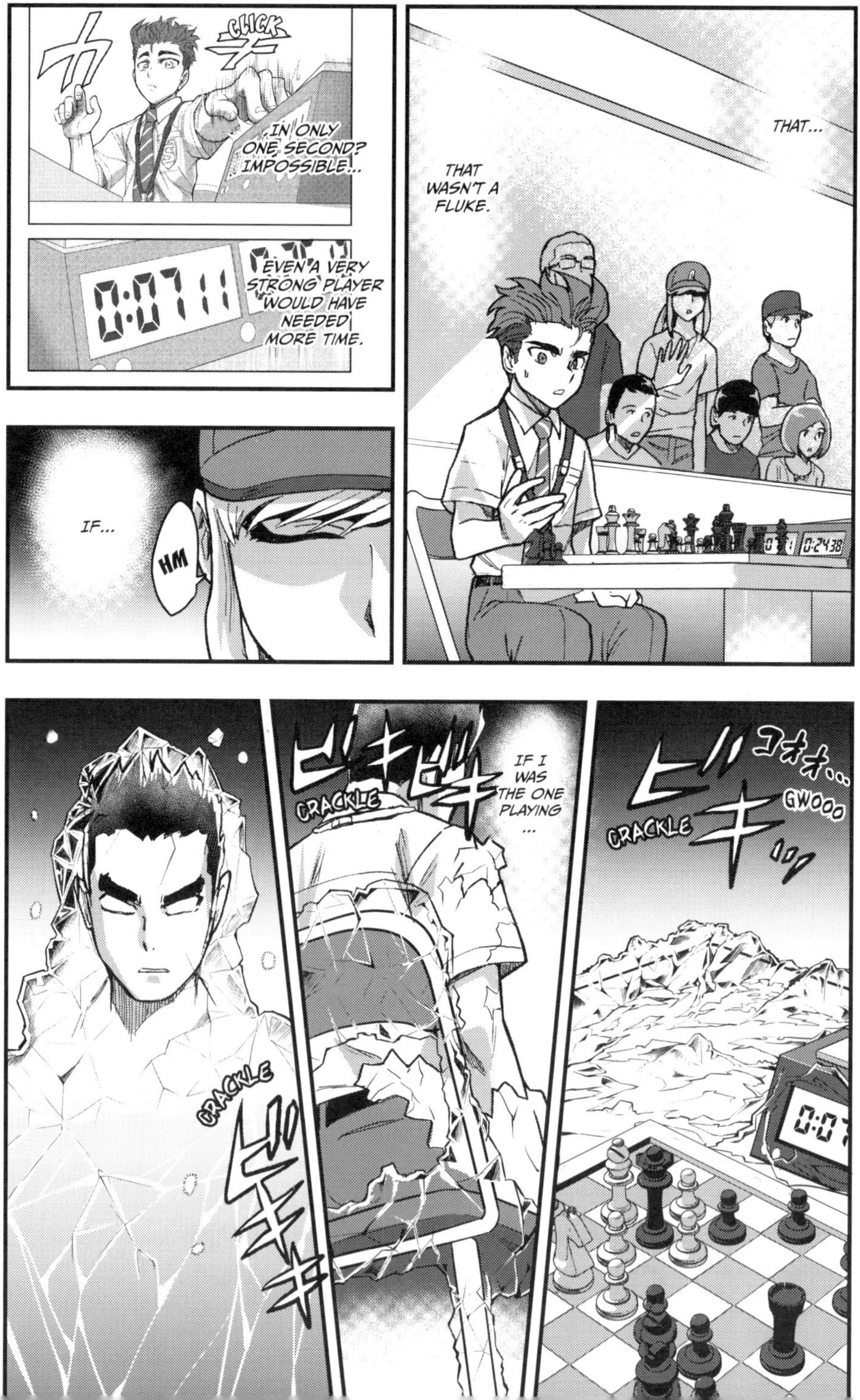
CLICK
IN ONLY ONE SECOND? IMPOSSIBLE...
EVEN A VERY STRONG PLAYER WOULD HAVE NEEDED MORE TIME.
THAT...
THAT WASN'T A FLUKE.
IF...
HM
CRACKLE
CRACKLE
IF I WAS THE ONE PLAYING ...
CRACKLE
GWOOO

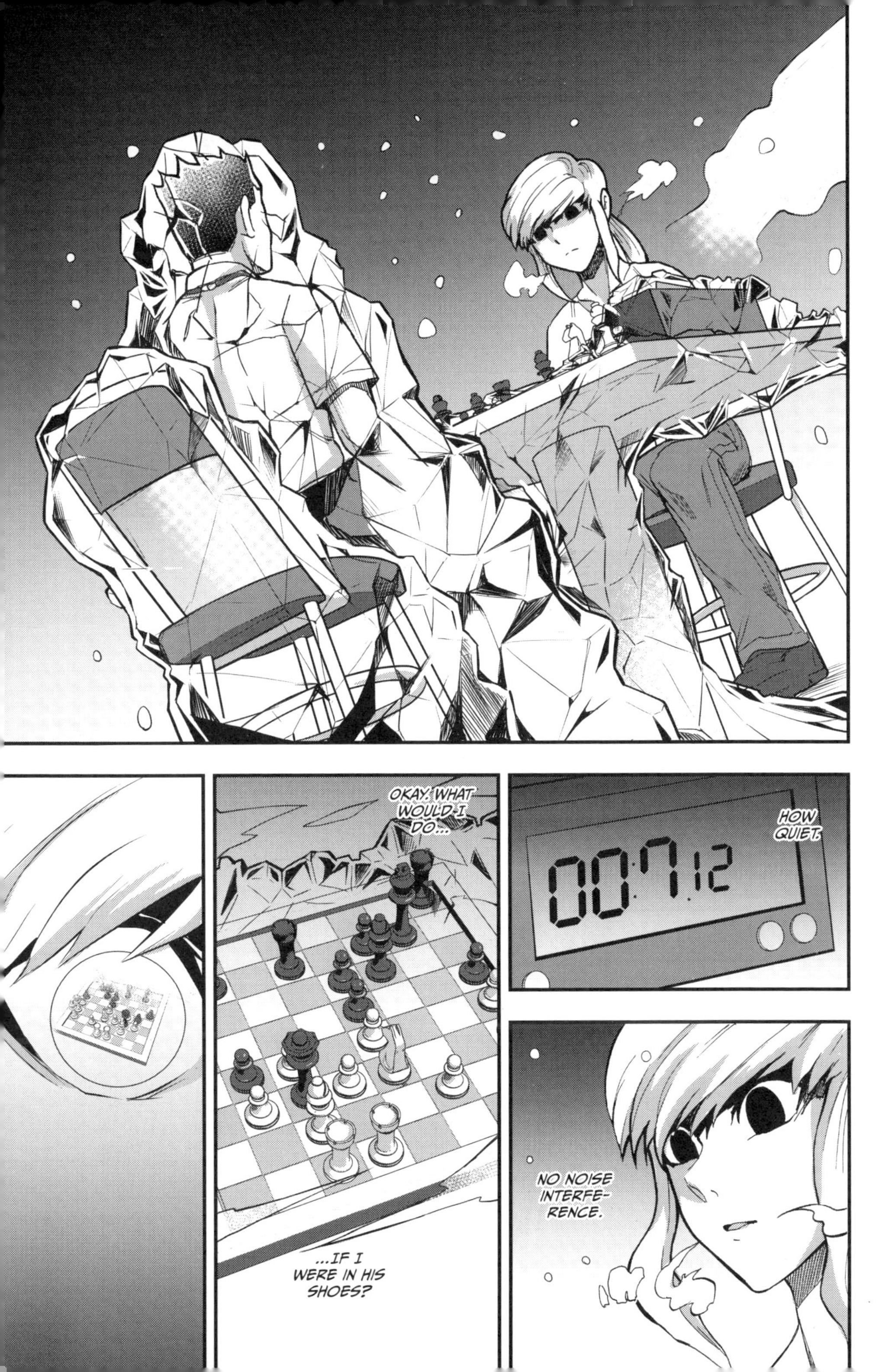
HOW QUIET.
NO NOISE INTERFERENCE.
OKAY, WHAT WOULD I DO...
...IF I WERE IN HIS SHOES?

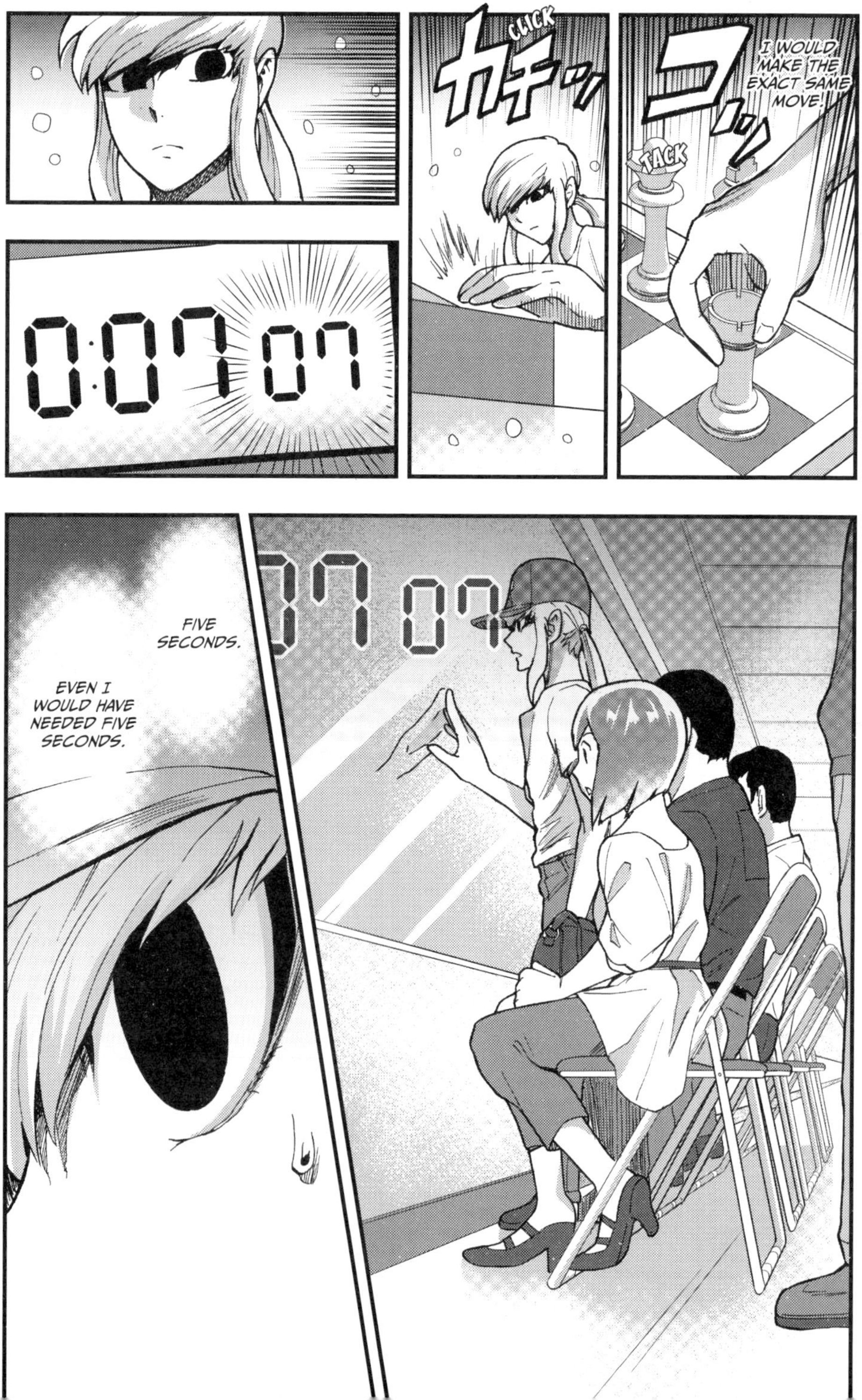

コ
I WOULD MAKE THE EXACT SAME MOVE!
TACK
カチッ
CLICK
FIVE SECONDS.
EVEN I WOULD HAVE NEEDED FIVE SECONDS.

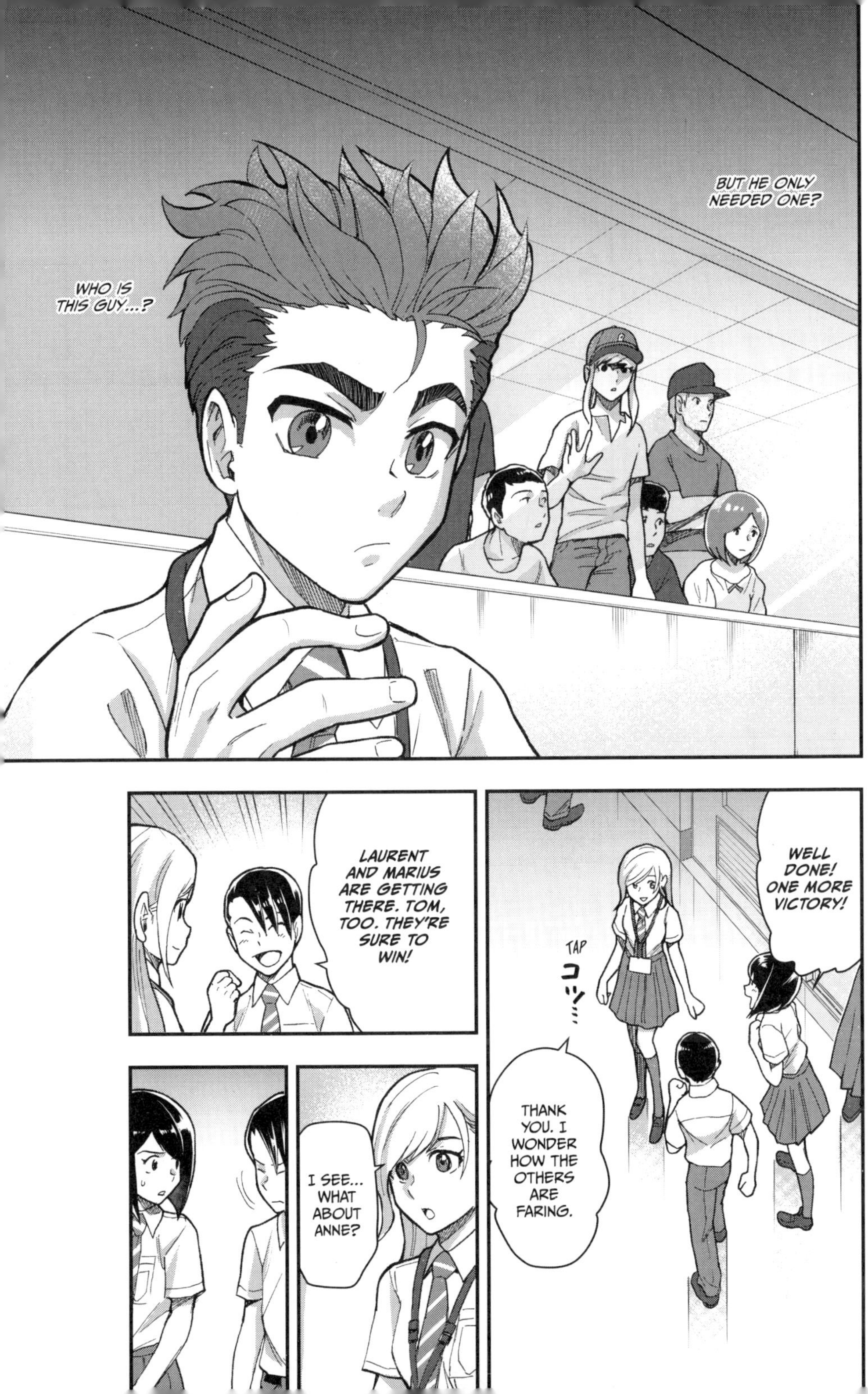
BUT HE ONLY NEEDED ONE?
WHO IS THIS GUY...?
WELL DONE! ONE MORE VICTORY!
TAP
コツ…
THANK YOU. I WONDER HOW THE OTHERS ARE FARING.
LAURENT AND MARIUS ARE GETTING THERE. TOM, TOO. THEY'RE SURE TO WIN!
I SEE... WHAT ABOUT ANNE?

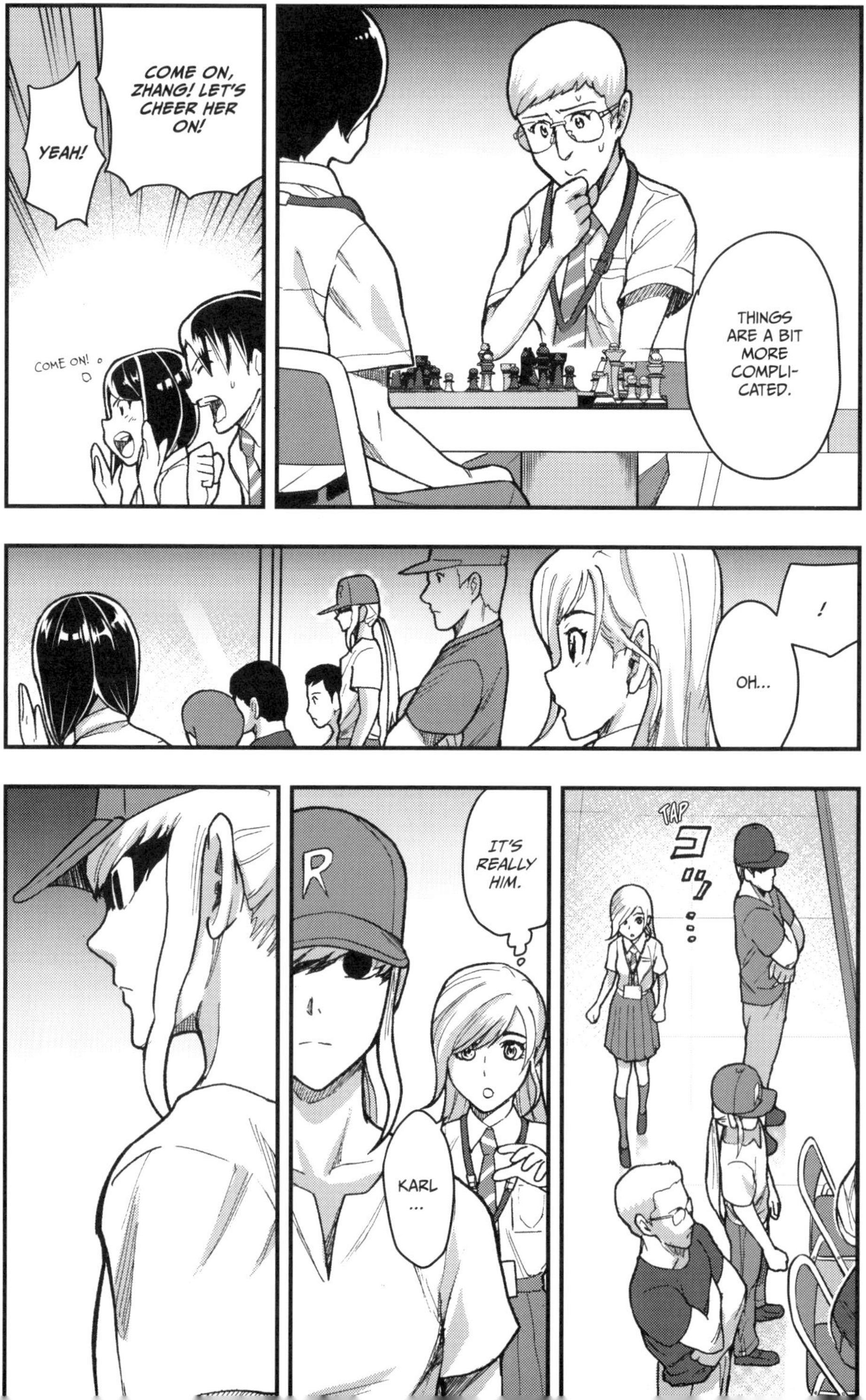
THINGS ARE A BIT MORE COMPLI- CATED.
COME ON, ZHANG! LET'S CHEER HER ON!
YEAH!
COME ON!
!
OH...
TAP
IT'S REALLY HIM.
KARL ...

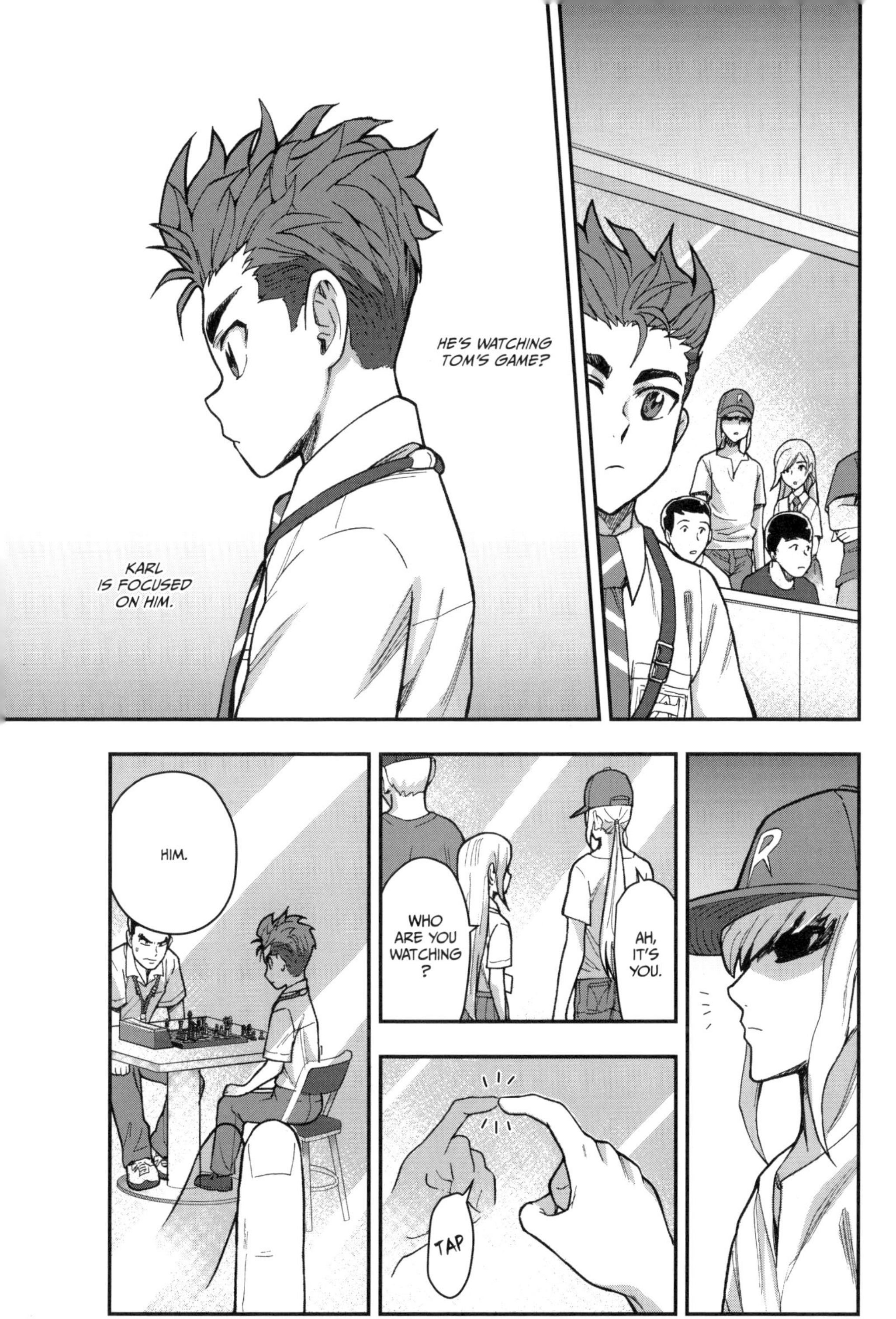
HE'S WATCHING TOM'S GAME?
KARL IS FOCUSED ON HIM.
AH, IT'S YOU.
WHO ARE YOU WATCHING ?
TAP
HIM.

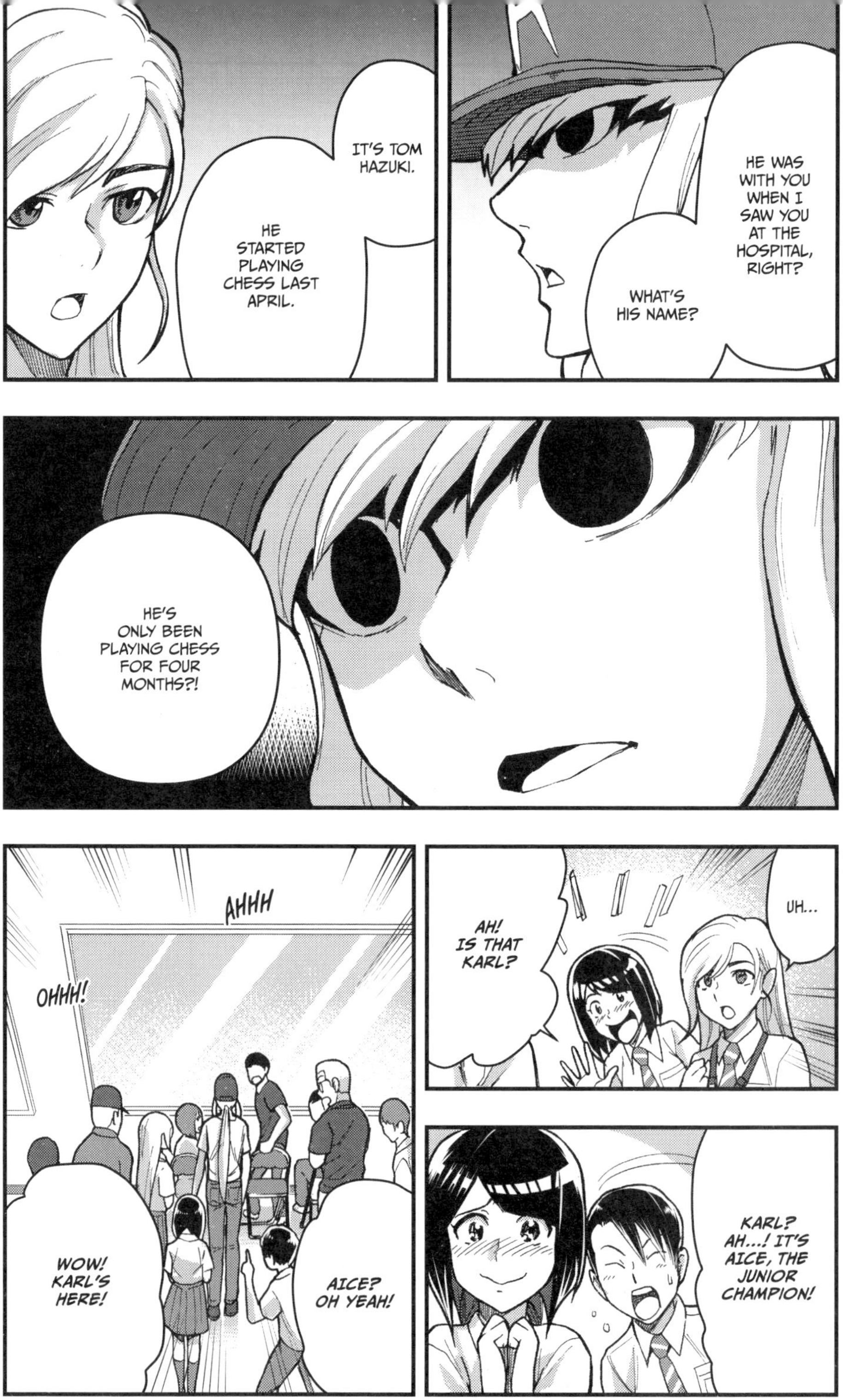
HE WAS WITH YOU WHEN I SAW YOU AT THE HOSPITAL, RIGHT?
WHAT'S HIS NAME?
IT'S TOM HAZUKI.
HE STARTED PLAYING CHESS LAST APRIL.
HE'S ONLY BEEN PLAYING CHESS FOR FOUR MONTHS?!
UH...
AH! IS THAT KARL?
KARL? AH...! IT'S AICE, THE JUNIOR CHAMPION!
AHHH
OHHH!
AICE? OH YEAH!
WOW! KARL'S HERE!

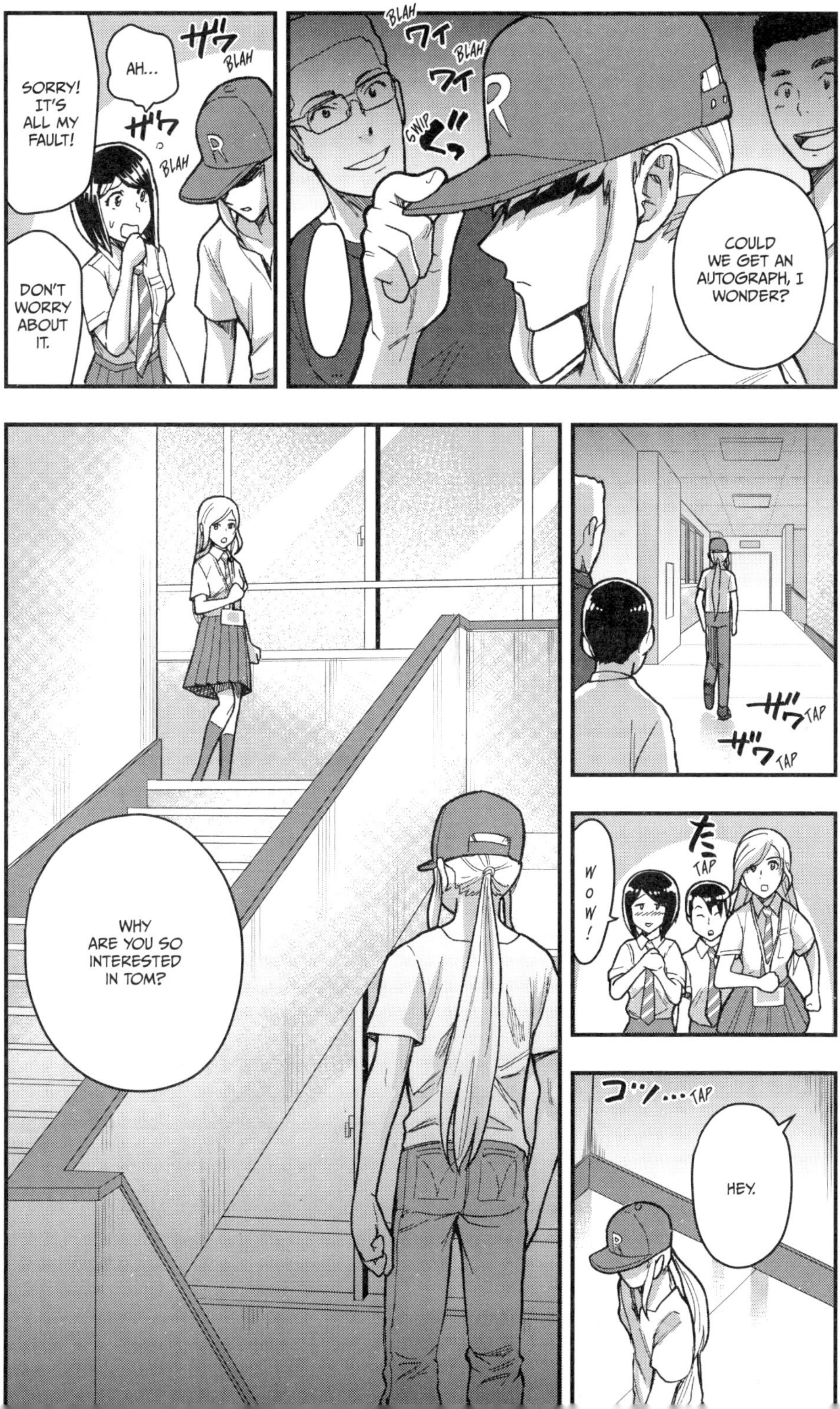
ワイ
BLAH
ワイ
BLAH
ぐっ
GWIP
COULD WE GET AN AUTOGRAPH, I WONDER?
ザワ
BLAH
AH...
SORRY! IT'S ALL MY FAULT!
ザワ
BLAH
DON'T WORRY ABOUT IT.
ザワ
TAP
ザワ
TAP
たっ
TAP
WOW!
コツ...
TAP
HEY.
WHY ARE YOU SO INTERESTED IN TOM?

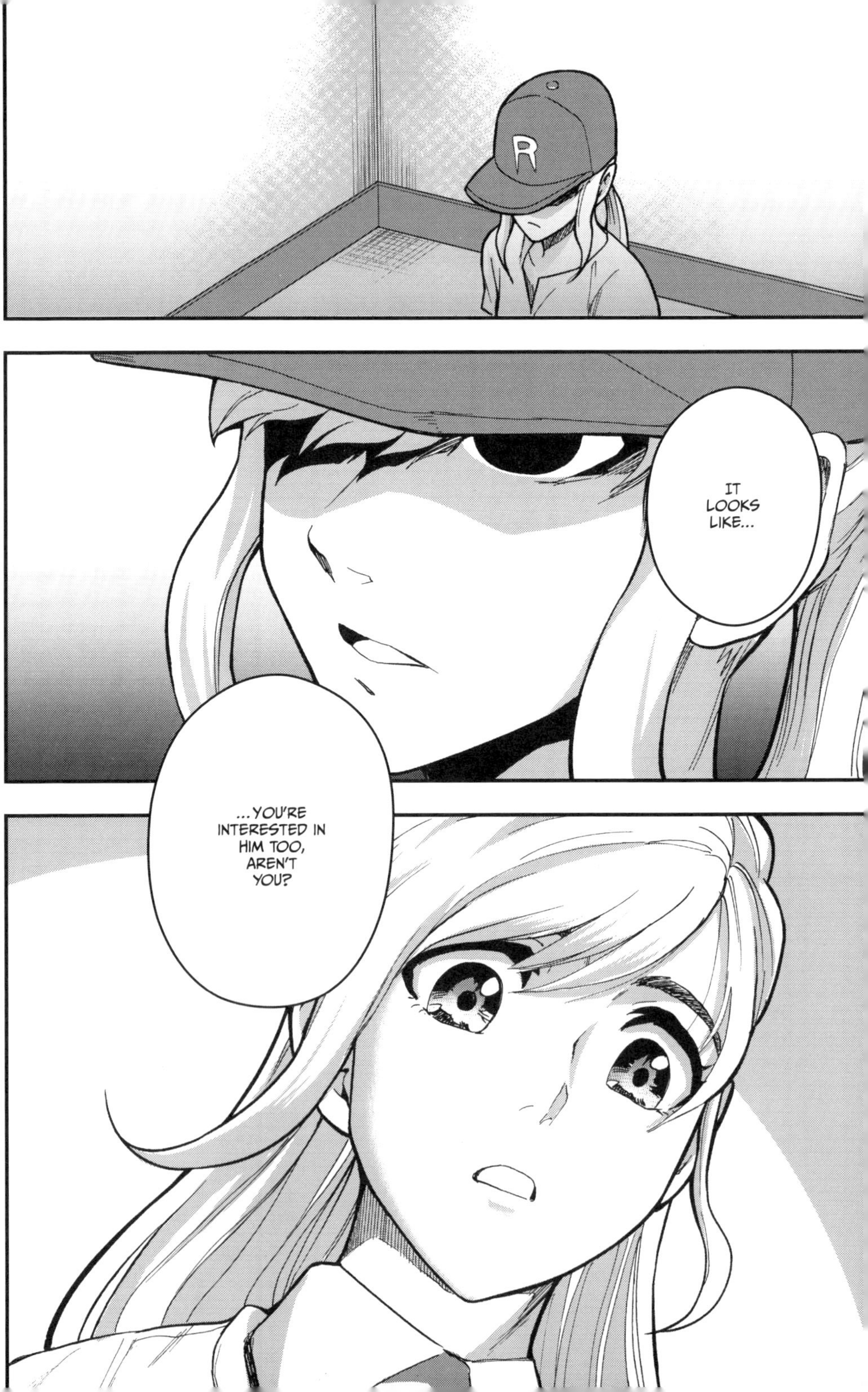
IT LOOKS LIKE...
...YOU'RE INTERESTED IN HIM TOO, AREN'T YOU?

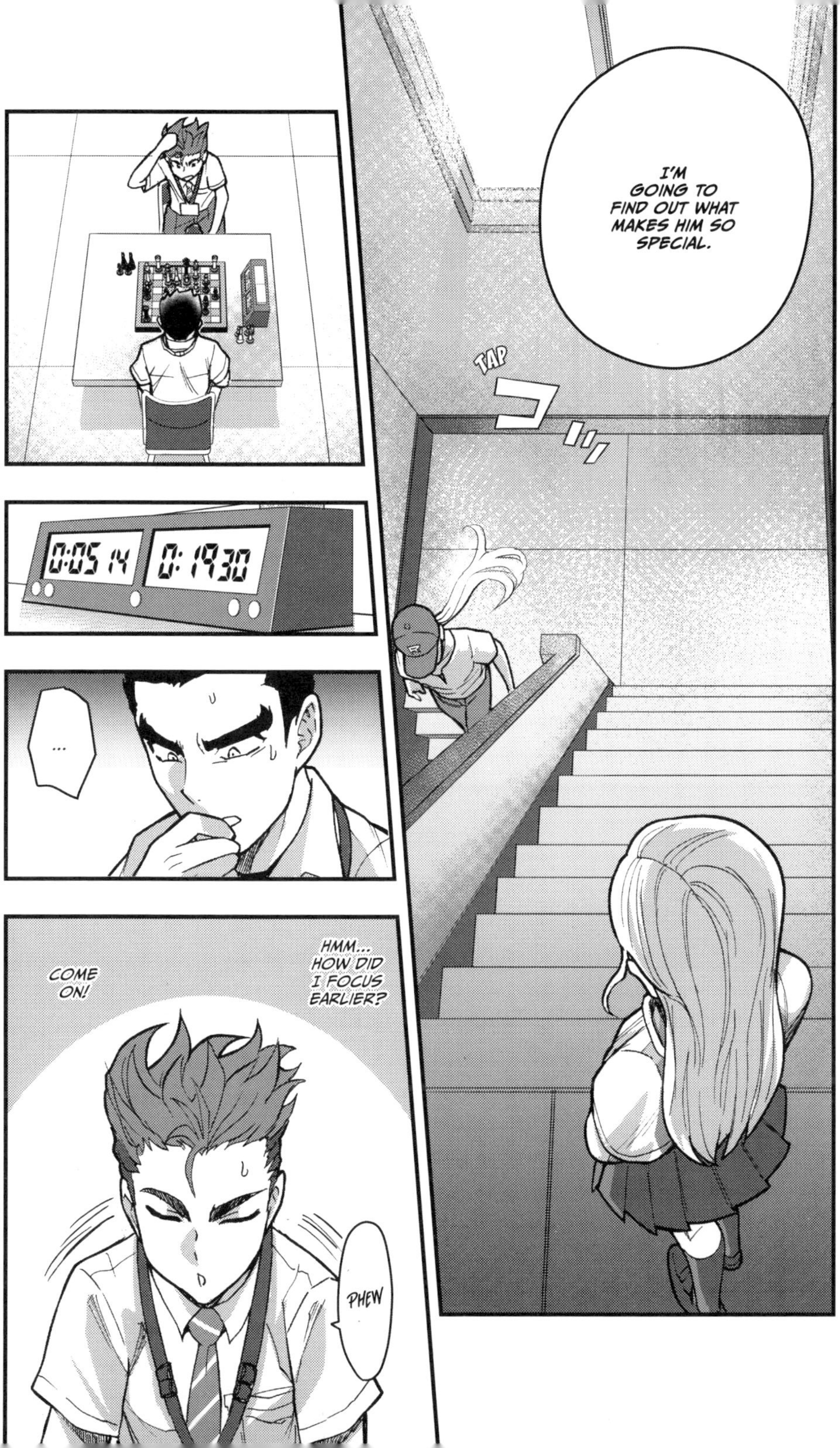
I'M GOING TO FIND OUT WHAT MAKES HIM SO SPECIAL.
TAP
0:05 14
0:19 30
...
HMM... HOW DID I FOCUS EARLIER?
COME ON!
PHEW

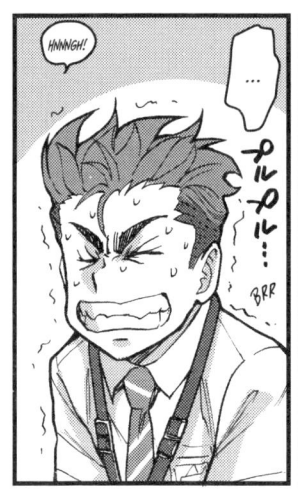

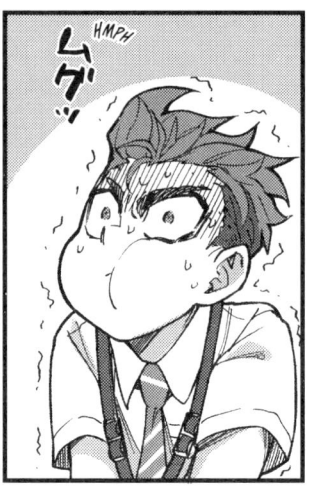

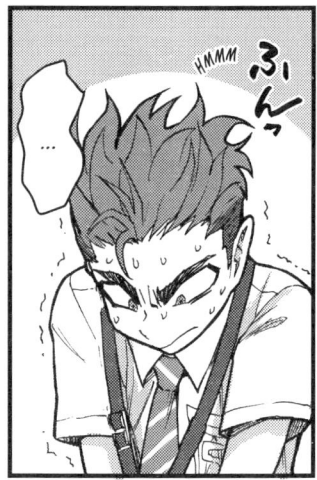

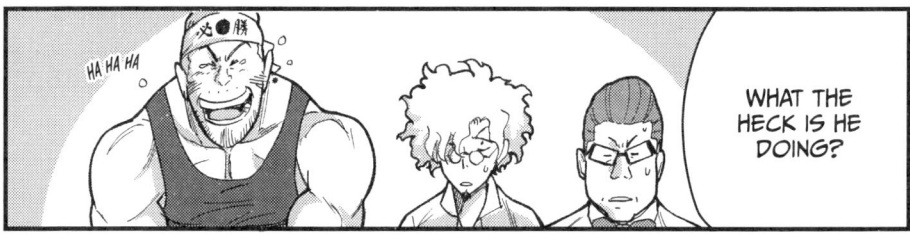

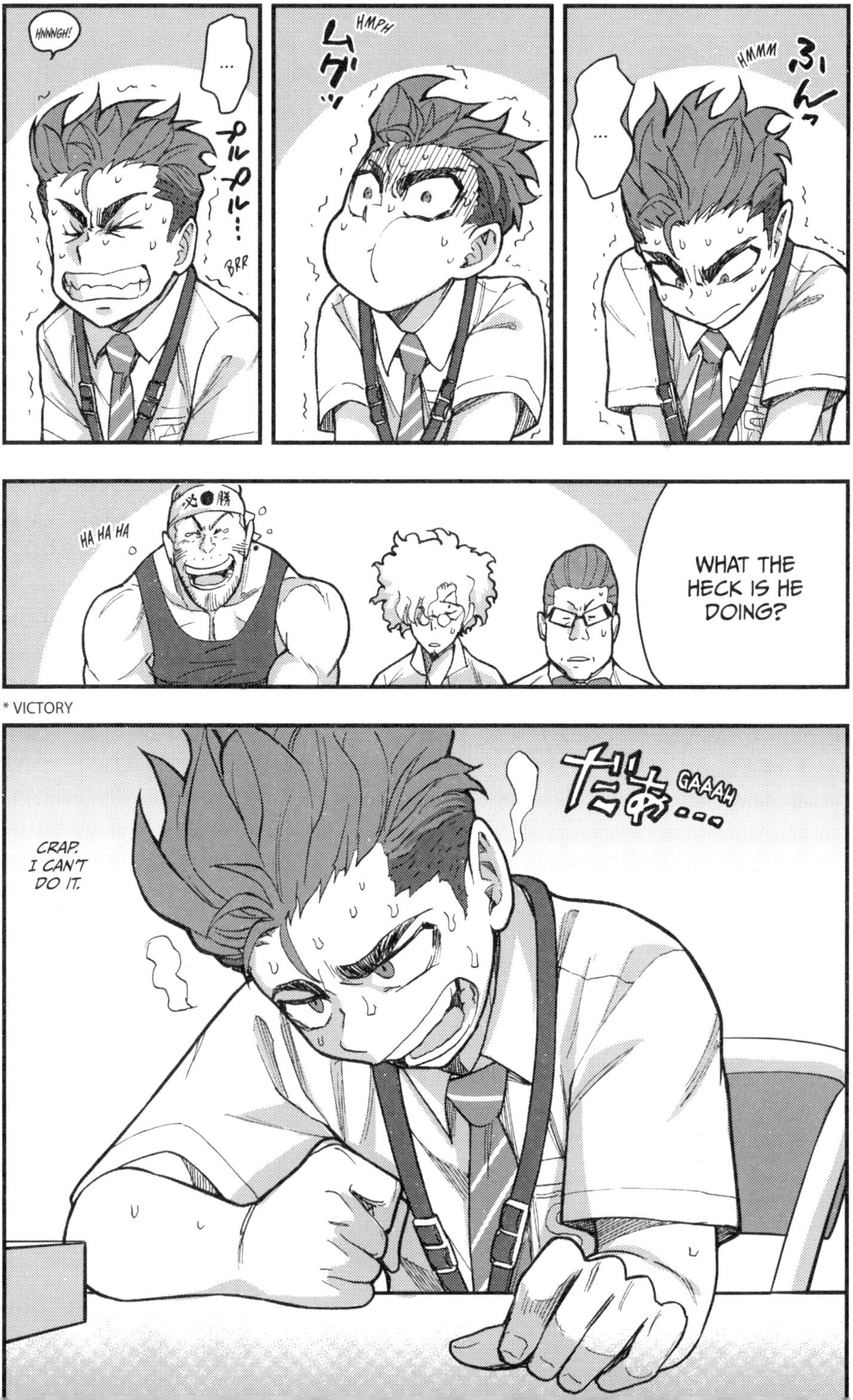
ふんっ
HMMM
...
ムグッ
HMPH
...
HNNNGH!
プルプル...
BRR
WHAT THE HECK IS HE DOING?
HA HA HA
だぁ...
GAAAH
CRAP. I CAN'T DO IT.

* VICTORY

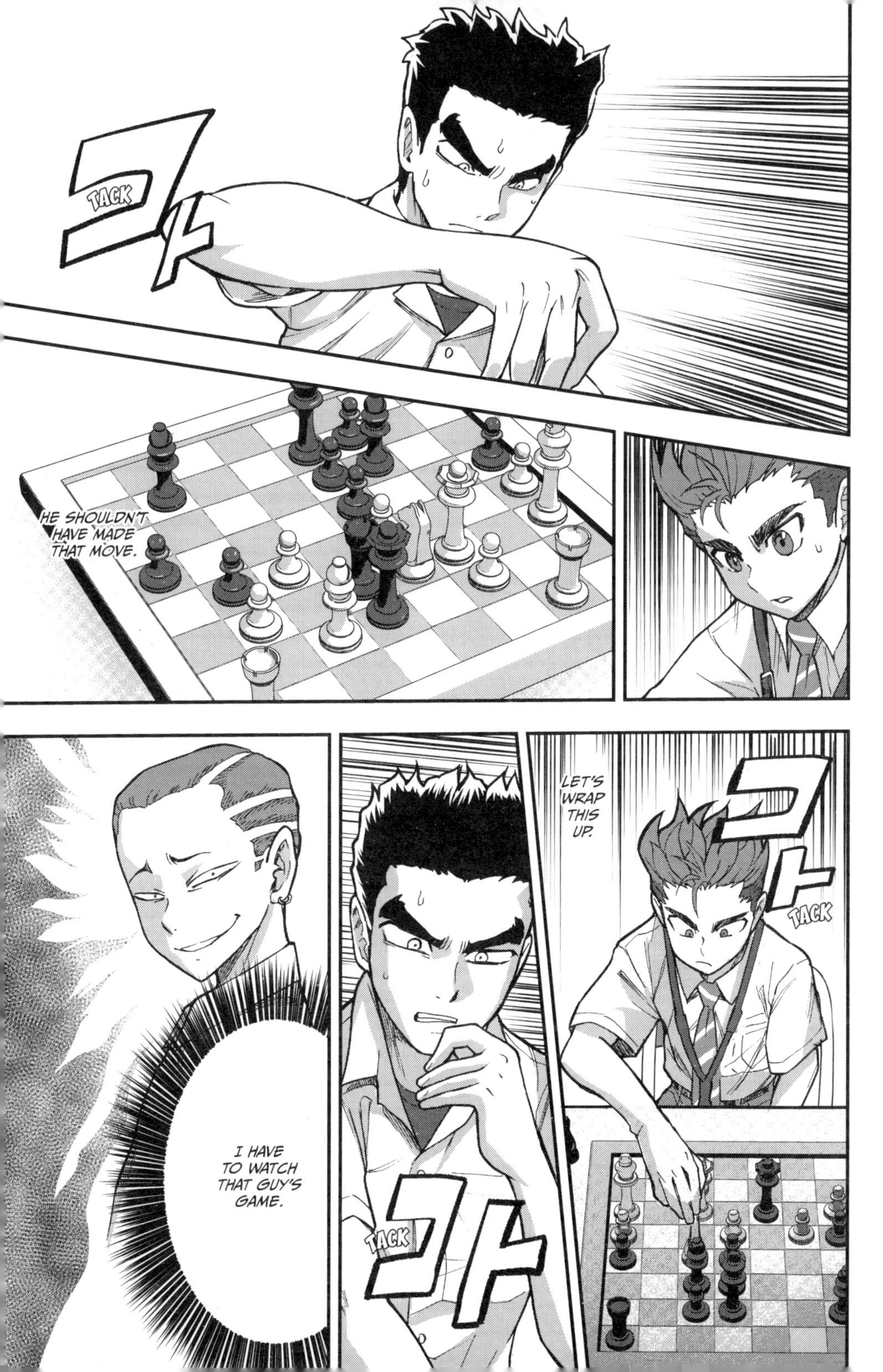
TACK
HE SHOULDN'T HAVE MADE THAT MOVE.
LET'S WRAP THIS UP.
TACK
TACK
I HAVE TO WATCH THAT GUY'S GAME.

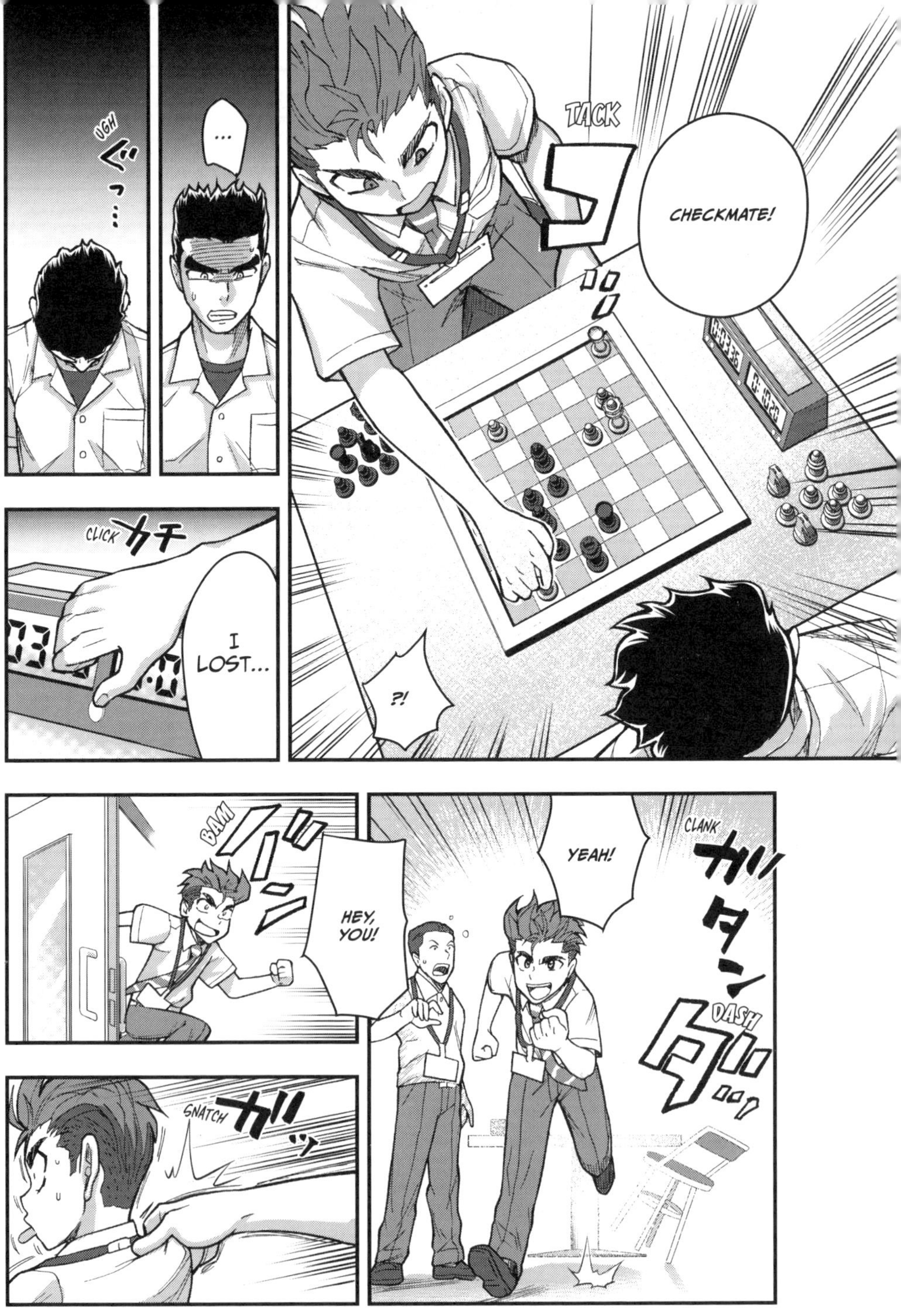
TACK
CHECKMATE!
?!
...
UGH
ぐっ…
CLICK
カチ
I LOST...
YEAH!
CLANK
ガタン
DASH
ダッ
BAM
バーン
HEY, YOU!
SNATCH
ガッ

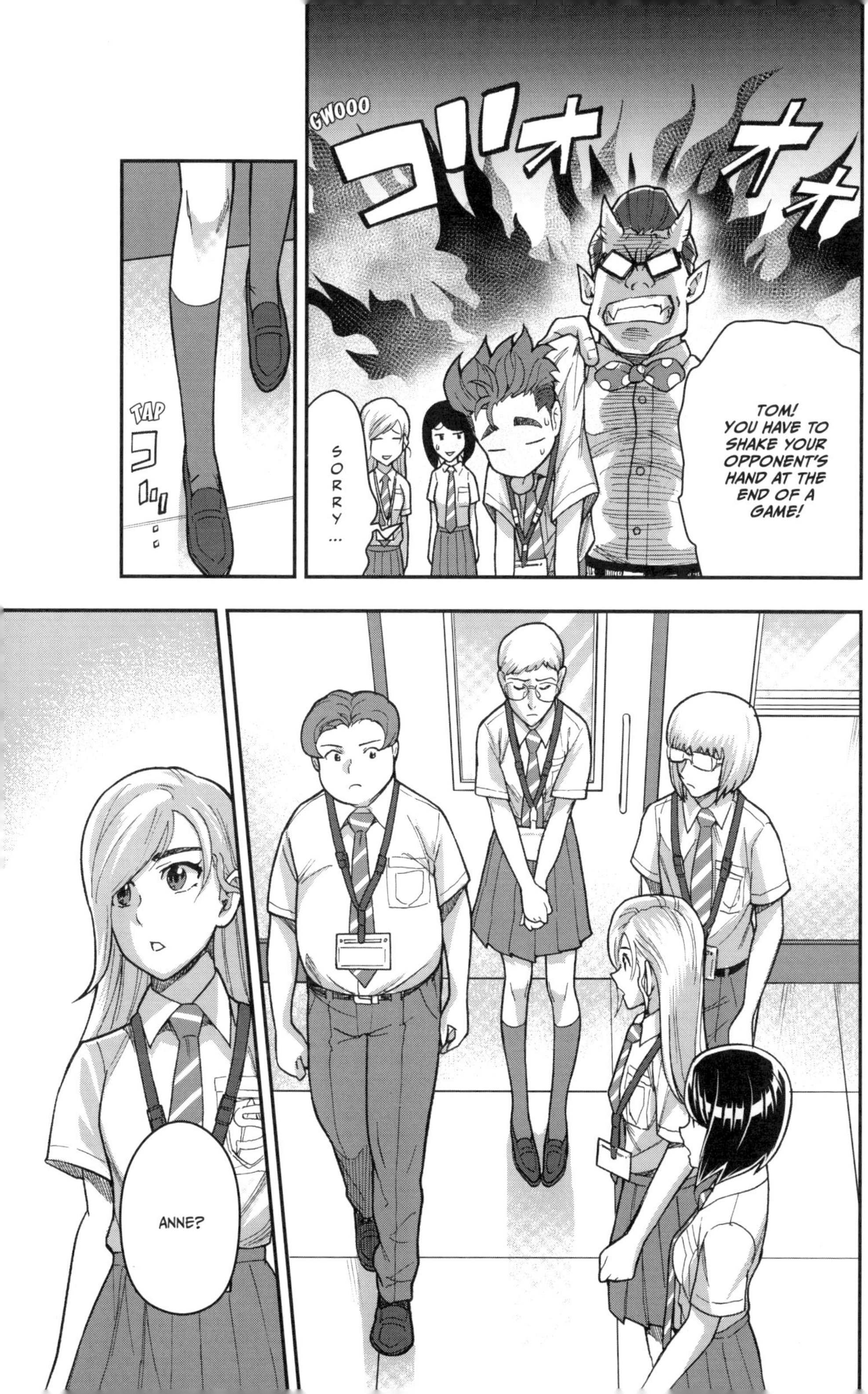
GWOOO
ゴォオオ
TOM! YOU HAVE TO SHAKE YOUR OPPONENT'S HAND AT THE END OF A GAME!
SORRY...
TAP
コッ...
ANNE?

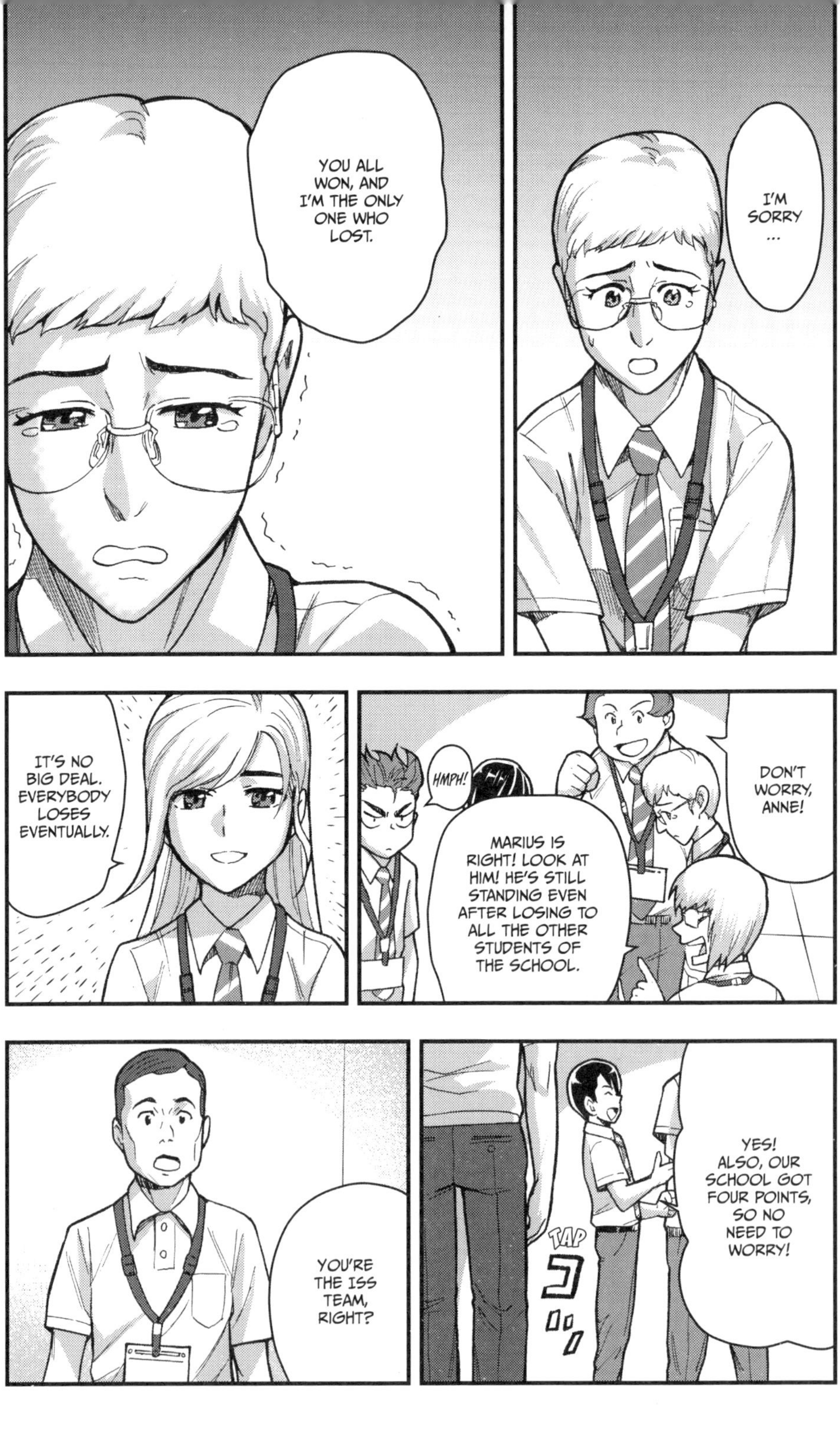
YOU ALL WON, AND I'M THE ONLY ONE WHO LOST.
I'M SORRY ...
IT'S NO BIG DEAL. EVERYBODY LOSES EVENTUALLY.
HMPH!
DON'T WORRY, ANNE!
MARIUS IS RIGHT! LOOK AT HIM! HE'S STILL STANDING EVEN AFTER LOSING TO ALL THE OTHER STUDENTS OF THE SCHOOL.
YOU'RE THE ISS TEAM, RIGHT?
TAP
YES! ALSO, OUR SCHOOL GOT FOUR POINTS, SO NO NEED TO WORRY!

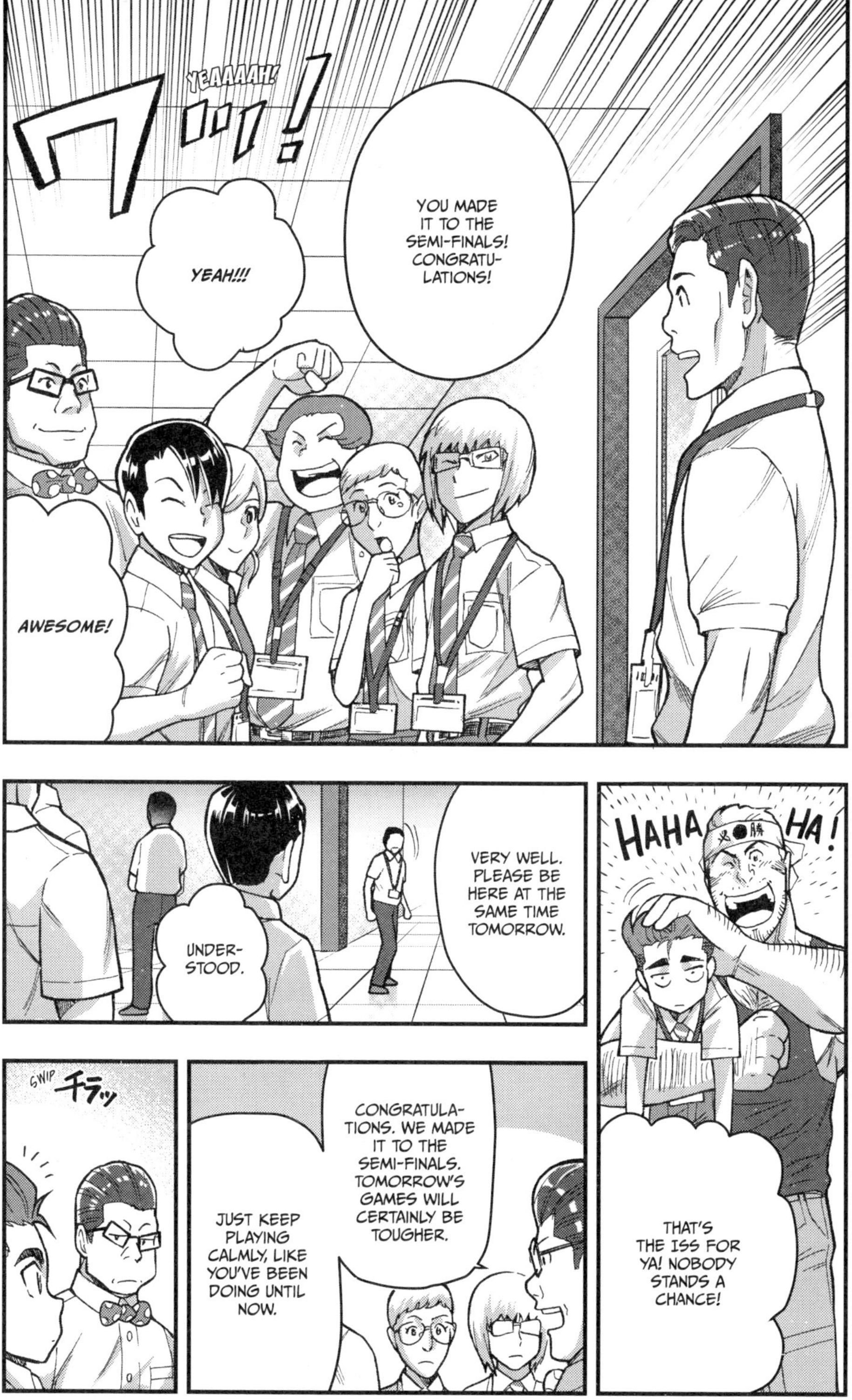

YEAAAAH!
YOU MADE IT TO THE SEMI-FINALS! CONGRATU-LATIONS!
YEAH!!!
AWESOME!
HAHAHA!
THAT'S THE ISS FOR YA! NOBODY STANDS A CHANCE!
VERY WELL. PLEASE BE HERE AT THE SAME TIME TOMORROW.
UNDER-STOOD.
CONGRATULA-TIONS. WE MADE IT TO THE SEMI-FINALS. TOMORROW'S GAMES WILL CERTAINLY BE TOUGHER.
JUST KEEP PLAYING CALMLY, LIKE YOU'VE BEEN DOING UNTIL NOW.
SWIP
チラッ

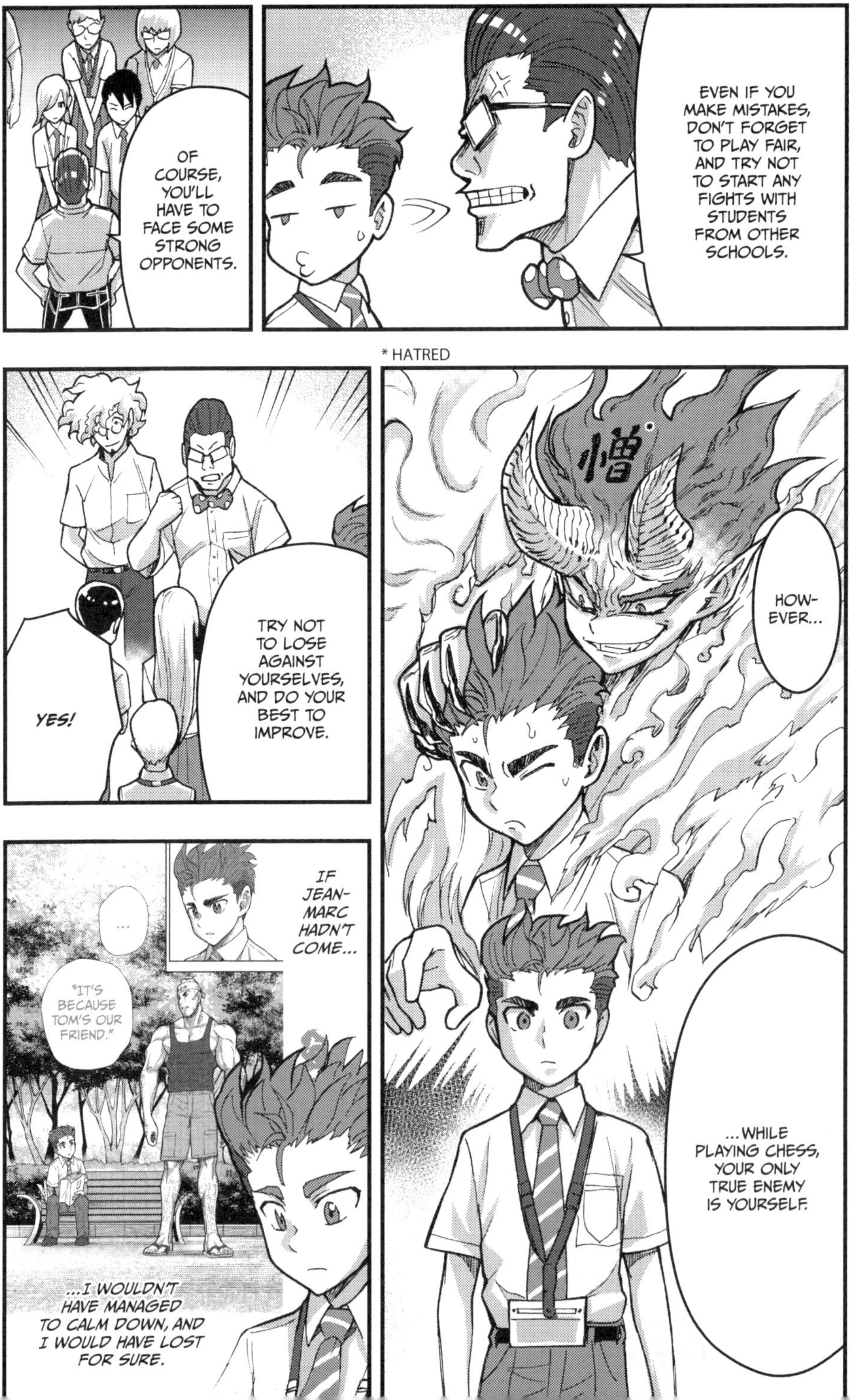
EVEN IF YOU MAKE MISTAKES, DON'T FORGET TO PLAY FAIR, AND TRY NOT TO START ANY FIGHTS WITH STUDENTS FROM OTHER SCHOOLS.
OF COURSE, YOU'LL HAVE TO FACE SOME STRONG OPPONENTS.
憎*
HOW-EVER...
...WHILE PLAYING CHESS, YOUR ONLY TRUE ENEMY IS YOURSELF.
* HATRED
TRY NOT TO LOSE AGAINST YOURSELVES, AND DO YOUR BEST TO IMPROVE.
YES!
IF JEAN-MARC HADN'T COME...
...
"IT'S BECAUSE TOM'S OUR FRIEND."
...I WOULDN'T HAVE MANAGED TO CALM DOWN, AND I WOULD HAVE LOST FOR SURE.

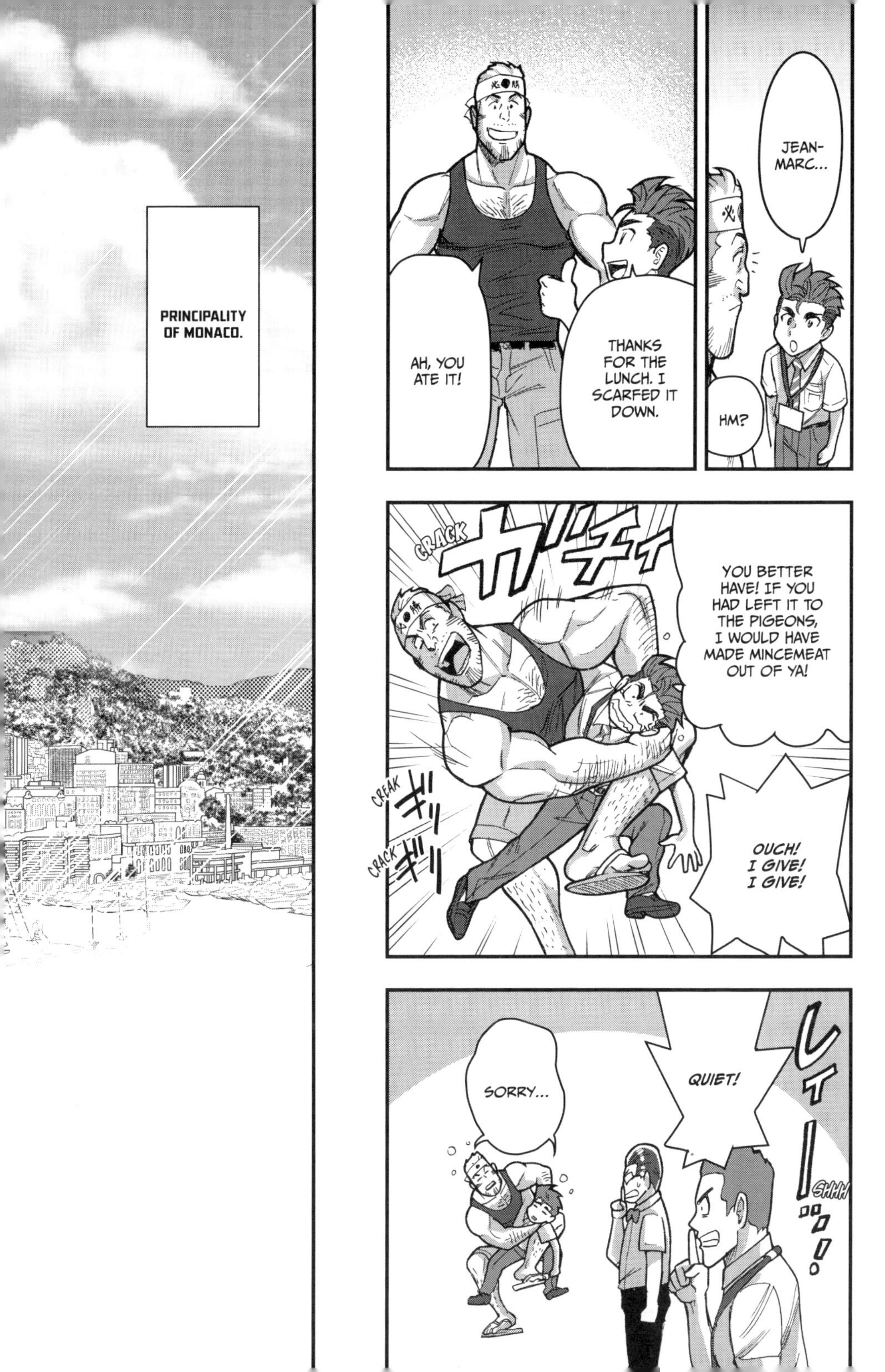
JEAN-MARC...
HM?
THANKS FOR THE LUNCH. I SCARFED IT DOWN.
AH, YOU ATE IT!
CRACK
YOU BETTER HAVE! IF YOU HAD LEFT IT TO THE PIGEONS, I WOULD HAVE MADE MINCEMEAT OUT OF YA!
OUCH! I GIVE! I GIVE!
CREAK
CRACK
QUIET!
SHHH
SORRY...
PRINCIPALITY OF MONACO.

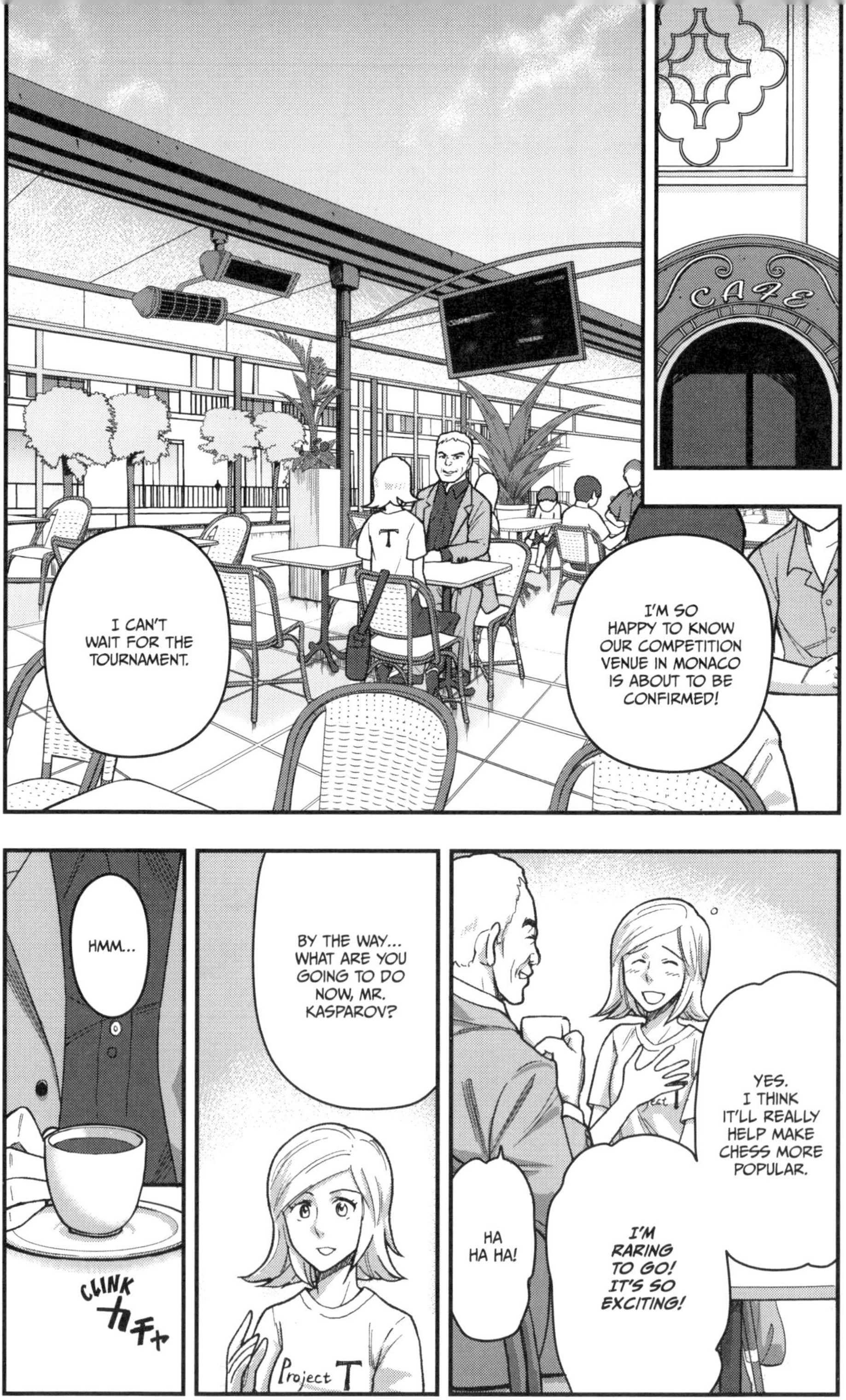
CAFE
I'M SO HAPPY TO KNOW OUR COMPETITION VENUE IN MONACO IS ABOUT TO BE CONFIRMED!
I CAN'T WAIT FOR THE TOURNAMENT.
YES. I THINK IT'LL REALLY HELP MAKE CHESS MORE POPULAR.
I'M RARING TO GO! IT'S SO EXCITING!
HA HA HA!
BY THE WAY... WHAT ARE YOU GOING TO DO NOW, MR. KASPAROV?
Project T
HMM...
CLINK カチャ

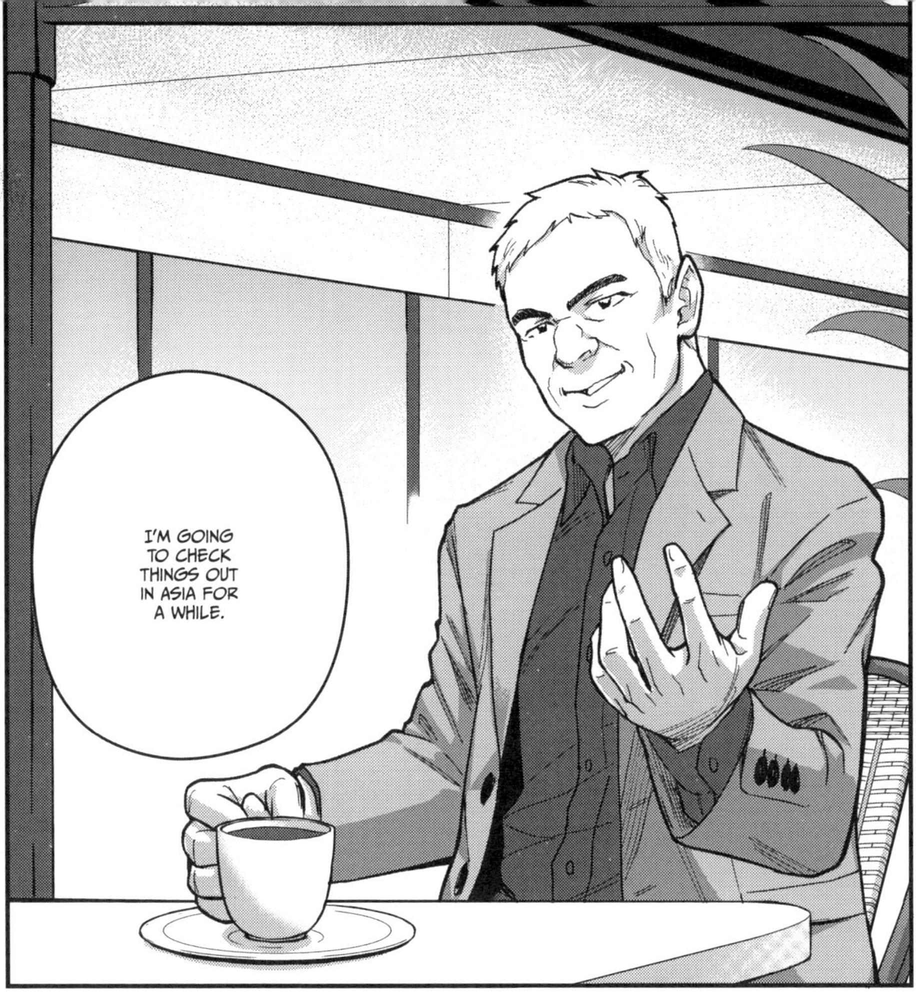
I'M GOING TO CHECK THINGS OUT IN ASIA FOR A WHILE.
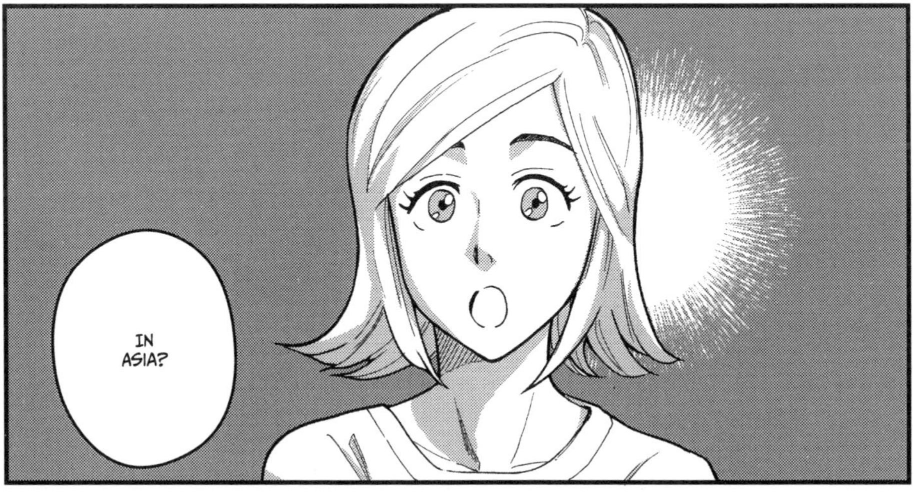
IN ASIA?

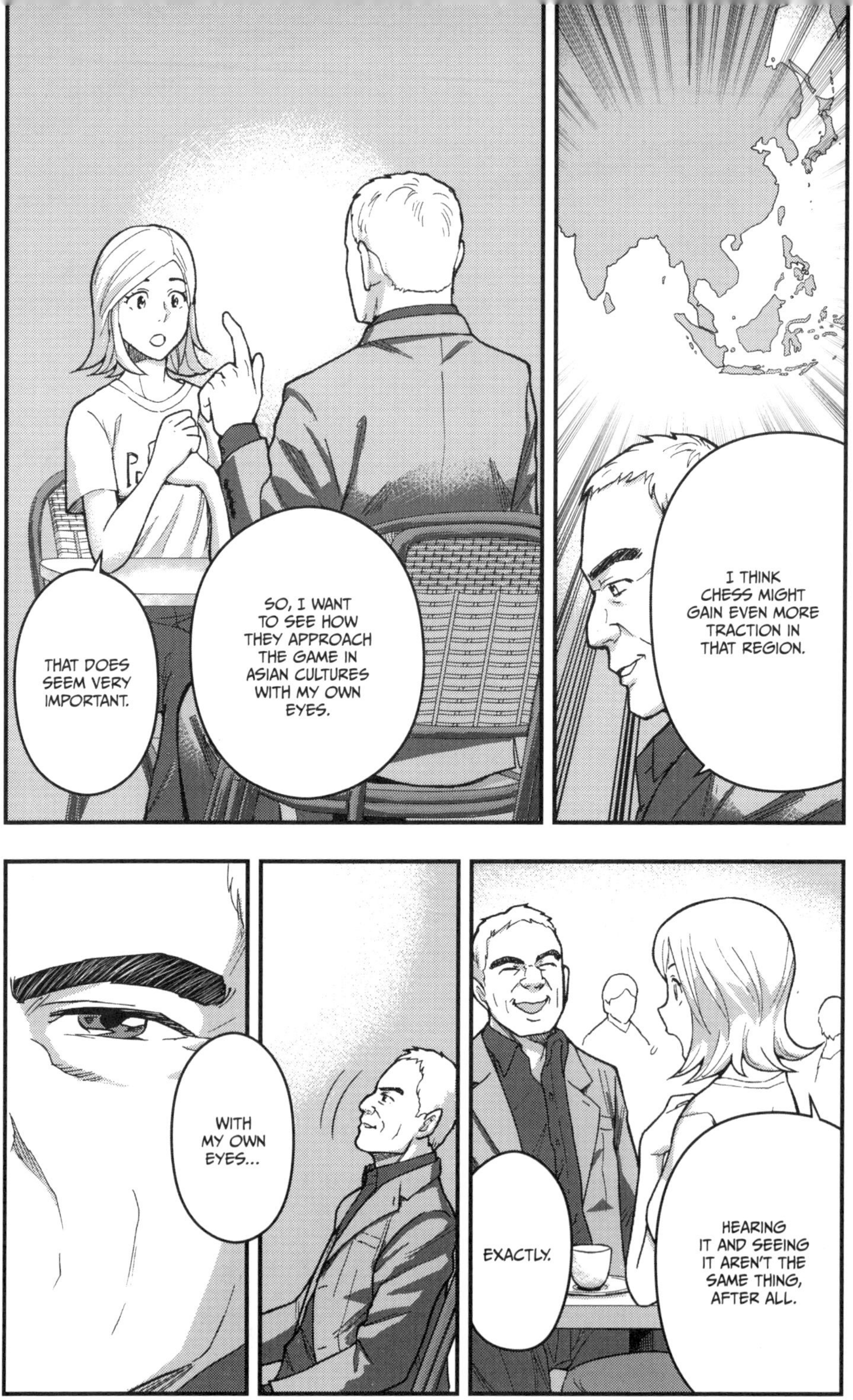
I THINK CHESS MIGHT GAIN EVEN MORE TRACTION IN THAT REGION.
SO, I WANT TO SEE HOW THEY APPROACH THE GAME IN ASIAN CULTURES WITH MY OWN EYES.
THAT DOES SEEM VERY IMPORTANT.
HEARING IT AND SEEING IT AREN'T THE SAME THING, AFTER ALL.
EXACTLY.
WITH MY OWN EYES...

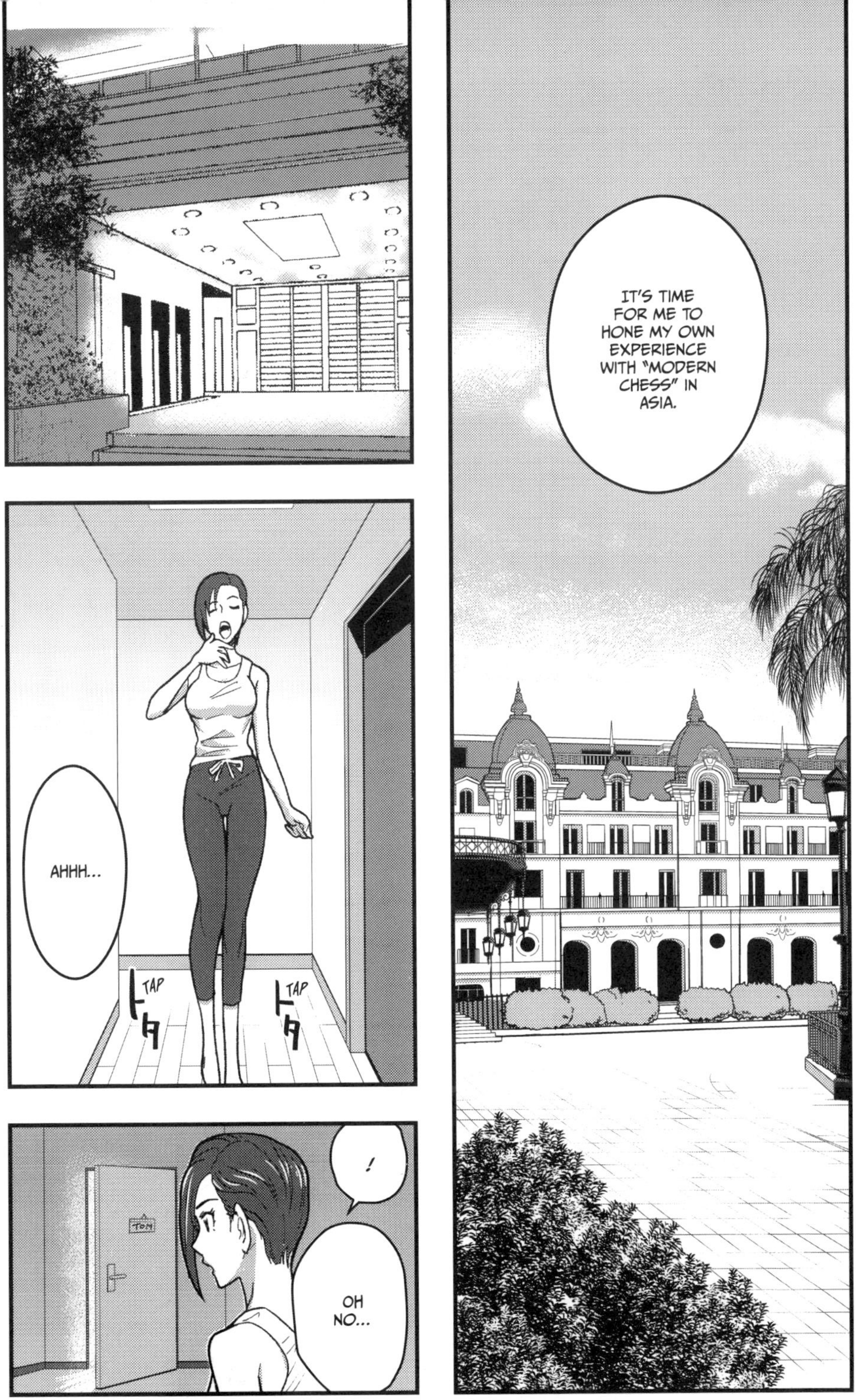
IT'S TIME FOR ME TO HONE MY OWN EXPERIENCE WITH "MODERN CHESS" IN ASIA.
AHHH...
TAP
TAP
!
OH NO...

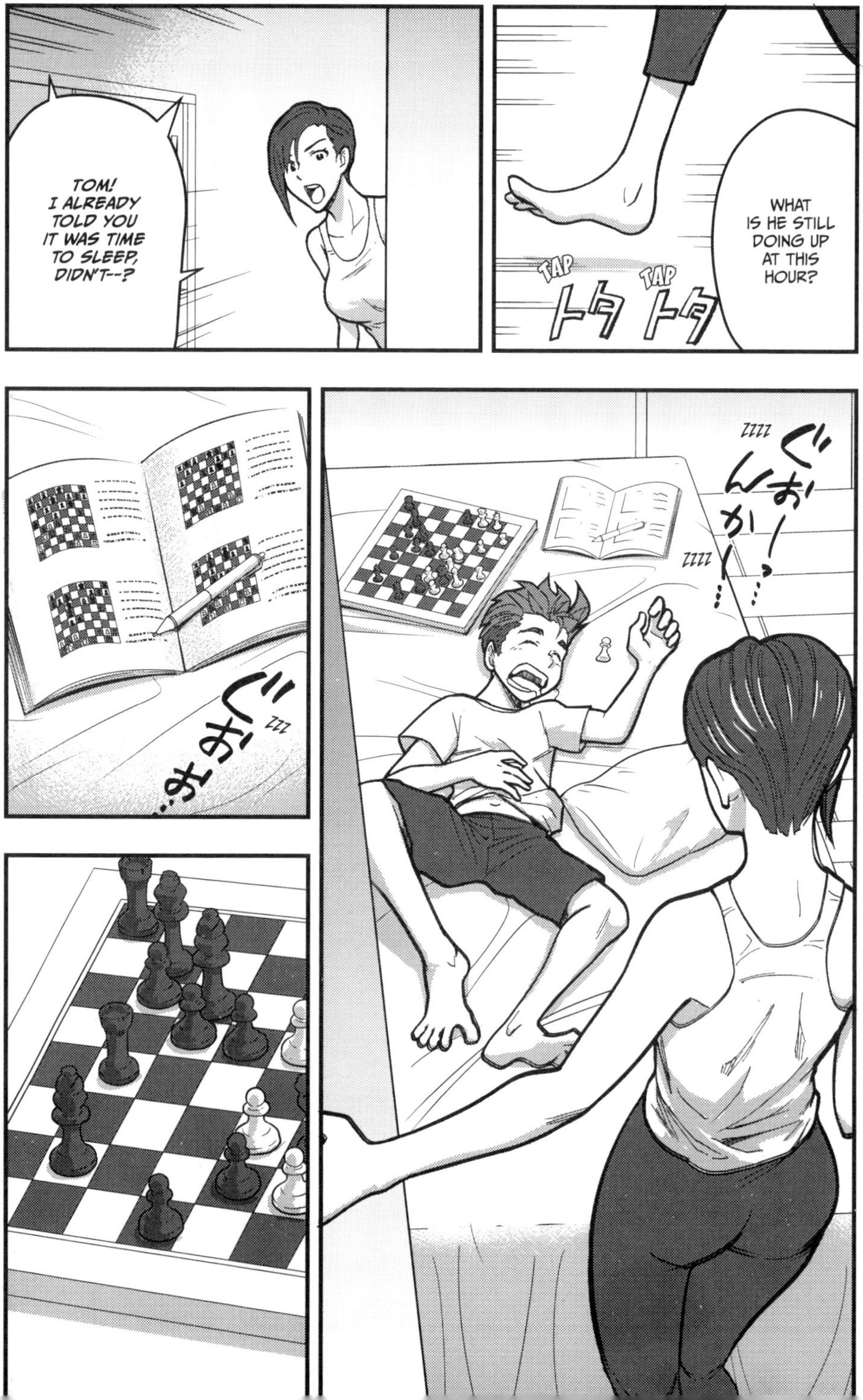
TAP TAP
トタ トタ
WHAT IS HE STILL DOING UP AT THIS HOUR?
TOM! I ALREADY TOLD YOU IT WAS TIME TO SLEEP, DIDN'T--?
ZZZZ
ぐおーんかー…
ZZZZ
ZZZ
ぐおお…

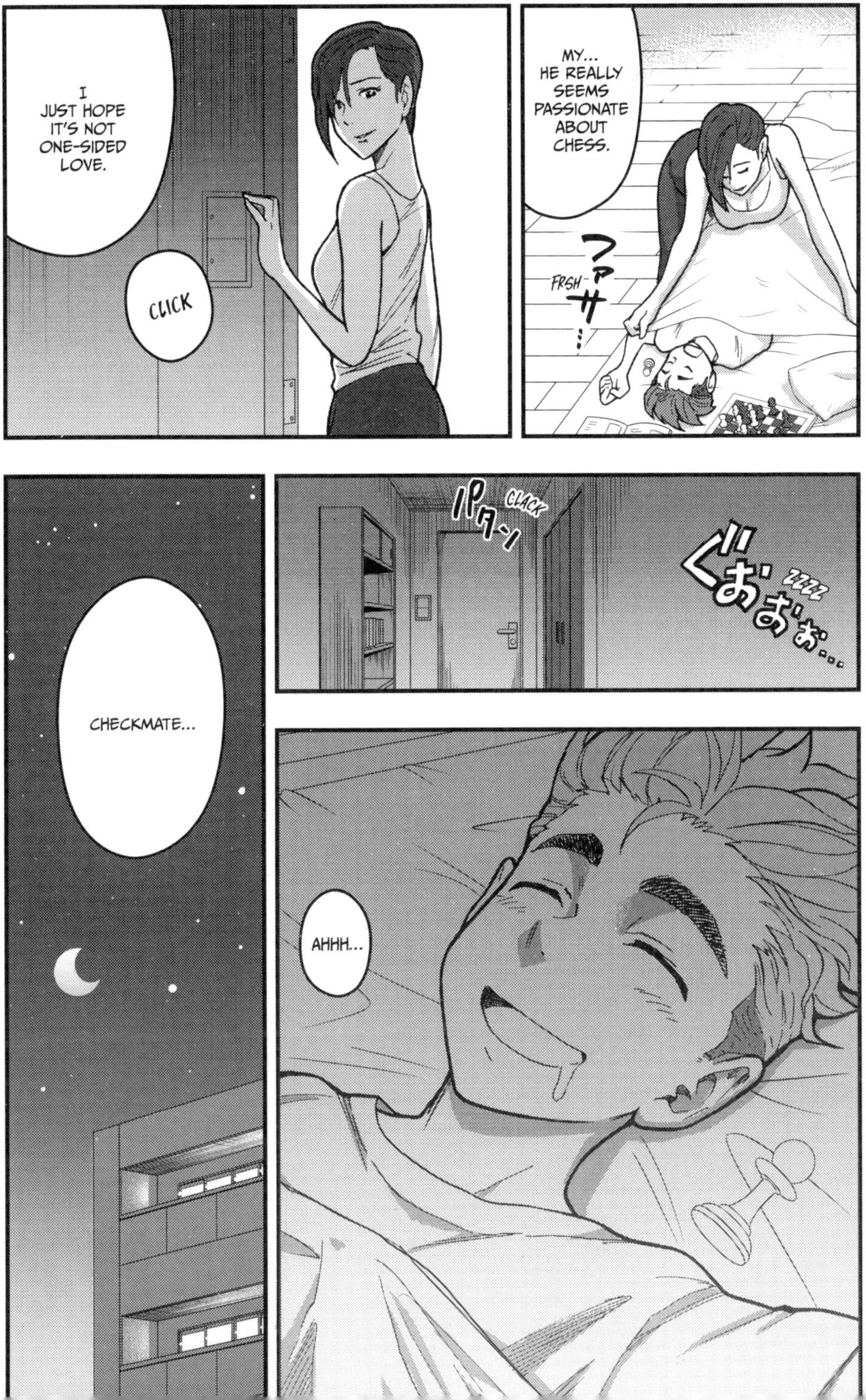
MY... HE REALLY SEEMS PASSIONATE ABOUT CHESS.
ファサ…
FRSH
I JUST HOPE IT'S NOT ONE-SIDED LOVE.
CLICK
パタン
CLACK
ぐおおお…
ZZZZ
AHHH...
CHECKMATE...

BLiTZ

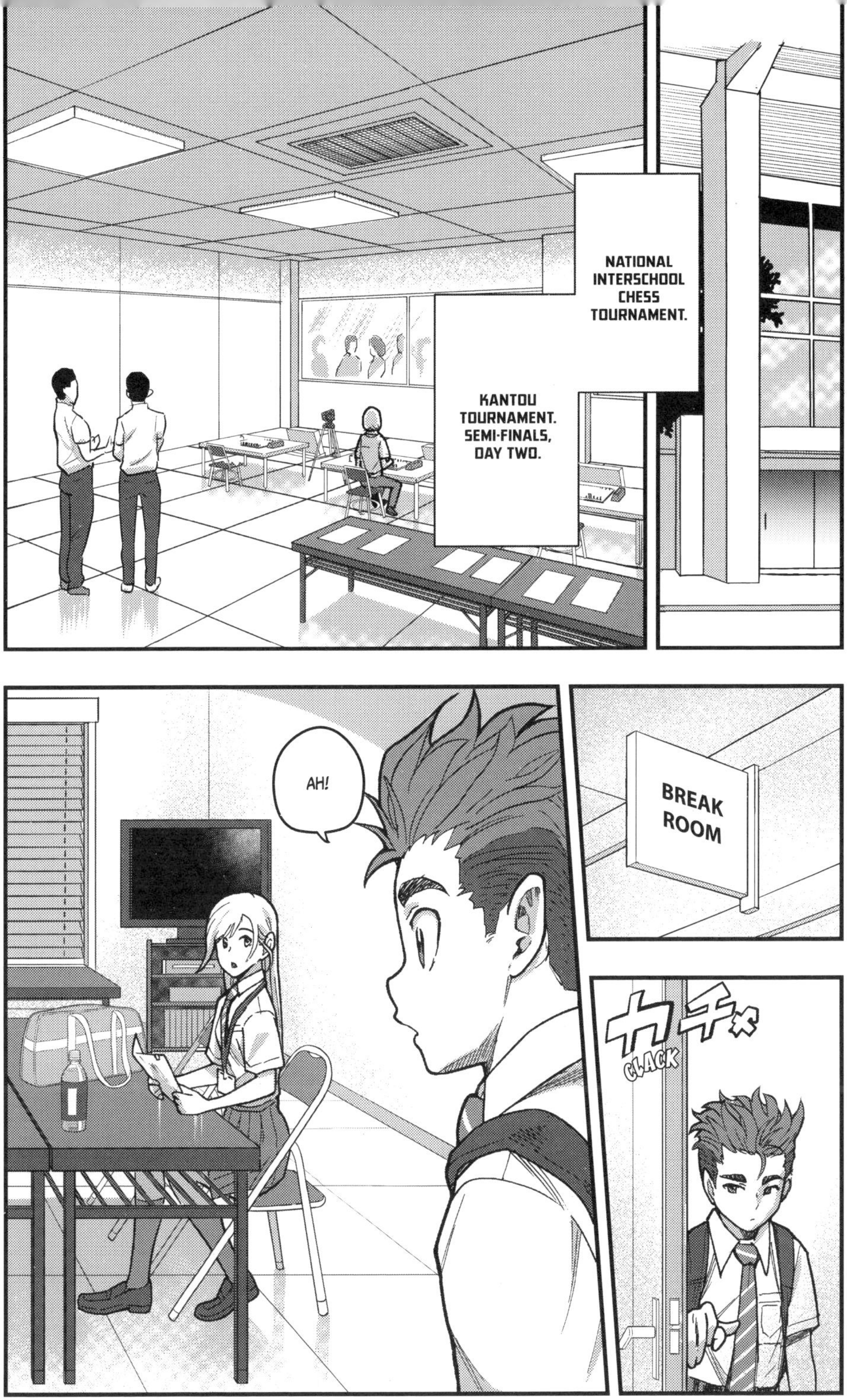
NATIONAL INTERSCHOOL CHESS TOURNAMENT.
KANTOU TOURNAMENT. SEMI-FINALS, DAY TWO.
BREAK ROOM
カチャ
CLACK
AH!

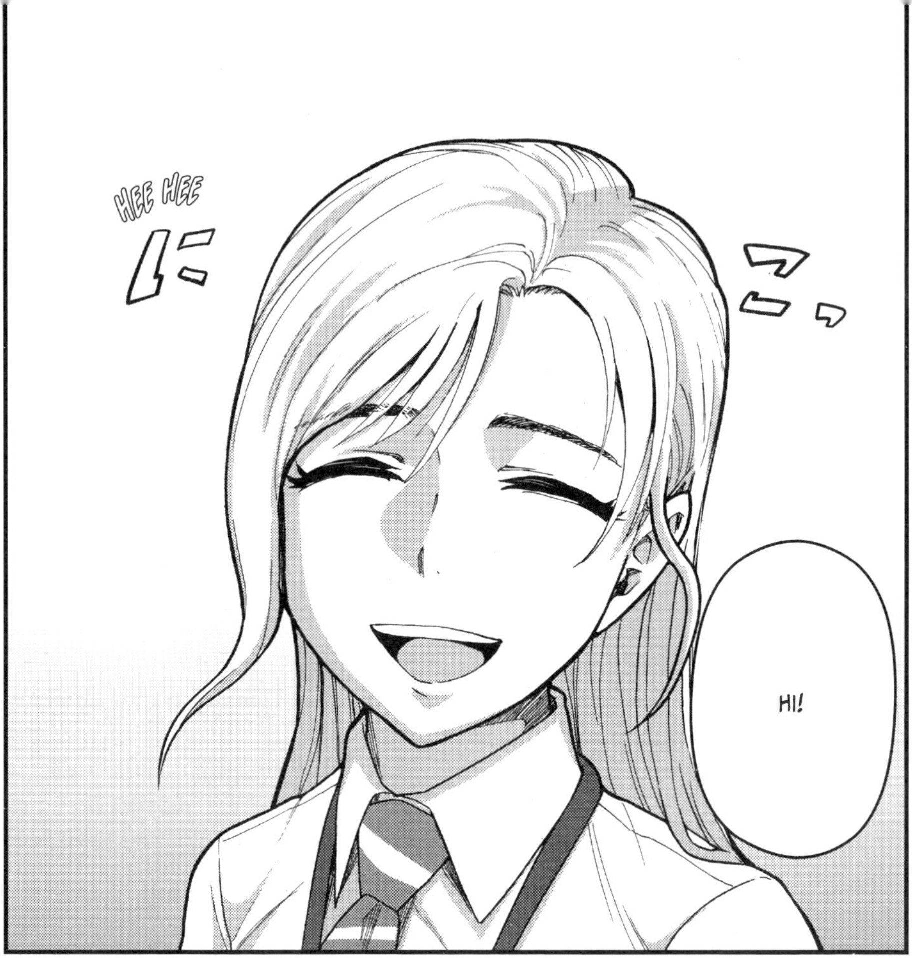
HEE HEE
HI!

Chapter 19: Princess

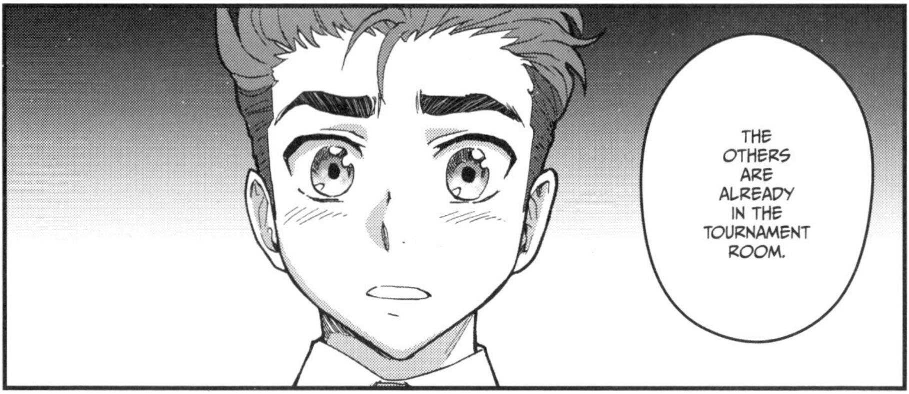
THE OTHERS ARE ALREADY IN THE TOURNAMENT ROOM.

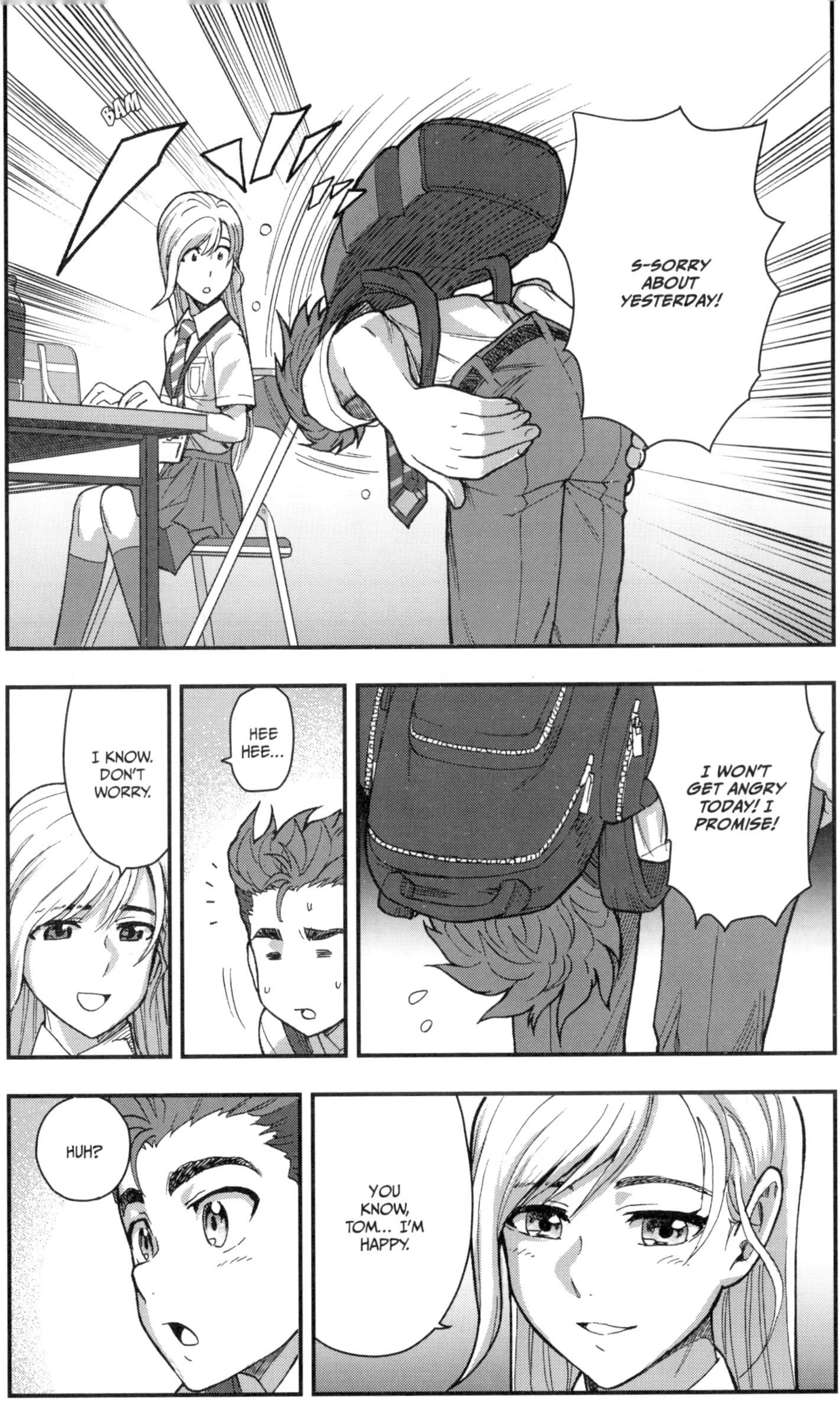
BAM
S-SORRY ABOUT YESTERDAY!
I WON'T GET ANGRY TODAY! I PROMISE!
HEE HEE...
I KNOW. DON'T WORRY.
YOU KNOW, TOM... I'M HAPPY.
HUH?

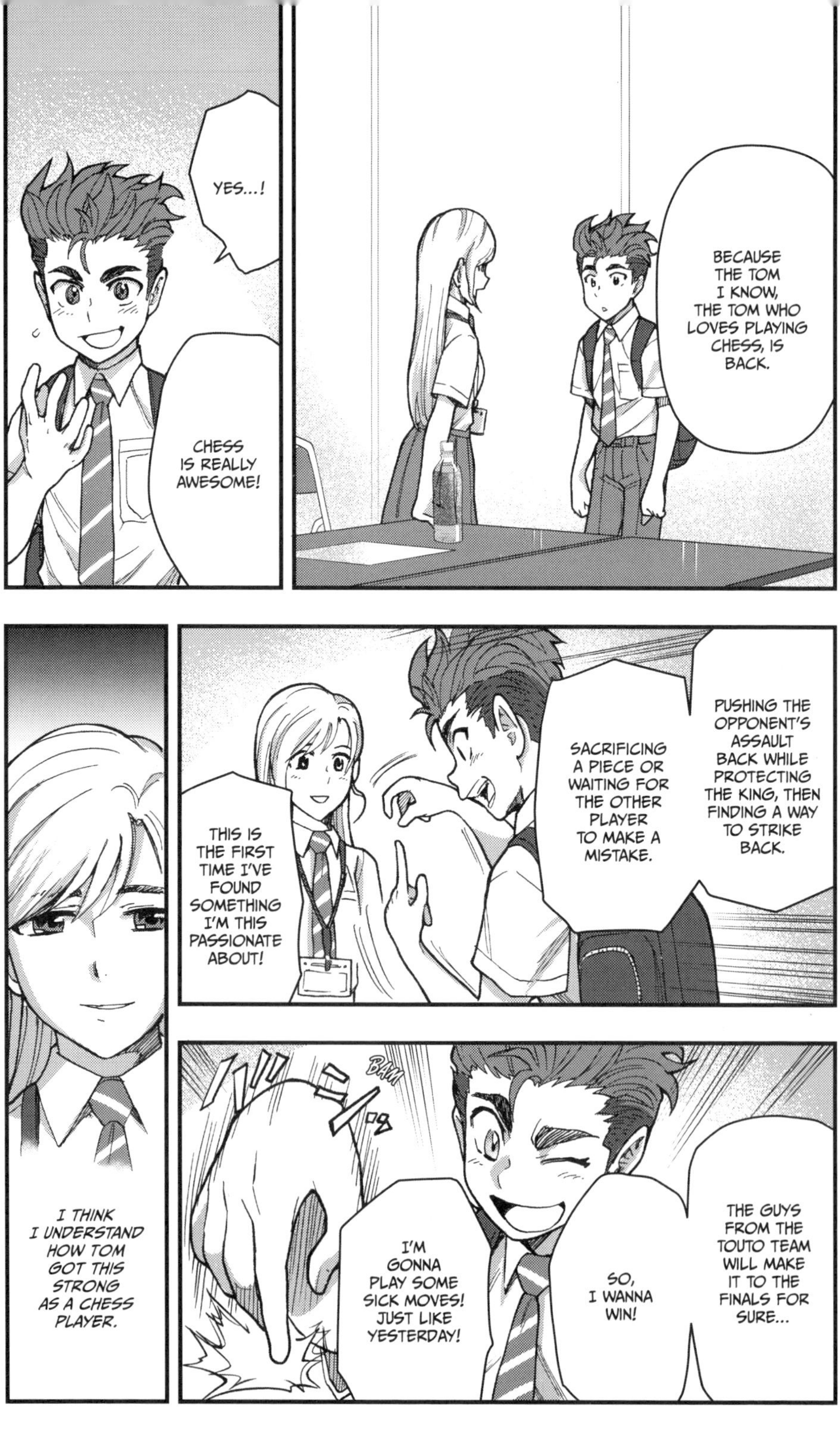
BECAUSE THE TOM I KNOW, THE TOM WHO LOVES PLAYING CHESS, IS BACK.
YES...!
CHESS IS REALLY AWESOME!
PUSHING THE OPPONENT'S ASSAULT BACK WHILE PROTECTING THE KING, THEN FINDING A WAY TO STRIKE BACK.
SACRIFICING A PIECE OR WAITING FOR THE OTHER PLAYER TO MAKE A MISTAKE.
THIS IS THE FIRST TIME I'VE FOUND SOMETHING I'M THIS PASSIONATE ABOUT!
BAM
THE GUYS FROM THE TOUTO TEAM WILL MAKE IT TO THE FINALS FOR SURE...
SO, I WANNA WIN!
I'M GONNA PLAY SOME SICK MOVES! JUST LIKE YESTERDAY!
I THINK I UNDERSTAND HOW TOM GOT THIS STRONG AS A CHESS PLAYER.

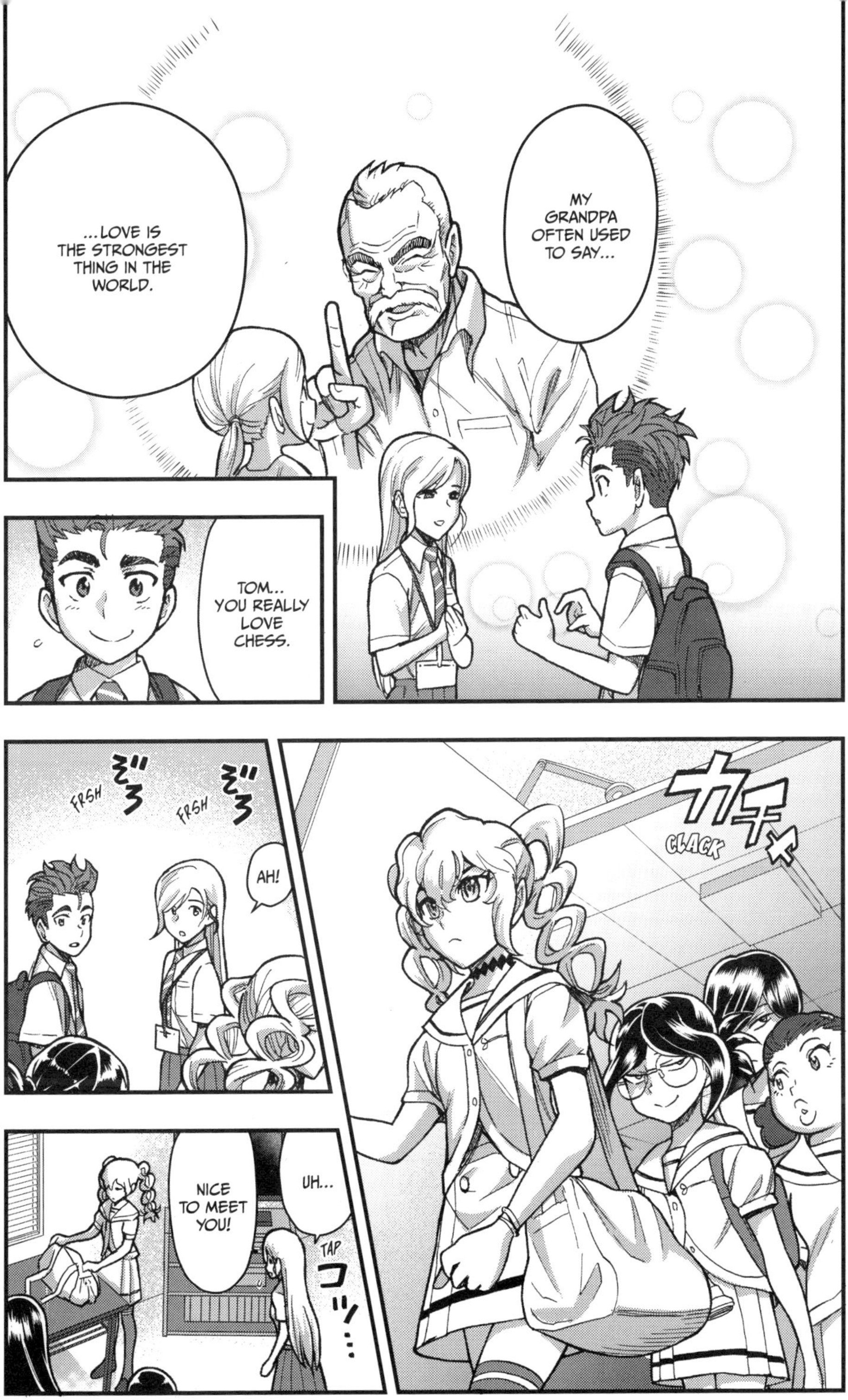
MY GRANDPA OFTEN USED TO SAY...
...LOVE IS THE STRONGEST THING IN THE WORLD.
TOM... YOU REALLY LOVE CHESS.
カチャ
CLACK
FRSH
ぞろ
FRSH
ぞろ
AH!
UH...
NICE TO MEET YOU!
TAP
コツ...

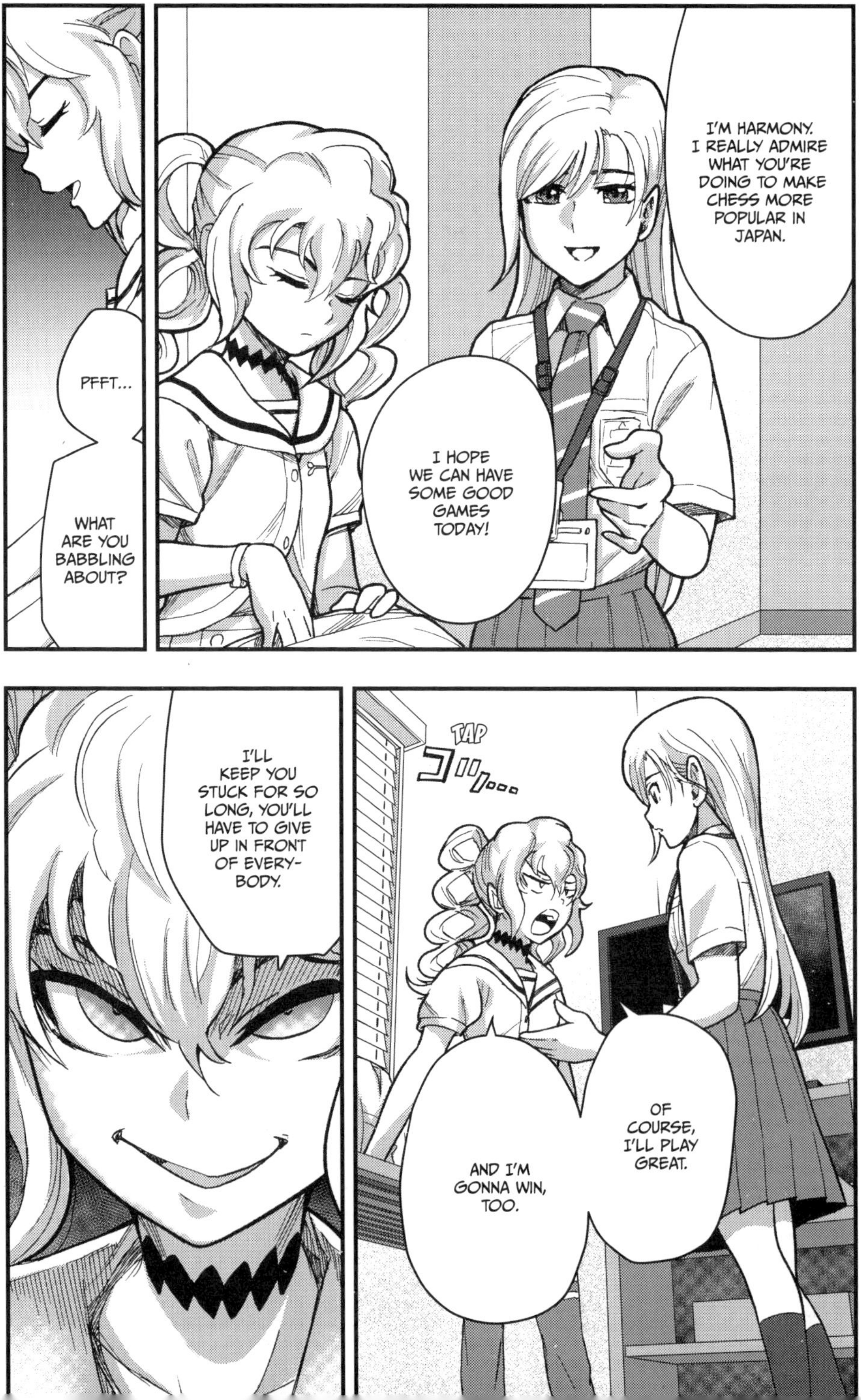
I'M HARMONY. I REALLY ADMIRE WHAT YOU'RE DOING TO MAKE CHESS MORE POPULAR IN JAPAN.
I HOPE WE CAN HAVE SOME GOOD GAMES TODAY!
PFFT...
WHAT ARE YOU BABBLING ABOUT?
TAP
OF COURSE, I'LL PLAY GREAT.
AND I'M GONNA WIN, TOO.
I'LL KEEP YOU STUCK FOR SO LONG, YOU'LL HAVE TO GIVE UP IN FRONT OF EVERY-BODY.

DON'T SWEAT IT, HARMONY.

I'M NOT WORRIED. THIS HAPPENS ALL THE TIME IN TOURNAMENTS.

バタン CLACK

ビクビク

HMPH!

ACTUALLY... SHE'S SO PASSIONATE ABOUT CHESS THAT I ALMOST WANT HER TO WIN.

HARMONY?

BUT...

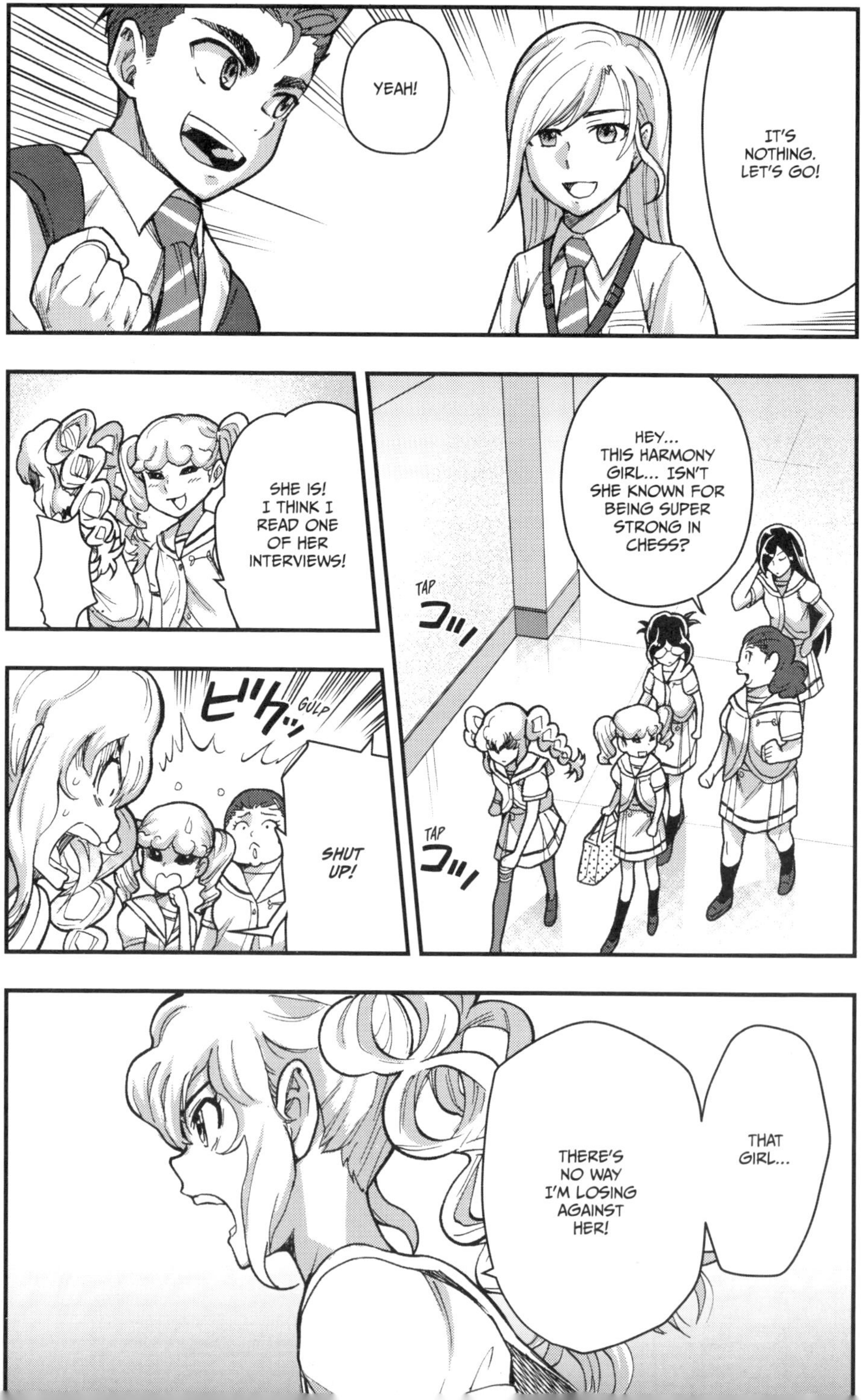
IT'S NOTHING. LET'S GO!
YEAH!
HEY... THIS HARMONY GIRL... ISN'T SHE KNOWN FOR BEING SUPER STRONG IN CHESS?
TAP
TAP
SHE IS! I THINK I READ ONE OF HER INTERVIEWS!
GULP
SHUT UP!
THAT GIRL...
THERE'S NO WAY I'M LOSING AGAINST HER!

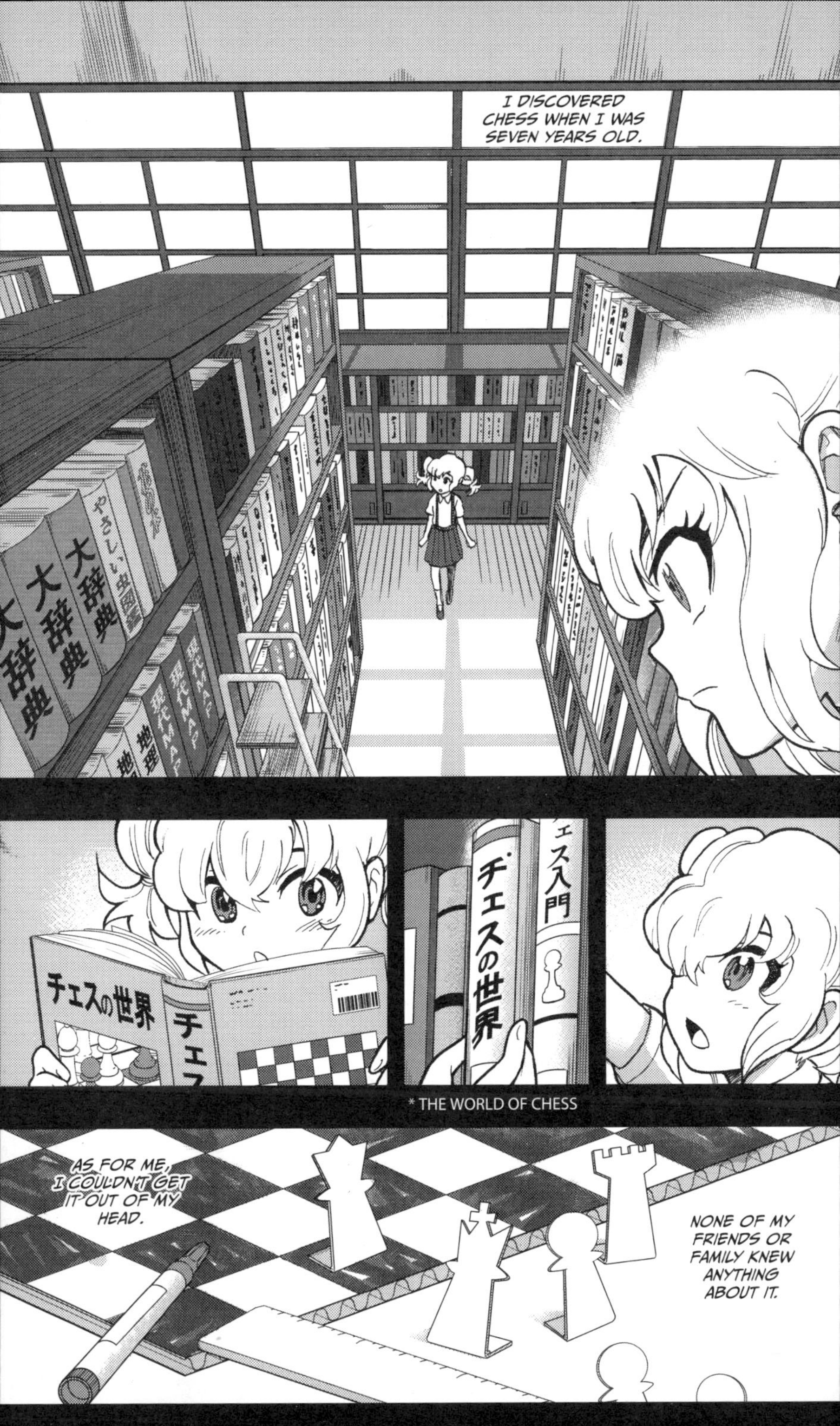
I DISCOVERED CHESS WHEN I WAS SEVEN YEARS OLD.
大辞典
大辞典
大辞典
やさしい虫図鑑
チェス入門
チェスの世界
チェスの世界
NONE OF MY FRIENDS OR FAMILY KNEW ANYTHING ABOUT IT.
AS FOR ME, I COULDN'T GET IT OUT OF MY HEAD.
* THE WORLD OF CHESS

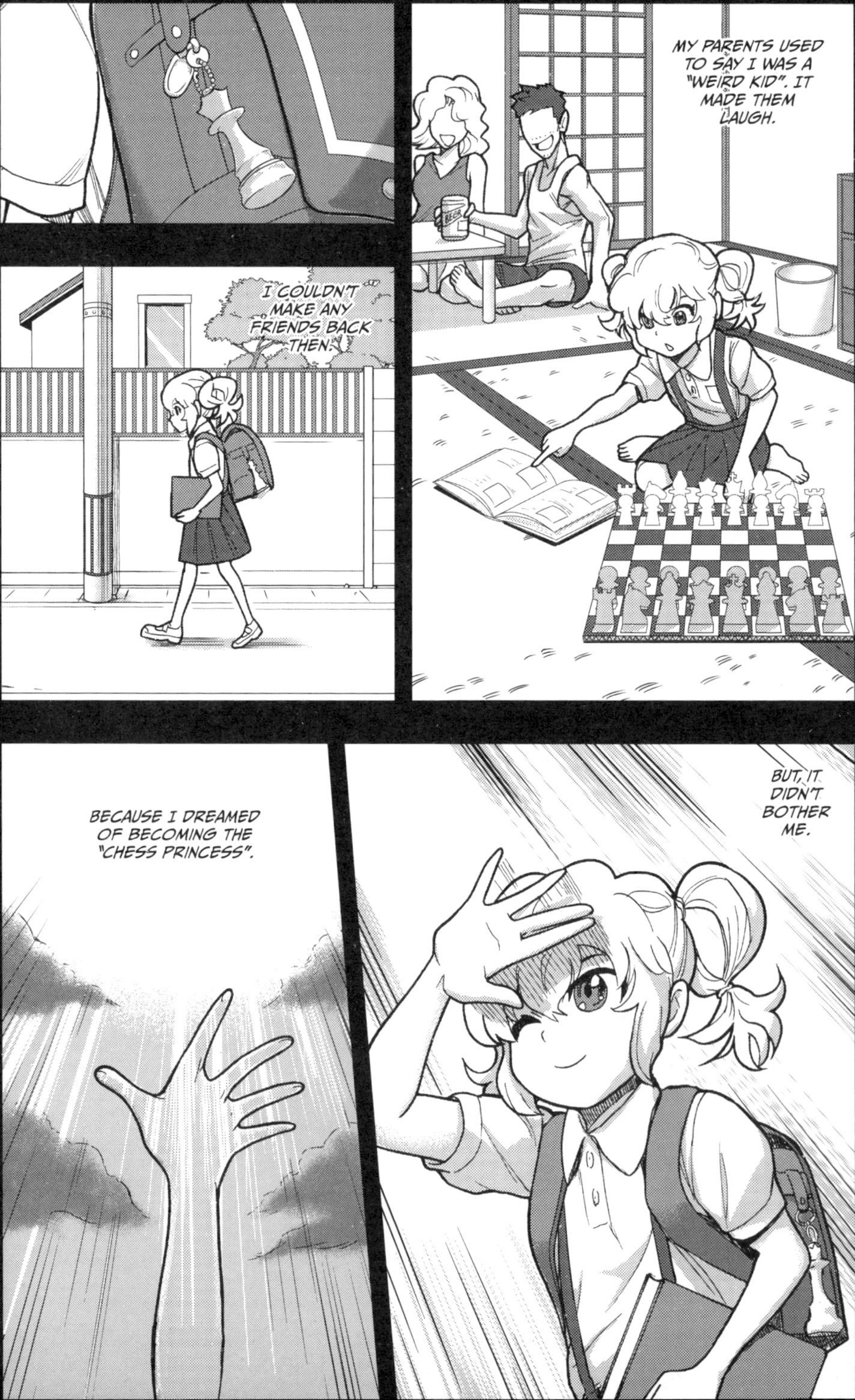
MY PARENTS USED TO SAY I WAS A "WEIRD KID". IT MADE THEM LAUGH.
BEER
I COULDN'T MAKE ANY FRIENDS BACK THEN.
BUT, IT DIDN'T BOTHER ME.
BECAUSE I DREAMED OF BECOMING THE "CHESS PRINCESS".

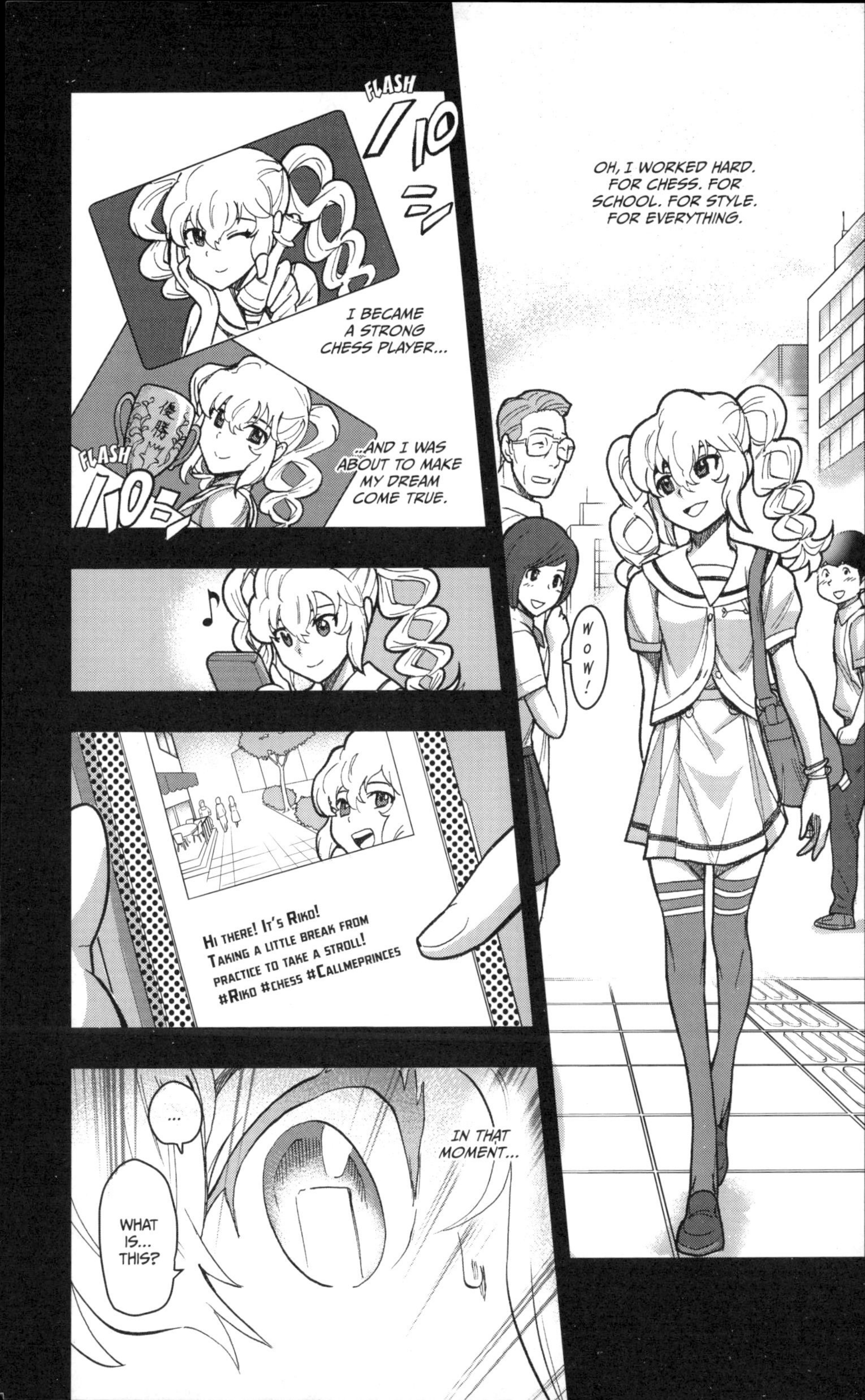
OH, I WORKED HARD. FOR CHESS. FOR SCHOOL. FOR STYLE. FOR EVERYTHING.
WOW!
FLASH
I BECAME A STRONG CHESS PLAYER...
FLASH
...AND I WAS ABOUT TO MAKE MY DREAM COME TRUE.
Hi there! It's Riko! Taking a little break from practice to take a stroll! #Riko #chess #Callmeprinces
IN THAT MOMENT...
...
WHAT IS... THIS?

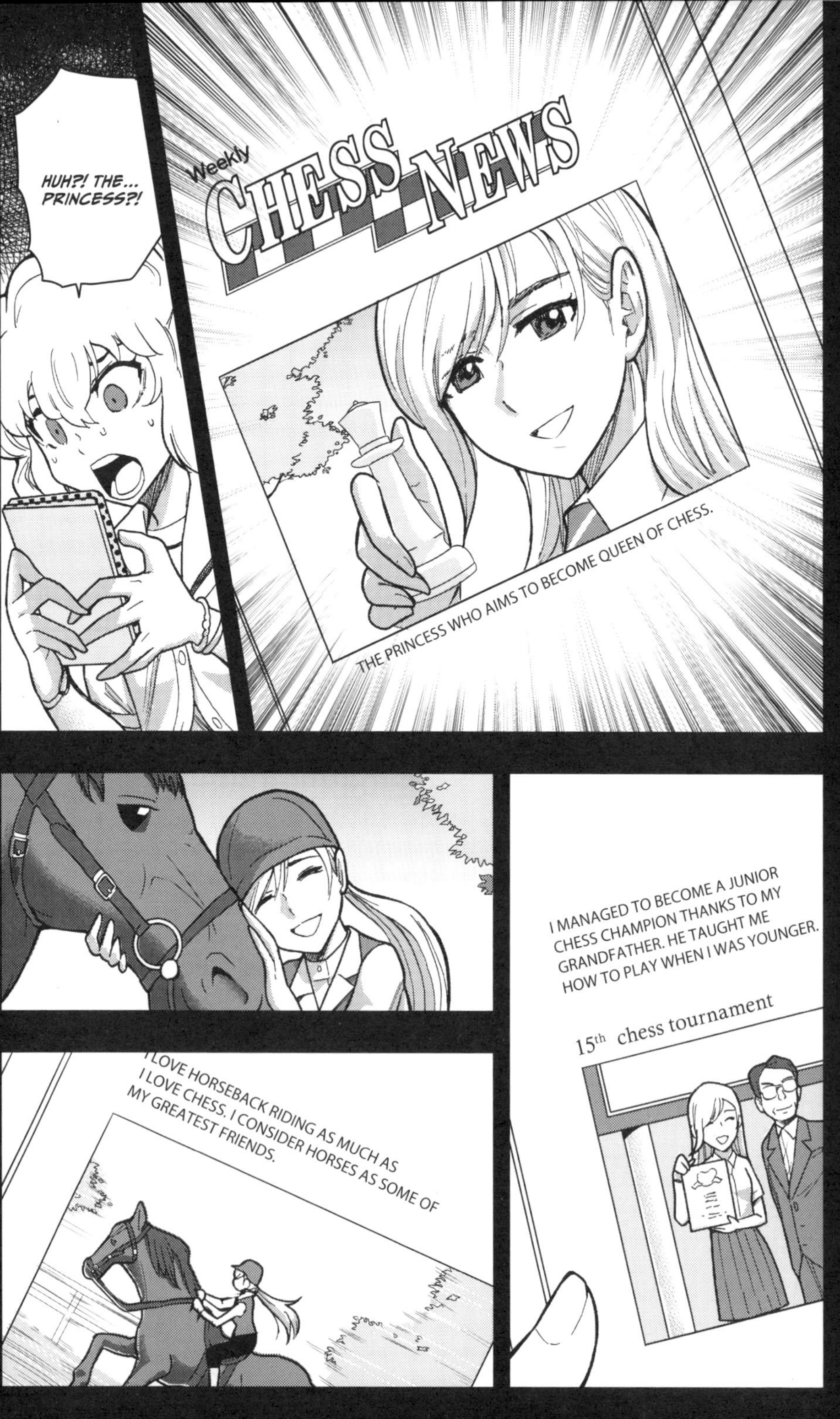
Weekly
CHESS NEWS
THE PRINCESS WHO AIMS TO BECOME QUEEN OF CHESS.
HUH?! THE... PRINCESS?!
I MANAGED TO BECOME A JUNIOR CHESS CHAMPION THANKS TO MY GRANDFATHER. HE TAUGHT ME HOW TO PLAY WHEN I WAS YOUNGER.
15th chess tournament
I LOVE HORSEBACK RIDING AS MUCH AS I LOVE CHESS. I CONSIDER HORSES AS SOME OF MY GREATEST FRIENDS.

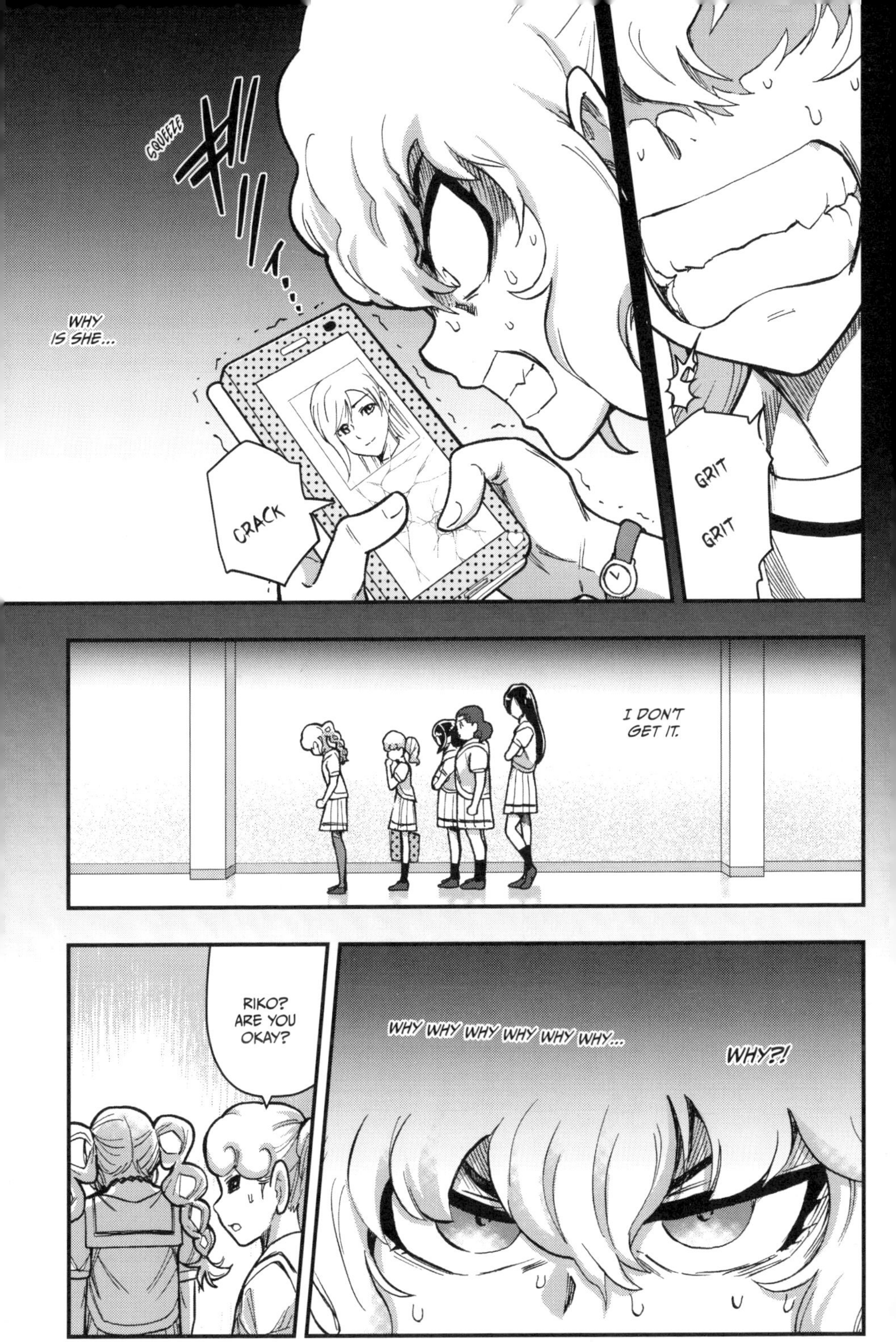
SQUEEZE
WHY IS SHE...
CRACK
GRIT GRIT
I DON'T GET IT.
RIKO? ARE YOU OKAY?
WHY WHY WHY WHY WHY WHY...
WHY?!

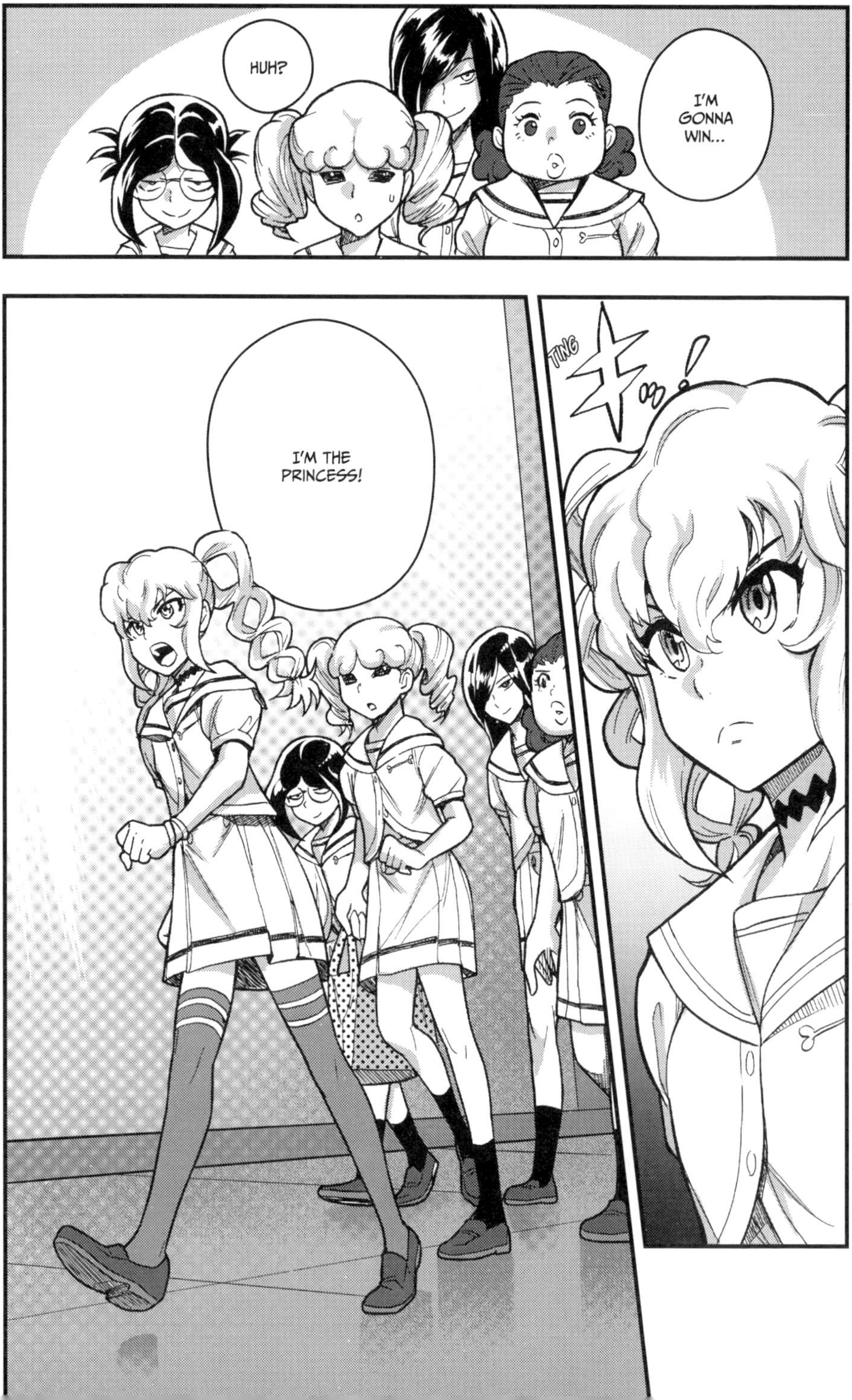
I'M GONNA WIN...
HUH?
TING
I'M THE PRINCESS!

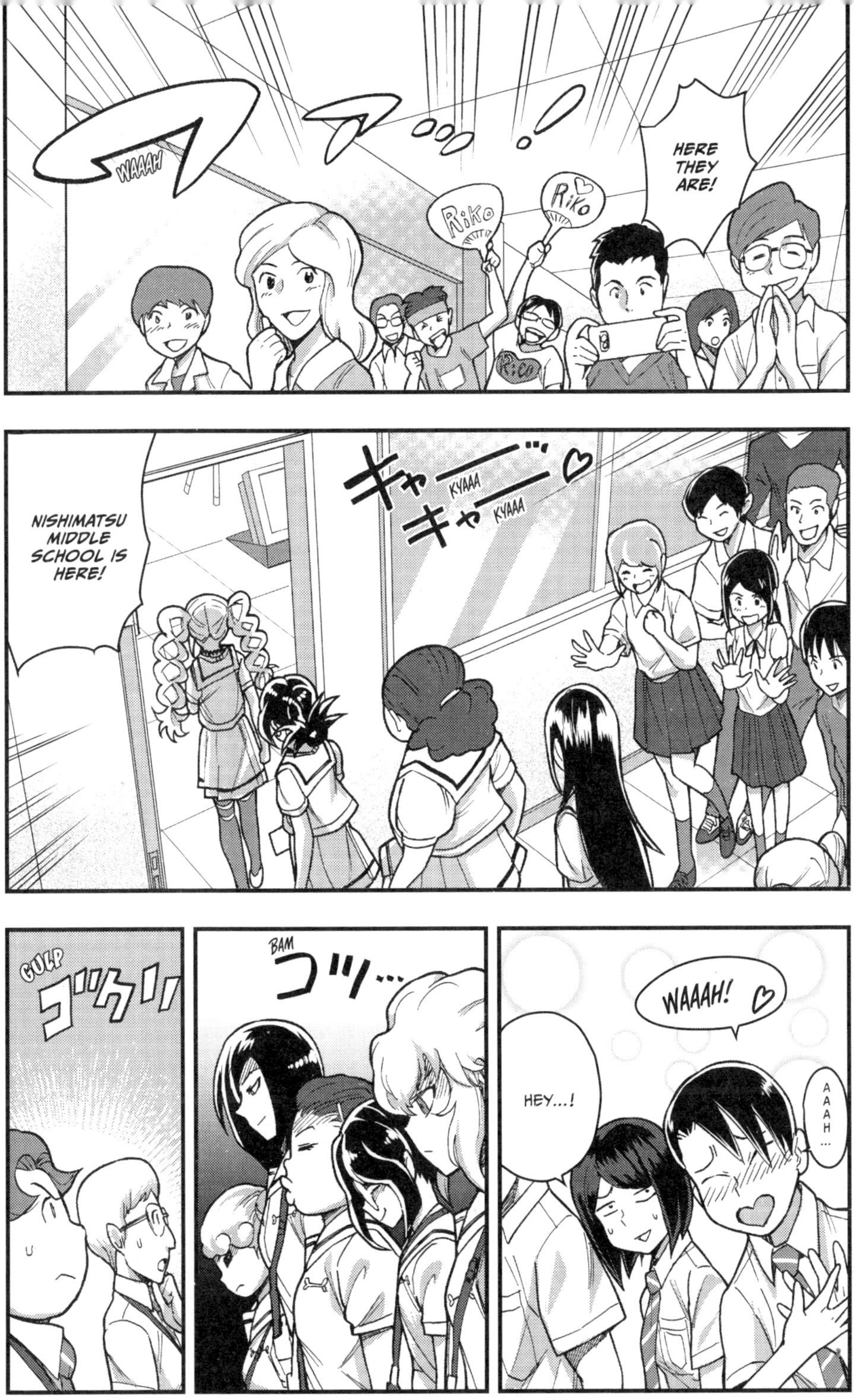
HERE THEY ARE!
WAAAH
RiKo
RiKo
NISHIMATSU MIDDLE SCHOOL IS HERE!
キャーーー KYAAA
キャー KYAAA
WAAAH!
AAAH...
HEY...!
コツ... BAM
ゴクリ GULP

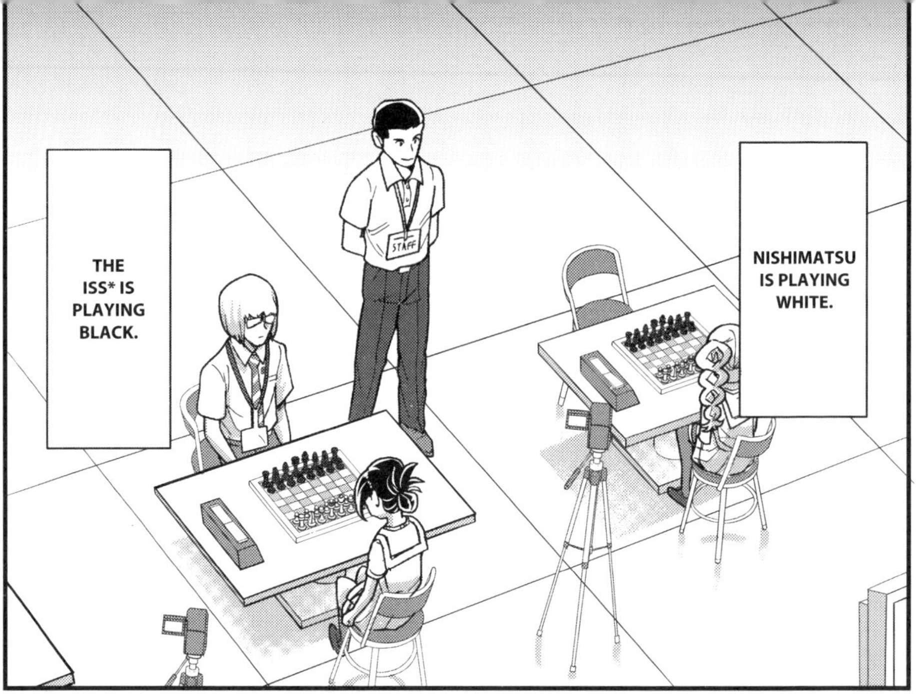
NISHIMATSU IS PLAYING WHITE.
THE ISS* IS PLAYING BLACK.

* INTERNATIONAL SCHOOL OF SHIBUYA

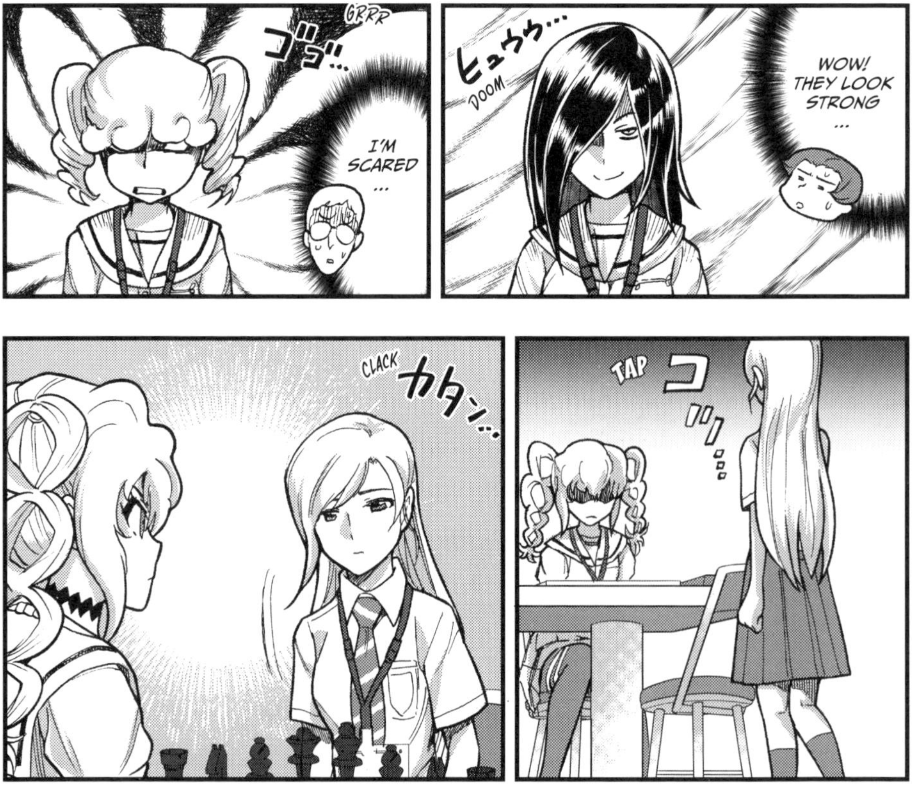
ヒュウウ…
DOOM
WOW! THEY LOOK STRONG ...
ゴゴ…
GRRR
I'M SCARED ...
TAP
コツ…
CLACK
カタン…

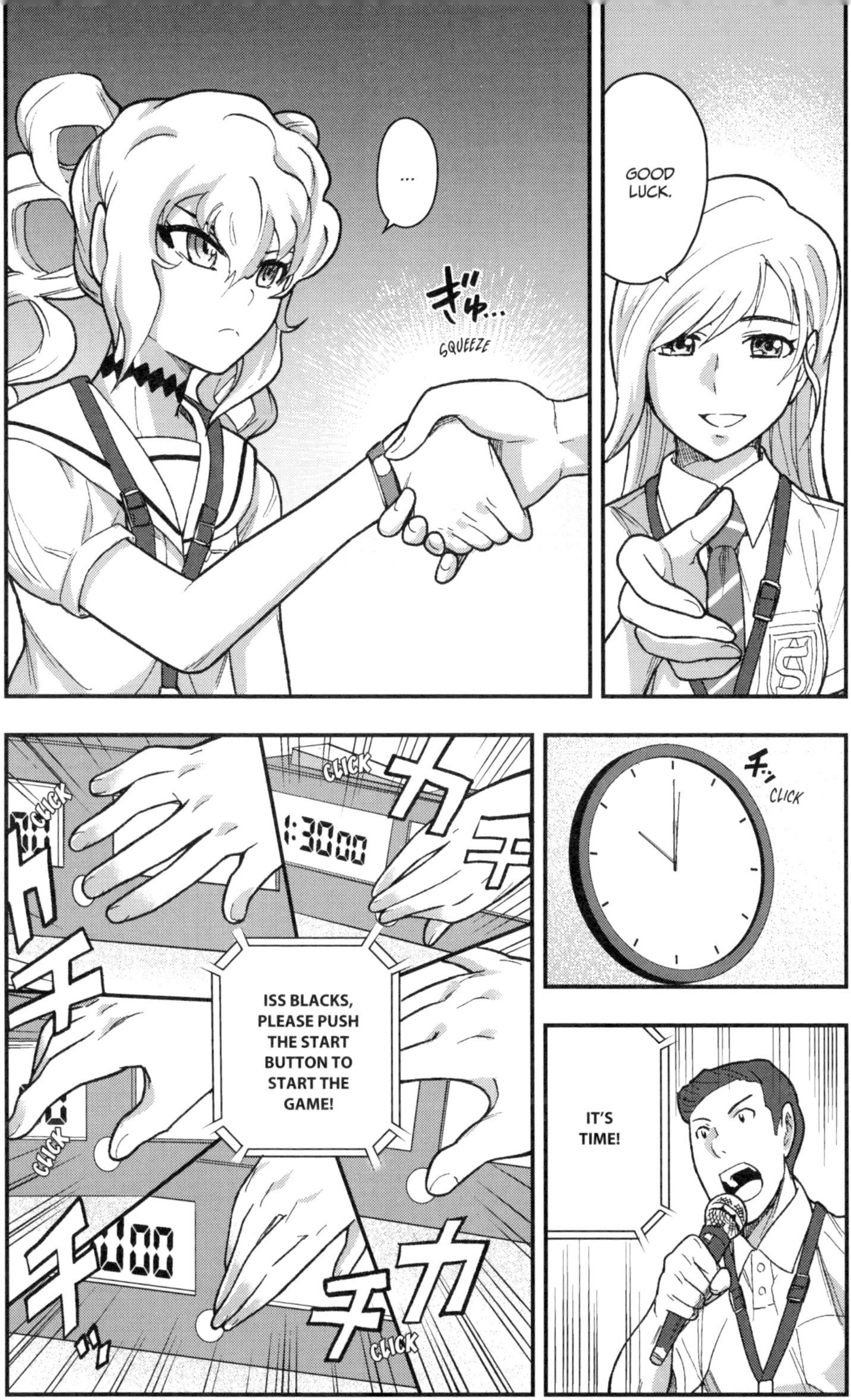
GOOD LUCK.
...
ぎゅ...
SQUEEZE
チッ
CLICK
IT'S TIME!
ISS BLACKS, PLEASE PUSH THE START BUTTON TO START THE GAME!
カチ
CLICK
カチ
CLICK
カチ
CLICK
カチ
CLICK
カチ
CLICK

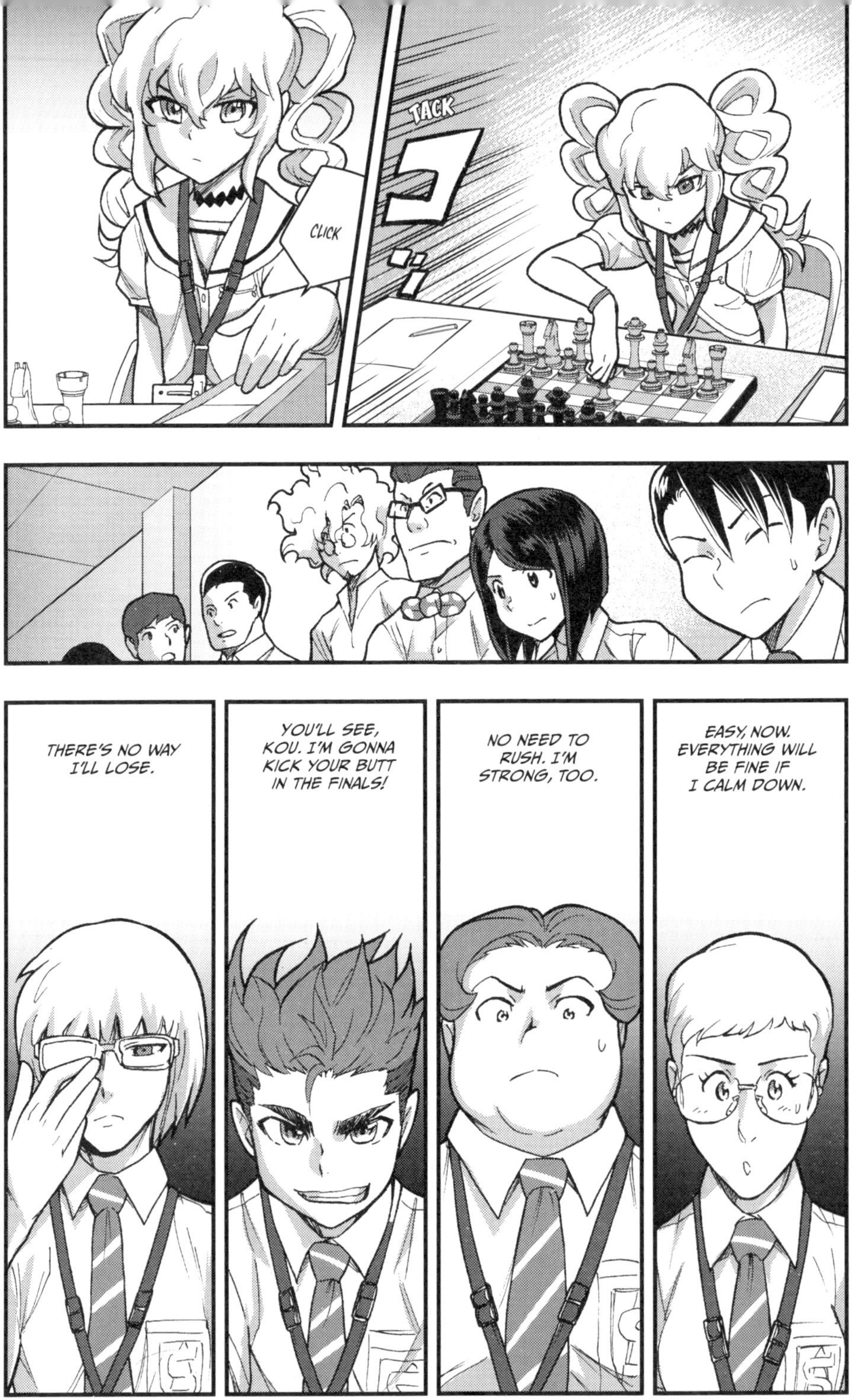
TACK
CLICK
EASY, NOW. EVERYTHING WILL BE FINE IF I CALM DOWN.
NO NEED TO RUSH. I'M STRONG, TOO.
YOU'LL SEE, KOU. I'M GONNA KICK YOUR BUTT IN THE FINALS!
THERE'S NO WAY I'LL LOSE.

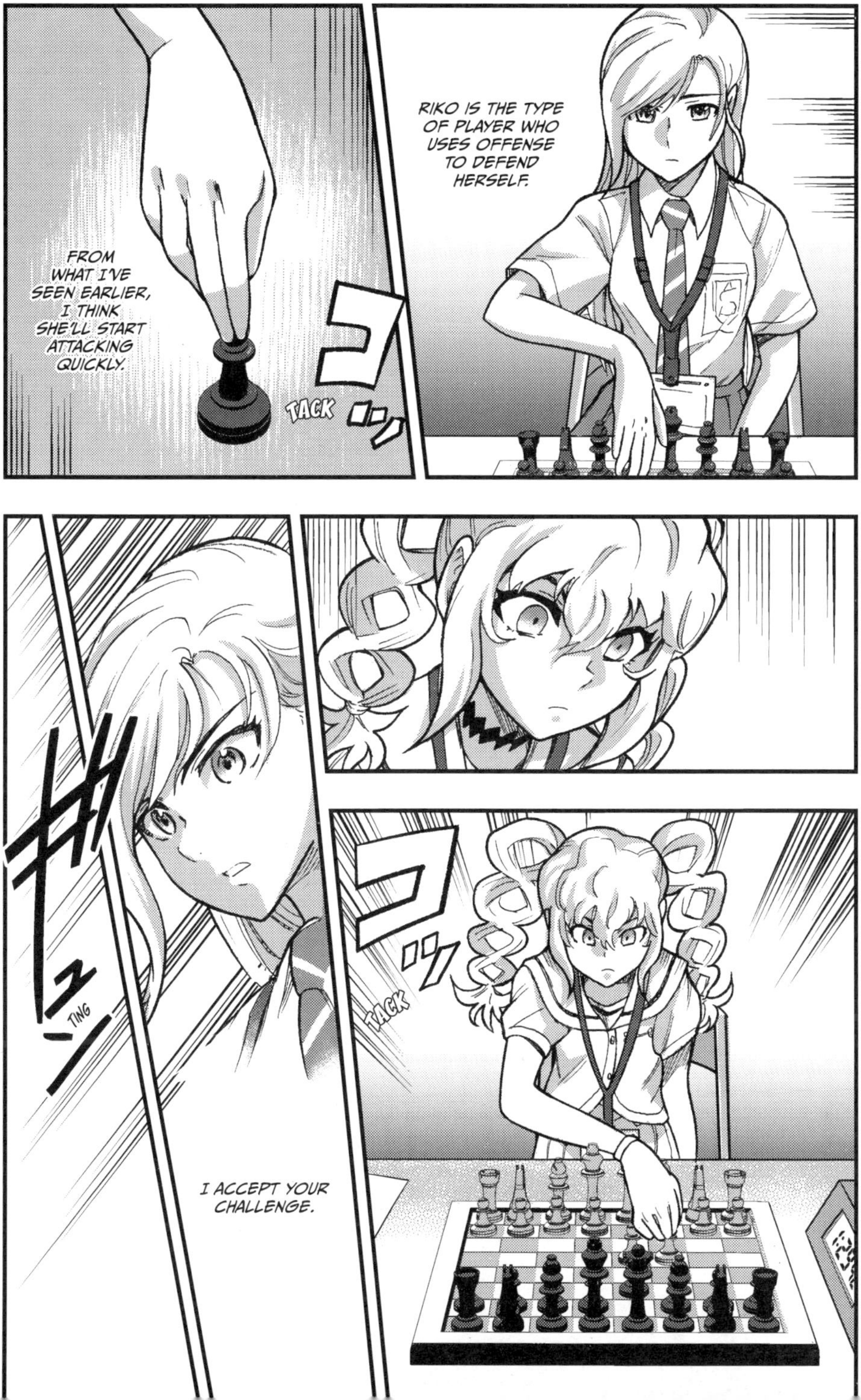
RIKO IS THE TYPE OF PLAYER WHO USES OFFENSE TO DEFEND HERSELF.
FROM WHAT I'VE SEEN EARLIER, I THINK SHE'LL START ATTACKING QUICKLY.
TACK
TACK
TING
I ACCEPT YOUR CHALLENGE.

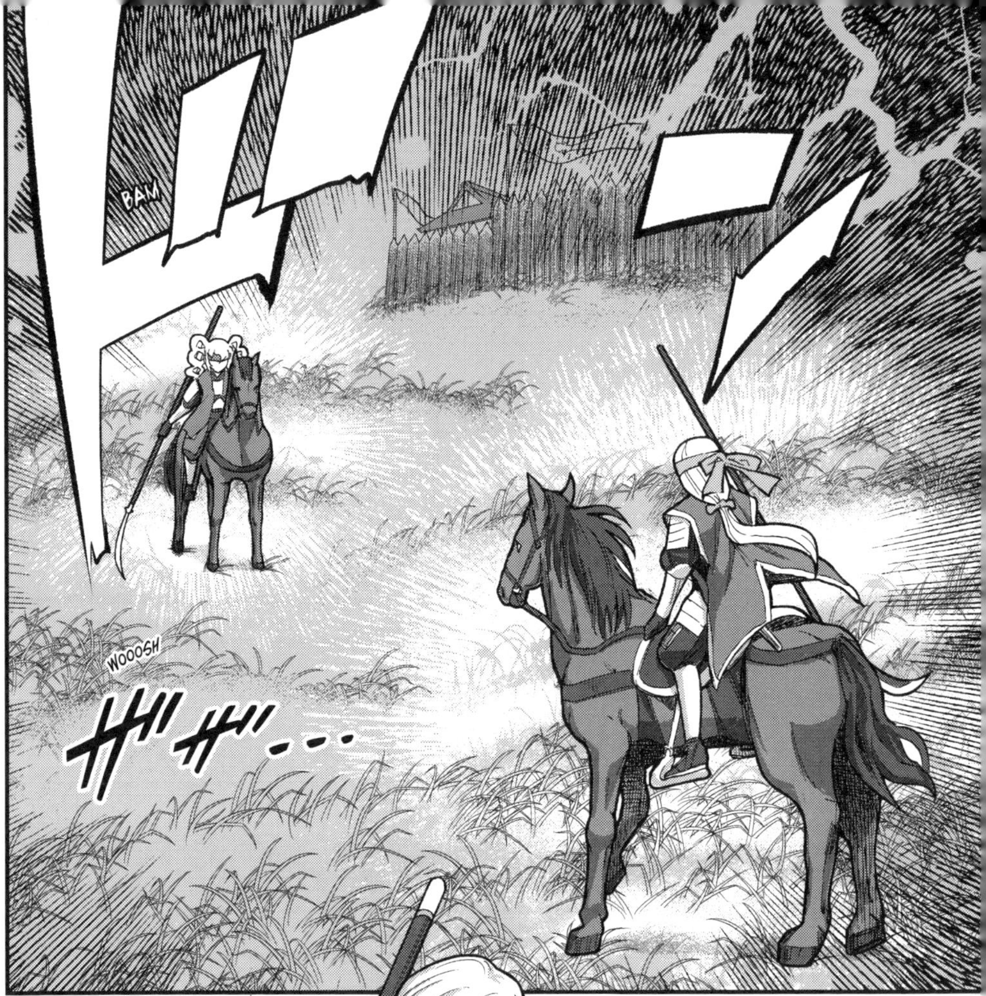
BAM
WOOOSH
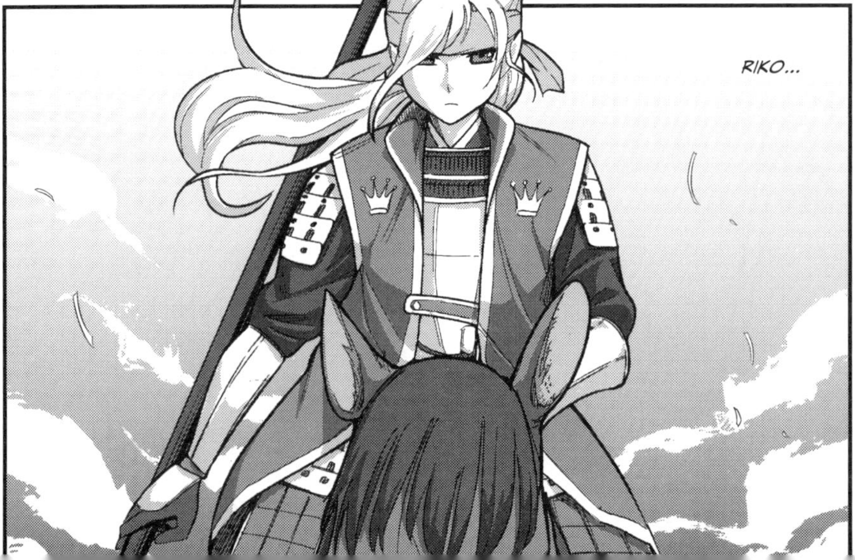
RIKO...

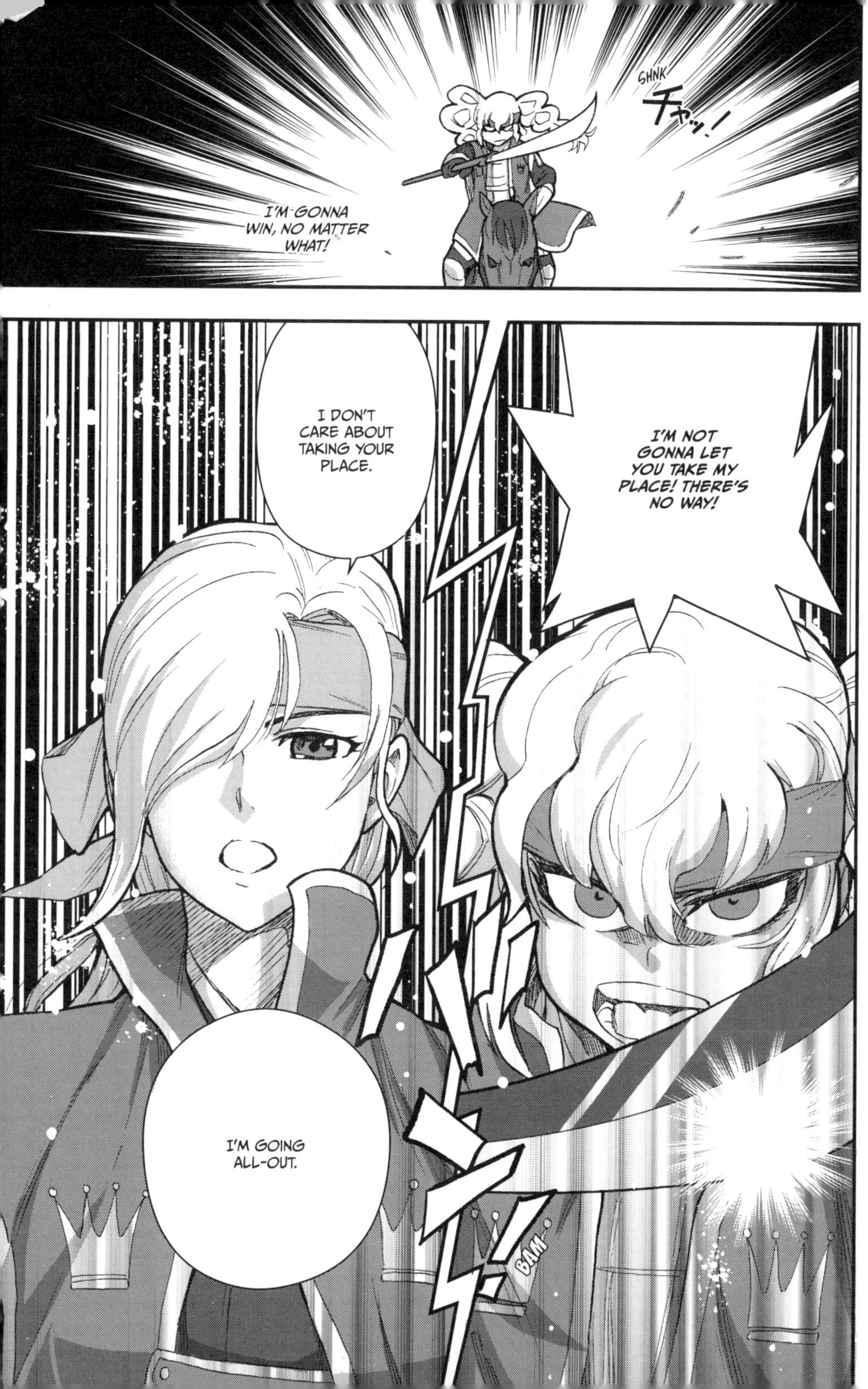
SHNK
チャッ!
I'M GONNA WIN, NO MATTER WHAT!
I'M NOT GONNA LET YOU TAKE MY PLACE! THERE'S NO WAY!
I DON'T CARE ABOUT TAKING YOUR PLACE.
I'M GOING ALL-OUT.
BAM

BLITZ

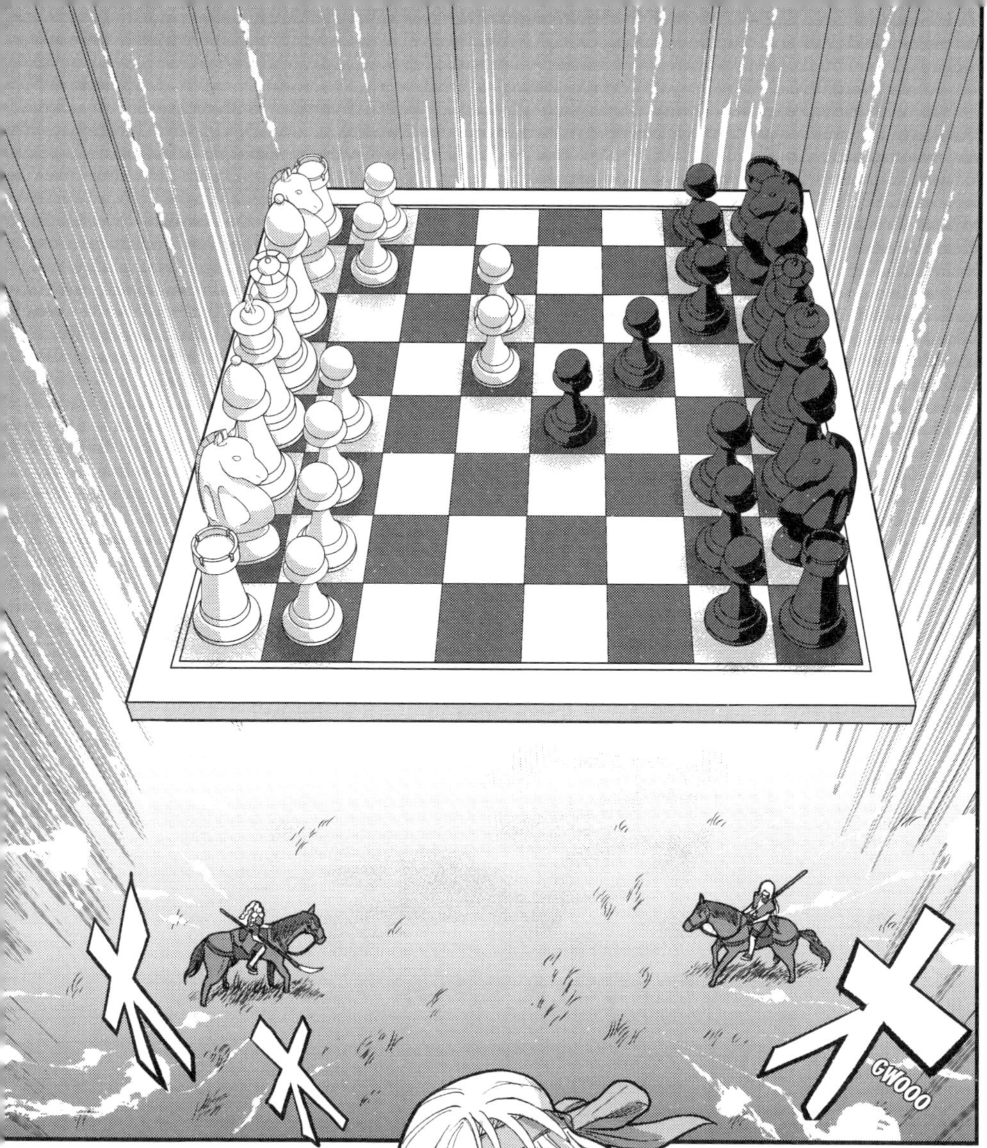
GWOOO
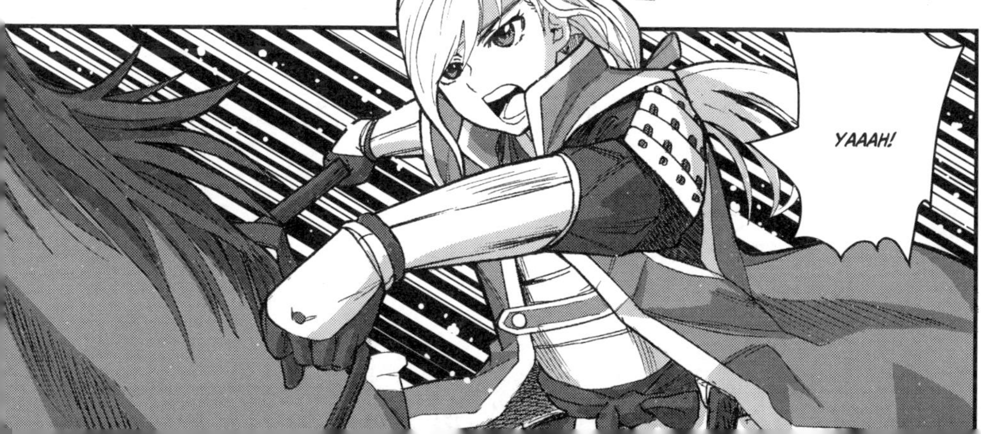
YAAAH!

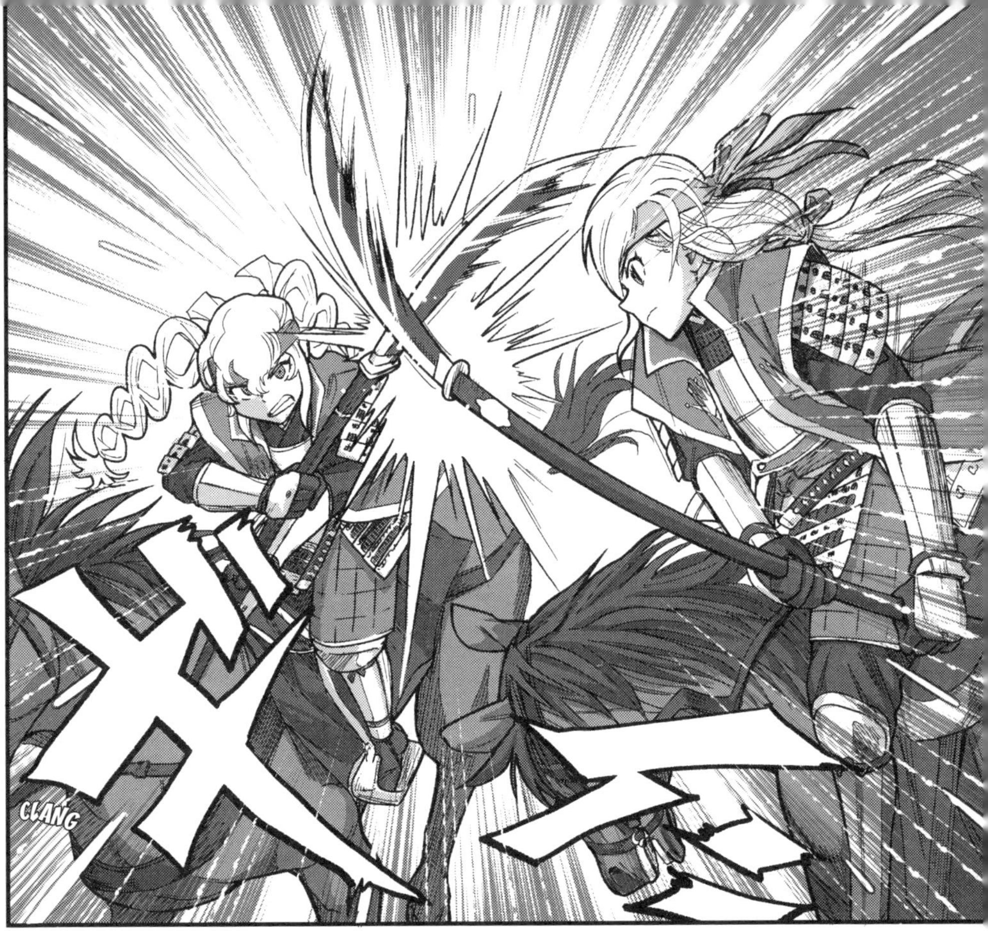
CLANG

Chapter 20: A bitter victory

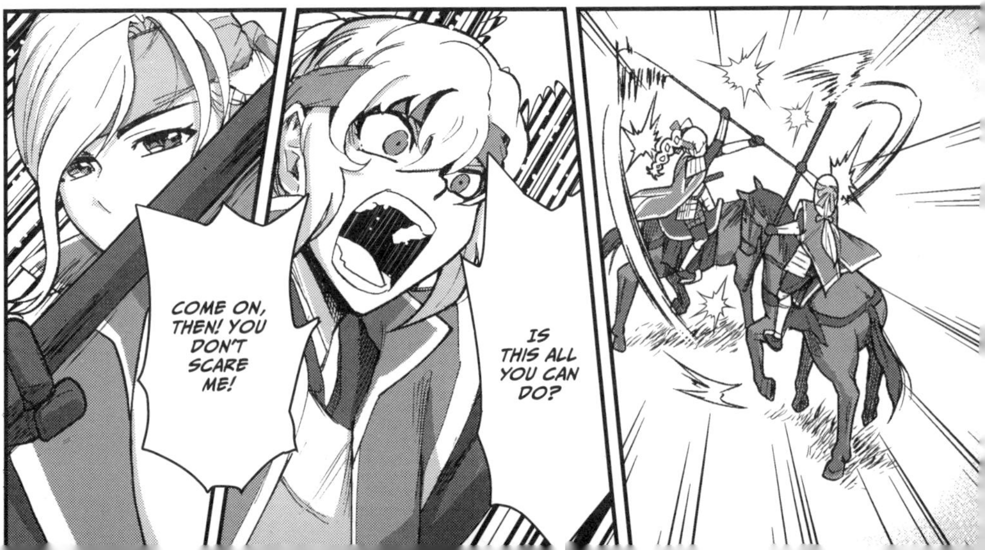
IS THIS ALL YOU CAN DO?
COME ON, THEN! YOU DON'T SCARE ME!

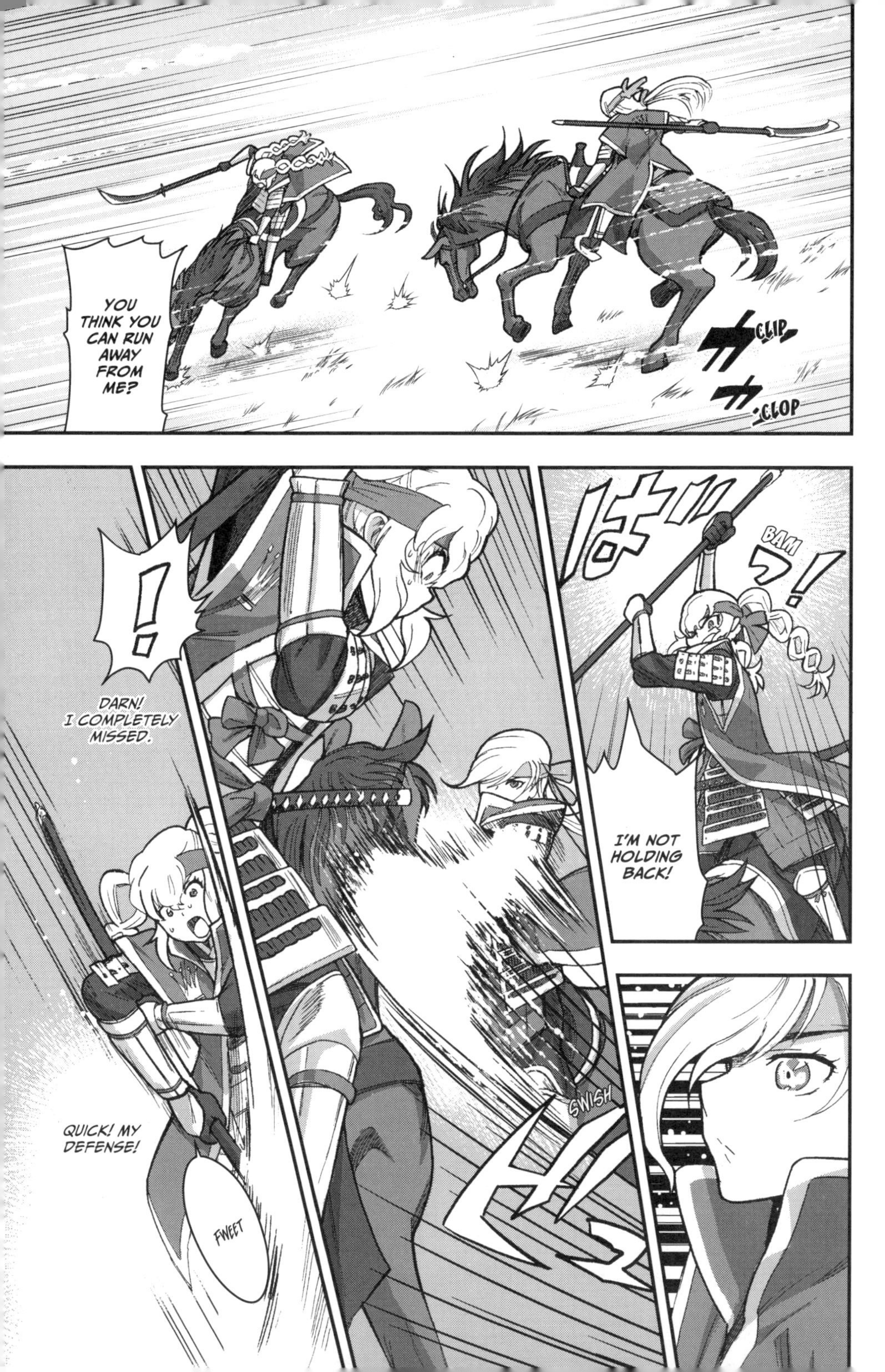
YOU THINK YOU CAN RUN AWAY FROM ME?
CLIP
CLOP
BAM
I'M NOT HOLDING BACK!
!
DARN! I COMPLETELY MISSED.
SWISH
QUICK! MY DEFENSE!
FWEET

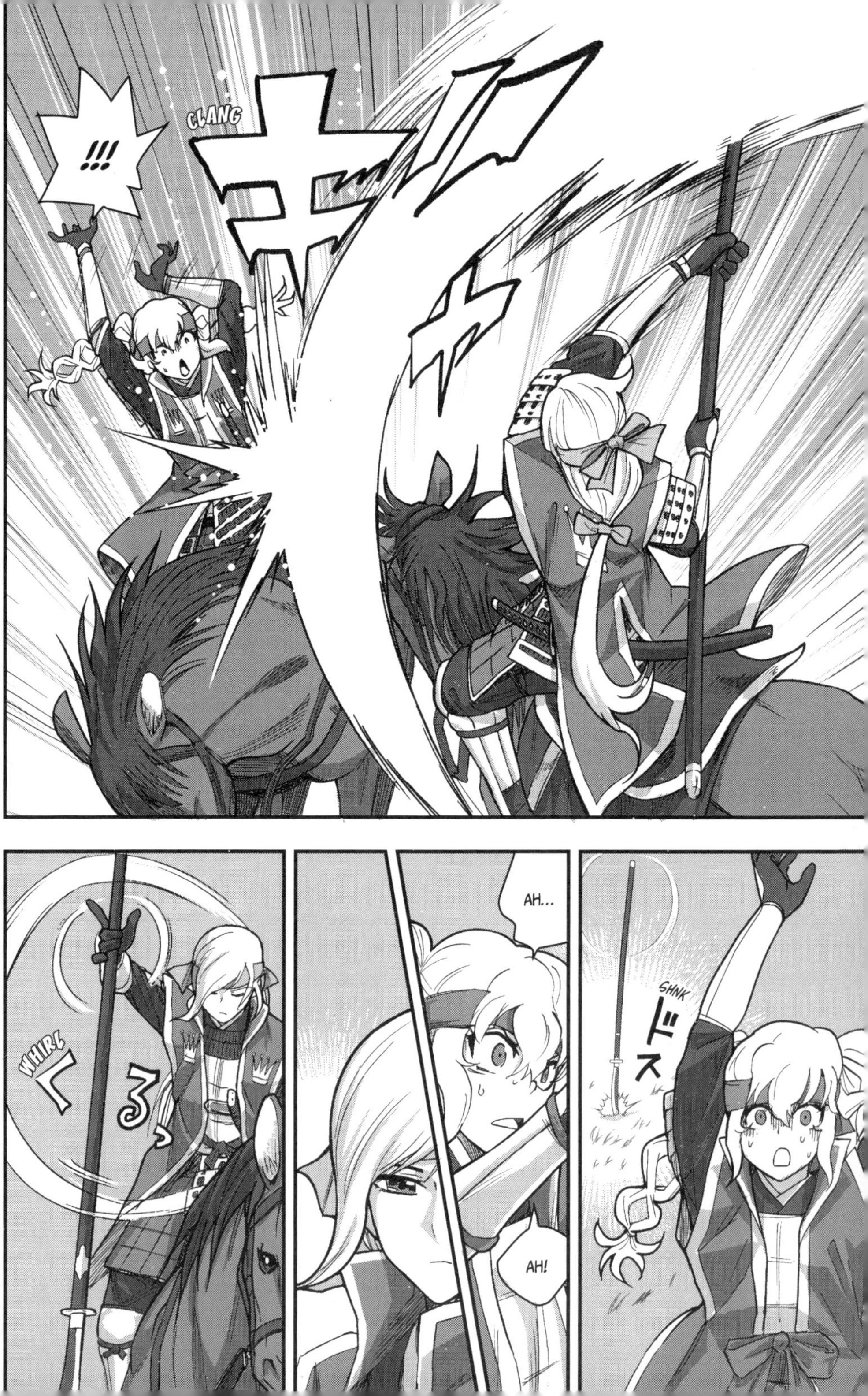
CLANG
!!!
SHNK
ドス
AH...
AH!
WHIRL
くる

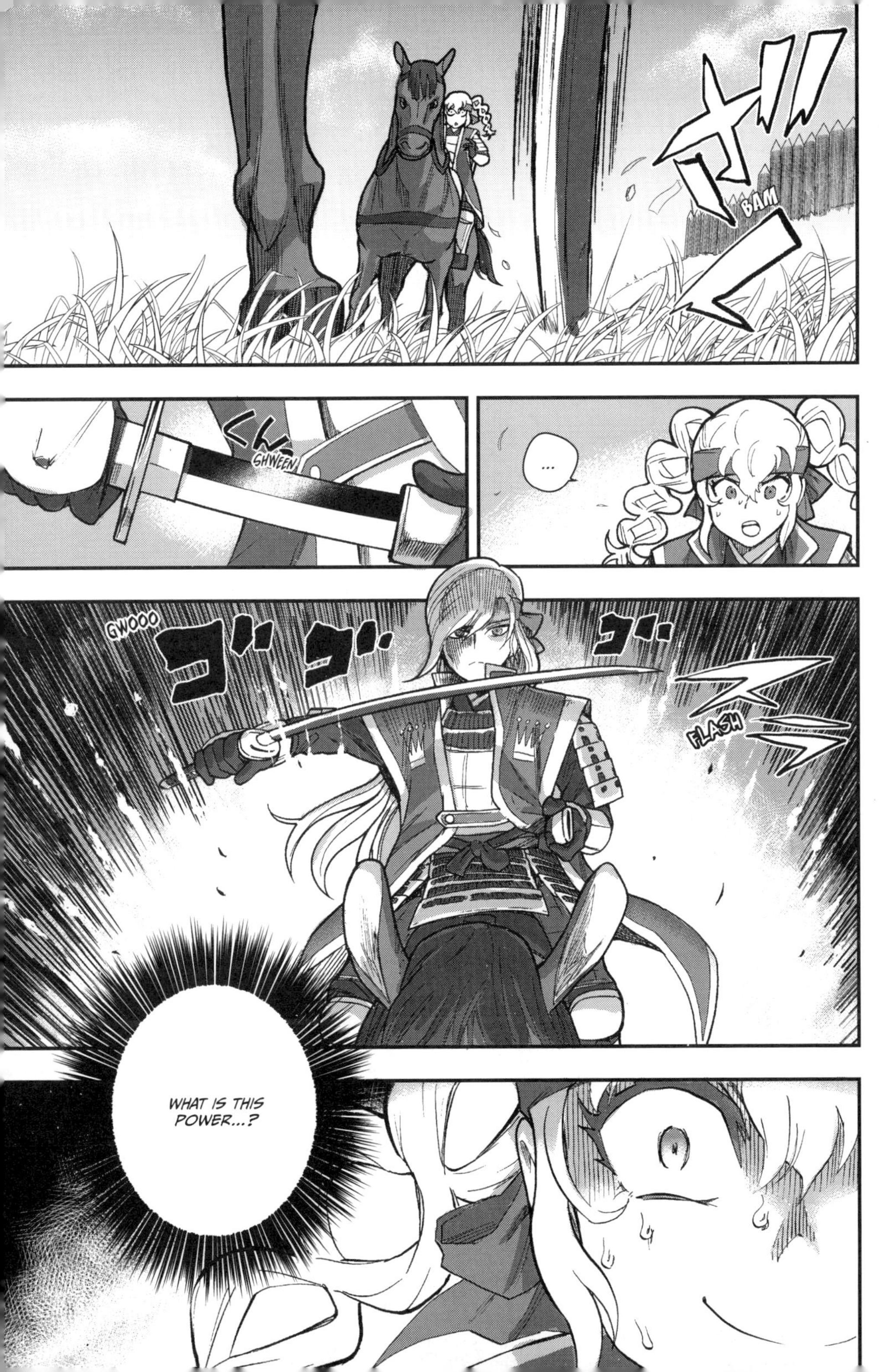

ザッ
BAM
...
くん
GHWEEN
ゴゴゴ
GWOOO
FLASH
WHAT IS THIS POWER...?

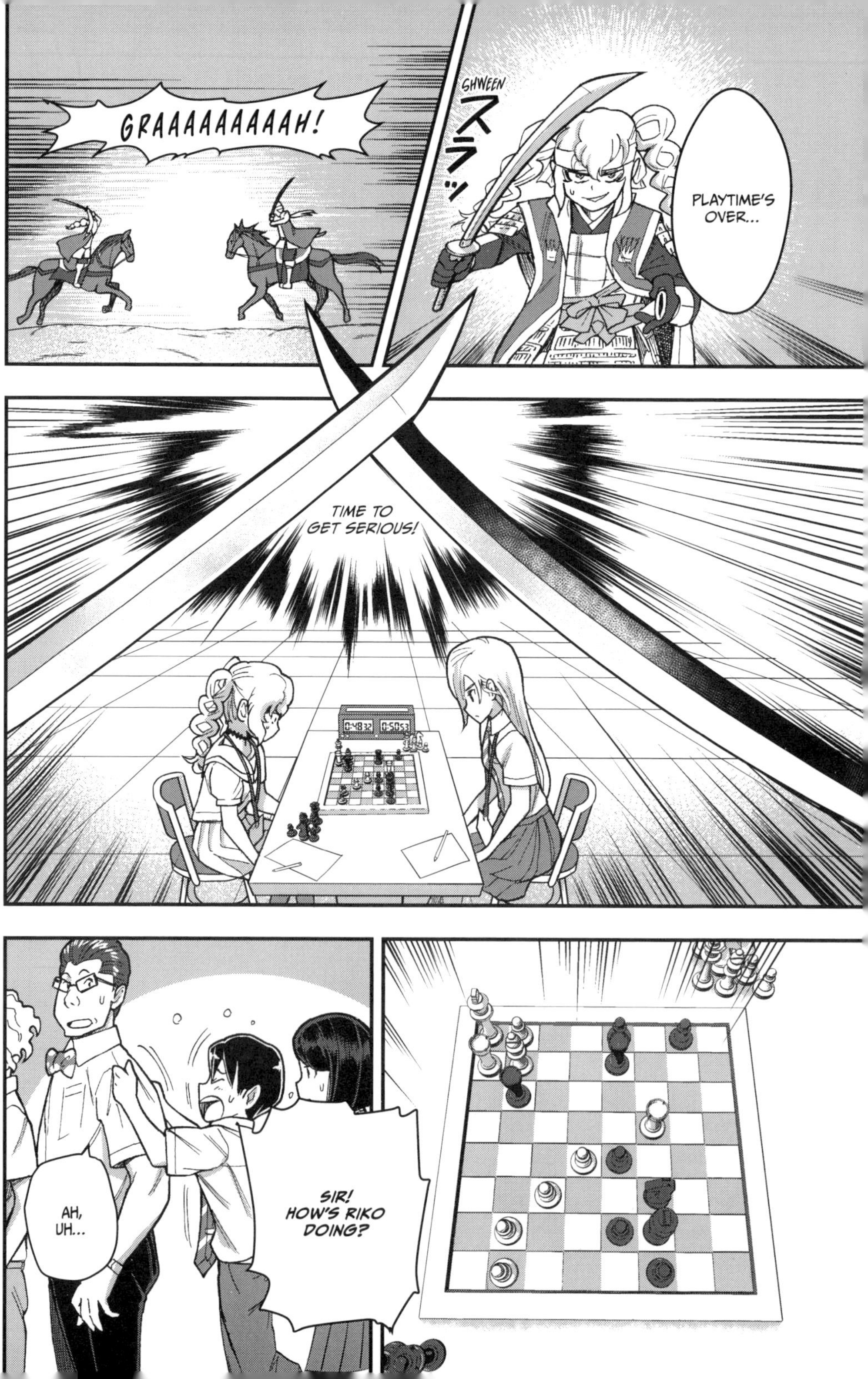
GRAAAAAAAAAH!
SHWEEN
スラッ
PLAYTIME'S OVER...
TIME TO GET SERIOUS!
SIR! HOW'S RIKO DOING?
AH, UH...

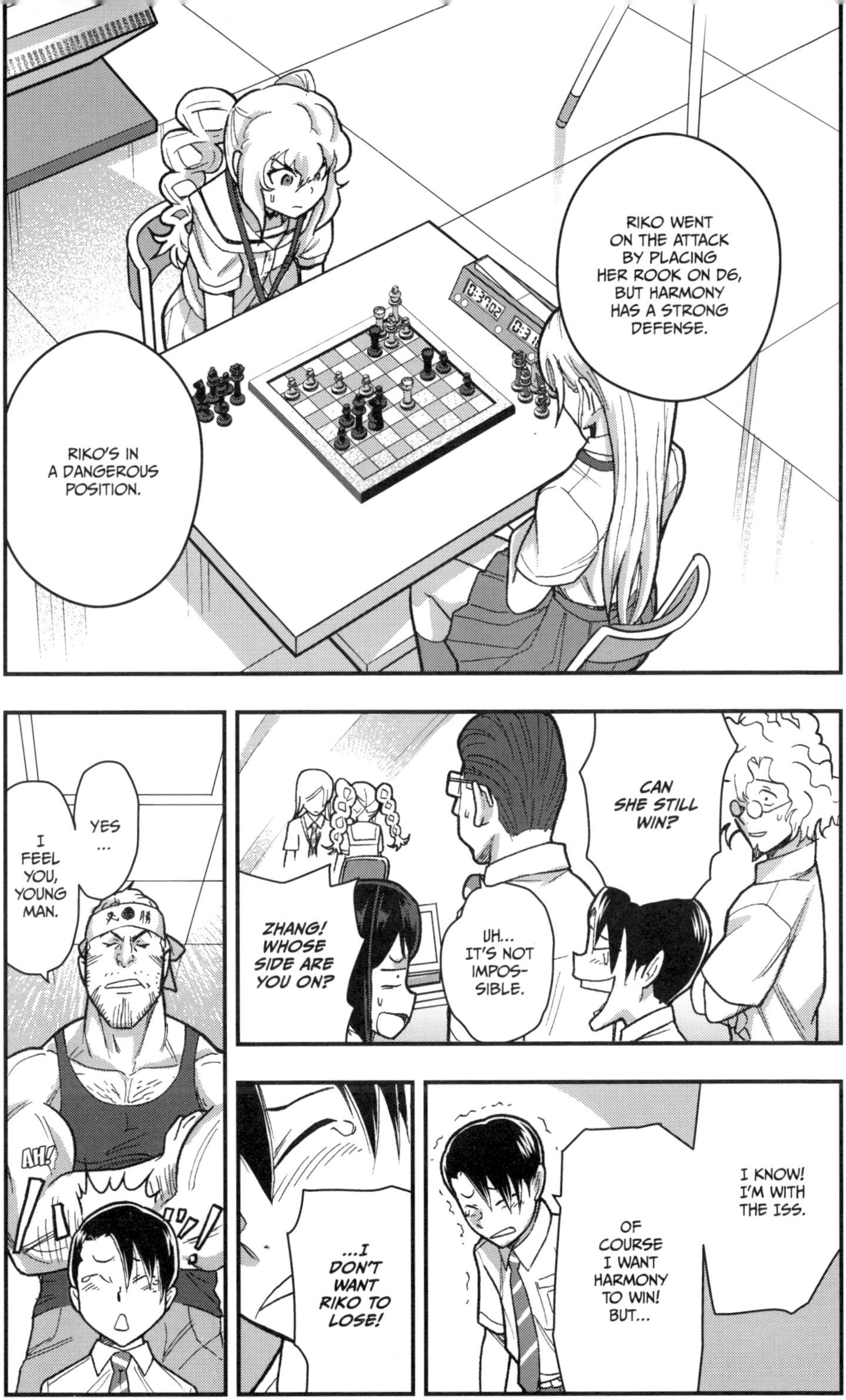
RIKO WENT ON THE ATTACK BY PLACING HER ROOK ON D6, BUT HARMONY HAS A STRONG DEFENSE.
RIKO'S IN A DANGEROUS POSITION.
CAN SHE STILL WIN?
UH... IT'S NOT IMPOSSIBLE.
ZHANG! WHOSE SIDE ARE YOU ON?
I KNOW! I'M WITH THE ISS.
OF COURSE I WANT HARMONY TO WIN! BUT...
...I DON'T WANT RIKO TO LOSE!
YES...
I FEEL YOU, YOUNG MAN.
AH!

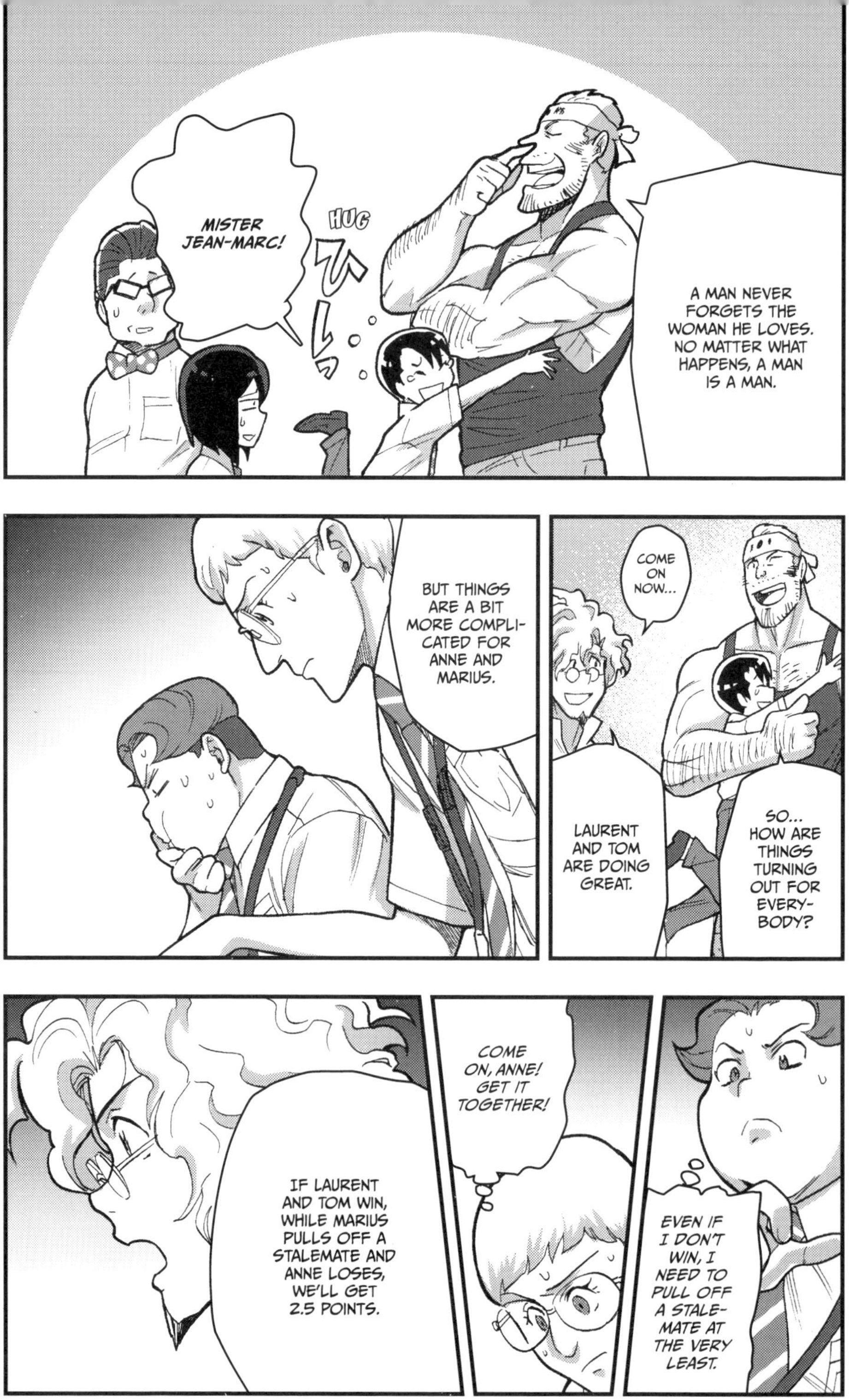
MISTER JEAN-MARC!
HUG
A MAN NEVER FORGETS THE WOMAN HE LOVES. NO MATTER WHAT HAPPENS, A MAN IS A MAN.
COME ON NOW...
SO... HOW ARE THINGS TURNING OUT FOR EVERYBODY?
LAURENT AND TOM ARE DOING GREAT.
BUT THINGS ARE A BIT MORE COMPLICATED FOR ANNE AND MARIUS.
EVEN IF I DON'T WIN, I NEED TO PULL OFF A STALEMATE AT THE VERY LEAST.
COME ON, ANNE! GET IT TOGETHER!
IF LAURENT AND TOM WIN, WHILE MARIUS PULLS OFF A STALEMATE AND ANNE LOSES, WE'LL GET 2.5 POINTS.

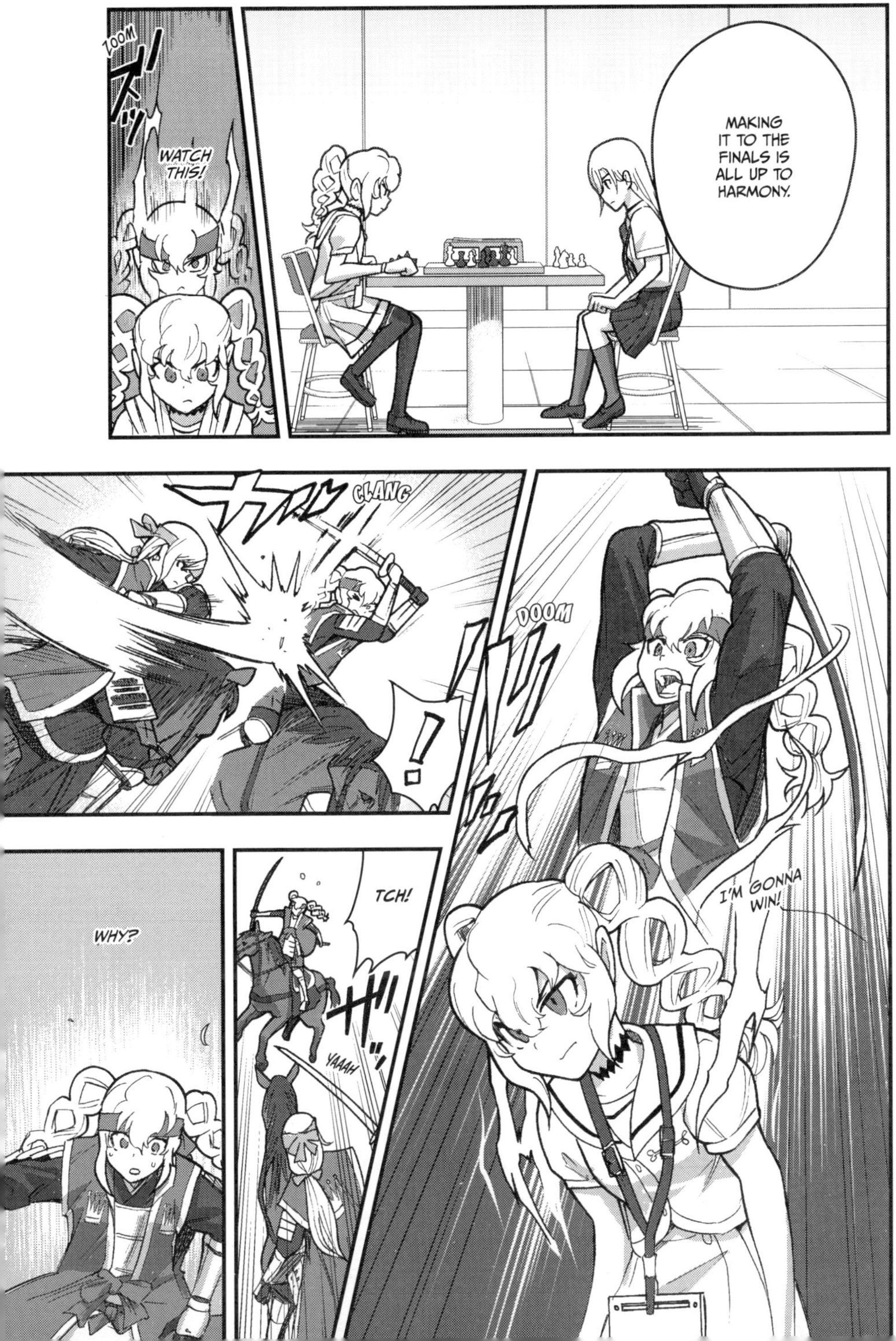
MAKING IT TO THE FINALS IS ALL UP TO HARMONY.
ZOOM
WATCH THIS!
DOOM
I'M GONNA WIN!
CLANG
!
TCH!
YAAAH
WHY?

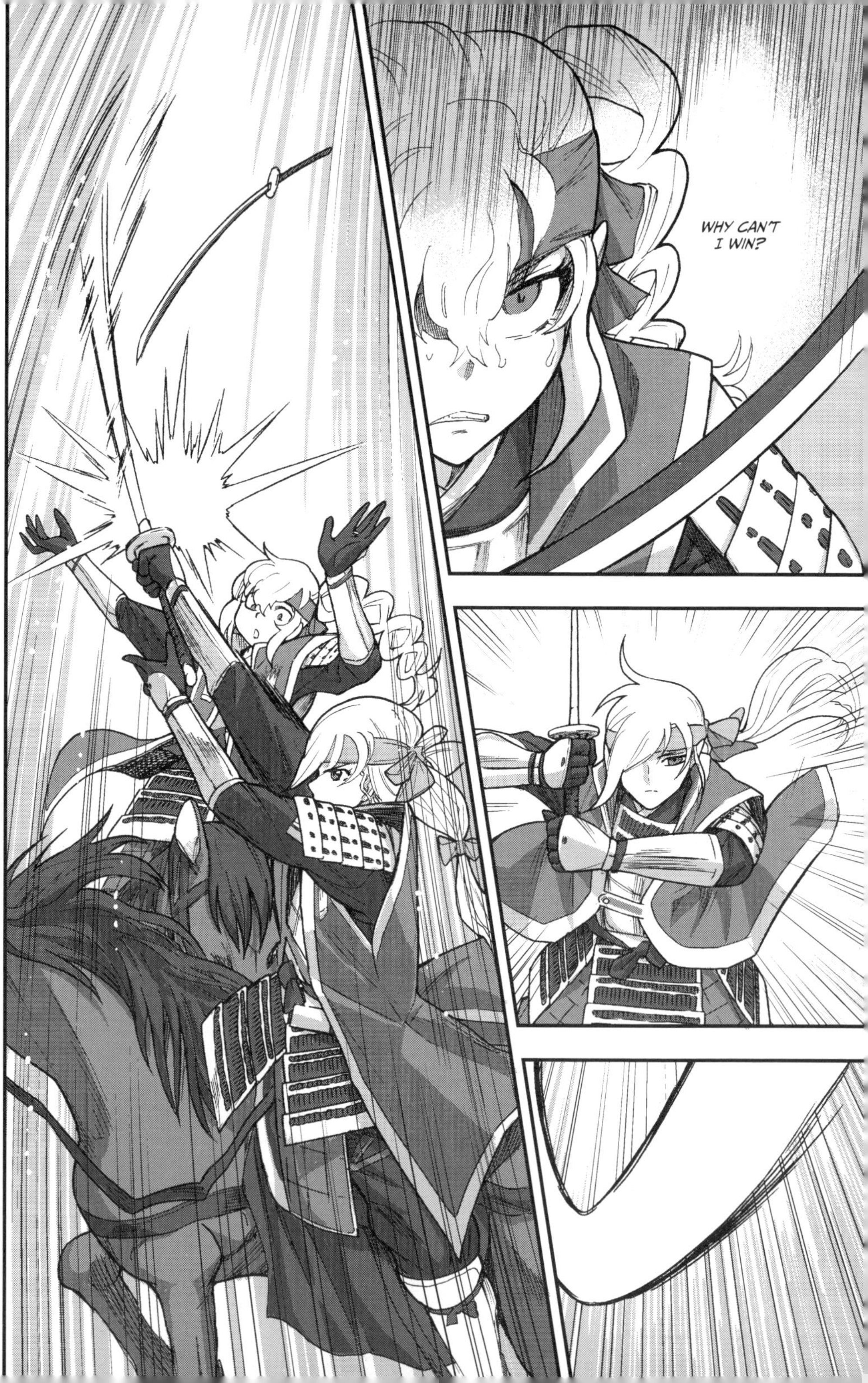
WHY CAN'T I WIN?

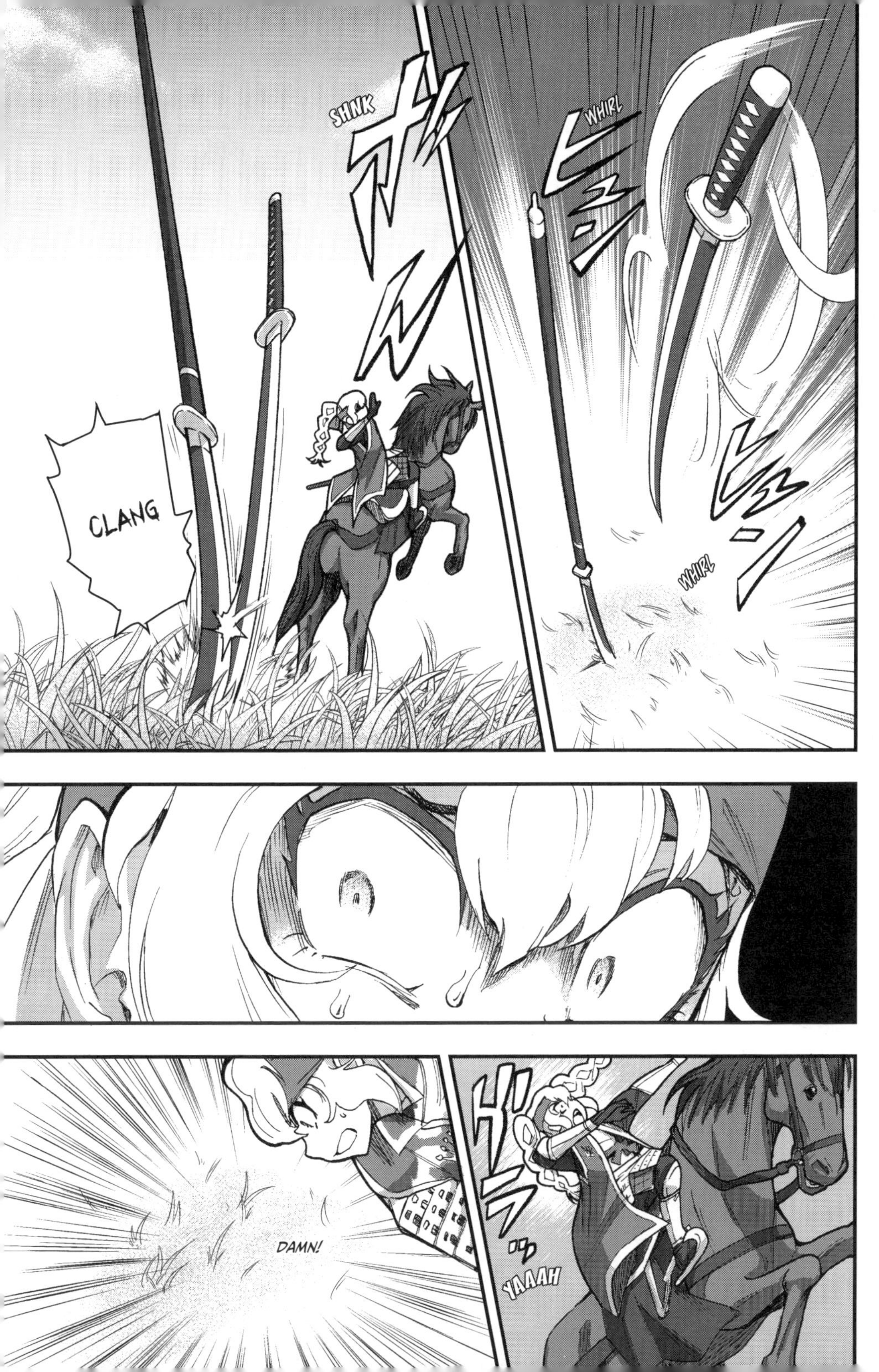
SHNK
WHIRL
WHIRL
CLANG
DAMN!
YAAAH

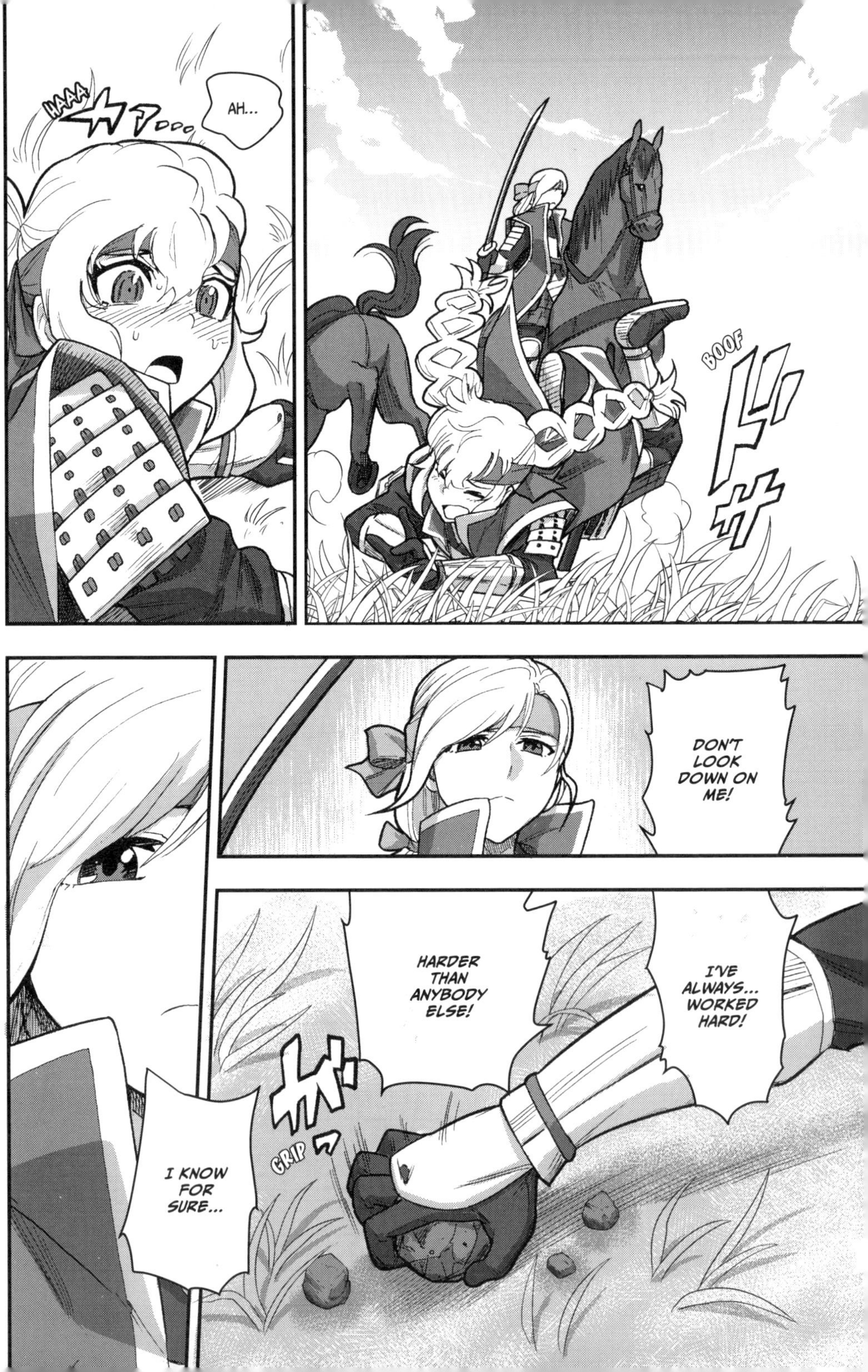
BOOF
ドサ
HAAA
ハァ...
AH...
DON'T LOOK DOWN ON ME!
I'VE ALWAYS... WORKED HARD!
HARDER THAN ANYBODY ELSE!
GRIP
ガッ
I KNOW FOR SURE...

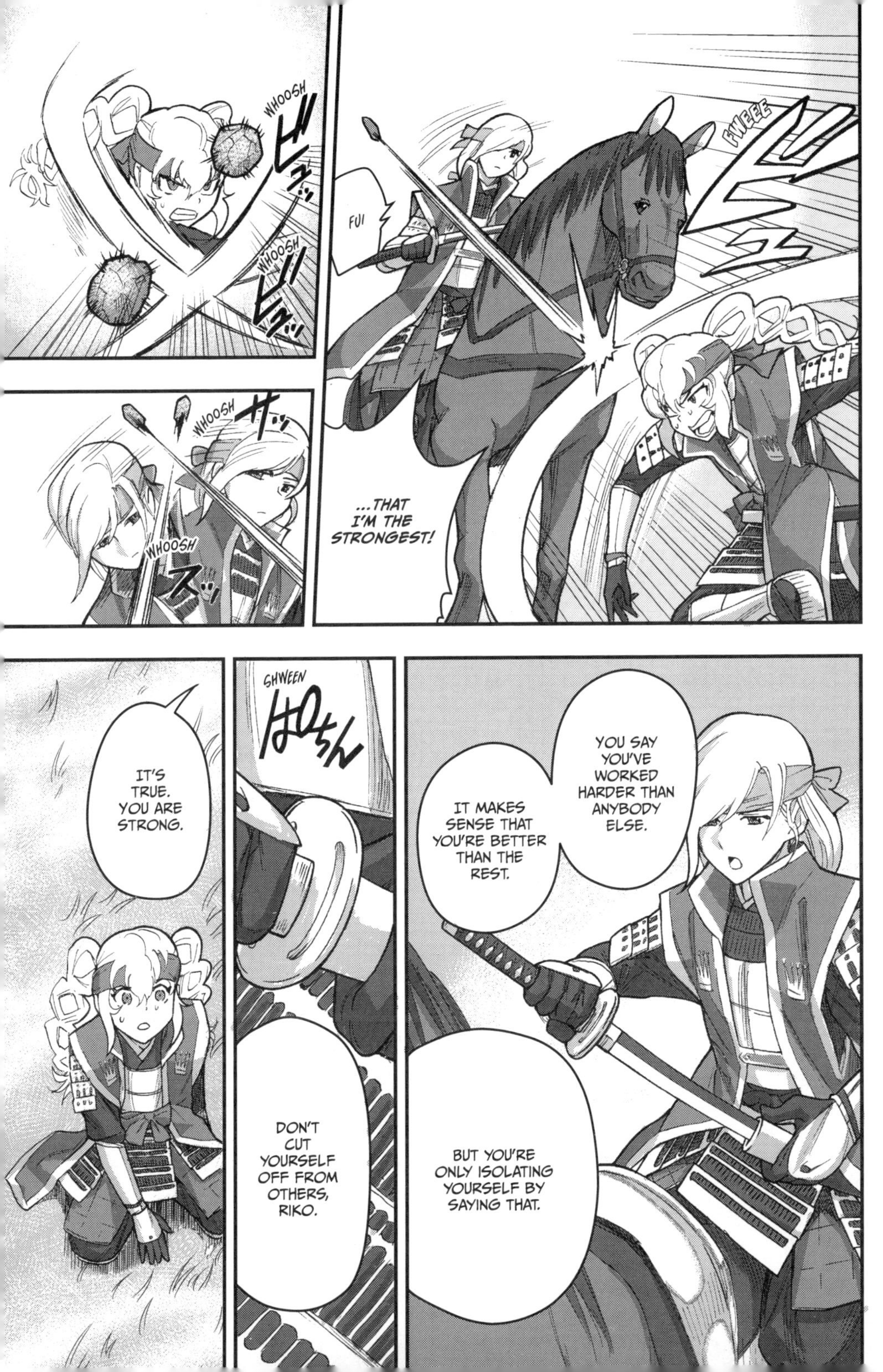
FWEEE
FUI
...THAT I'M THE STRONGEST!
WHOOSH
WHOOSH
WHOOSH
WHOOSH
YOU SAY YOU'VE WORKED HARDER THAN ANYBODY ELSE.
IT MAKES SENSE THAT YOU'RE BETTER THAN THE REST.
BUT YOU'RE ONLY ISOLATING YOURSELF BY SAYING THAT.
SHWEEN
DON'T CUT YOURSELF OFF FROM OTHERS, RIKO.
IT'S TRUE. YOU ARE STRONG.

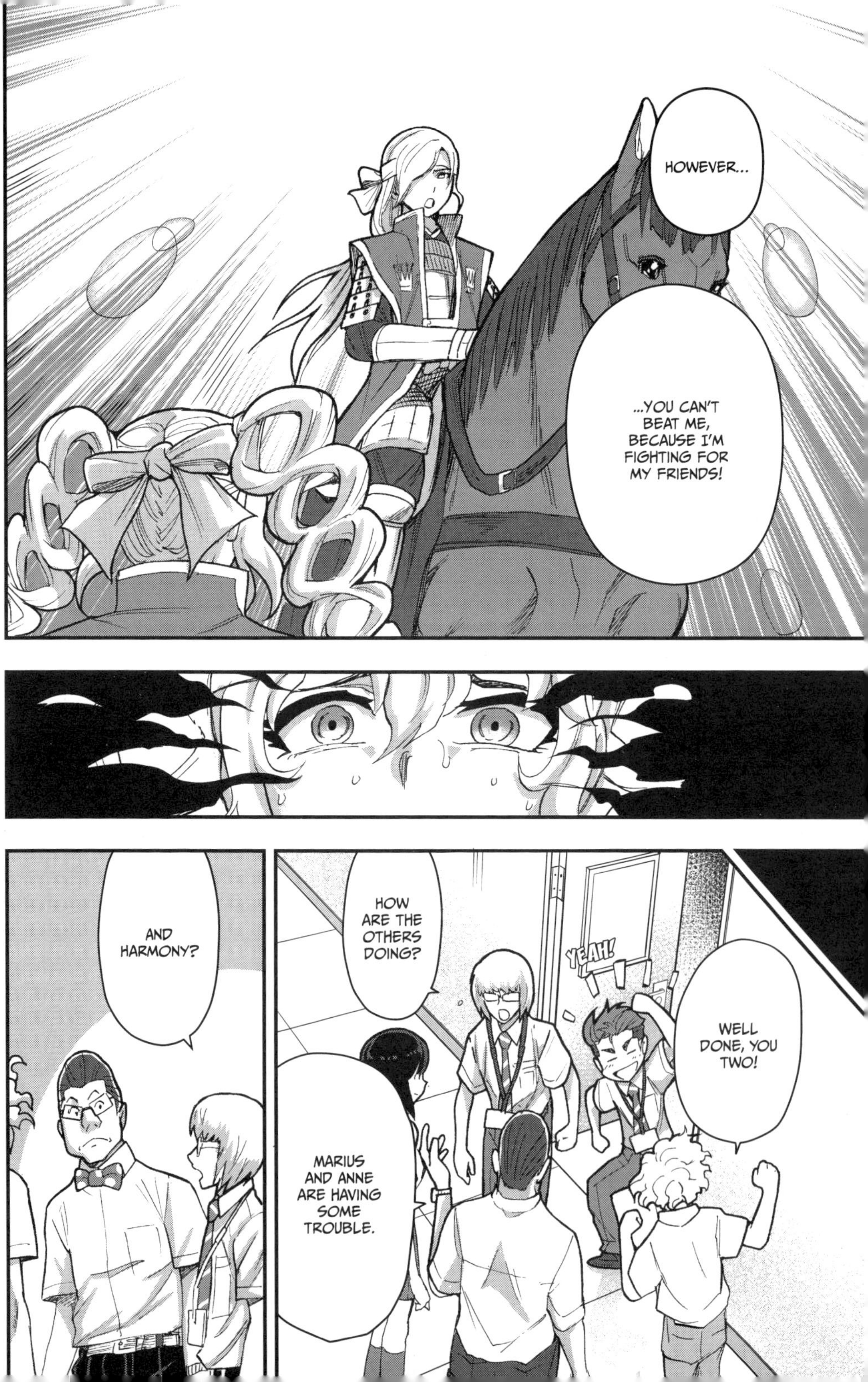
HOWEVER...
...YOU CAN'T BEAT ME, BECAUSE I'M FIGHTING FOR MY FRIENDS!
HOW ARE THE OTHERS DOING?
YEAH!
WELL DONE, YOU TWO!
AND HARMONY?
MARIUS AND ANNE ARE HAVING SOME TROUBLE.

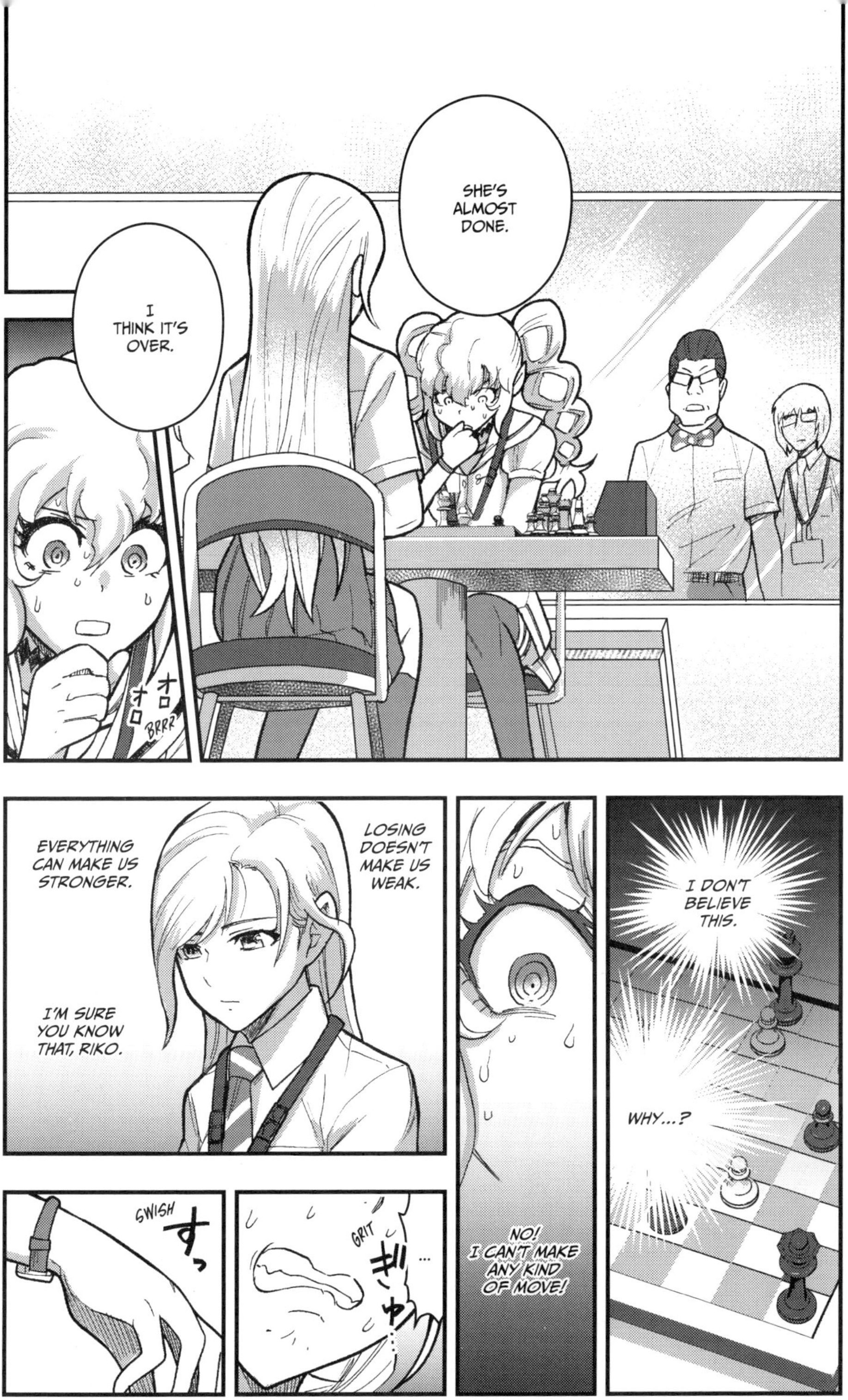
SHE'S ALMOST DONE.
I THINK IT'S OVER.
オロオロ
BRRR
I DON'T BELIEVE THIS.
WHY...?
NO! I CAN'T MAKE ANY KIND OF MOVE!
LOSING DOESN'T MAKE US WEAK.
EVERYTHING CAN MAKE US STRONGER.
I'M SURE YOU KNOW THAT, RIKO.
GRIT
ぎゅ…
SWISH
すっ

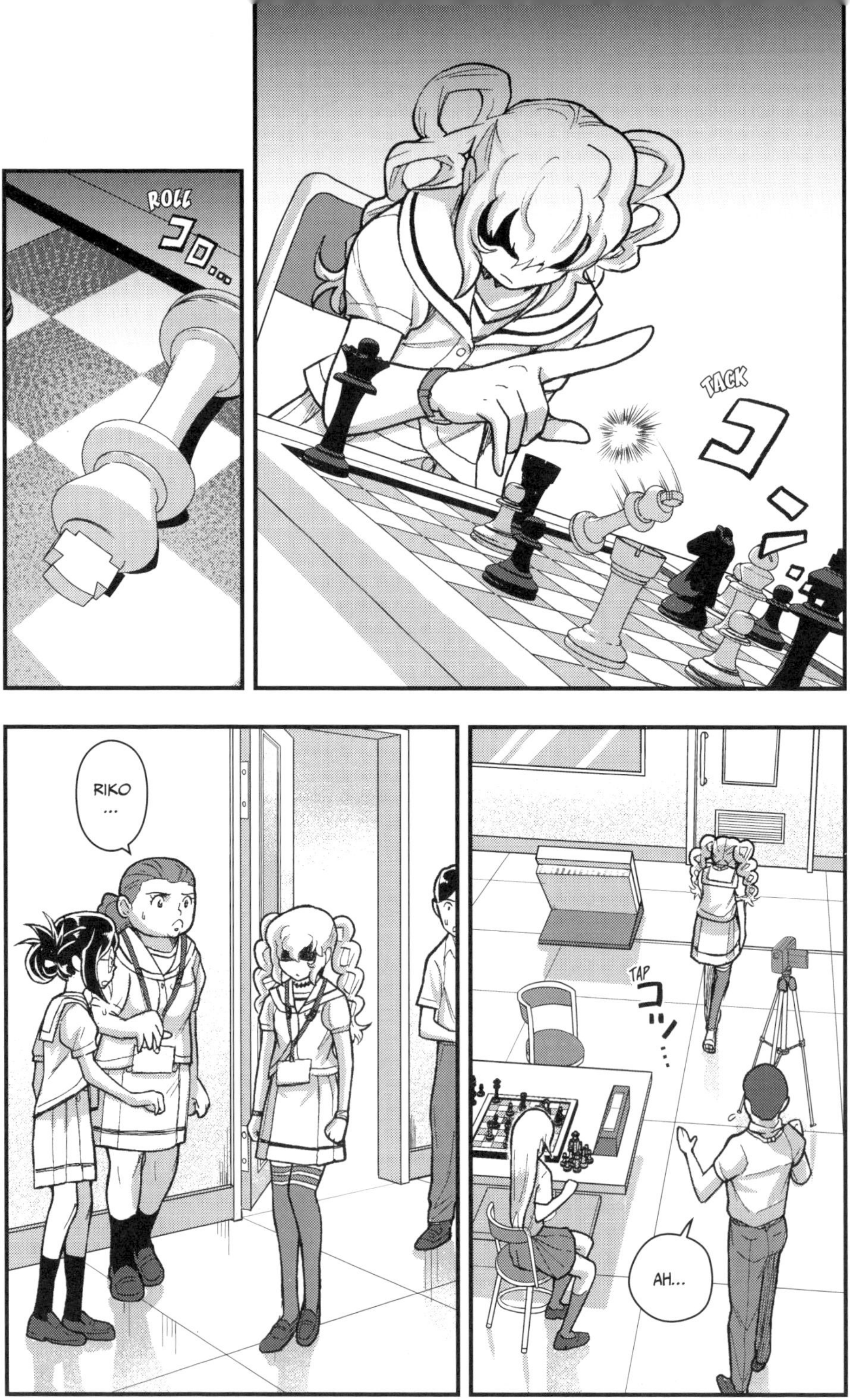
TACK
コッ
ROLL
コロ...
TAP
コツ...
AH...
RIKO
...

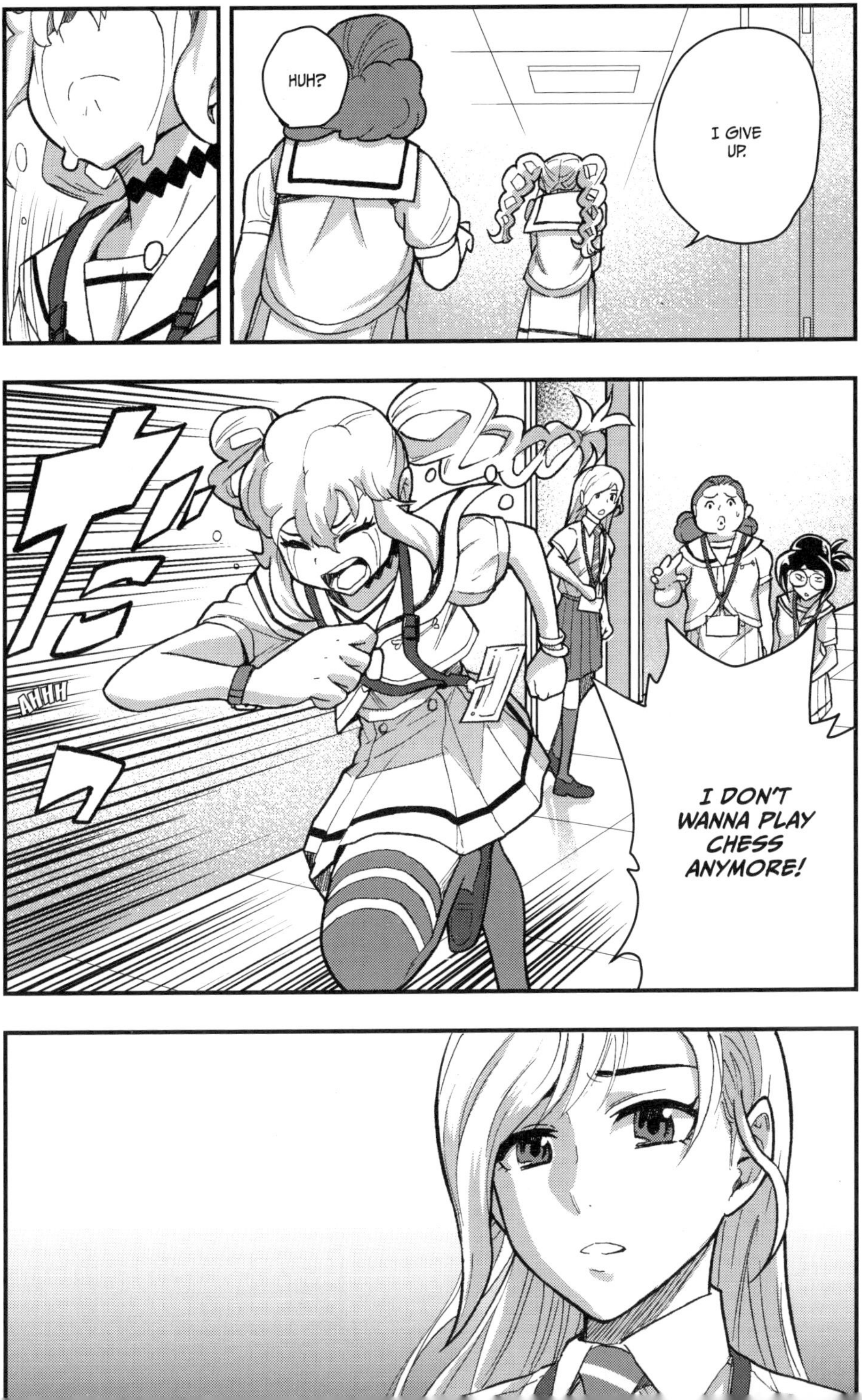
I GIVE UP.
HUH?
AHHH
I DON'T WANNA PLAY CHESS ANYMORE!

RIKO...

HARMONY...

I'M SORRY. I LOST AGAIN.

HOW DID IT GO FOR YOU GUYS? I HAD A STALEMATE.

AWESOME!

YEAH!

IT'S OKAY. THE OTHER THREE HAVE WON. WE'RE GOING TO THE FINALS!

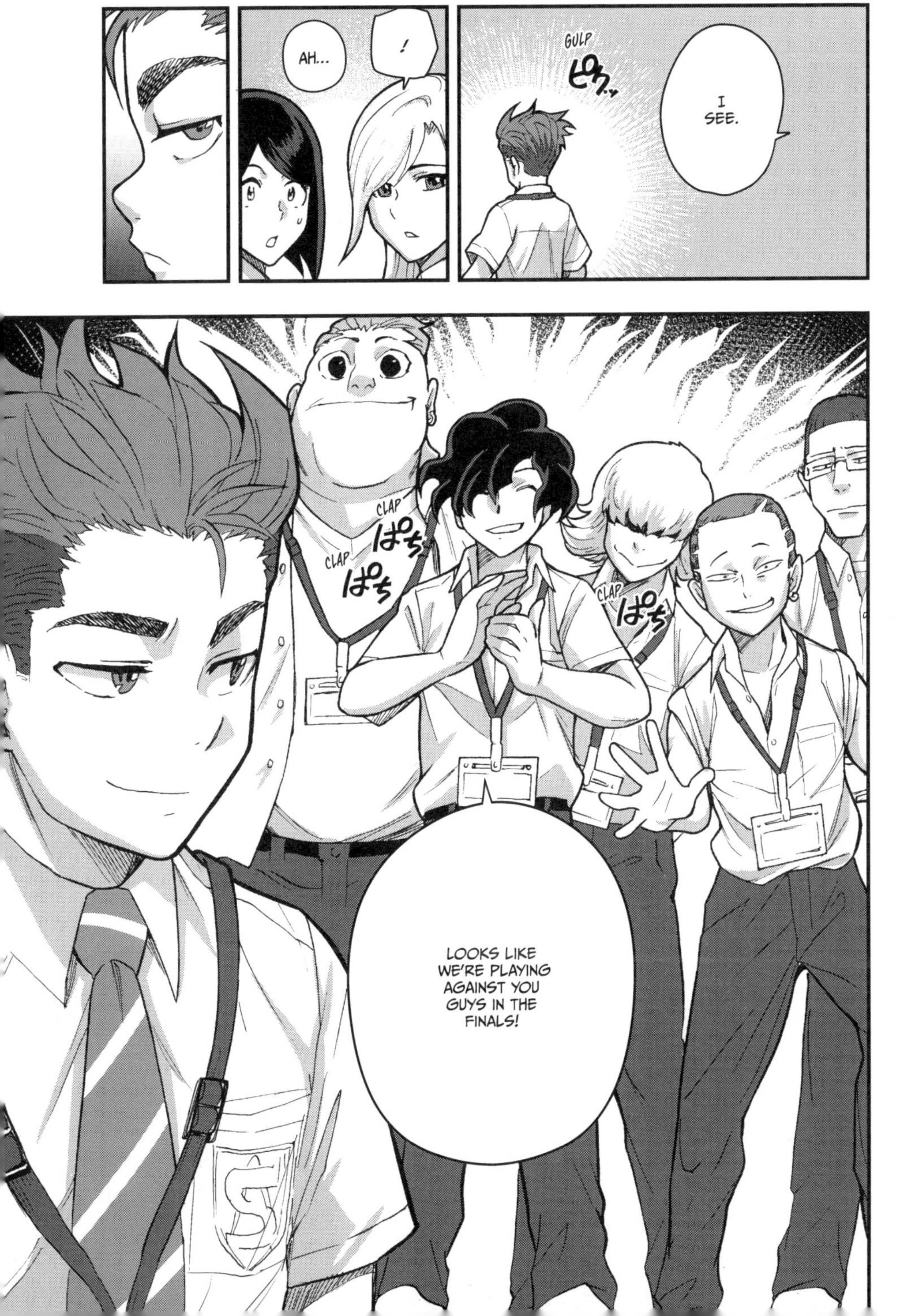
GULP
I SEE.
!
AH...
CLAP ぱち
CLAP ぱち
CLAP ぱち
LOOKS LIKE WE'RE PLAYING AGAINST YOU GUYS IN THE FINALS!

BLiTZ

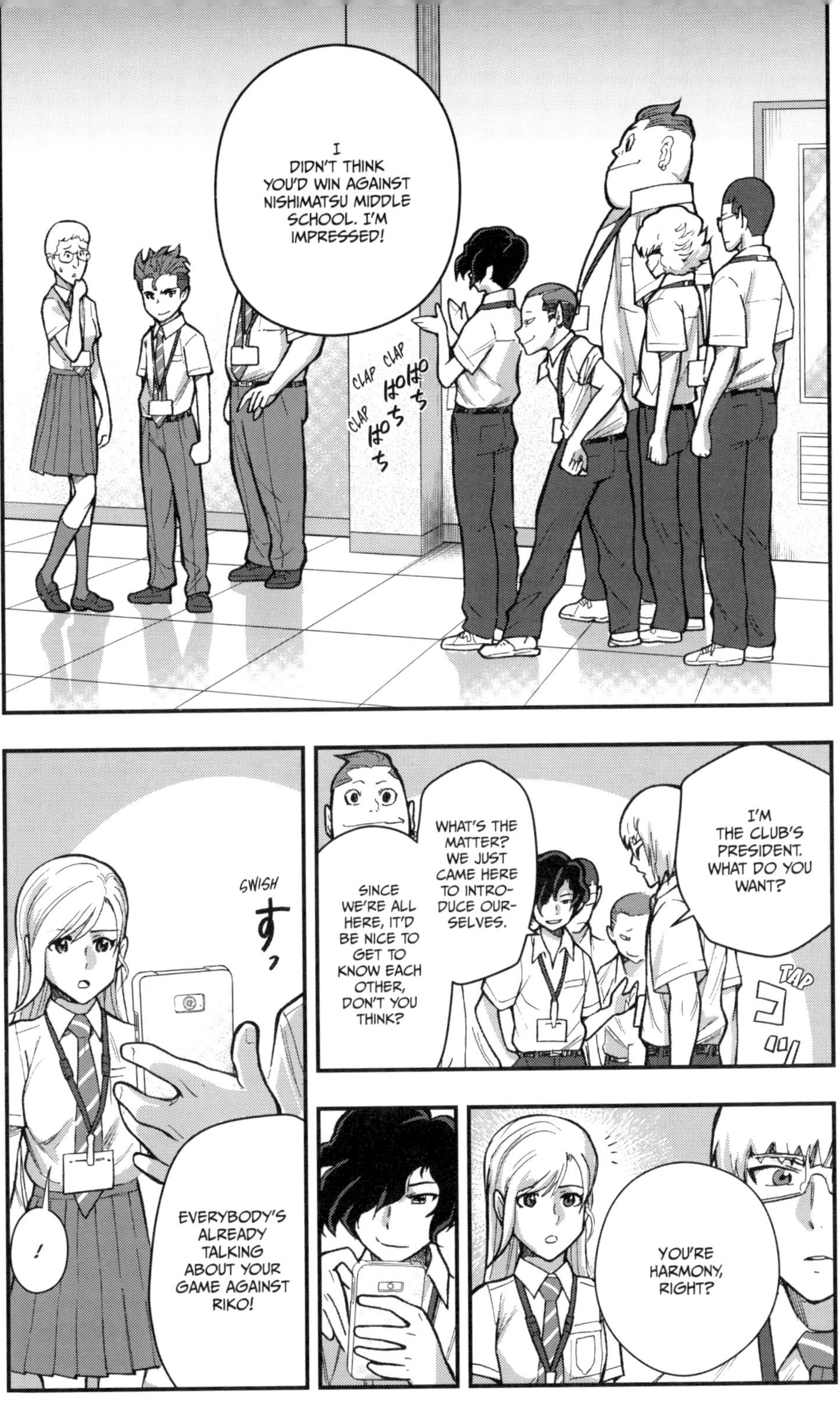
I DIDN'T THINK YOU'D WIN AGAINST NISHIMATSU MIDDLE SCHOOL. I'M IMPRESSED!
CLAP CLAP CLAP
ぱちぱち ぱち
I'M THE CLUB'S PRESIDENT. WHAT DO YOU WANT?
TAP
WHAT'S THE MATTER? WE JUST CAME HERE TO INTRODUCE OURSELVES.
SINCE WE'RE ALL HERE, IT'D BE NICE TO GET TO KNOW EACH OTHER, DON'T YOU THINK?
YOU'RE HARMONY, RIGHT?
SWISH
すっ
!
EVERYBODY'S ALREADY TALKING ABOUT YOUR GAME AGAINST RIKO!

💬 1	↻ 0	♡ 15	⤒

Yoshi — 5 minutes
Riko lost!

💬 2	↻ 0	♡ 4	⤒

JJ — 10 minutes
She actually sucks...

Is Riko really giving up on chess?!

...

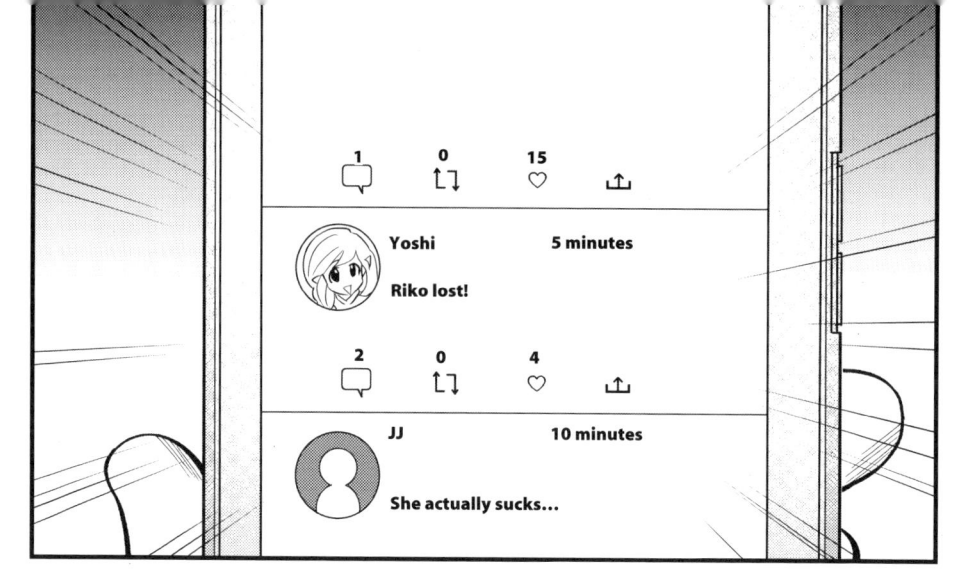

Chapter 21: Here comes Touto middle school!

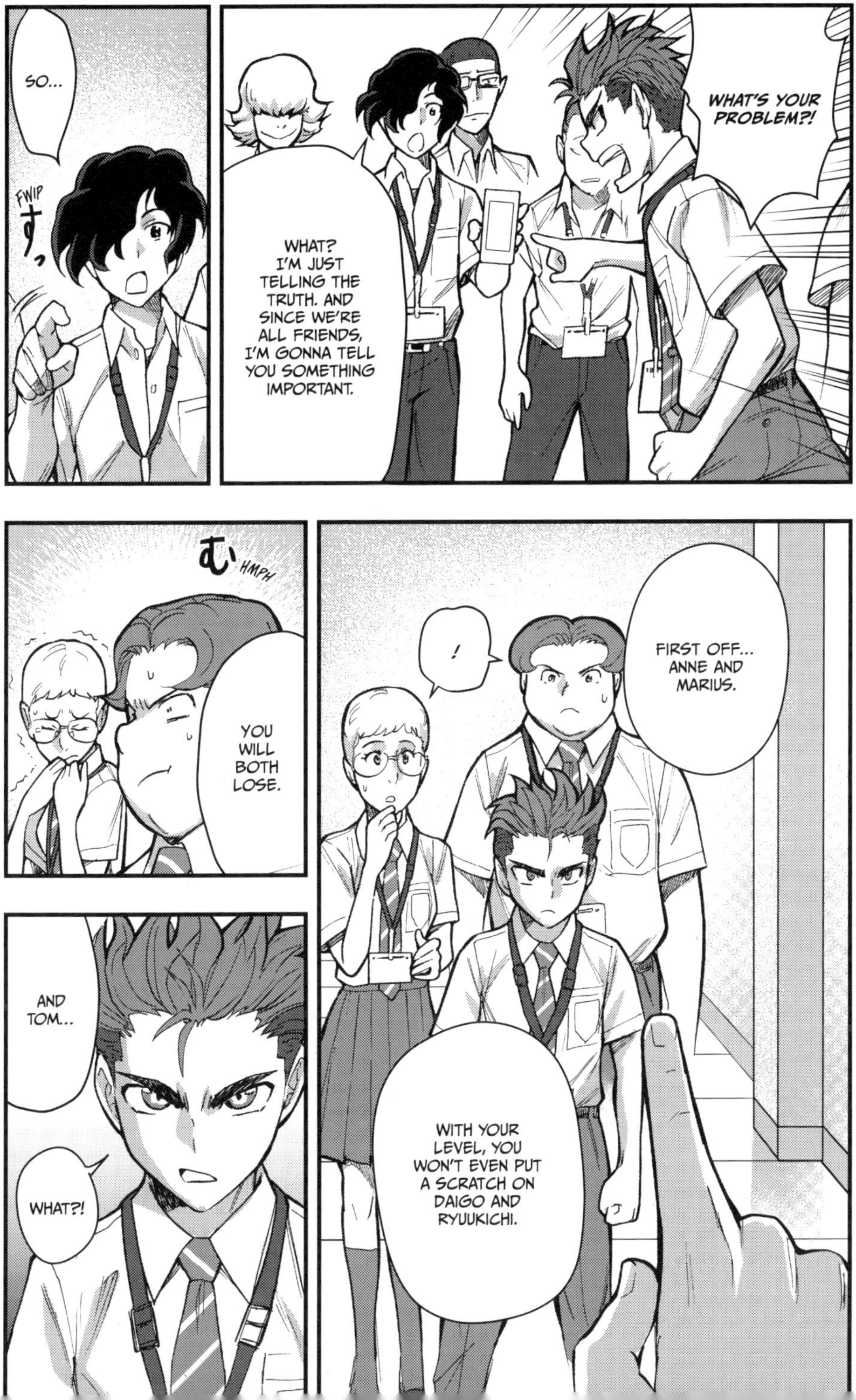
SO...
FWIP
すっ
WHAT? I'M JUST TELLING THE TRUTH. AND SINCE WE'RE ALL FRIENDS, I'M GONNA TELL YOU SOMETHING IMPORTANT.
WHAT'S YOUR PROBLEM?!
むっ
HMPH
YOU WILL BOTH LOSE.
!
FIRST OFF... ANNE AND MARIUS.
AND TOM...
WHAT?!
WITH YOUR LEVEL, YOU WON'T EVEN PUT A SCRATCH ON DAIGO AND RYUUKICHI.

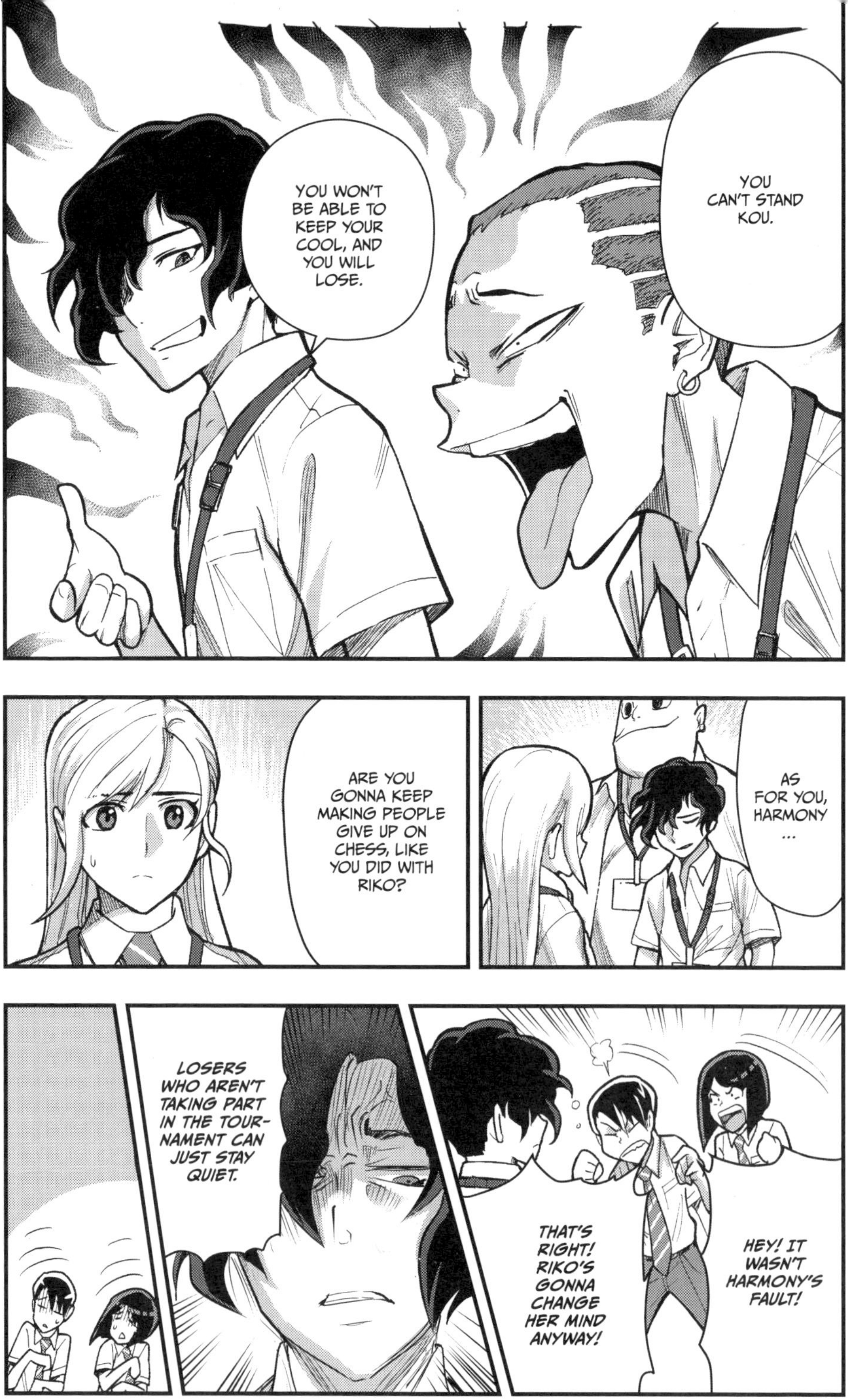
YOU CAN'T STAND KOU.
YOU WON'T BE ABLE TO KEEP YOUR COOL, AND YOU WILL LOSE.
AS FOR YOU, HARMONY...
ARE YOU GONNA KEEP MAKING PEOPLE GIVE UP ON CHESS, LIKE YOU DID WITH RIKO?
HEY! IT WASN'T HARMONY'S FAULT!
THAT'S RIGHT! RIKO'S GONNA CHANGE HER MIND ANYWAY!
LOSERS WHO AREN'T TAKING PART IN THE TOUR-NAMENT CAN JUST STAY QUIET.

AND YOU, LAURENT...

YOU ONLY MADE IT THIS FAR BECAUSE YOUR OPPONENTS WERE WEAK.

THAT'S WHY YOU'LL FAIL IN THE FINALS.

SUCKS FOR YOU GUYS, BUT THIS IS THE END OF THE LINE!

WAS THAT ALL?

SHEESH, HOW SERIOUS!

BAH...

YOUR STUPID TAUNTS ARE USELESS.

OUR TEAM WILL BE THE ONE TO WIN.

YEAH!

WELL, SEE YA.

LET'S DITCH THESE CLOWNS!

WE'LL SEE ABOUT THAT SOON ENOUGH.

DON'T GET WORKED UP BECAUSE OF THOSE IDIOTS.

GRRR...!

YEAH!!!

SO... ARE YOU GUYS READY TO WIN THIS TOURNAMENT?

IF THEY CAME HERE TO TAUNT US, THAT MEANS THEY'RE NOT AS CALM AND COLLECTED AS THEY WANT US TO THINK.

THEY MUST FEEL THREATENED.

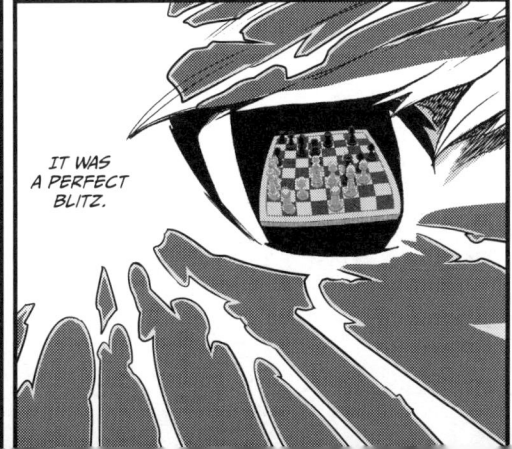

TACK

WHEN I THINK BACK TO THAT GUY'S GAME...

CLICK

THAT QUICK THINKING.

RIIING

IT WAS A PERFECT BLITZ.

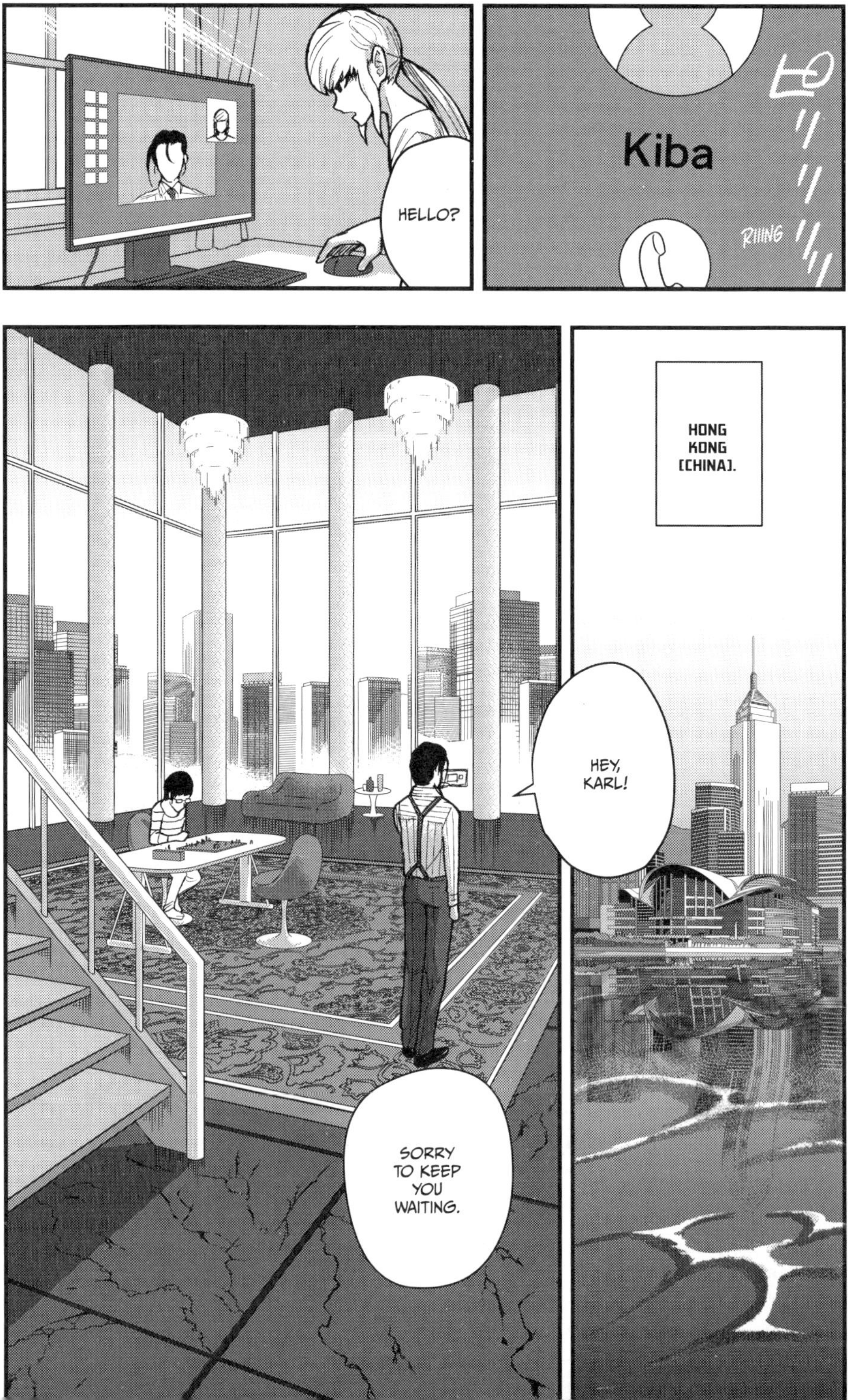
Kiba
RIIING
HELLO?
HONG KONG [CHINA].
HEY, KARL!
SORRY TO KEEP YOU WAITING.

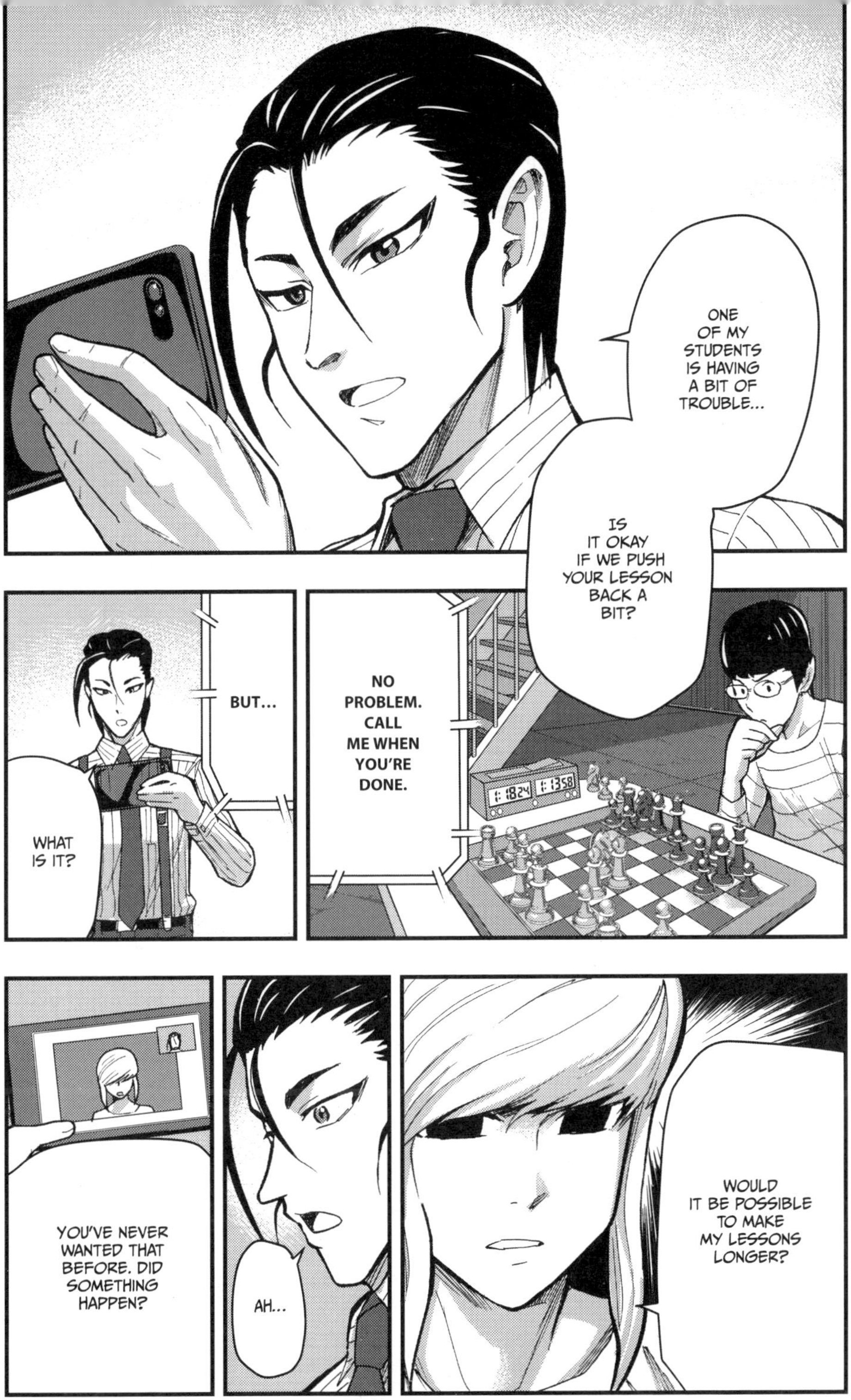
ONE OF MY STUDENTS IS HAVING A BIT OF TROUBLE...
IS IT OKAY IF WE PUSH YOUR LESSON BACK A BIT?
NO PROBLEM. CALL ME WHEN YOU'RE DONE.
BUT...
WHAT IS IT?
WOULD IT BE POSSIBLE TO MAKE MY LESSONS LONGER?
AH...
YOU'VE NEVER WANTED THAT BEFORE. DID SOMETHING HAPPEN?

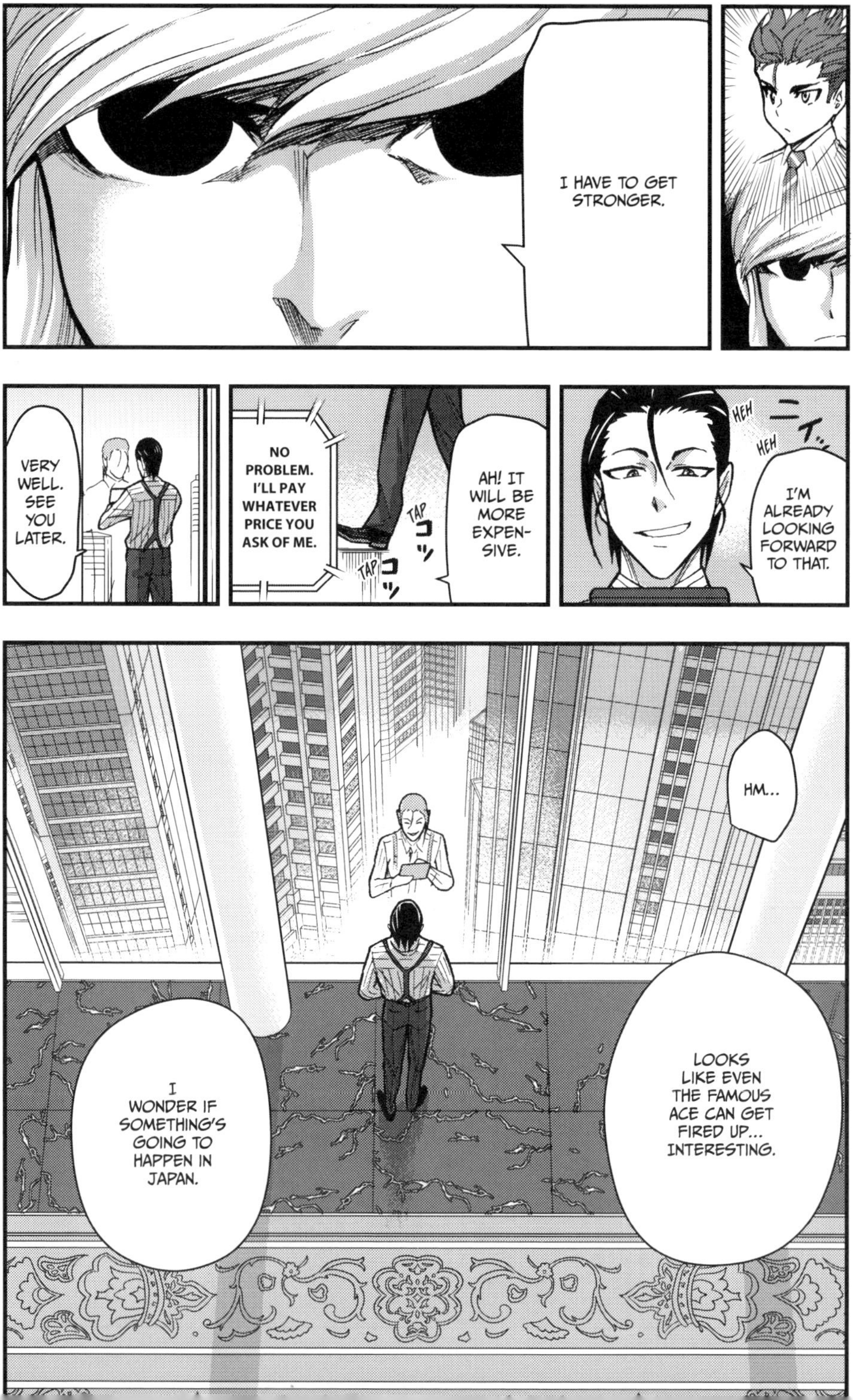
I HAVE TO GET STRONGER.
HEH HEH
I'M ALREADY LOOKING FORWARD TO THAT.
AH! IT WILL BE MORE EXPENSIVE.
TAP TAP
NO PROBLEM. I'LL PAY WHATEVER PRICE YOU ASK OF ME.
VERY WELL. SEE YOU LATER.
HM...
LOOKS LIKE EVEN THE FAMOUS ACE CAN GET FIRED UP... INTERESTING.
I WONDER IF SOMETHING'S GOING TO HAPPEN IN JAPAN.

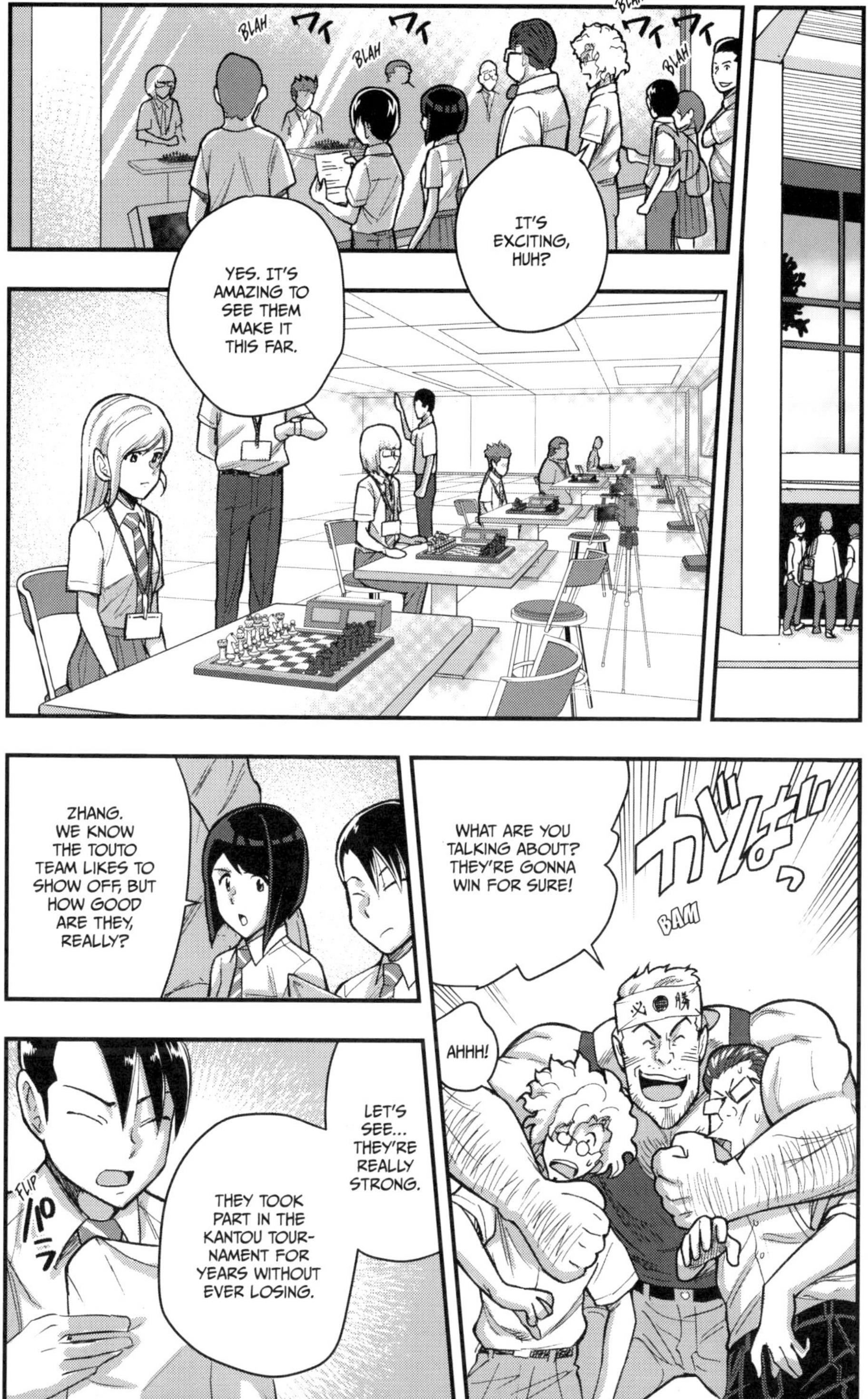
IT'S EXCITING, HUH?
YES. IT'S AMAZING TO SEE THEM MAKE IT THIS FAR.
BLAH ワイ ワイ
BLAH
BLAH ワイ ワイ
BLAH
ZHANG. WE KNOW THE TOUTO TEAM LIKES TO SHOW OFF, BUT HOW GOOD ARE THEY, REALLY?
WHAT ARE YOU TALKING ABOUT? THEY'RE GONNA WIN FOR SURE!
BAM
AHHH!
LET'S SEE... THEY'RE REALLY STRONG.
THEY TOOK PART IN THE KANTOU TOUR-NAMENT FOR YEARS WITHOUT EVER LOSING.
FLIP

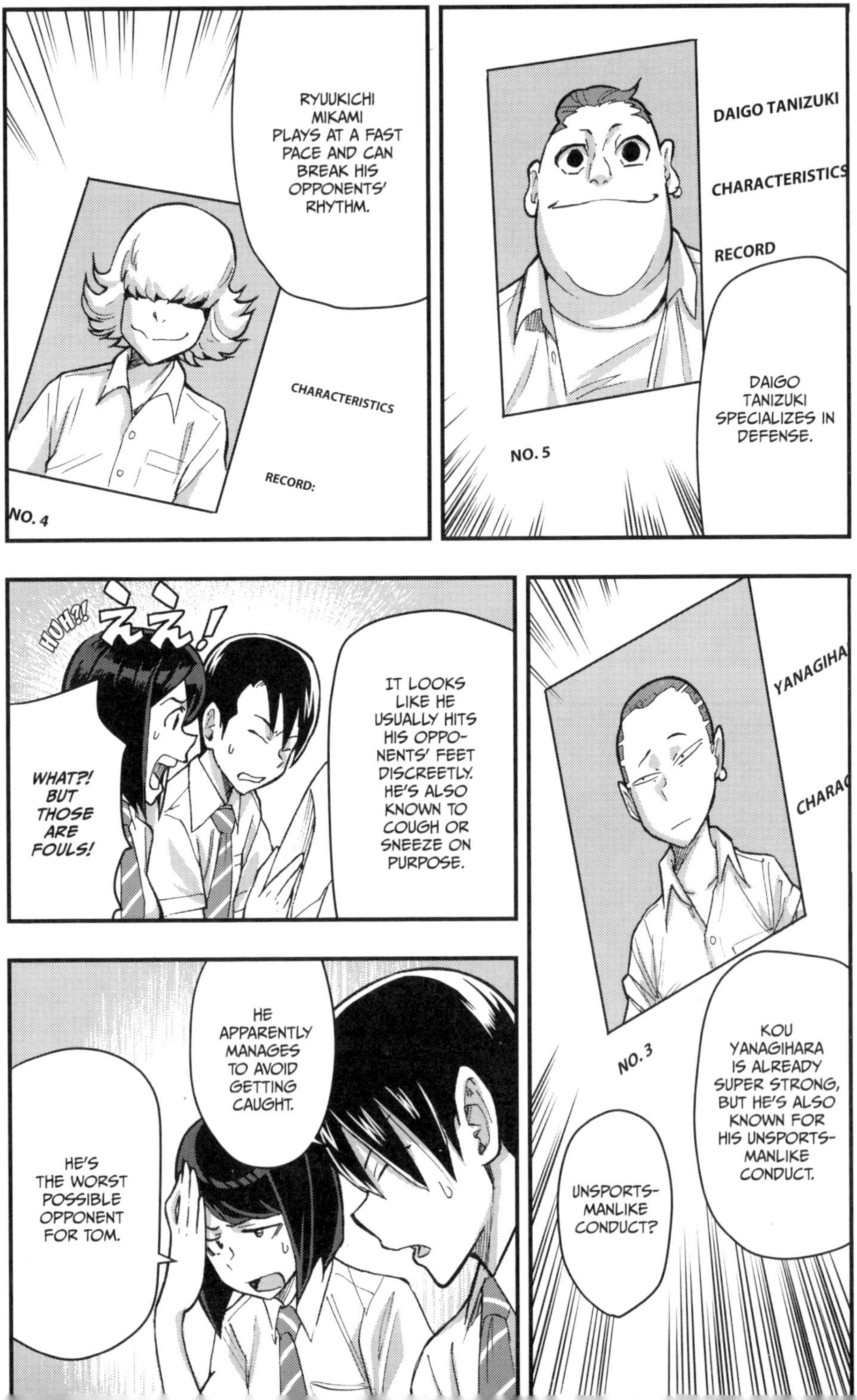
DAIGO TANIZUKI
CHARACTERISTICS
RECORD
NO. 5
DAIGO TANIZUKI SPECIALIZES IN DEFENSE.
RYUUKICHI MIKAMI PLAYS AT A FAST PACE AND CAN BREAK HIS OPPONENTS' RHYTHM.
CHARACTERISTICS
RECORD:
NO. 4
YANAGIHA
CHARAC
NO. 3
KOU YANAGIHARA IS ALREADY SUPER STRONG, BUT HE'S ALSO KNOWN FOR HIS UNSPORTS-MANLIKE CONDUCT.
UNSPORTS-MANLIKE CONDUCT?
IT LOOKS LIKE HE USUALLY HITS HIS OPPO-NENTS' FEET DISCREETLY. HE'S ALSO KNOWN TO COUGH OR SNEEZE ON PURPOSE.
HUH?!
WHAT?! BUT THOSE ARE FOULS!
HE APPARENTLY MANAGES TO AVOID GETTING CAUGHT.
HE'S THE WORST POSSIBLE OPPONENT FOR TOM.

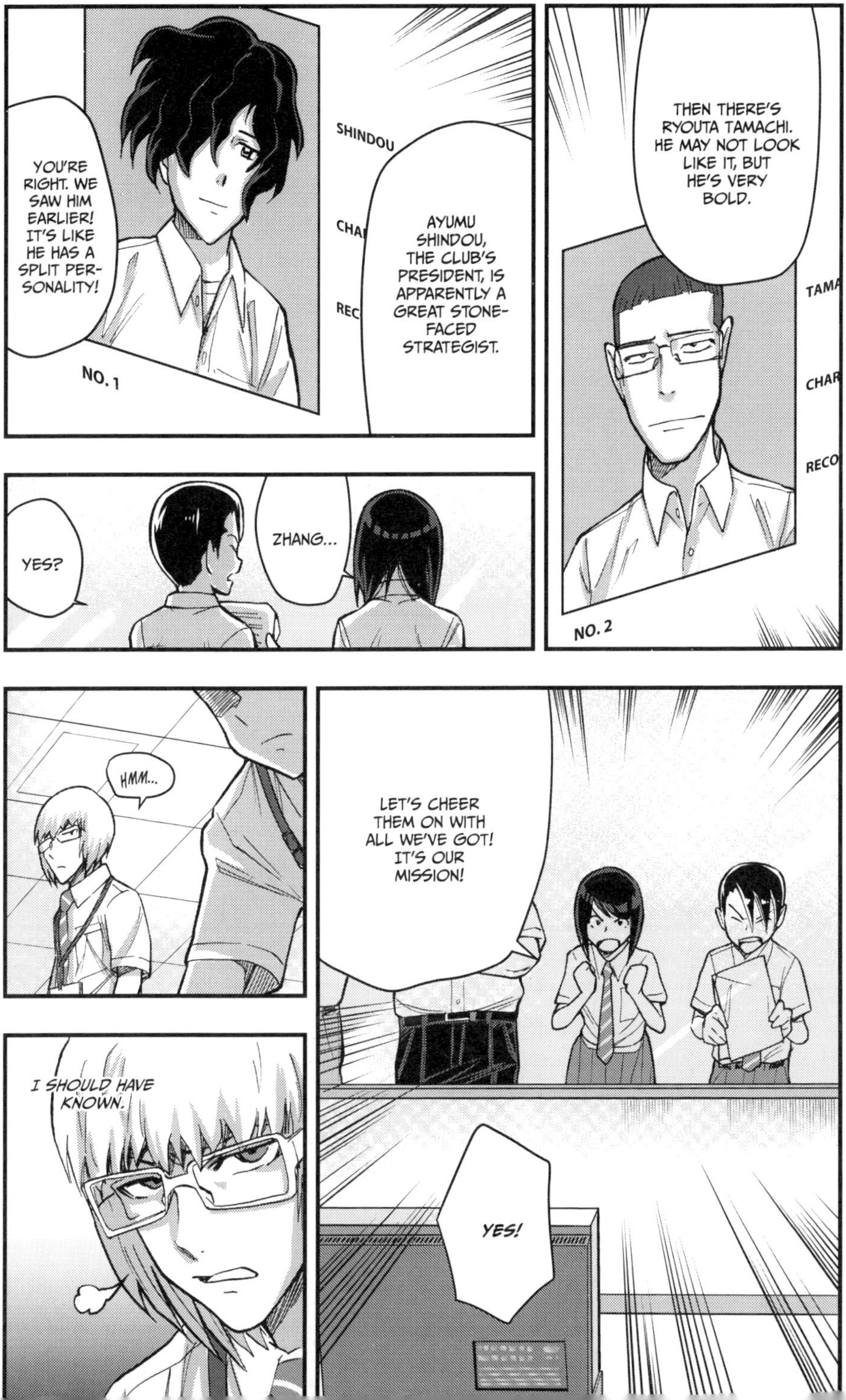
SHINDOU
AYUMU SHINDOU, THE CLUB'S PRESIDENT, IS APPARENTLY A GREAT STONE-FACED STRATEGIST.
YOU'RE RIGHT. WE SAW HIM EARLIER! IT'S LIKE HE HAS A SPLIT PER-SONALITY!
NO. 1
THEN THERE'S RYOUTA TAMACHI. HE MAY NOT LOOK LIKE IT, BUT HE'S VERY BOLD.
NO. 2
ZHANG...
YES?
HMM...
LET'S CHEER THEM ON WITH ALL WE'VE GOT! IT'S OUR MISSION!
YES!
I SHOULD HAVE KNOWN.

IT'LL BE OKAY. JUST DON'T PANIC, AND GIVE IT YOUR ALL.

ANNE...

MARIUS. YOU'LL WIN EASILY IF YOU MANAGE TO RELAX. YOU HAVE TO BE MORE CONFIDENT.

YOU KNOW... THERE ARE ALWAYS WINNERS AND LOSERS IN COMPETITIONS.

TOM. YOU REALLY HAVE TO CALM DOWN. IF YOU GET ANGRY, THINGS WILL END QUICKLY.

VSH

AS FOR ME...

HERE THEY COME.

...I WILL OBVIOUSLY WIN.

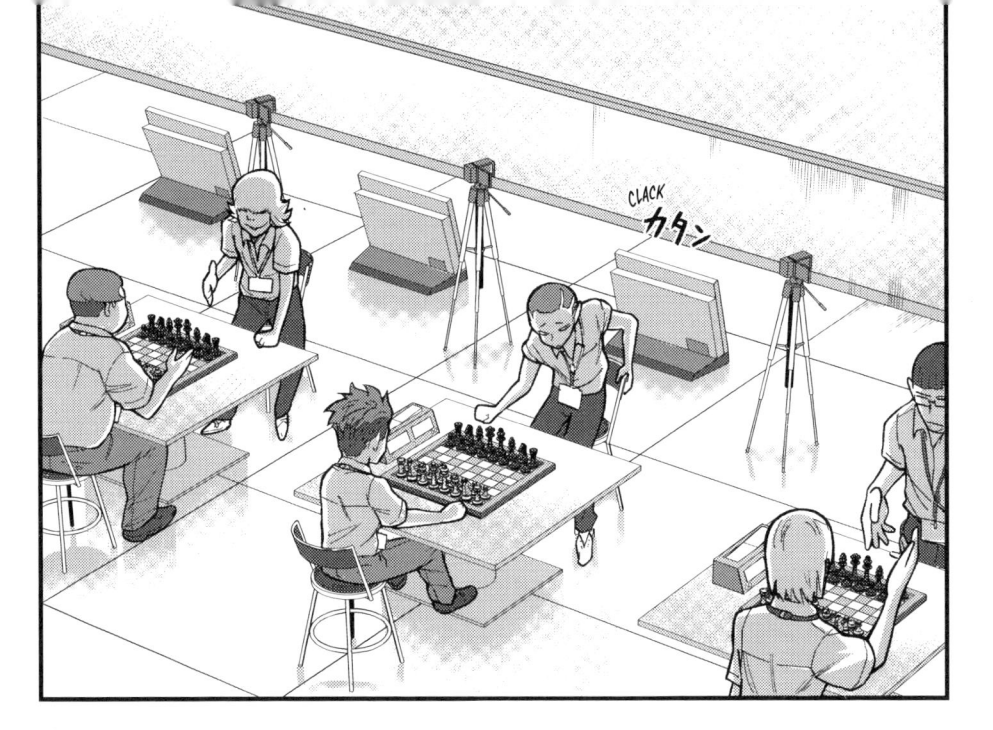

CLACK

SNEER

GOOD LUCK...

HEH HEH

GOOD LUCK, FOUR EYES!

YOU'RE THE FOUR EYES!

IN YOUR DREAMS! YOU'LL BE THE ONE CRYING LIKE A BABY.

I CAN'T WAIT TO SEE YOU BAWL YOUR EYES OUT.

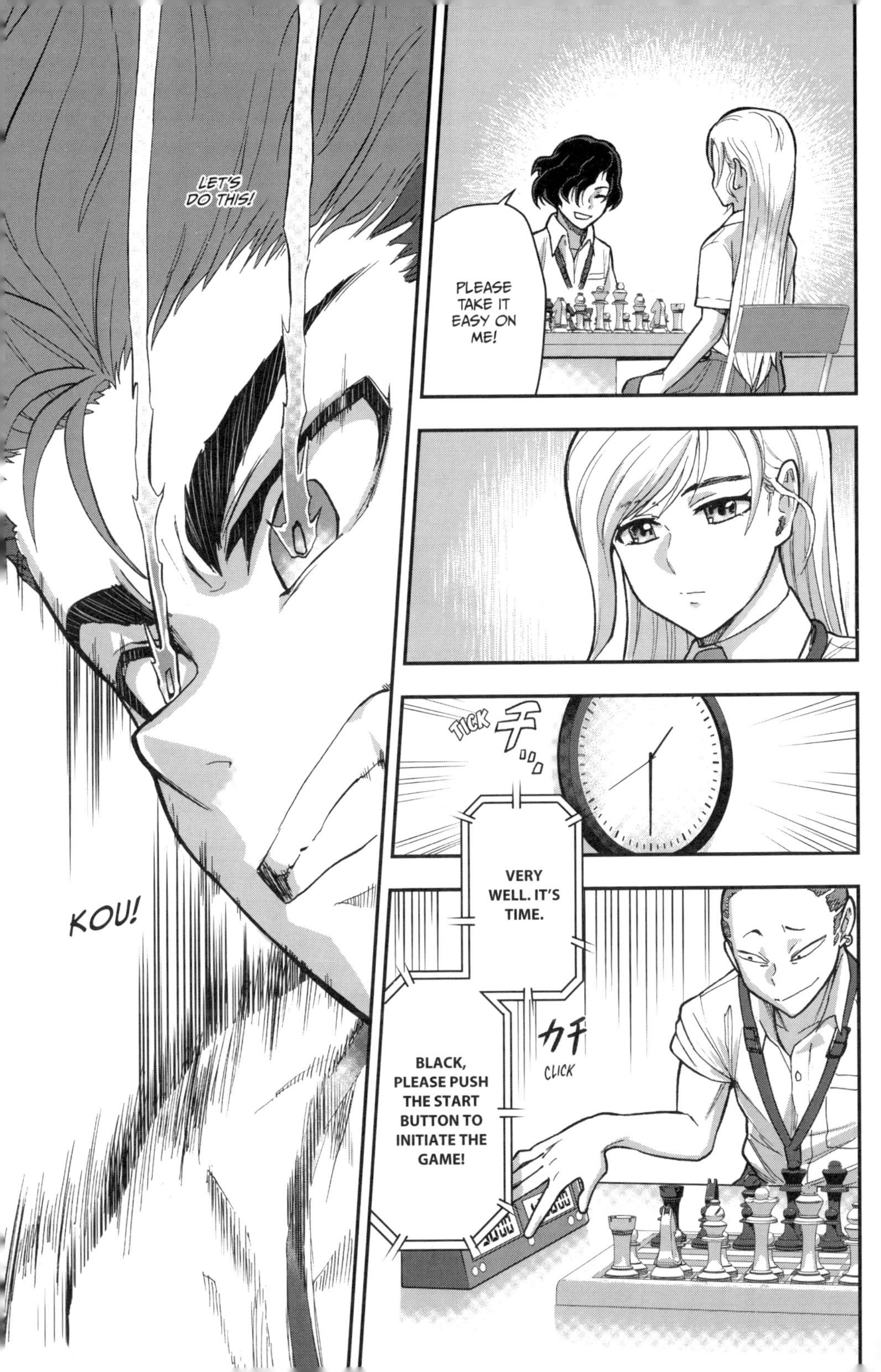
PLEASE TAKE IT EASY ON ME!
TICK
チ
VERY WELL. IT'S TIME.
BLACK, PLEASE PUSH THE START BUTTON TO INITIATE THE GAME!
カチ
CLICK
LET'S DO THIS!
KOU!

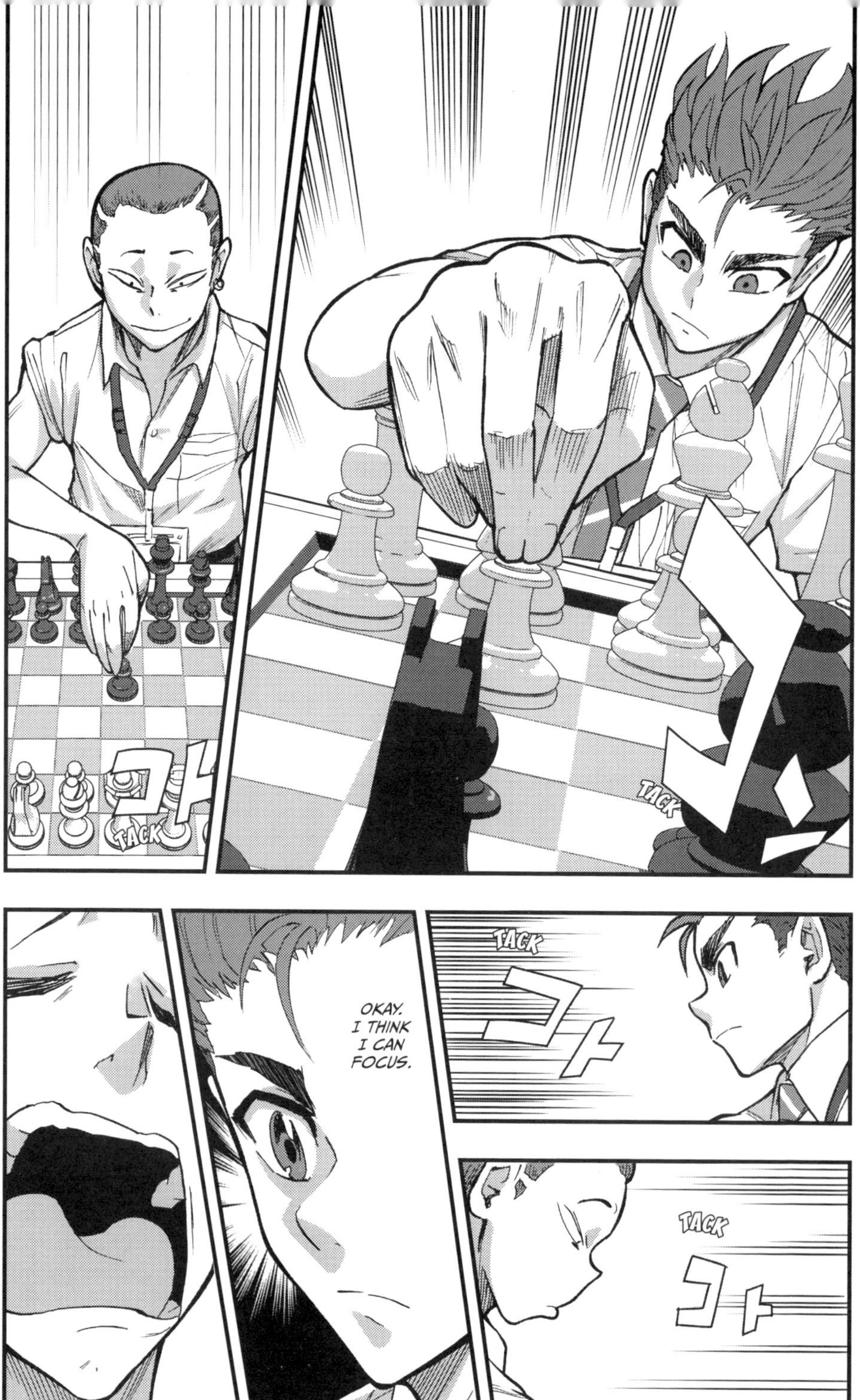
TACK
TACK
コト
TACK
コト
TACK
コト
OKAY. I THINK I CAN FOCUS.

ACHOO!

YES... SORRY! | **ARE YOU ALRIGHT? COVER YOUR MOUTH.**

TAP

CALM DOWN... I CAN'T LET HIM GET TO ME. TAKE IT EASY.

TACK

BASTARD!

AH... I CAN'T STOP SNEEZING TODAY.

SNIFF

?!

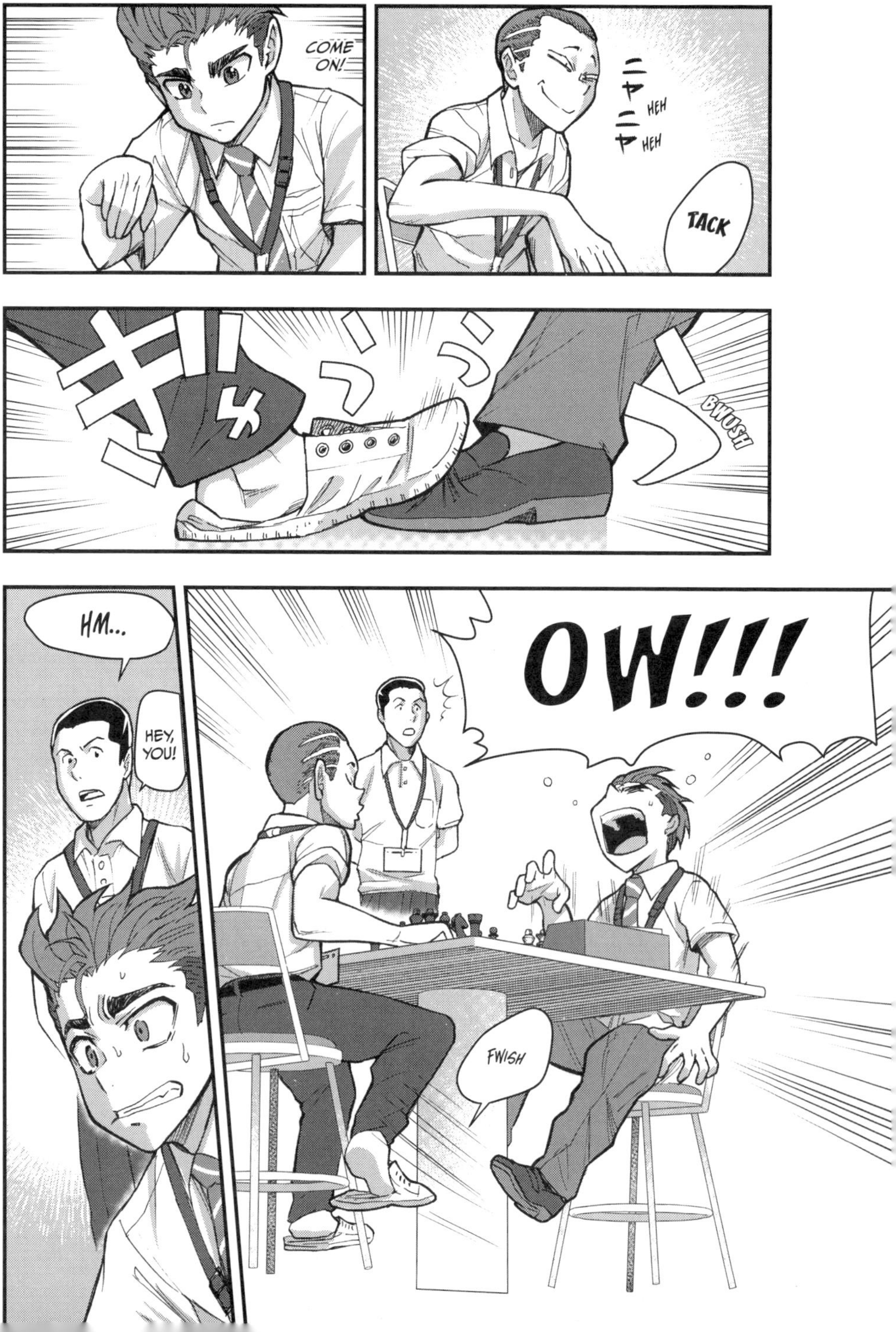

ニヤニヤ
HEH HEH
TACK
COME ON!
BWUSH
OW!!!
FWISH
HM...
HEY, YOU!

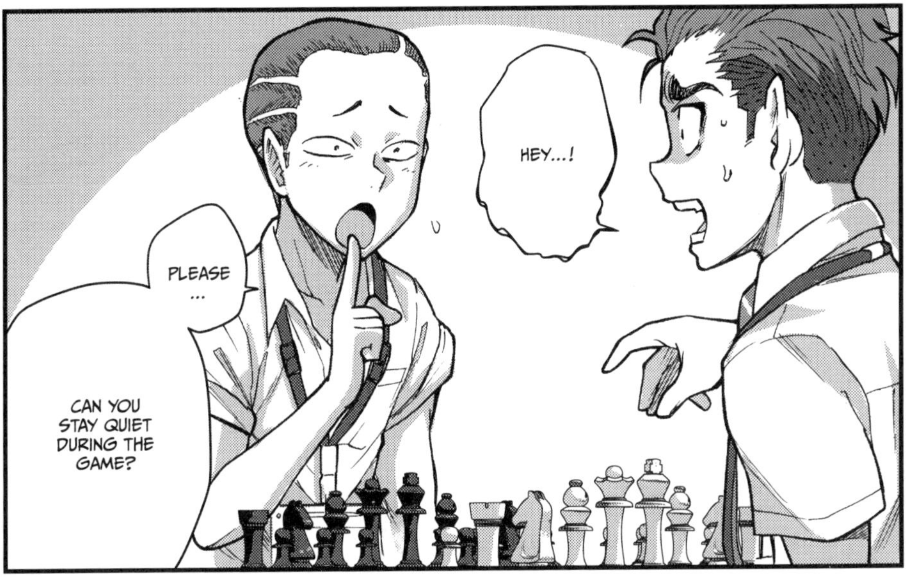
HEY...!
PLEASE...
CAN YOU STAY QUIET DURING THE GAME?
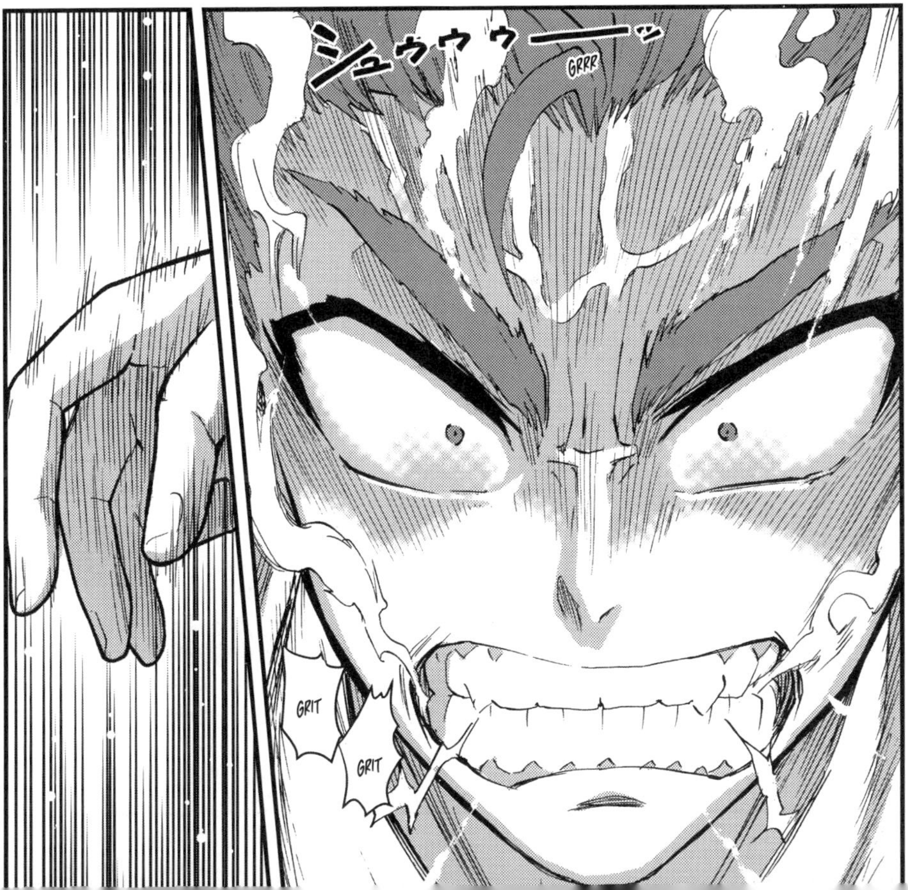
シュウウウーーッ
GRRR
GRIT
GRIT

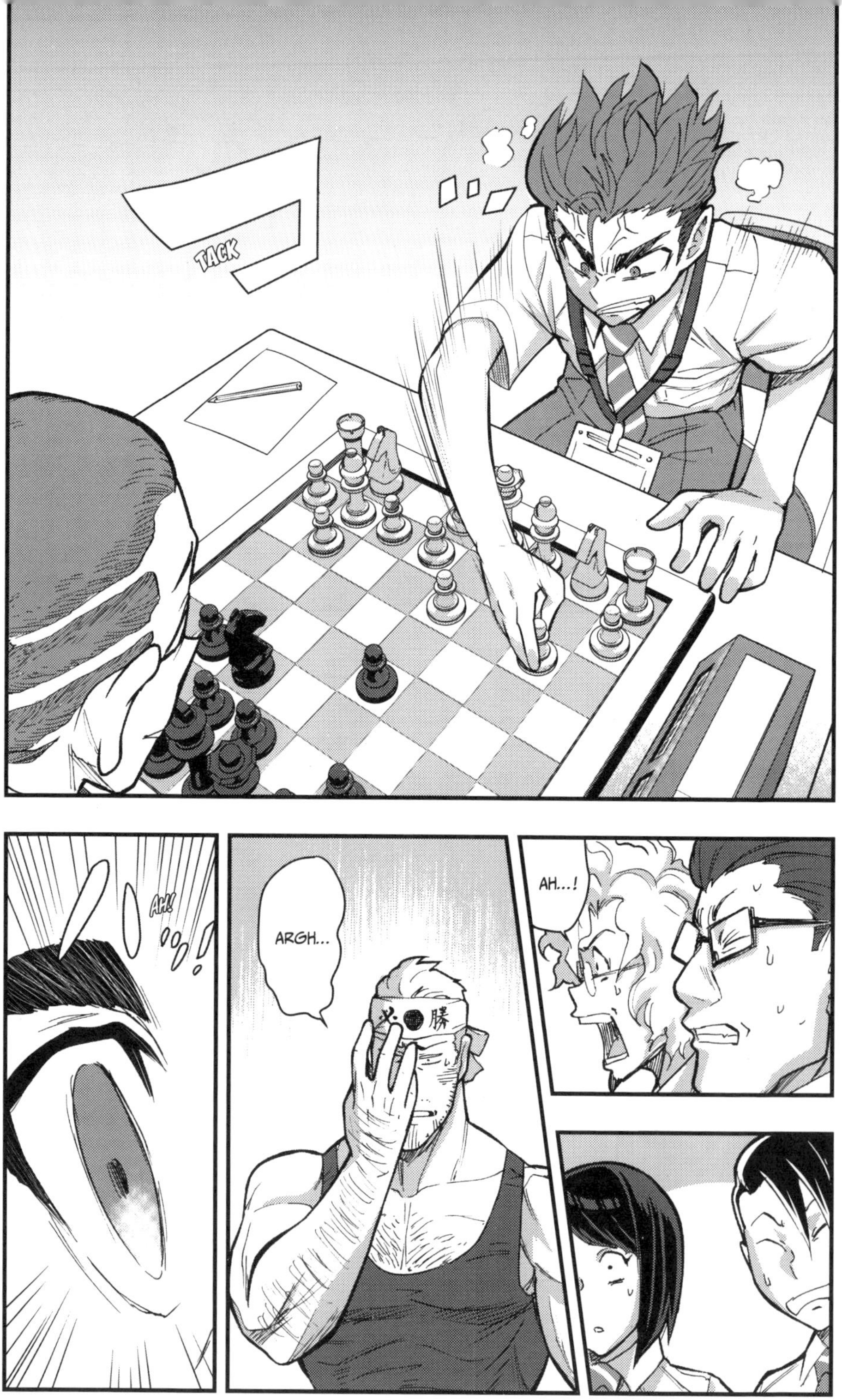
TACK
AH!
ARGH...
AH...!

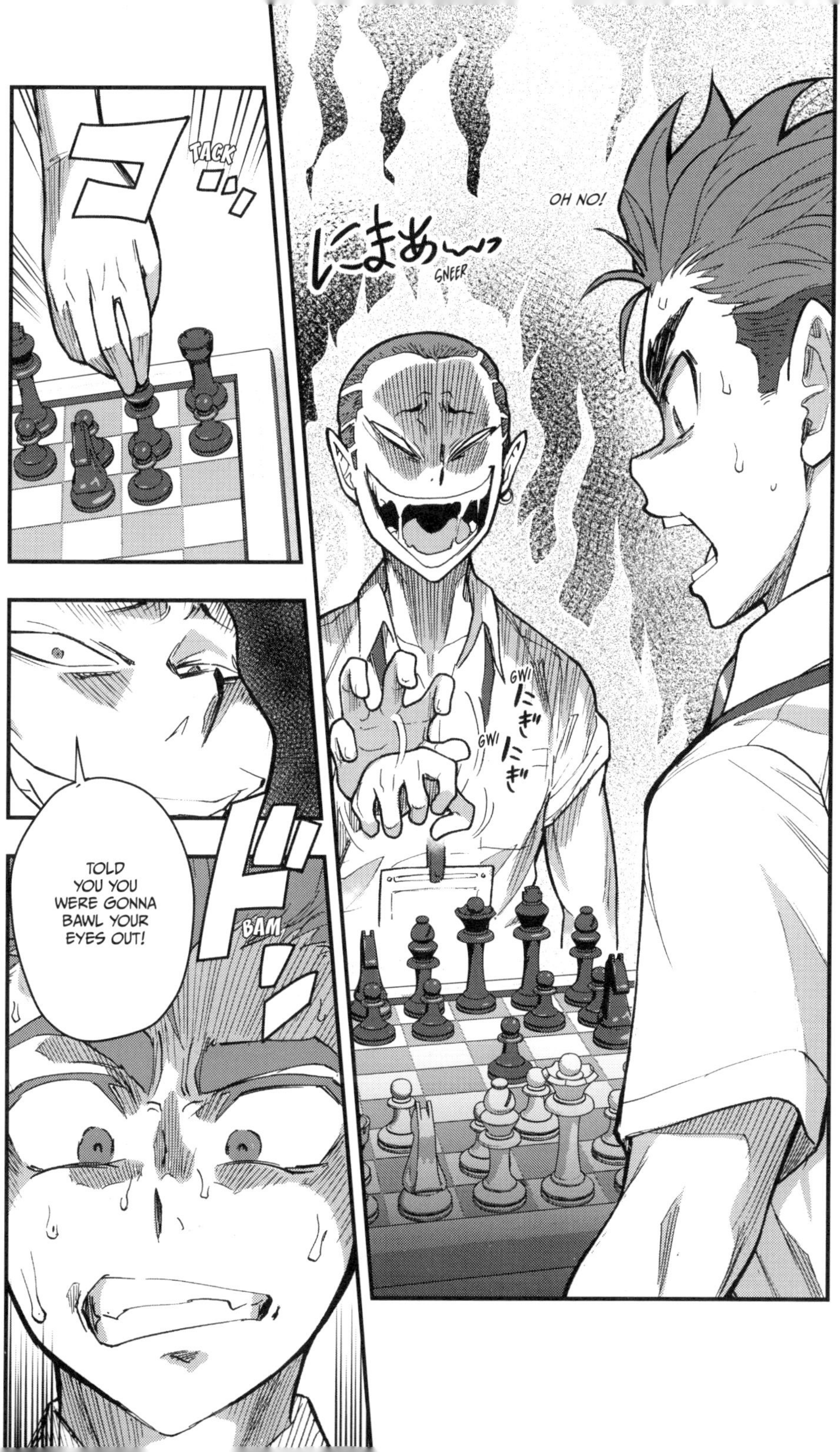

OH NO!
にまぁ～っ
SNEER
GWI
にぎ
GWI
にぎ
TACK
コ…
TOLD YOU YOU WERE GONNA BAWL YOUR EYES OUT!
ド
BAM

BLITZ

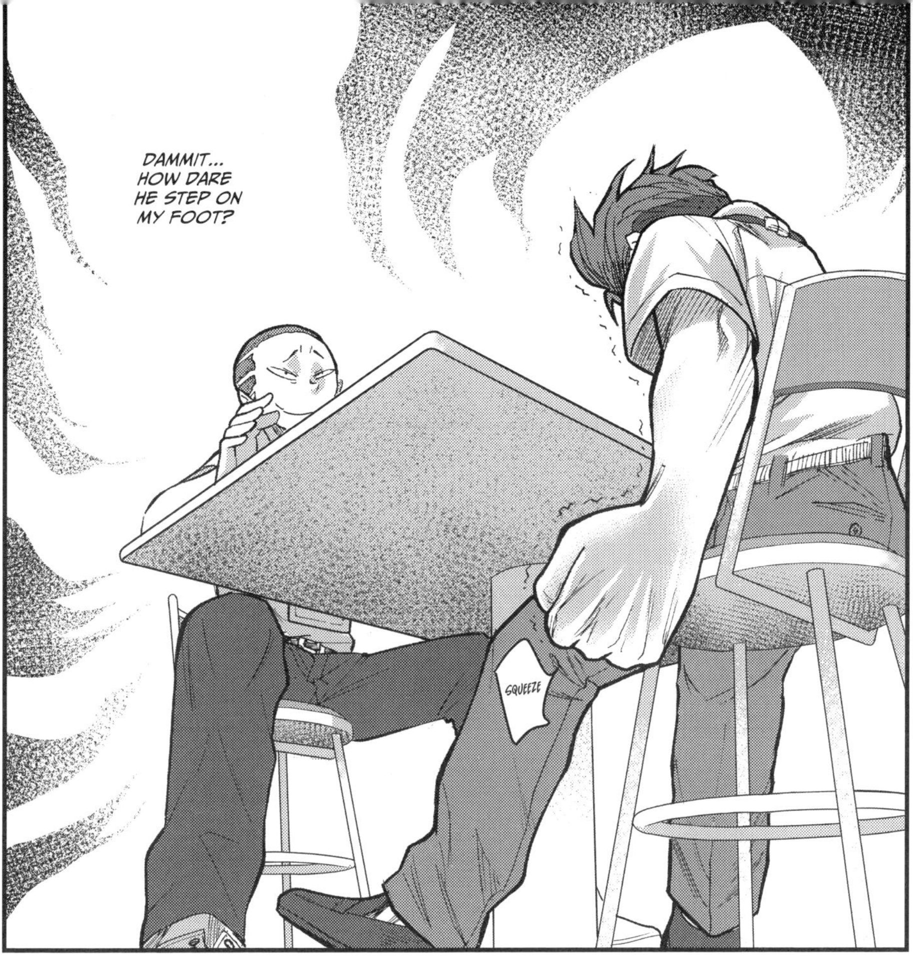
DAMMIT... HOW DARE HE STEP ON MY FOOT?
SQUEEZE

Chapter 22: All-out battle

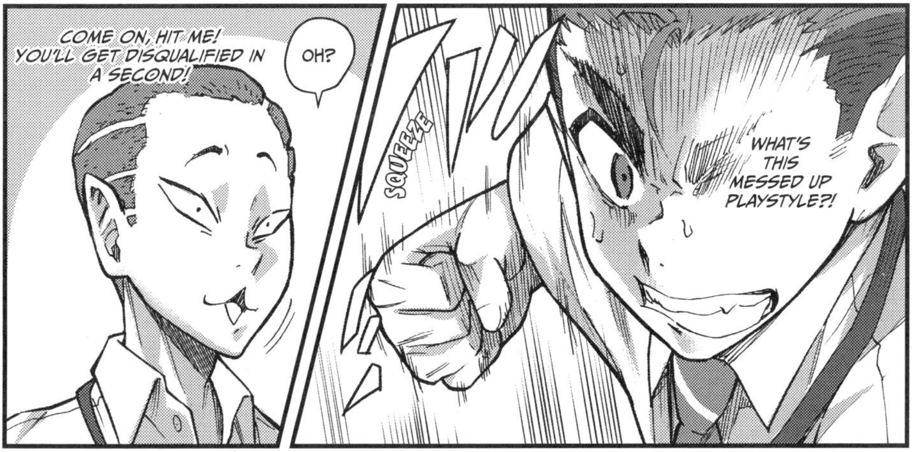
SQUEEEZE
WHAT'S THIS MESSED UP PLAYSTYLE?!
COME ON, HIT ME! YOU'LL GET DISQUALIFIED IN A SECOND!
OH?

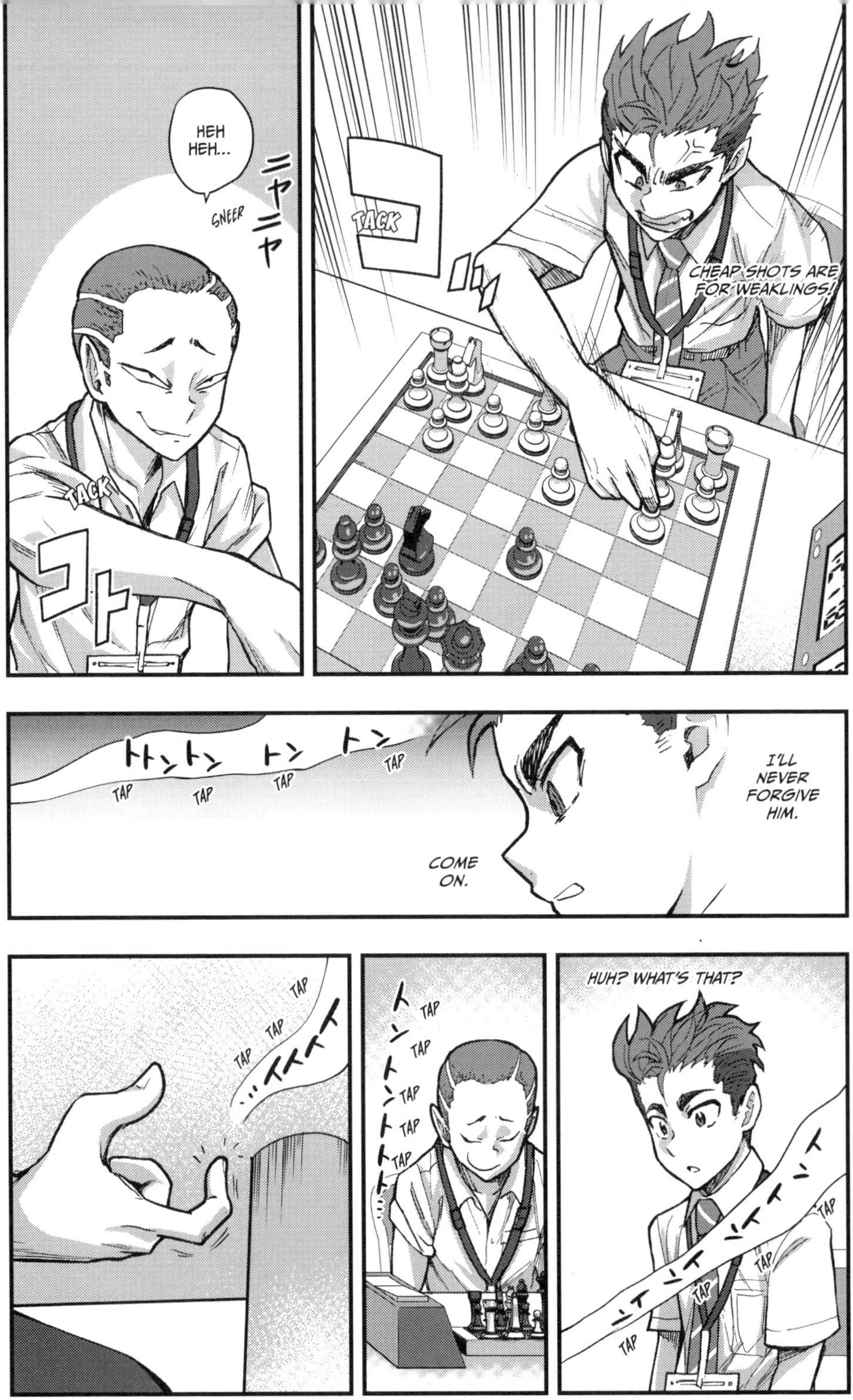
TACK
CHEAP SHOTS ARE FOR WEAKLINGS!
HEH HEH...
ニヤニヤ
SNEER
TACK
コト
I'LL NEVER FORGIVE HIM.
COME ON.
トントン トン トン
TAP
TAP
TAP
TAP
HUH? WHAT'S THAT?
TAP
TAP
TAP
TAP
TAP
TAP
TAP
TAP
TAP
TAP
TAP
TAP
TAP

UNBELIEVABLE!

HE'S A GOOD PLAYER. WHY IS HE DOING THIS?!

I DON'T GET IT.

HE'S DOING IT TO WIN!

DON'T LET HIM GET TO YOU.

FOCUS... FOCUS.

PHEW...

HE WANTS TO WIN NO MATTER WHAT.

WHAT AN IDIOT.

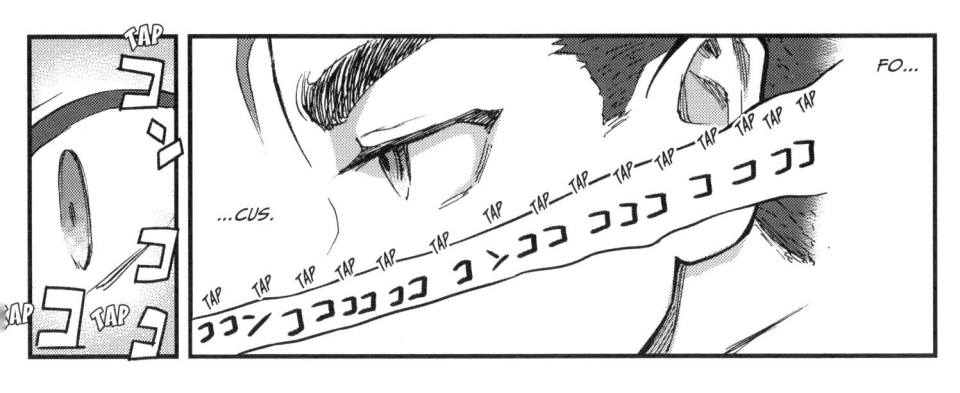

TAP TAP TAP TAP TAP TAP TAP TAP TAP TAP TAP TAP TAP TAP

FO...

...CUS.

SNAP

YES! THAT'S EXACTLY WHAT I WAS WAITING FOR! ♥

AHHH...

I'M GONNA KICK HIS ASS!

TOC

AH!

AGAIN?!

SLURP

THIS IS GONNA BE AN EASY WIN.

AH! LOOK! THE OTHERS ARE ALSO...

THAT'S THE FINALS FOR YOU.

TOM... GOT DUPED.

SHAKE SHAKE

IT IS... A FOUL.

HEY! HE STEPPED ON TOM'S FOOT ON PURPOSE! THAT'S A FOUL!

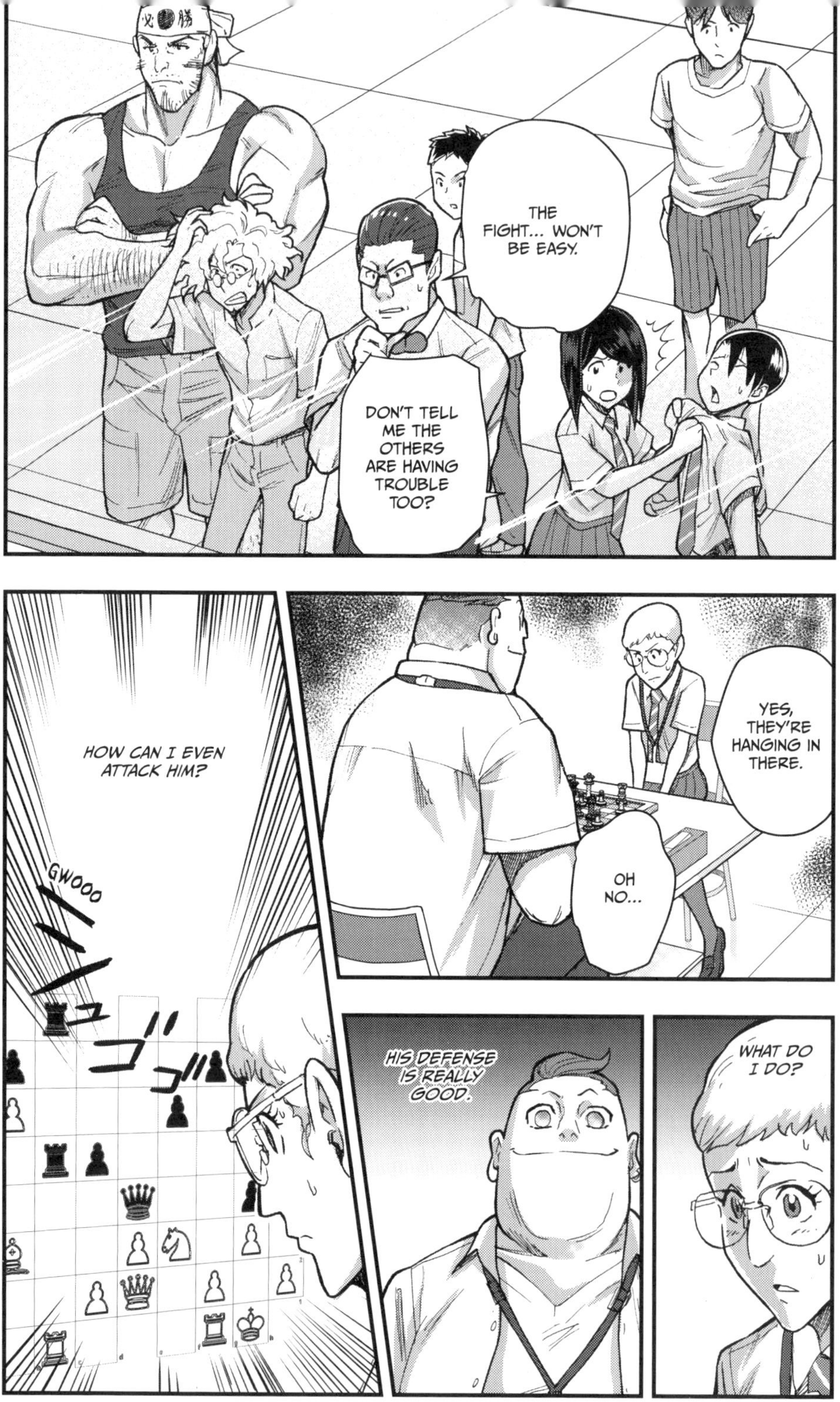
THE FIGHT... WON'T BE EASY.
DON'T TELL ME THE OTHERS ARE HAVING TROUBLE TOO?
YES, THEY'RE HANGING IN THERE.
OH NO...
WHAT DO I DO?
HIS DEFENSE IS REALLY GOOD.
HOW CAN I EVEN ATTACK HIM?
GWOOO

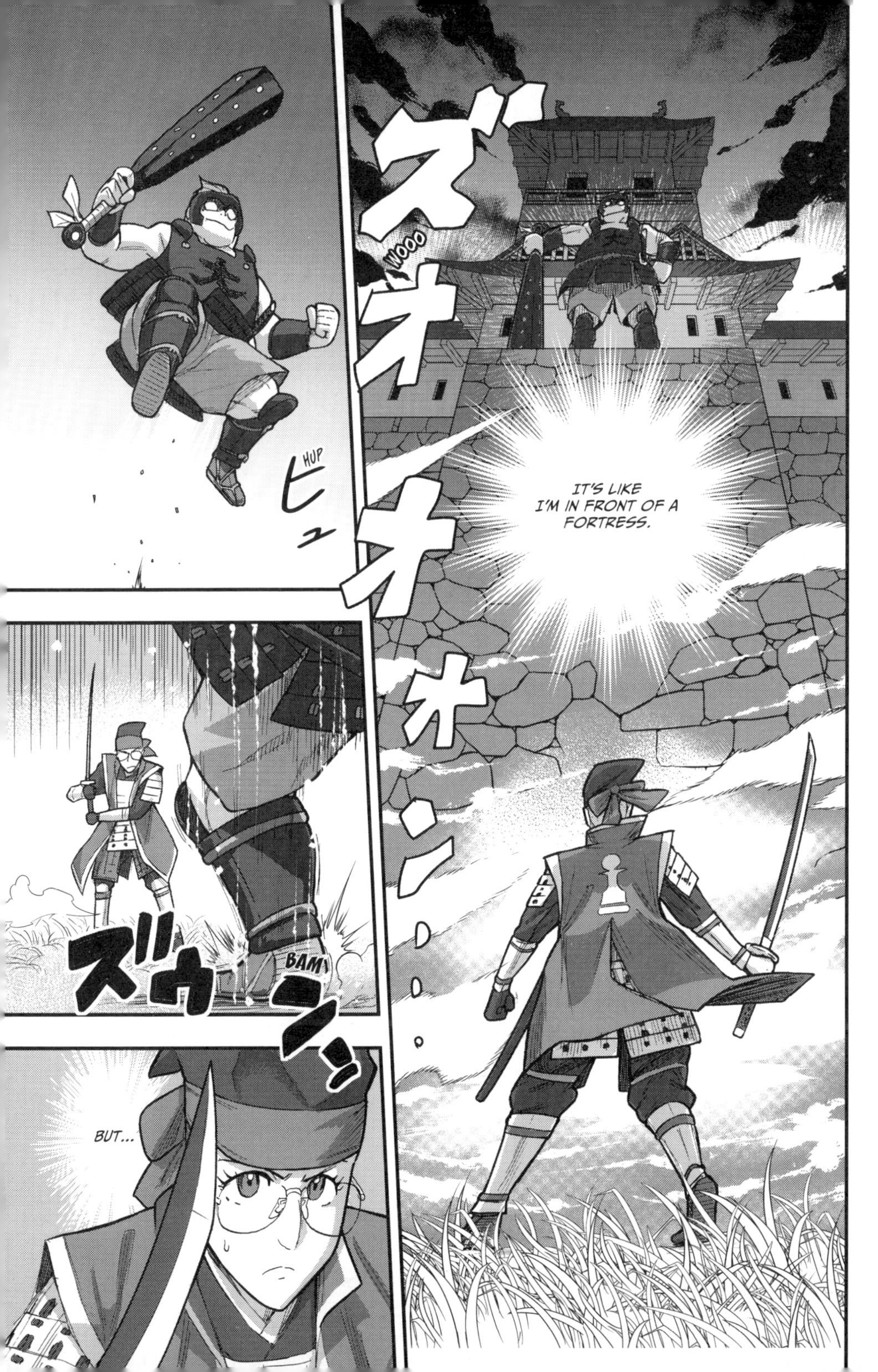
WOOO
IT'S LIKE I'M IN FRONT OF A FORTRESS.
HUP
BAM
BUT...

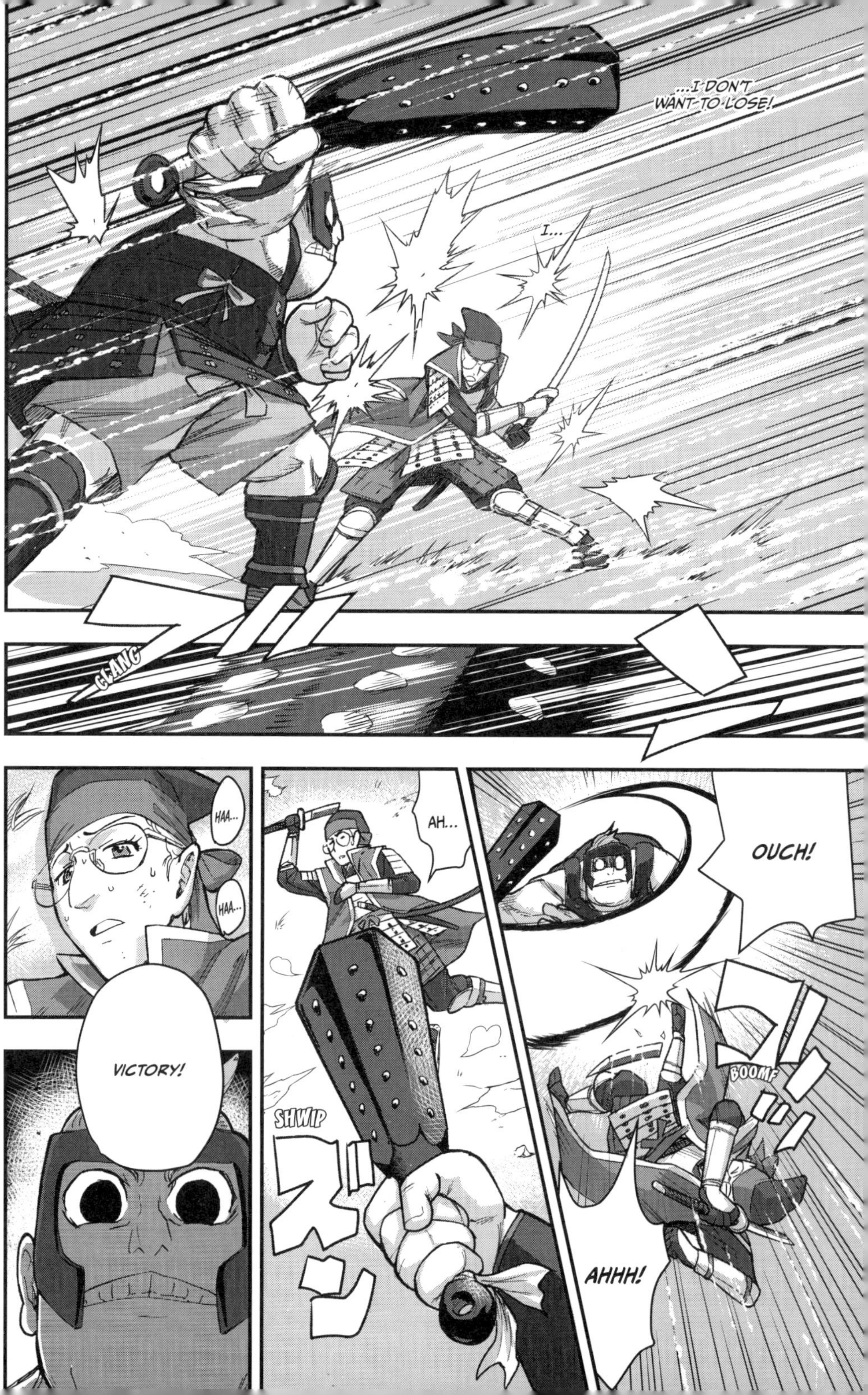
...I DON'T WANT TO LOSE!
I...
CLANG
HAA...
HAA...
VICTORY!
AH...
SHWIP
OUCH!
BOOMF
AHHH!

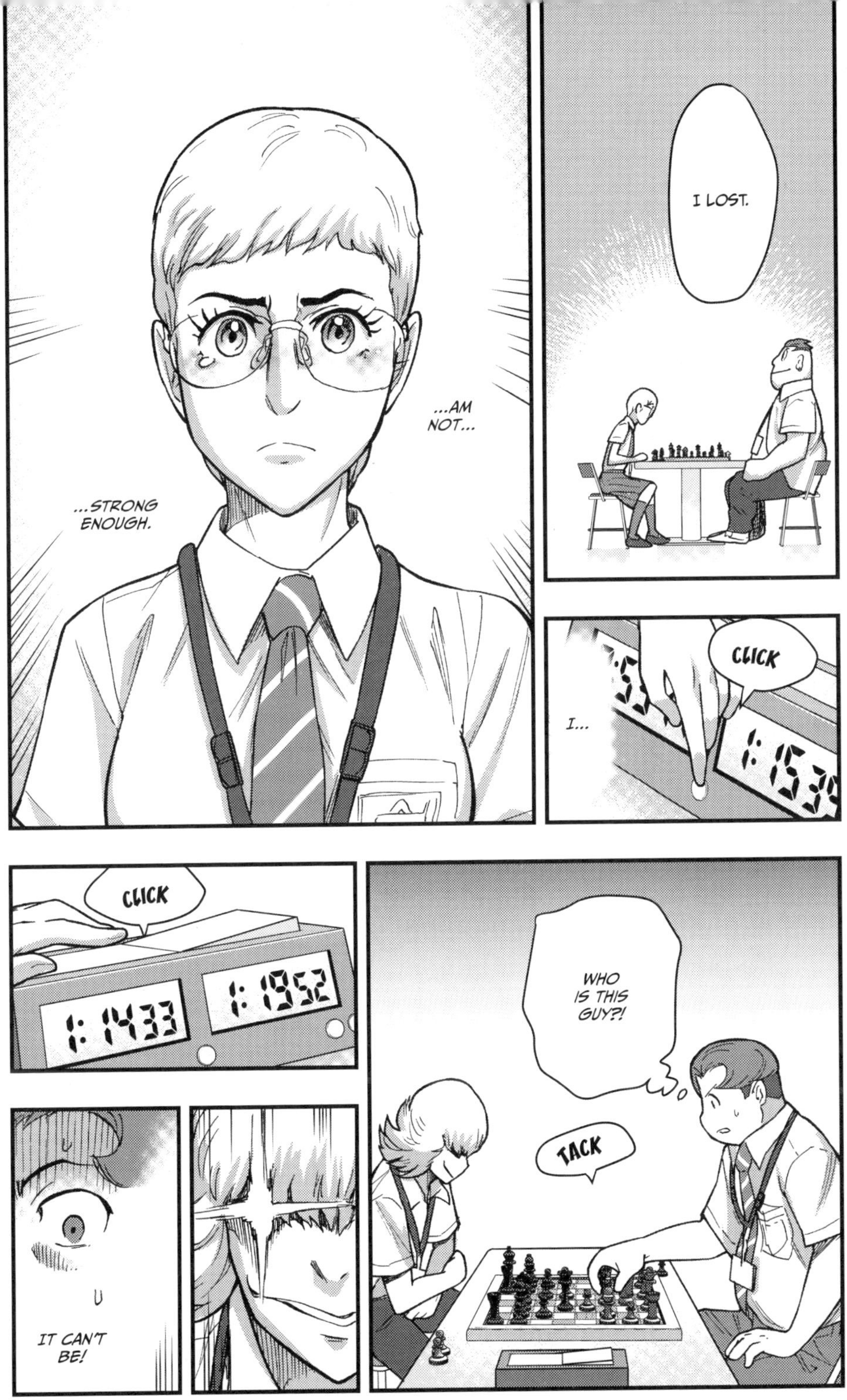
I LOST.
CLICK
I...
...AM NOT...
...STRONG ENOUGH.
WHO IS THIS GUY?!
TACK
CLICK
1: 1433
1: 1952
IT CAN'T BE!

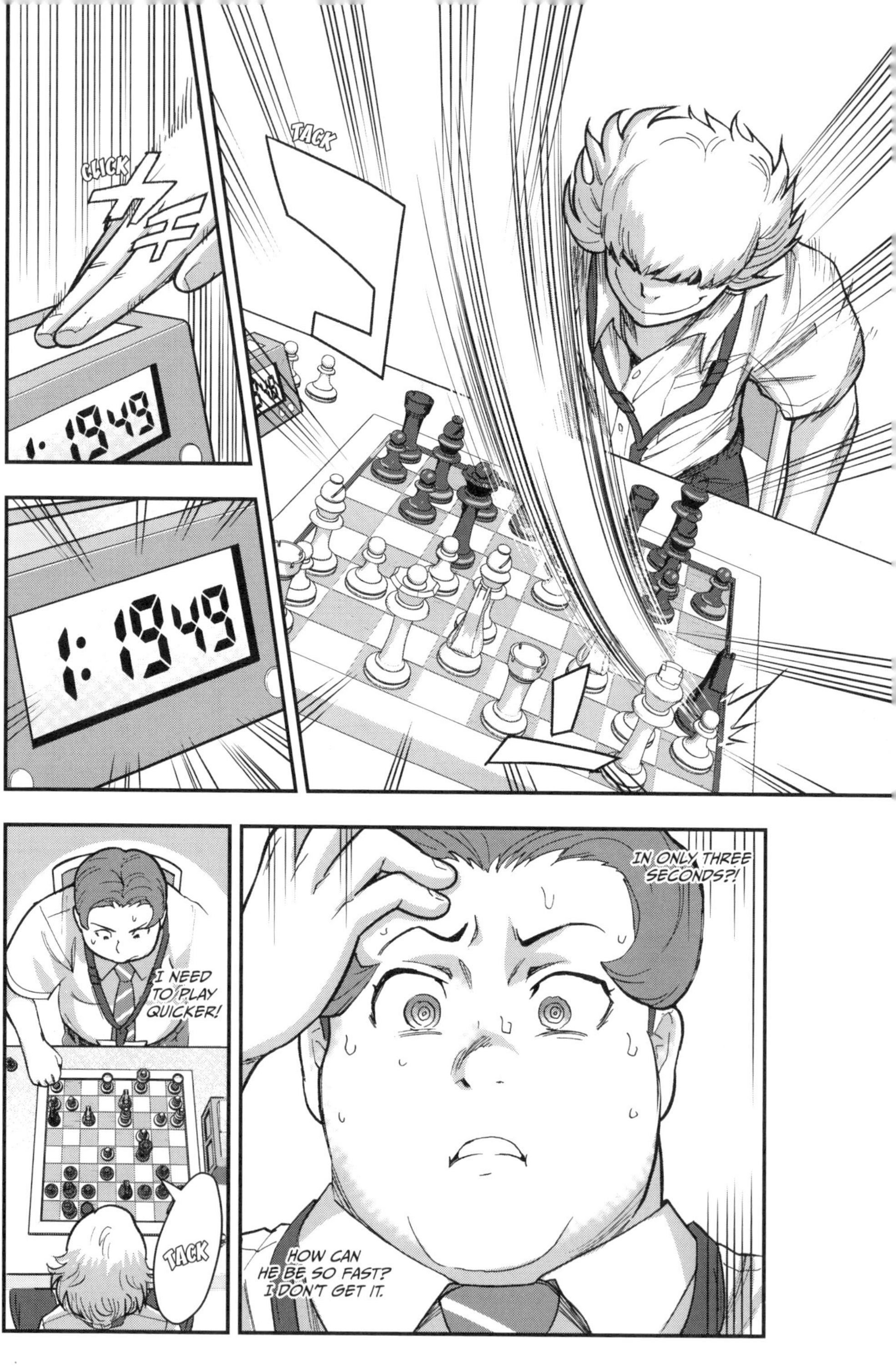TACK
CLICK
1:19 49
1:19 49
IN ONLY THREE SECONDS?!
HOW CAN HE BE SO FAST? I DON'T GET IT.
I NEED TO PLAY QUICKER!
TACK

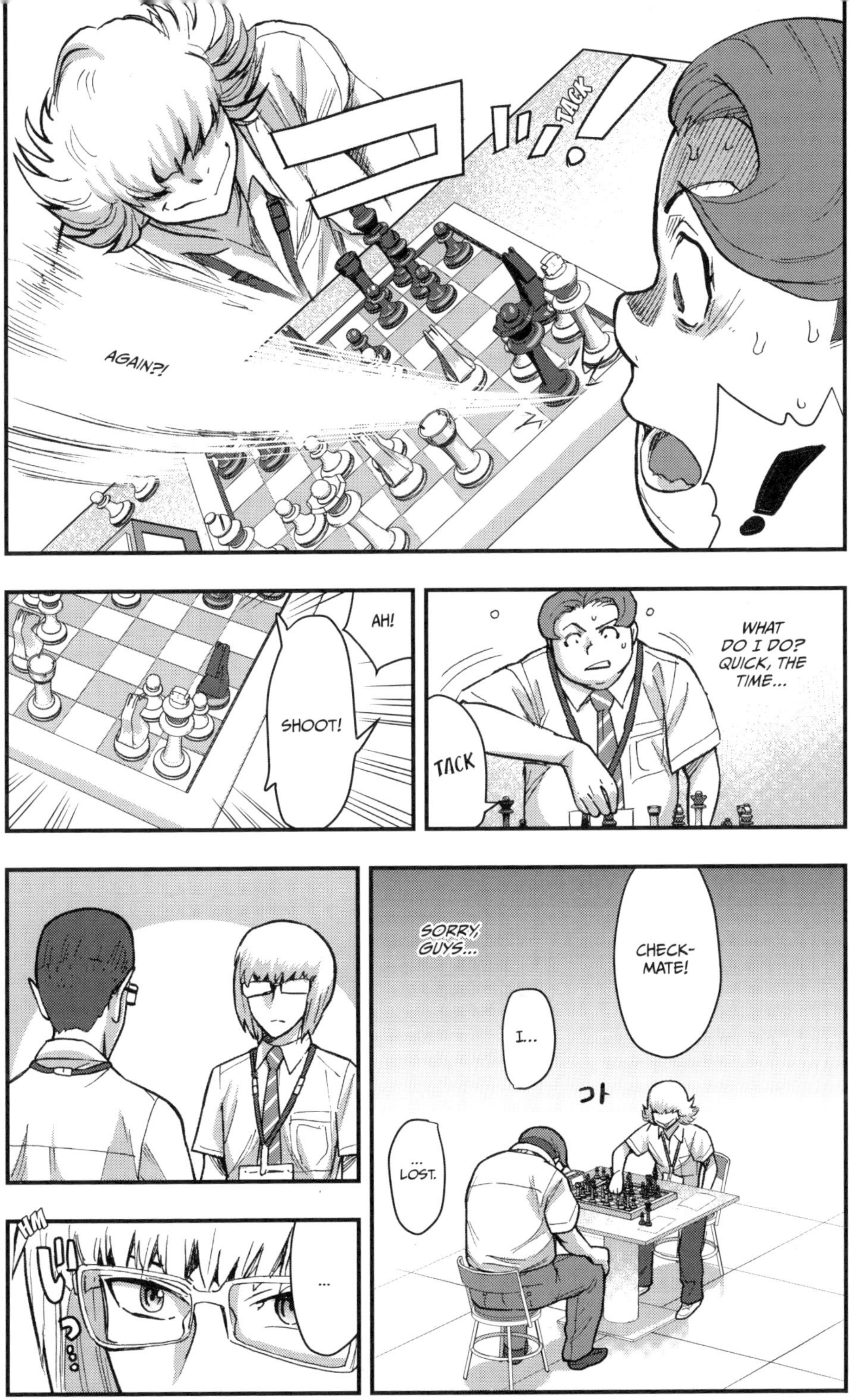

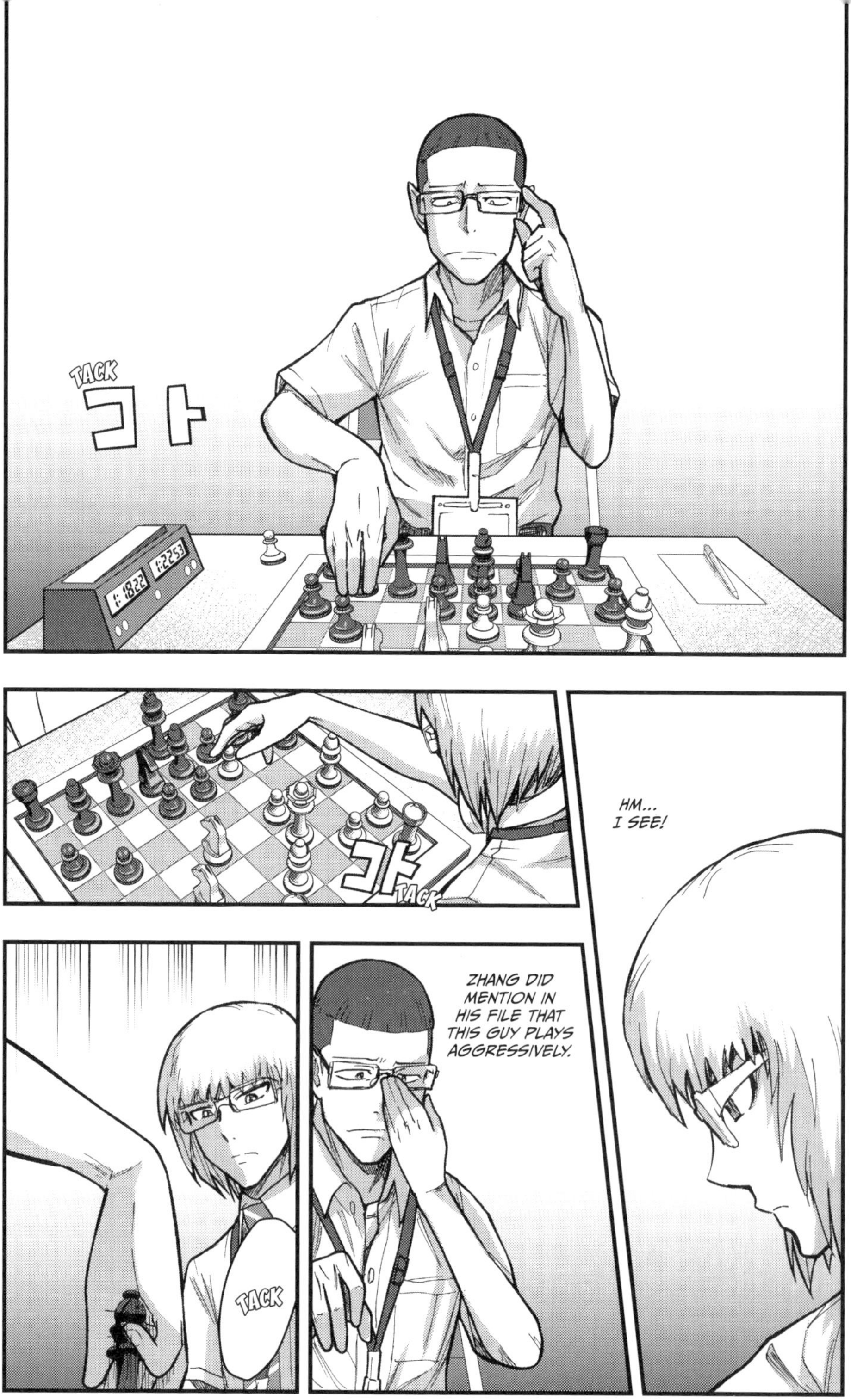
TACK
コト
HM... I SEE!
コト
TACK
ZHANG DID MENTION IN HIS FILE THAT THIS GUY PLAYS AGGRESSIVELY.
TACK

ARGH! HE TOOK MY QUEEN!

HE JUST GOES ALL-IN ON OFFENSE INSTEAD OF PLAYING DEFENSE!

THIS ISN'T GOOD.

IF THIS KEEPS GOING..!

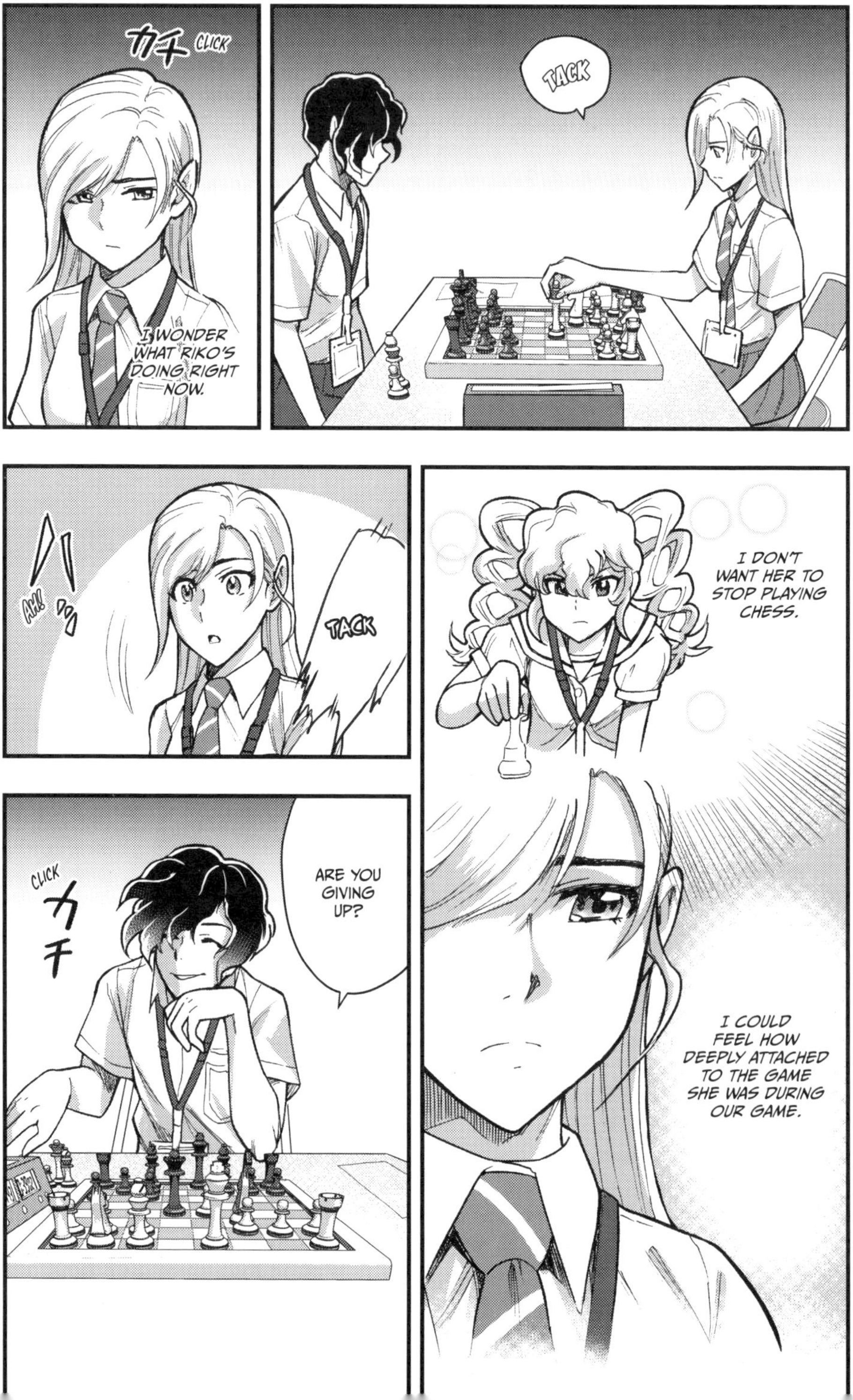
TACK
カチ CLICK
I WONDER WHAT RIKO'S DOING RIGHT NOW.
I DON'T WANT HER TO STOP PLAYING CHESS.
I COULD FEEL HOW DEEPLY ATTACHED TO THE GAME SHE WAS DURING OUR GAME.
ハッ AH!
TACK
CLICK カチ
ARE YOU GIVING UP?

I NEED TO FOCUS ON THE GAME.

NO.

OH NO! ANNE AND MARIUS LOST!

HEY, CALM DOWN! THE OTHER THREE ARE STILL PLAYING!

BUT THEY ABSOLUTELY NEED TO WIN!

TOM IS UNDER PRESSURE...

AND THINGS AREN'T GOING SO WELL FOR LAURENT AND HARMONY!

THEN WE NEED... TO CHEER THEM ON...

GO!

LAU-RENT...

!!!

HEY, LOOK! THINGS ARE GETTING SERIOUS FOR LAURENT!

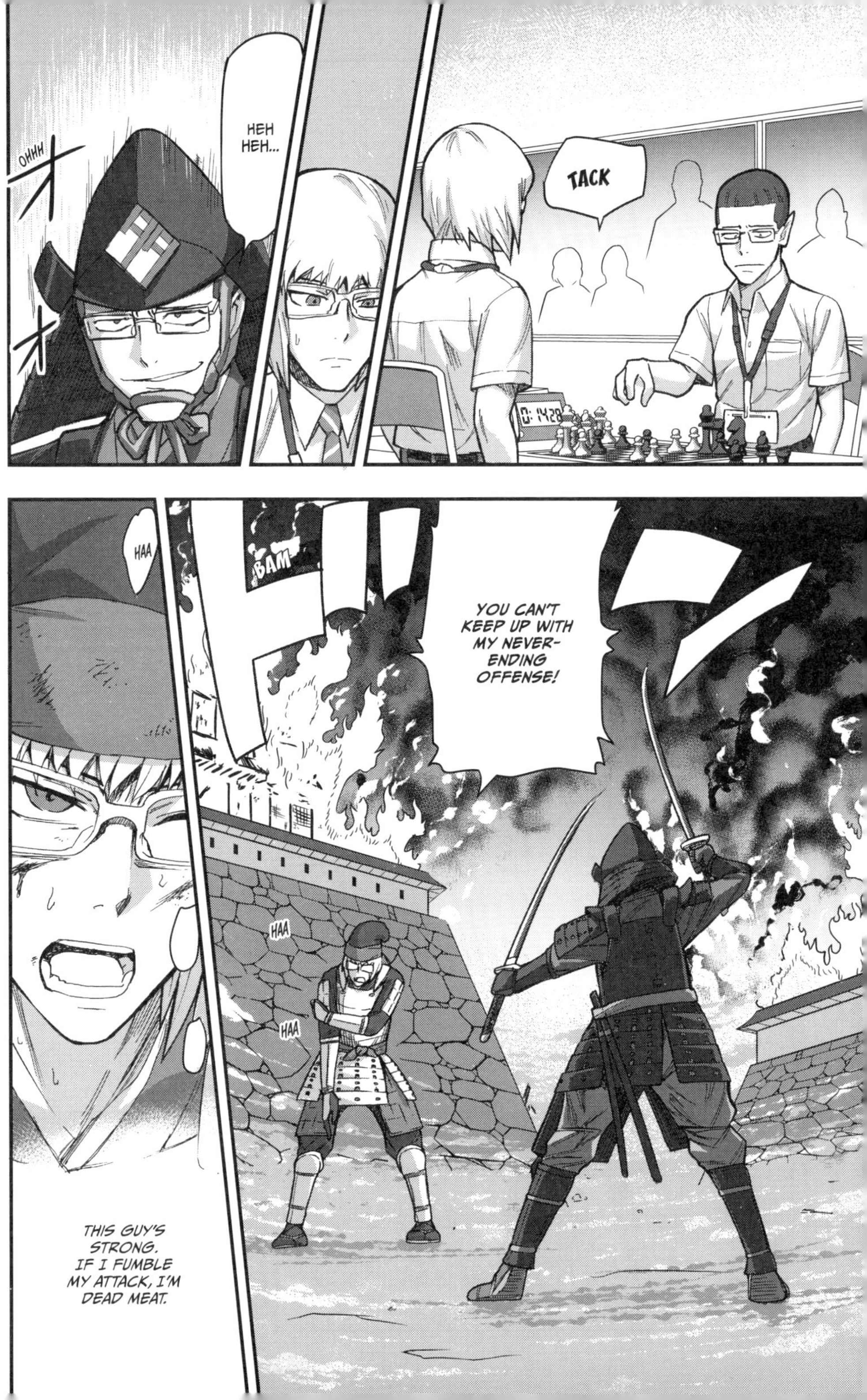
TACK
HEH HEH...
OHHH
YOU CAN'T KEEP UP WITH MY NEVER-ENDING OFFENSE!
BAM
HAA
HAA
HAA
THIS GUY'S STRONG. IF I FUMBLE MY ATTACK, I'M DEAD MEAT.

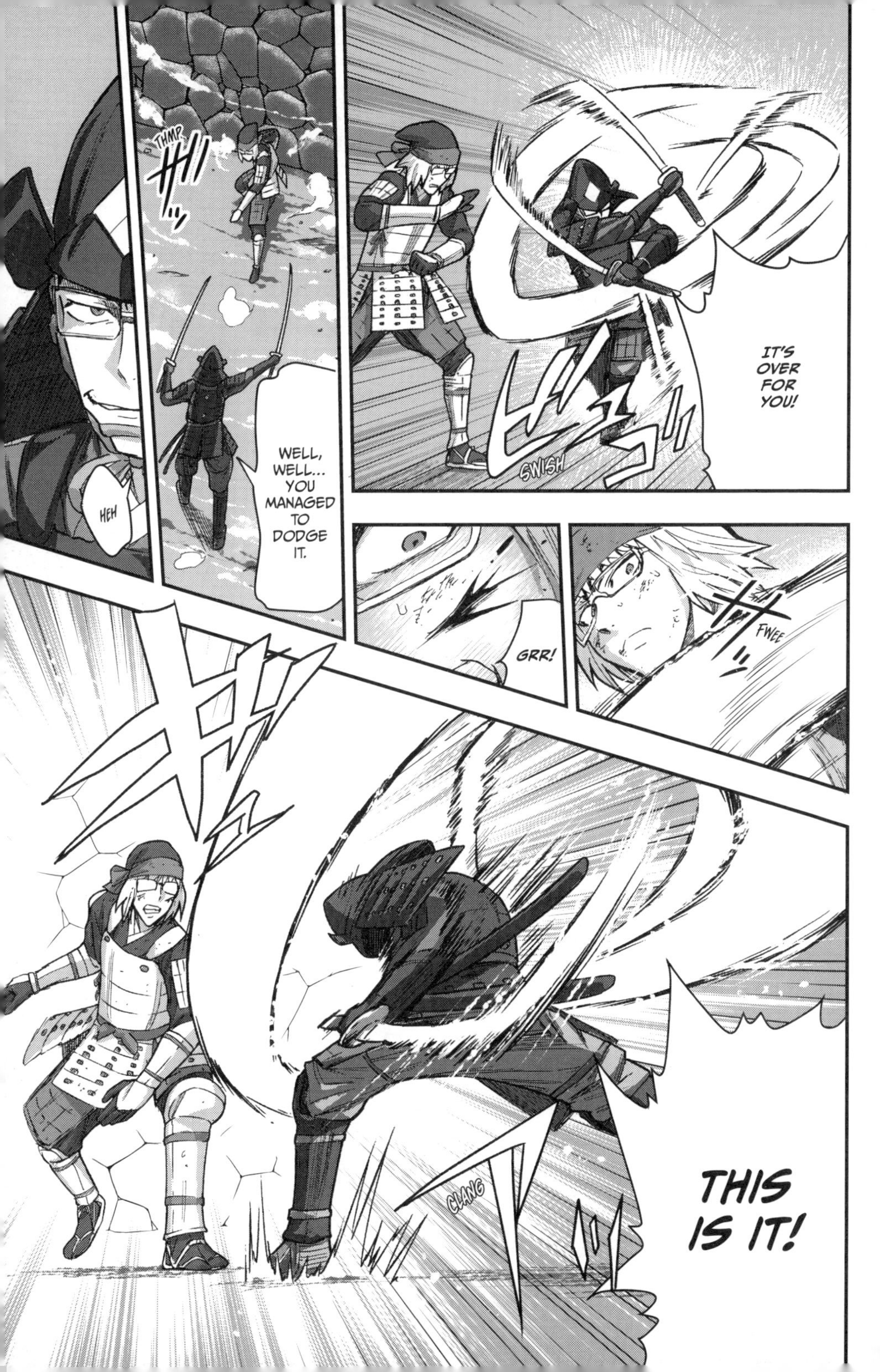
SWISH
IT'S OVER FOR YOU!
THMP
WELL, WELL... YOU MANAGED TO DODGE IT.
HEH
FWEE
GRR!
CLANG
THIS IS IT!

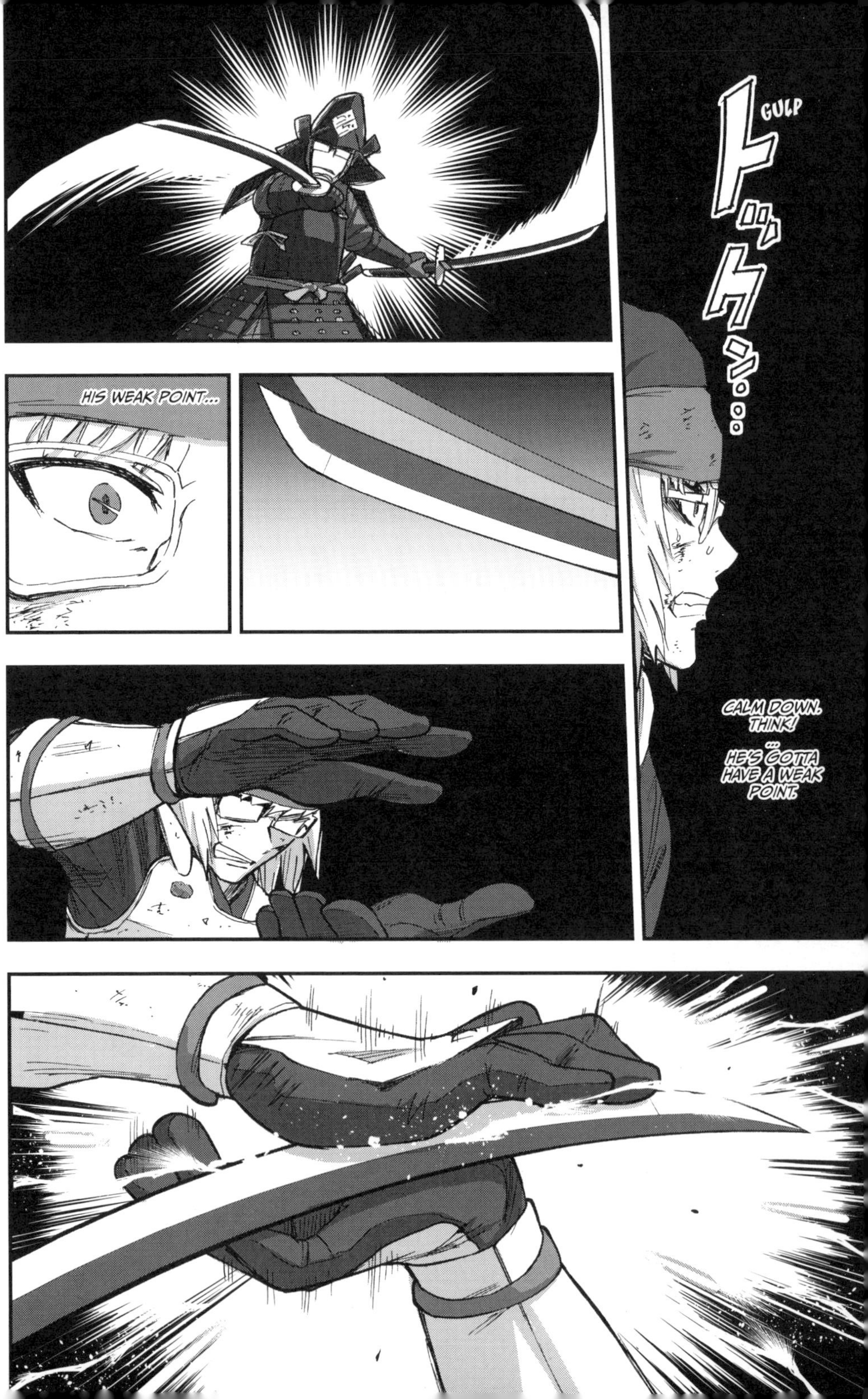
GULP
CALM DOWN. THINK!
... HE'S GOTTA HAVE A WEAK POINT.
HIS WEAK POINT...

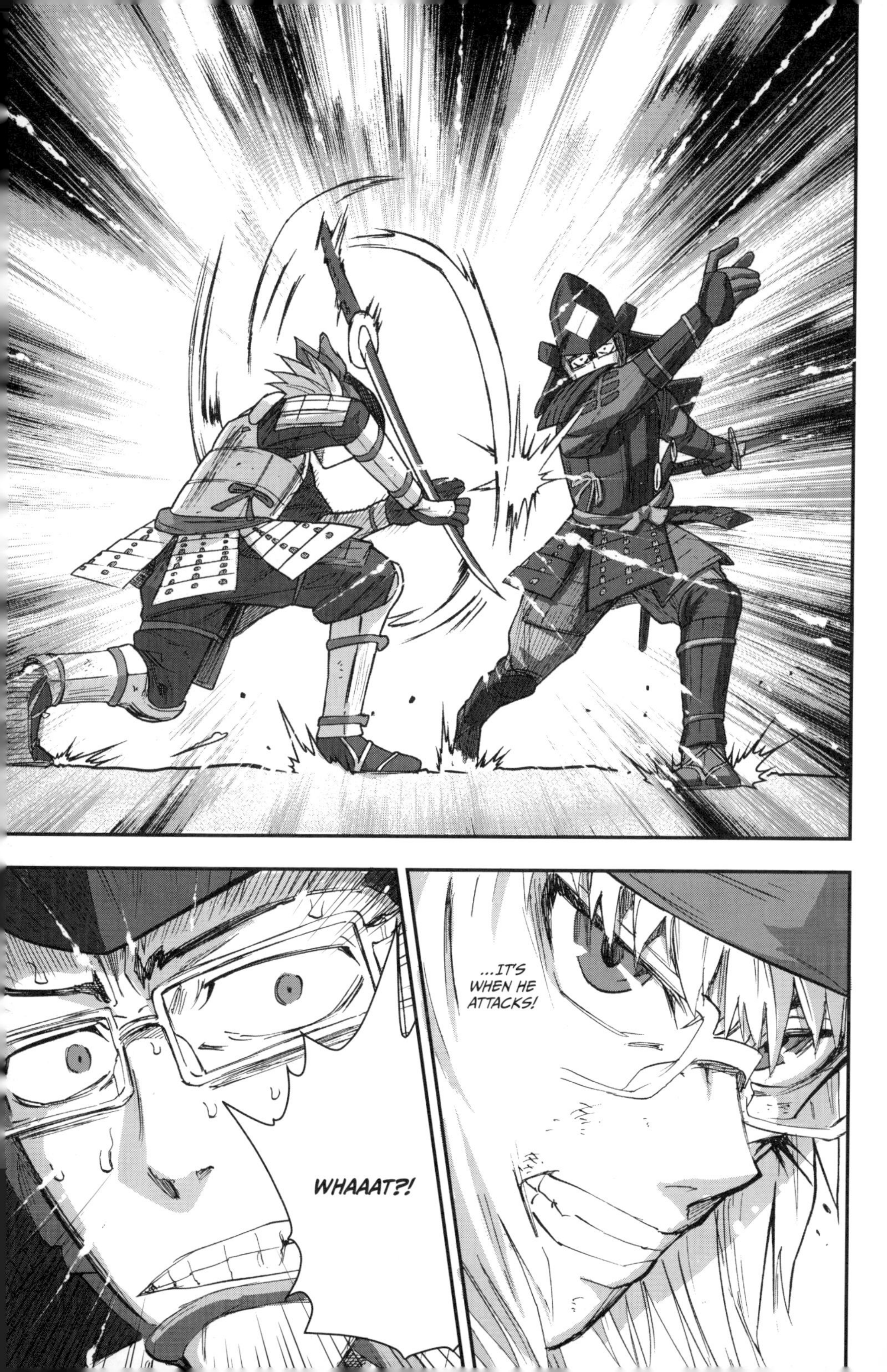
...IT'S WHEN HE ATTACKS!
WHAAAT?!

YOU LET YOUR GUARD DOWN! GOING ALL-OUT IS A WEAKNESS, TOO!

GWISH

CLANG

WOW... I HAD GOOSE-BUMPS.

IT'S NOT A CHECKMATE, BUT IT'S STILL A WIN.

CLICK

...

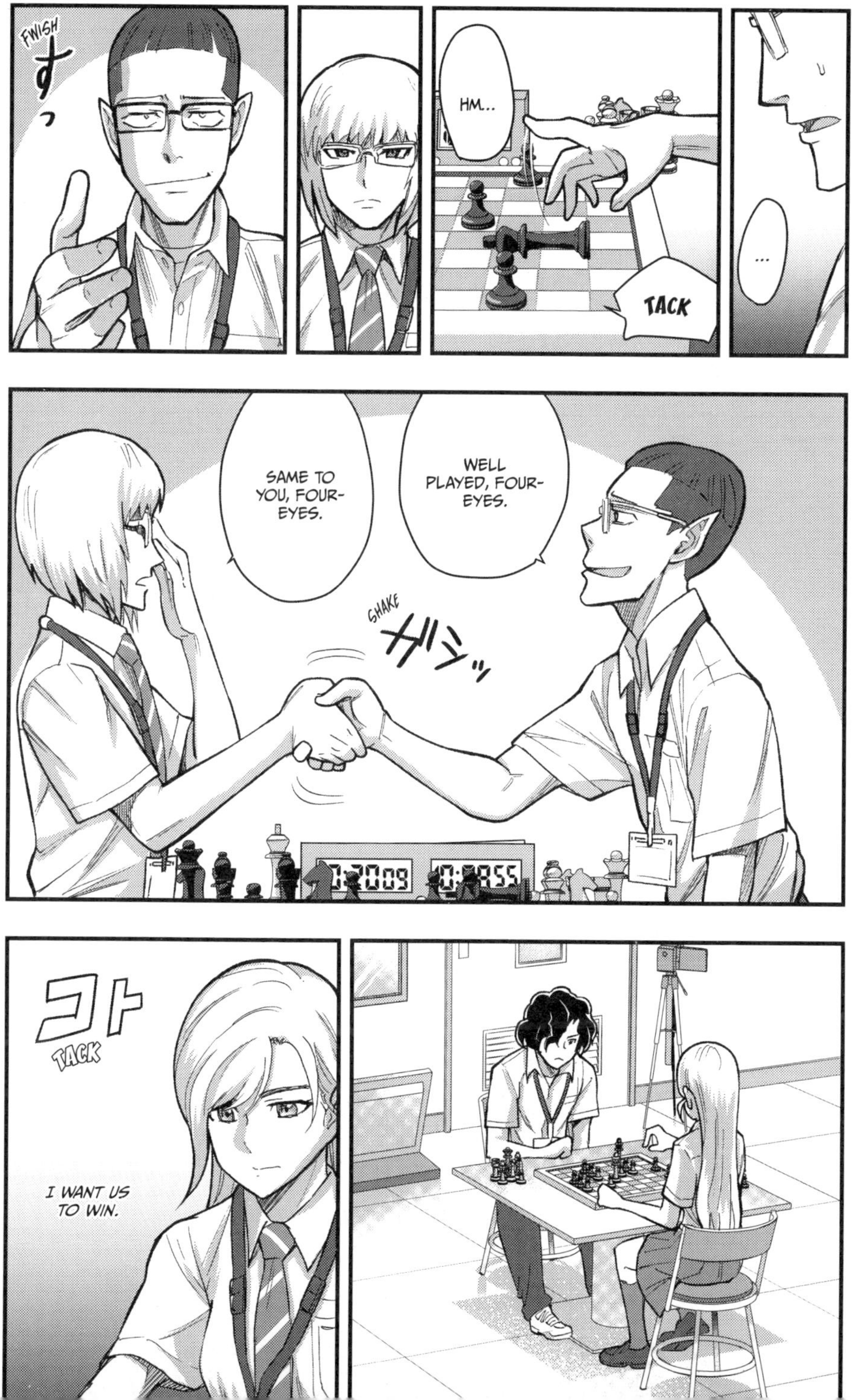
FWISH
すっ
HM...
TACK
...
WELL PLAYED, FOUR-EYES.
SAME TO YOU, FOUR-EYES.
SHAKE
ガシッ
コト
TACK
I WANT US TO WIN.

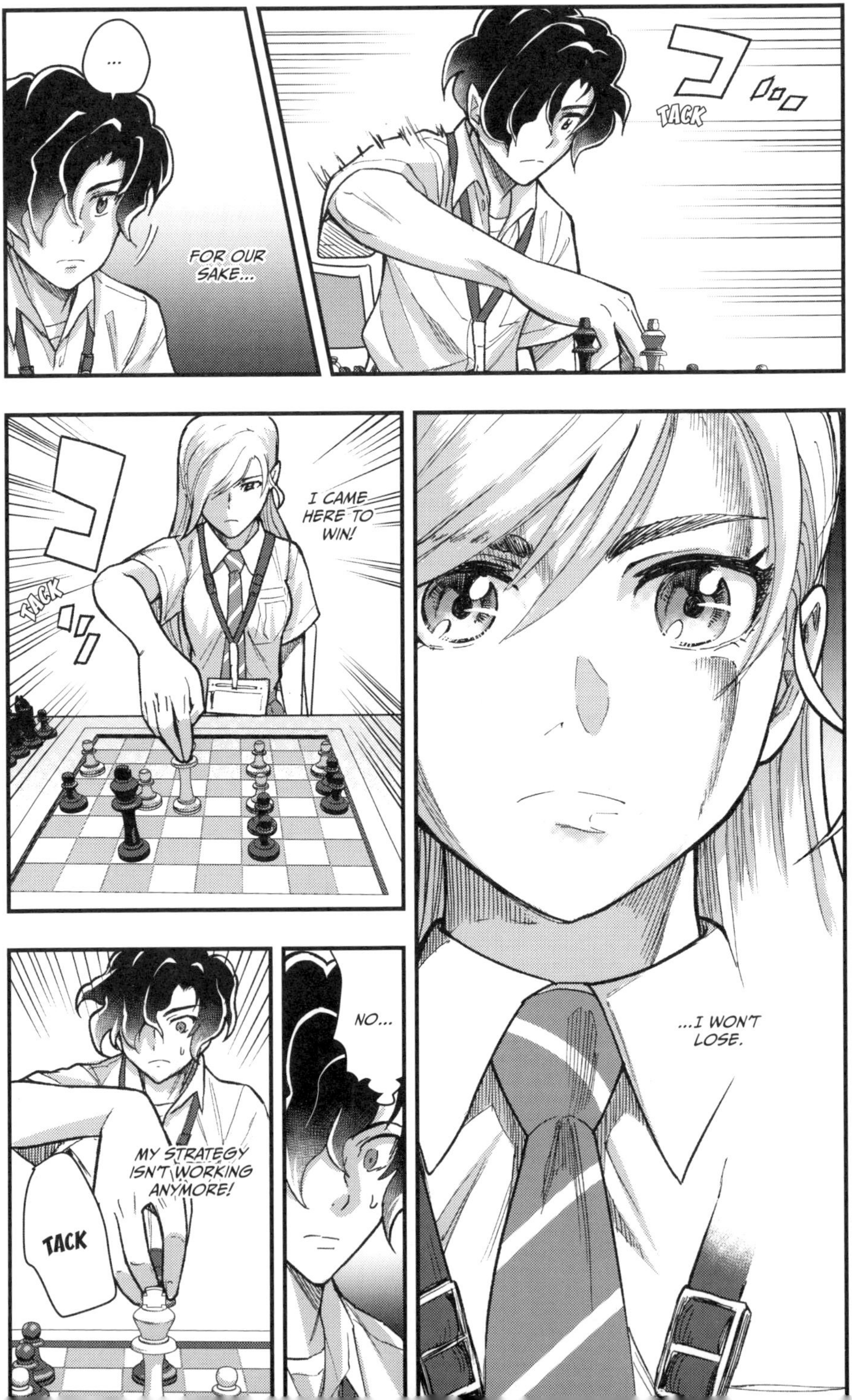
TACK
...
FOR OUR SAKE...
TACK
I CAME HERE TO WIN!
NO...
TACK
MY STRATEGY ISN'T WORKING ANYMORE!
...I WON'T LOSE.

TACK

TACK

OH NO...
I SHOULD HAVE
ATTACKED HARDER!

NO, IT
CAN'T BE!

AH

IF SHE BLOCKS MY PAWN ON H5, THEN THE GAME IS OVER.

...

I HEARD SHE WAS STRONG...

...BUT NOT LIKE THIS!

TACK

IF KOU WINS HIS GAME, VICTORY WILL BE OURS.

I THINK WE'LL HAVE ENOUGH POINTS, EVEN IF I LOSE.

HEH

FWISH

CLAP CLAP CLAP CLAP

CLICK

I LOST. YOU LIVED UP TO YOUR REPUTATION!

THANK YOU.

HOWEVER...

...TOUTO MIDDLE SCHOOL WILL STILL WIN.

BLITZ

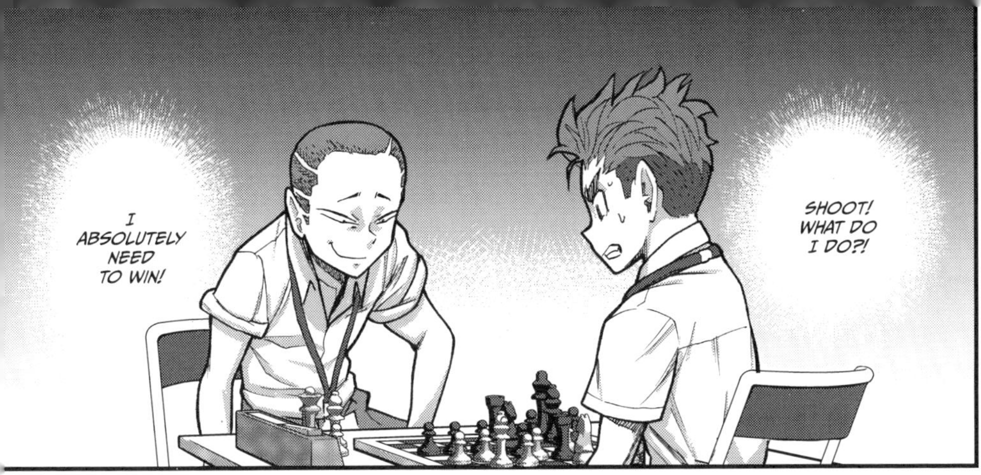
SHOOT! WHAT DO I DO?!
I ABSOLUTELY NEED TO WIN!

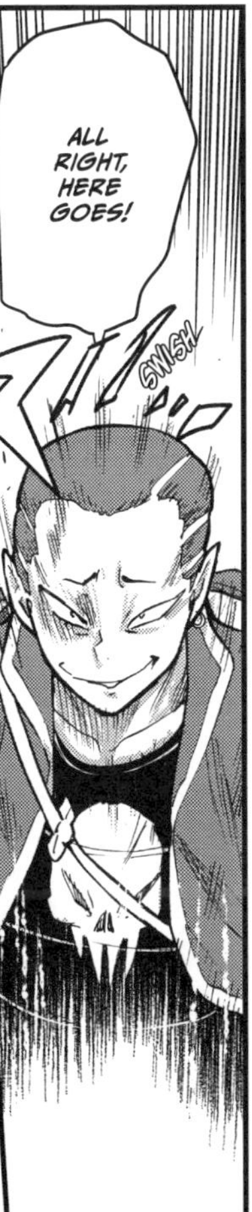
ALL RIGHT, HERE GOES!
SWISH

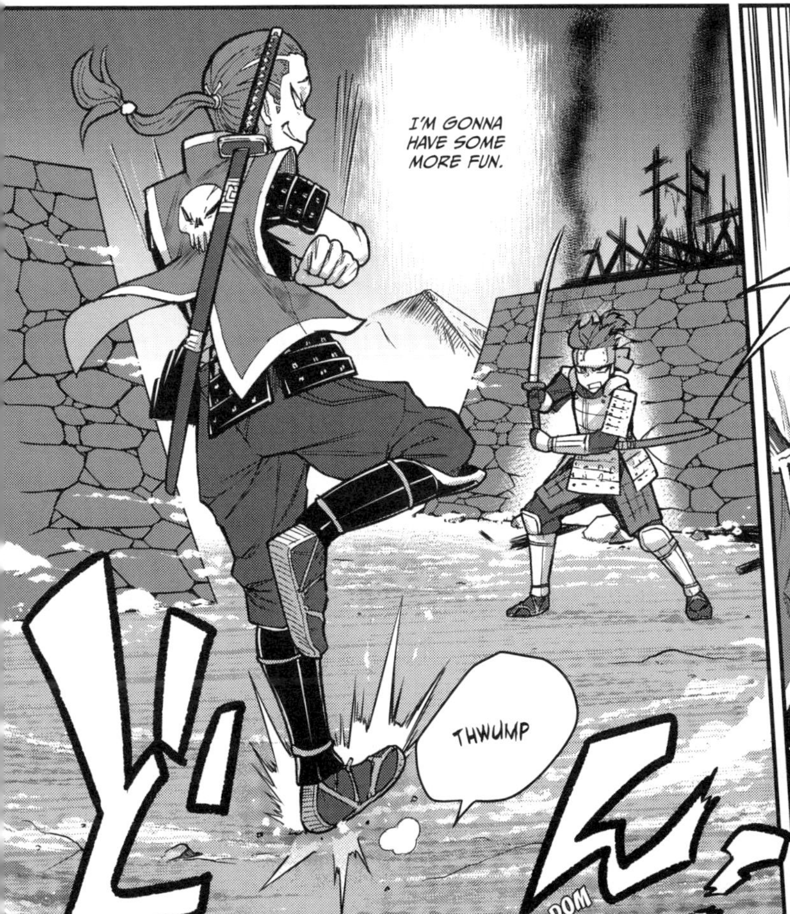
I'M GONNA HAVE SOME MORE FUN.
THWUMP
DOM

Chapter 23: Fatal blow

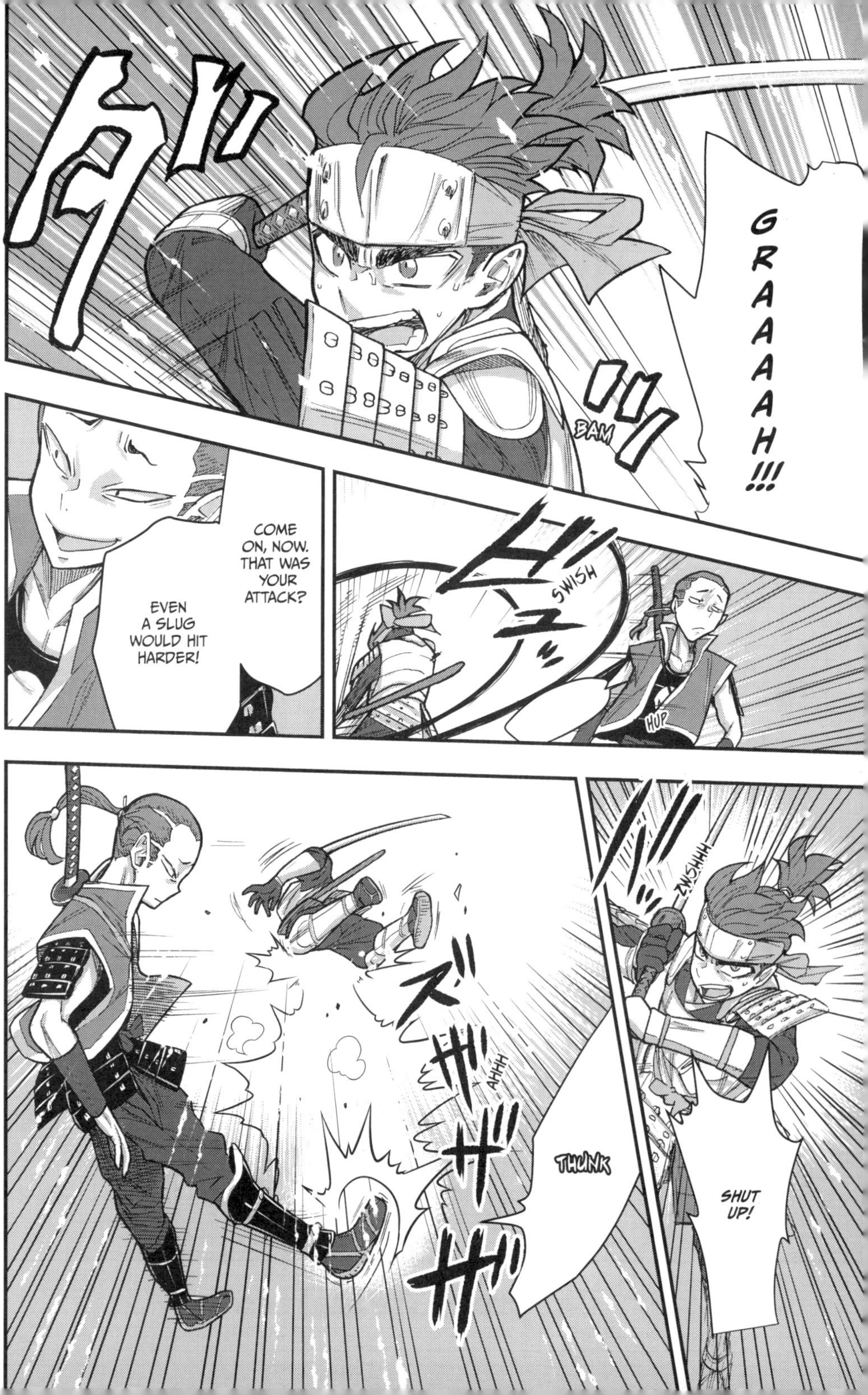
GRAAAAAH!!!
BAM
SWISH
COME ON, NOW. THAT WAS YOUR ATTACK?
EVEN A SLUG WOULD HIT HARDER!
HUP
ZWSHHH
SHUT UP!
THUNK
AHHH

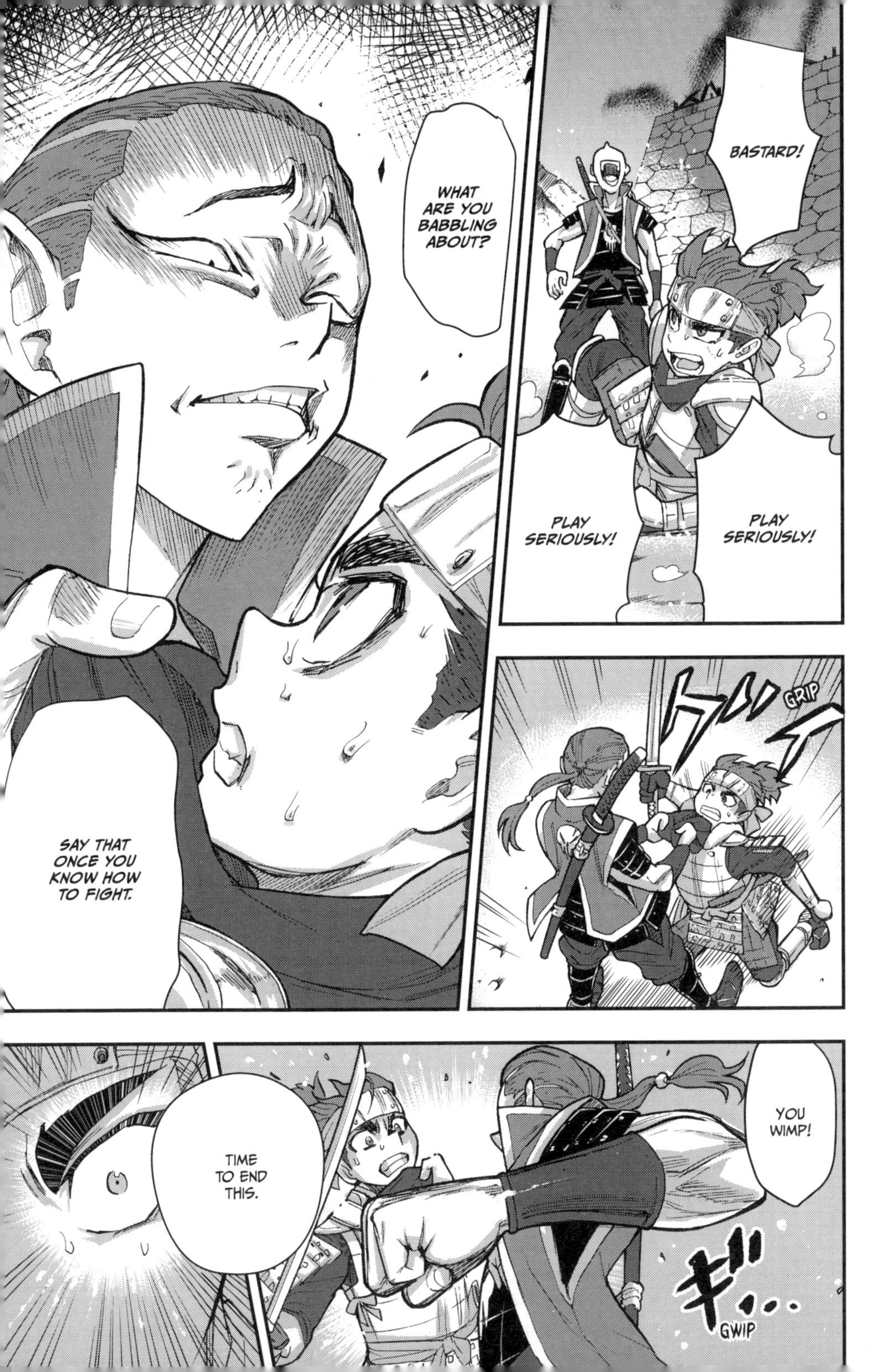
BASTARD!
PLAY SERIOUSLY!
PLAY SERIOUSLY!
GRIP
WHAT ARE YOU BABBLING ABOUT?
SAY THAT ONCE YOU KNOW HOW TO FIGHT.
YOU WIMP!
TIME TO END THIS.
GWIP

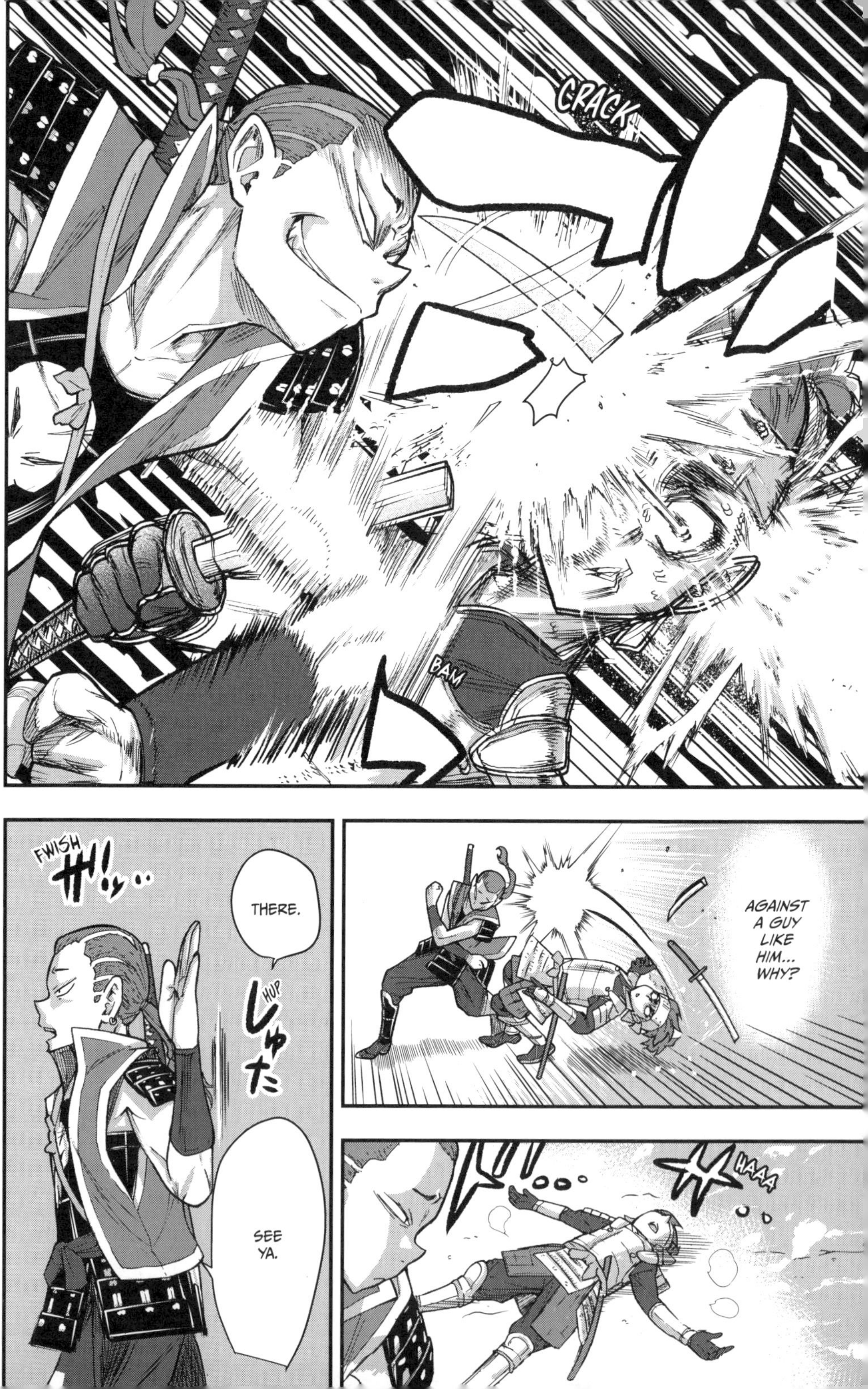
CRACK
BAM
FWISH
THERE.
HUP
SEE YA.
AGAINST A GUY LIKE HIM... WHY?
HAAA

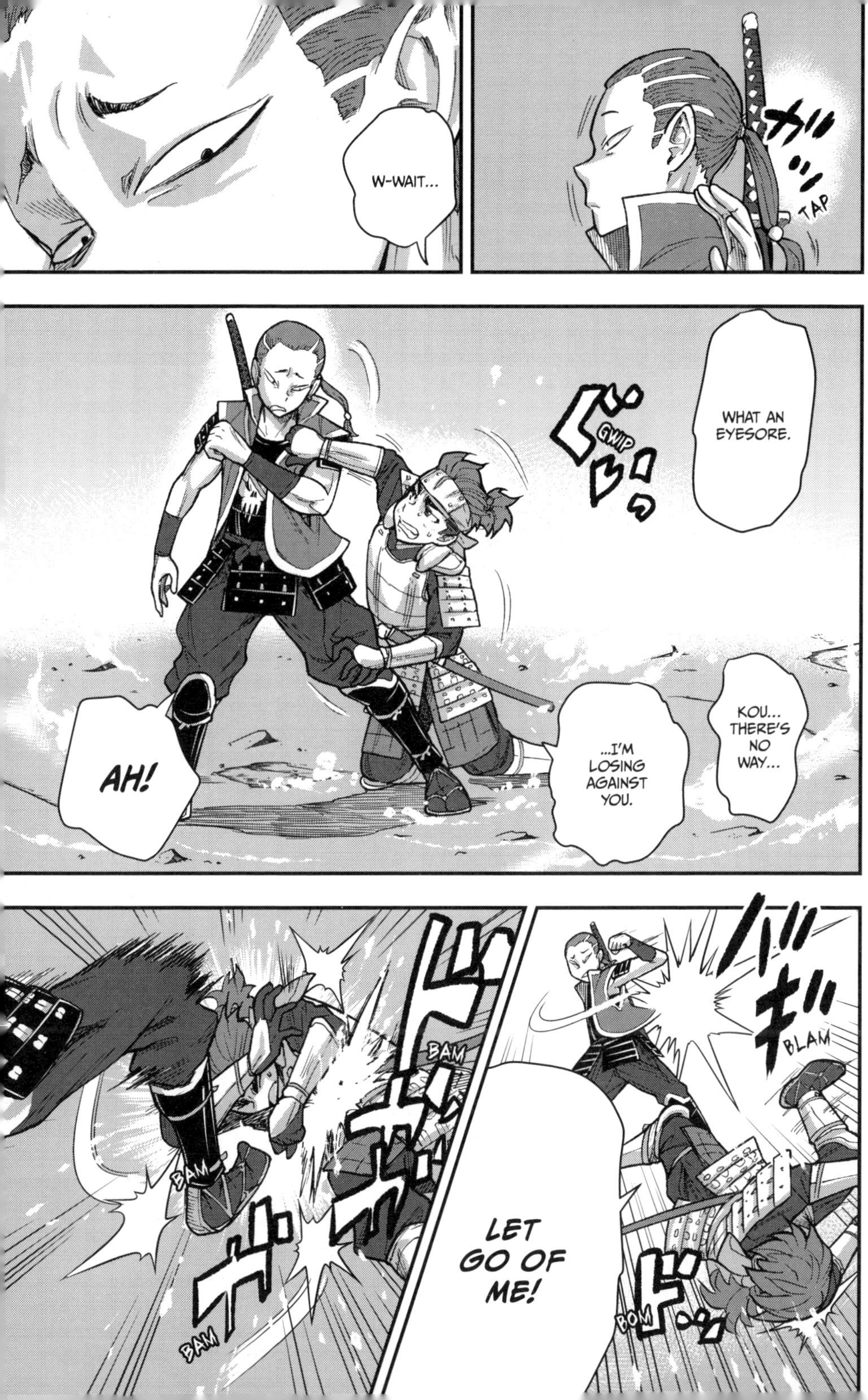
W-WAIT...
TAP
WHAT AN EYESORE.
GWIP
KOU... THERE'S NO WAY...
...I'M LOSING AGAINST YOU.
AH!
BLAM
BOM
LET GO OF ME!
BAM
BAM
BAM

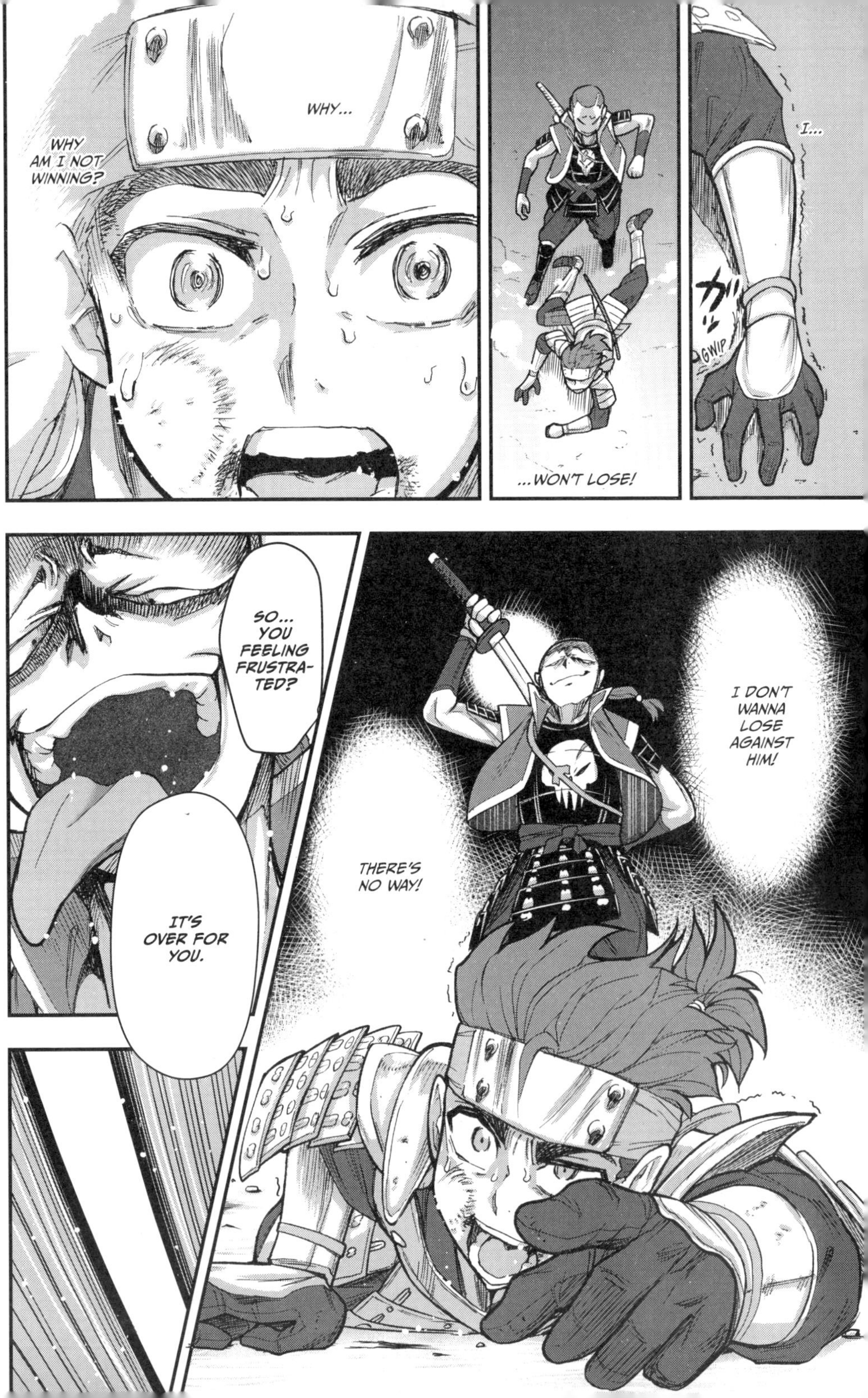
WHY...
WHY AM I NOT WINNING?
I...
...WON'T LOSE!
GWIP
SO... YOU FEELING FRUSTRA-TED?
IT'S OVER FOR YOU.
I DON'T WANNA LOSE AGAINST HIM!
THERE'S NO WAY!

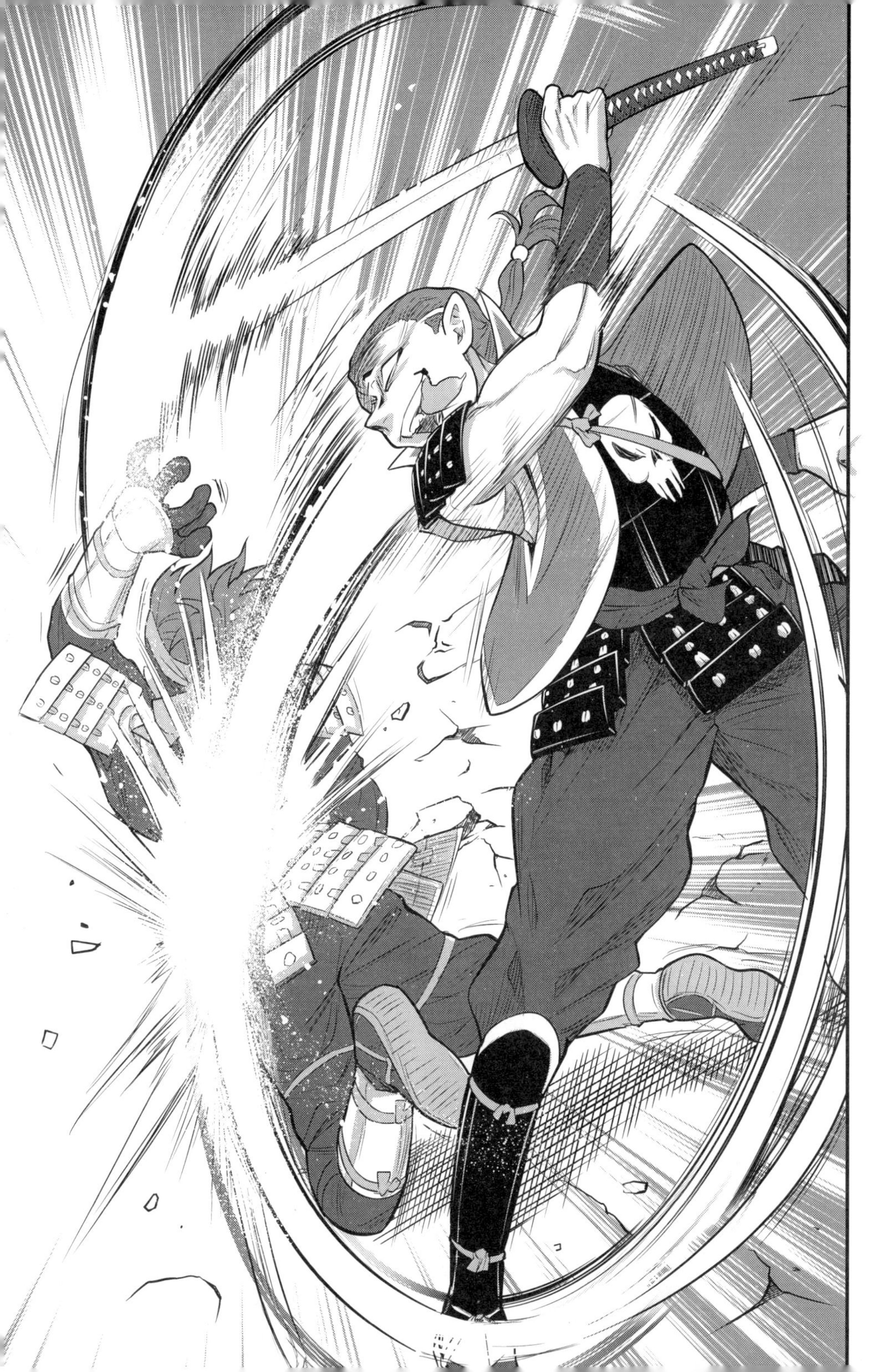

CLICK

...

I WAS SURE I'D WIN, THOUGH...

I CAN'T MAKE...

...ANOTHER MOVE!

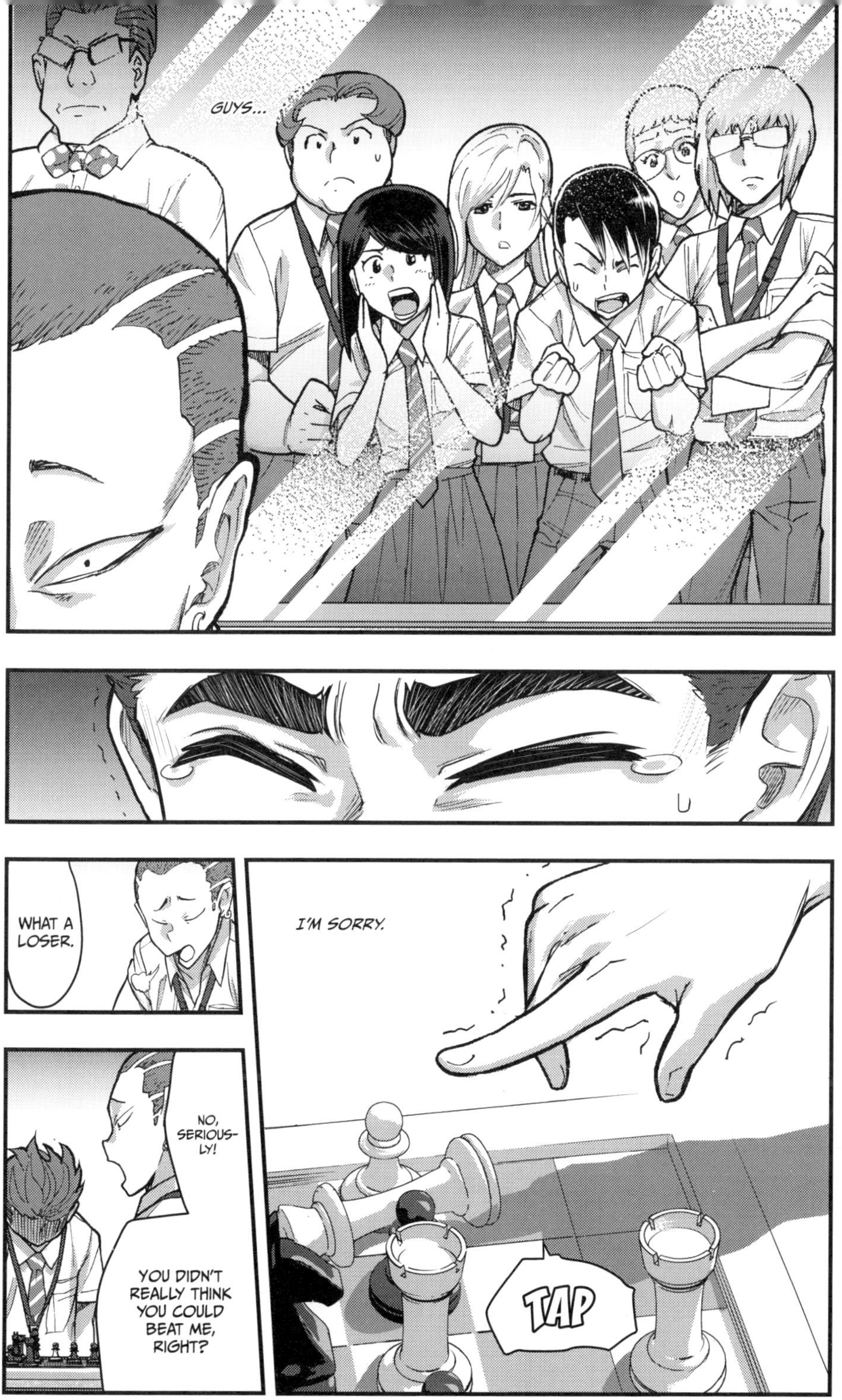
GUYS...
WHAT A LOSER.
I'M SORRY.
NO, SERIOUS-LY!
YOU DIDN'T REALLY THINK YOU COULD BEAT ME, RIGHT?
TAP

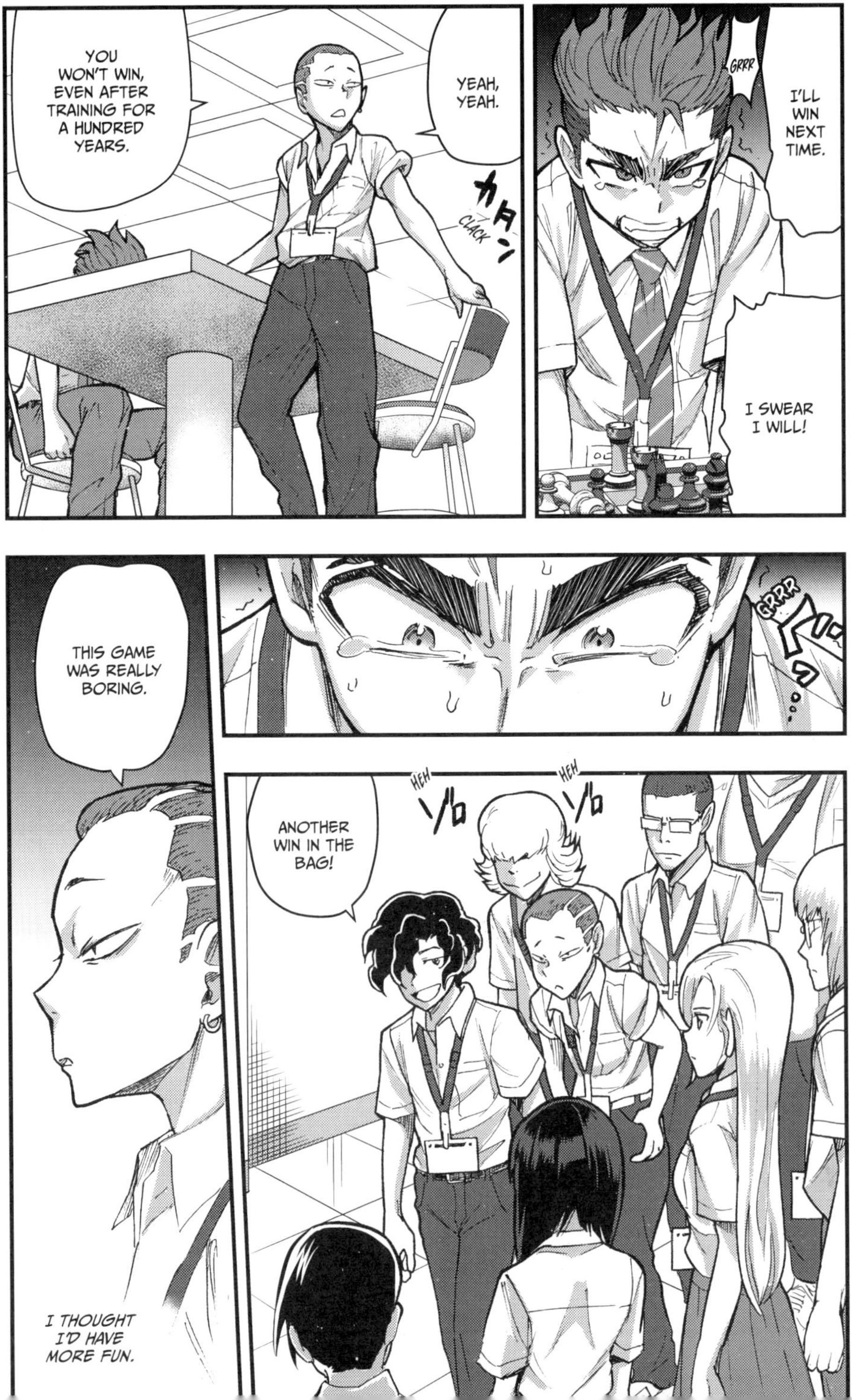
I'LL WIN NEXT TIME.
GRRR
I SWEAR I WILL!
YEAH, YEAH.
YOU WON'T WIN, EVEN AFTER TRAINING FOR A HUNDRED YEARS.
CLACK
GRRR
THIS GAME WAS REALLY BORING.
HEH
HEH
ANOTHER WIN IN THE BAG!
I THOUGHT I'D HAVE MORE FUN.

WE CAN'T WIN THE TOURNAMENT, AND IT'S ALL MY FAULT. SORRY.

I LOST.

HE'S RIGHT. I MESSED UP TOO!

I DIDN'T WIN EITHER, YOU KNOW. IT'S NOT YOUR FAULT.

I COULDN'T FOCUS.

YEAH! THAT'S GREAT!

YOU DID YOUR BEST! ESPECIALLY AGAINST A CHEAT LIKE HIM!

TOM...

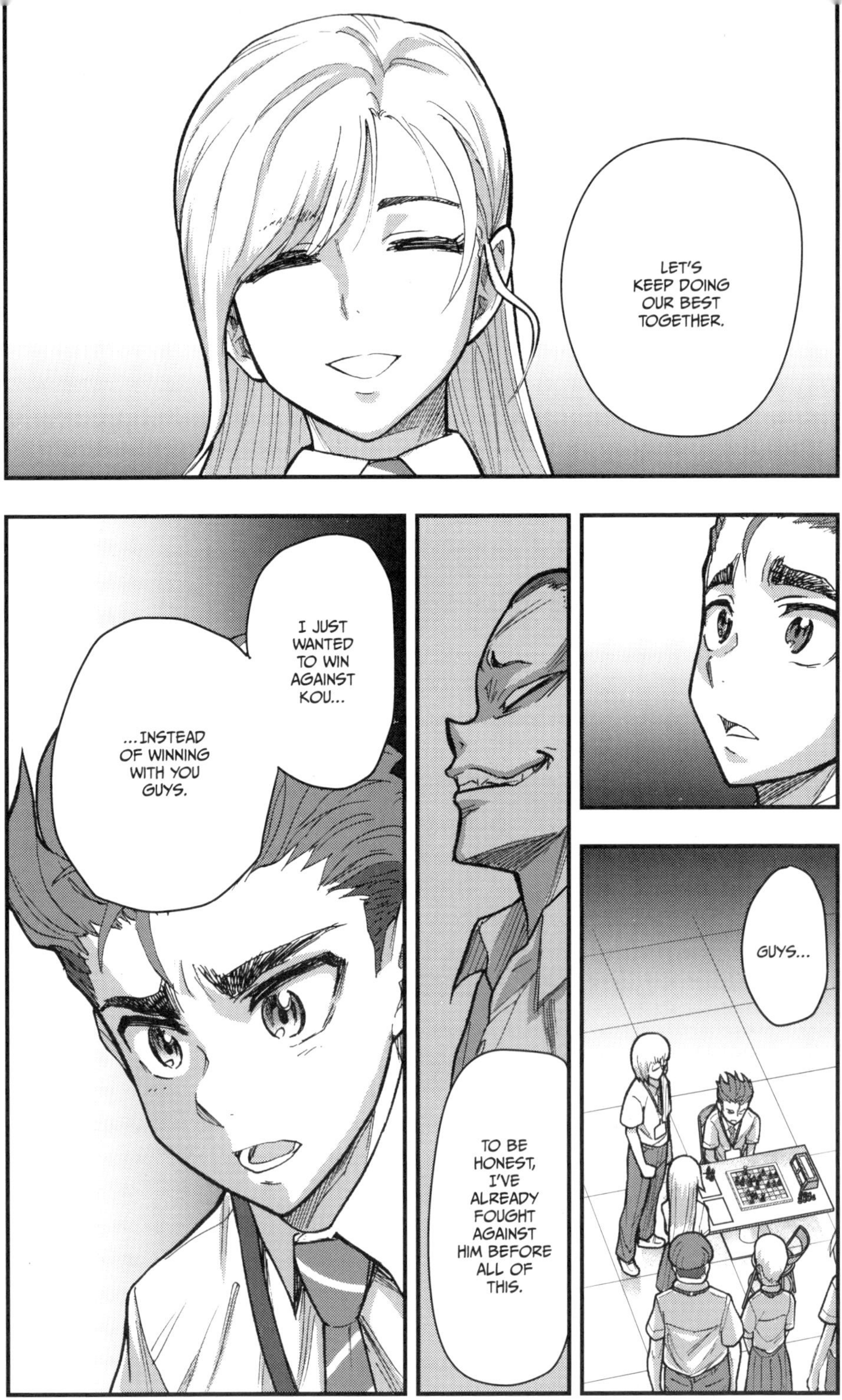
LET'S KEEP DOING OUR BEST TOGETHER.
GUYS...
TO BE HONEST, I'VE ALREADY FOUGHT AGAINST HIM BEFORE ALL OF THIS.
I JUST WANTED TO WIN AGAINST KOU...
...INSTEAD OF WINNING WITH YOU GUYS.

I'M REALLY SORRY!

THAT'S WHY WE LOST. IT WAS ALL MY FAULT. I WAS STUPID...

AH, WELL... FORGET ABOUT IT.

IF WE WIN THE EASTERN JAPAN LAST CHANCE TOURNAMENT, WE'LL BE ABLE TO TAKE PART IN THE NATIONALS.

ISN'T THAT RIGHT, ZHANG?

YES!

YES! A ROUND-ROBIN TOURNAMENT WILL TAKE PLACE WITH ALL THE SCHOOLS WHO MADE IT TO SECOND PLACE IN THE PRELIMINARIES FOR EASTERN JAPAN.

THE WINNING MIDDLE SCHOOL WILL TAKE PART IN THE NATIONAL CHAMPIONSHIP!

AND TO TOP IT OFF, OUR SCHOOL HAS PLANNED A TRAINING CAMP RIGHT BEFORE THAT. WE'RE SURE TO MAKE SOME PROGRESS BY THEN!

WE HAVE ANOTHER CHANCE.

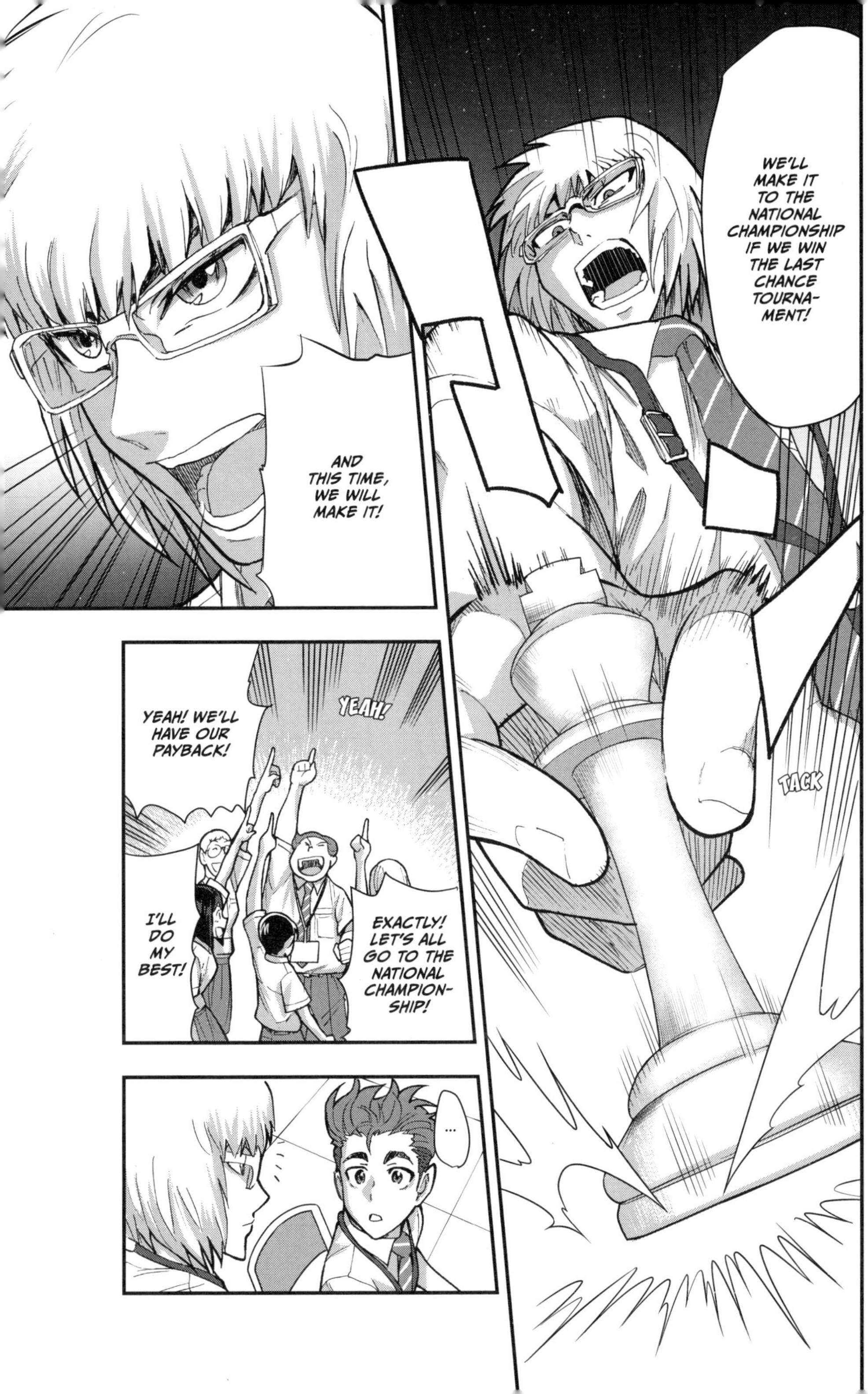
WE'LL MAKE IT TO THE NATIONAL CHAMPIONSHIP IF WE WIN THE LAST CHANCE TOURNAMENT!
AND THIS TIME, WE WILL MAKE IT!
TACK
YEAH!
YEAH! WE'LL HAVE OUR PAYBACK!
EXACTLY! LET'S ALL GO TO THE NATIONAL CHAMPIONSHIP!
I'LL DO MY BEST!
...

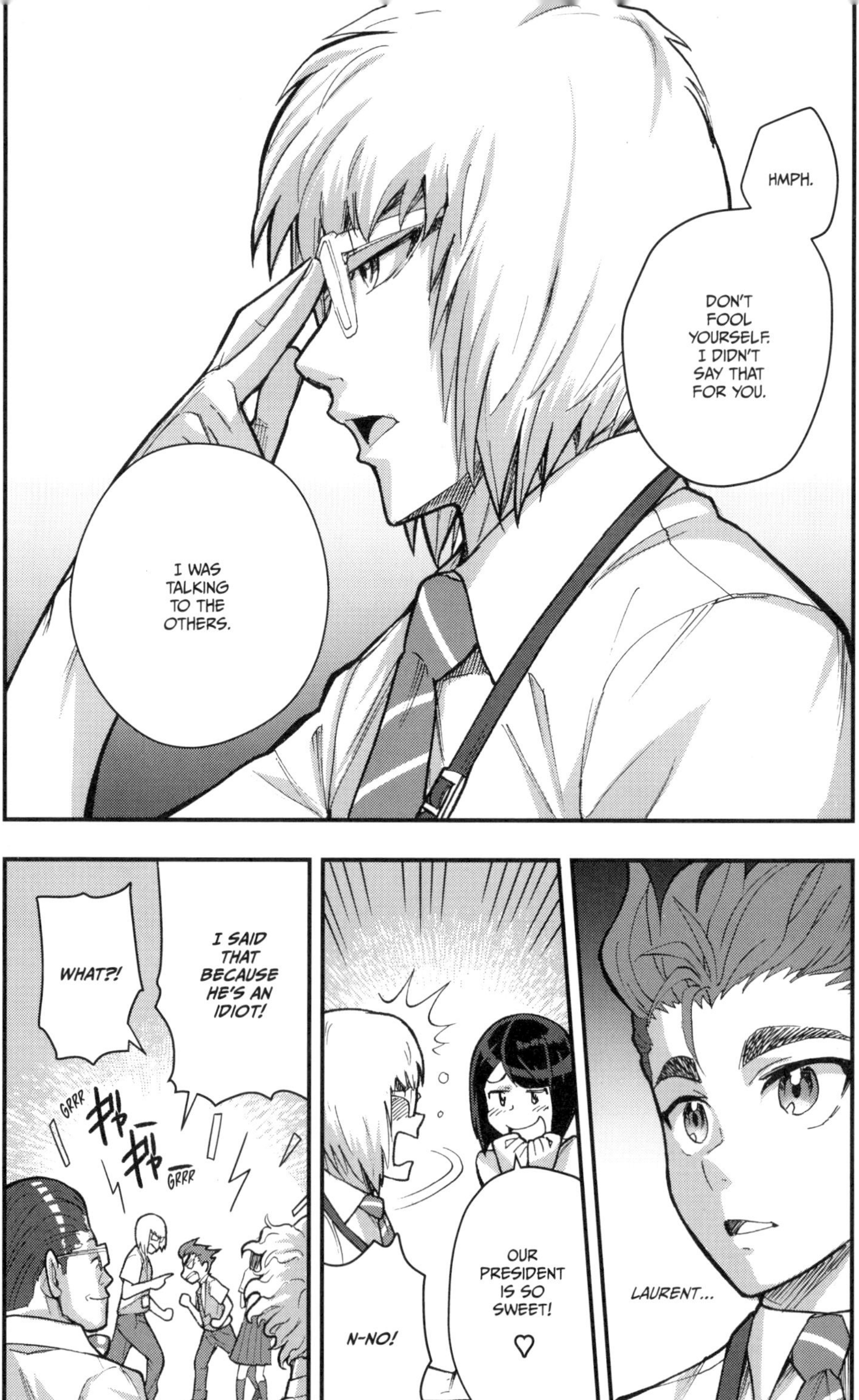
HMPH.
DON'T FOOL YOURSELF. I DIDN'T SAY THAT FOR YOU.
I WAS TALKING TO THE OTHERS.
LAURENT...
OUR PRESIDENT IS SO SWEET! ♡
N-NO!
I SAID THAT BECAUSE HE'S AN IDIOT!
WHAT?!
GRRR
GRRR

SOME DAYS LATER...
BLOCK B
3RD FLOOR – MRI 1 & 2
3RD FLOOR – NEUROSURGERY
GOOD.
EVERYTHING SEEMS IN ORDER.
CLICK
CLICK
LOOKS LIKE ALL'S WELL THAT ENDS WELL.
YES! I CAN'T WAIT TO START THE TRAINING CAMP!
SNIFF ...
HEH HEH
THANK YOU ALL... THAT WAS BEAUTIFUL!

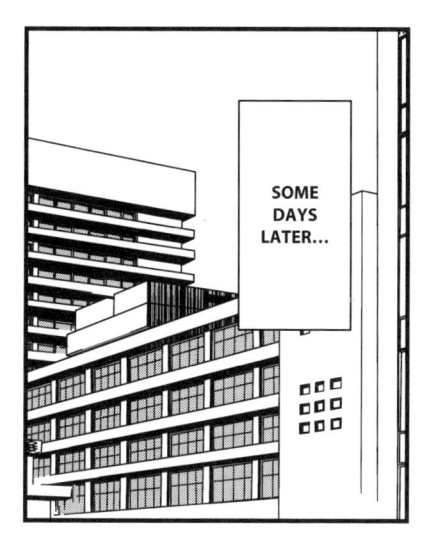

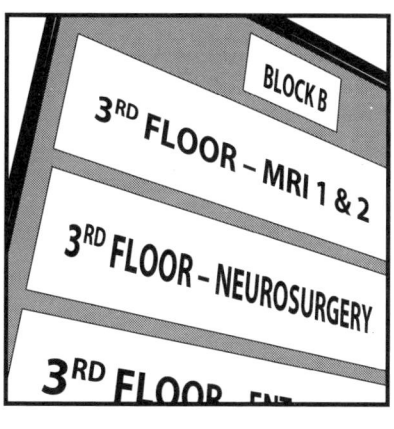

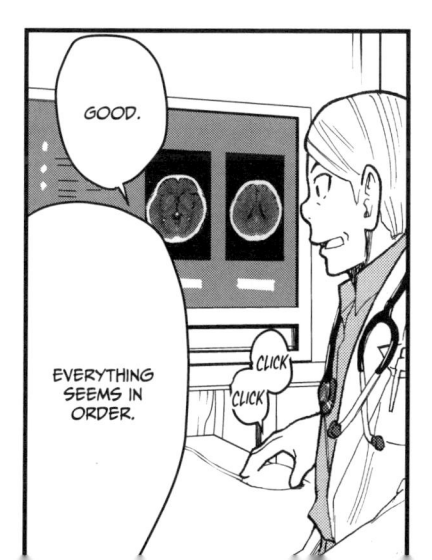

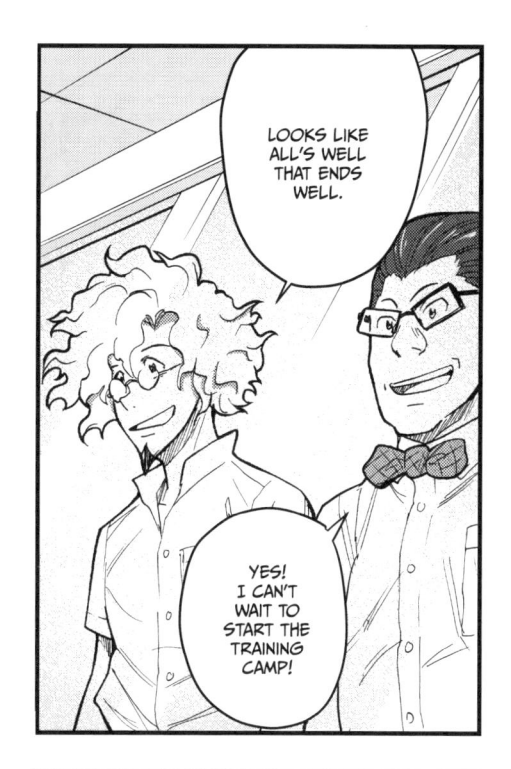

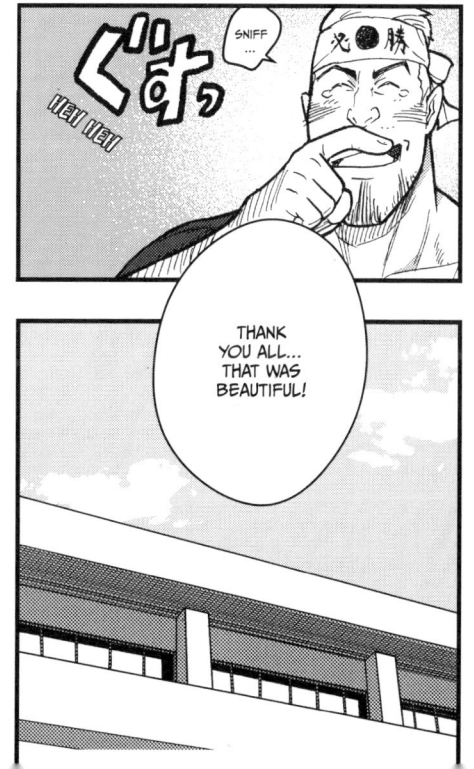

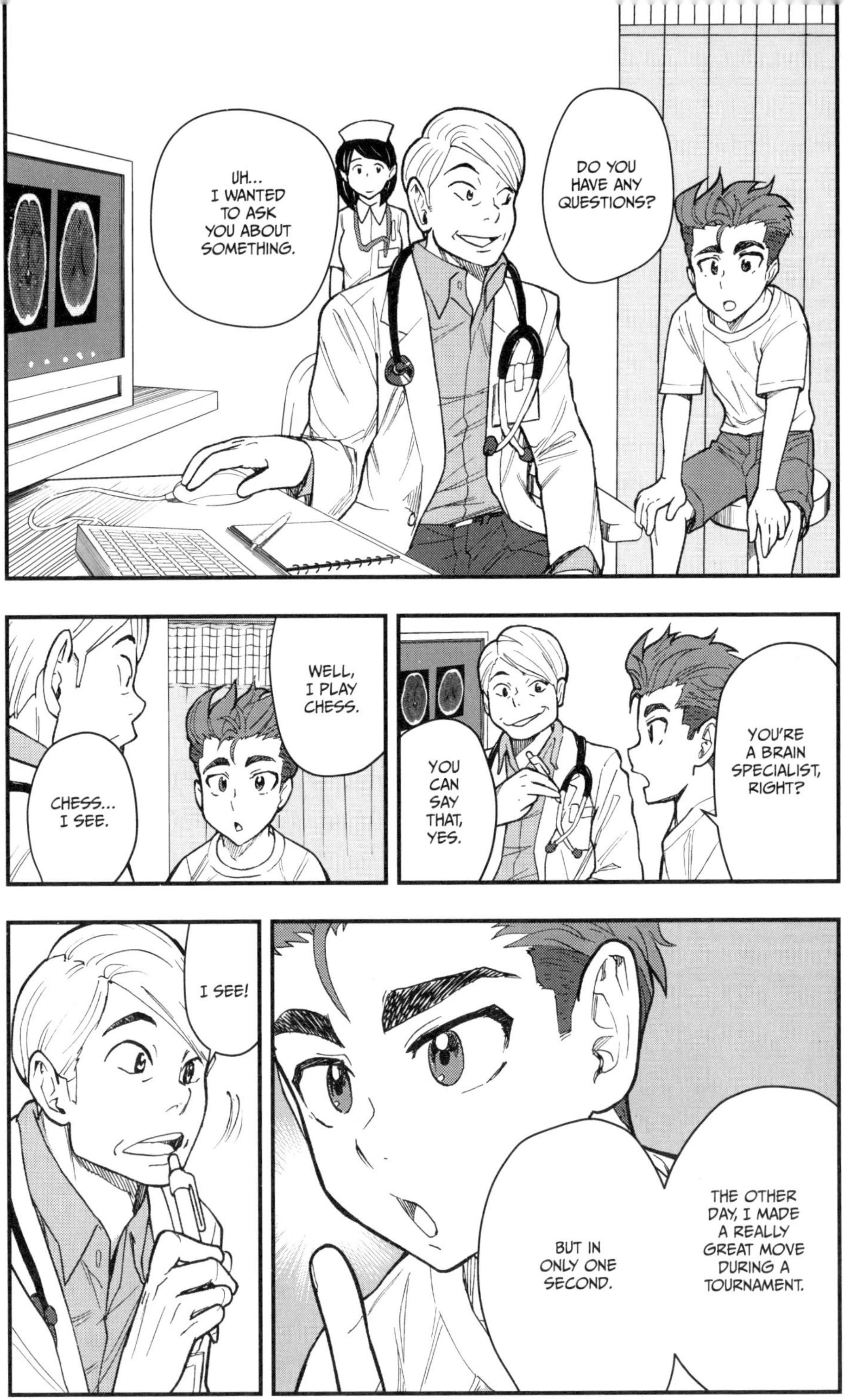
DO YOU HAVE ANY QUESTIONS?
UH... I WANTED TO ASK YOU ABOUT SOMETHING.
YOU'RE A BRAIN SPECIALIST, RIGHT?
YOU CAN SAY THAT, YES.
WELL, I PLAY CHESS.
CHESS... I SEE.
THE OTHER DAY, I MADE A REALLY GREAT MOVE DURING A TOURNAMENT.
BUT IN ONLY ONE SECOND.
I SEE!

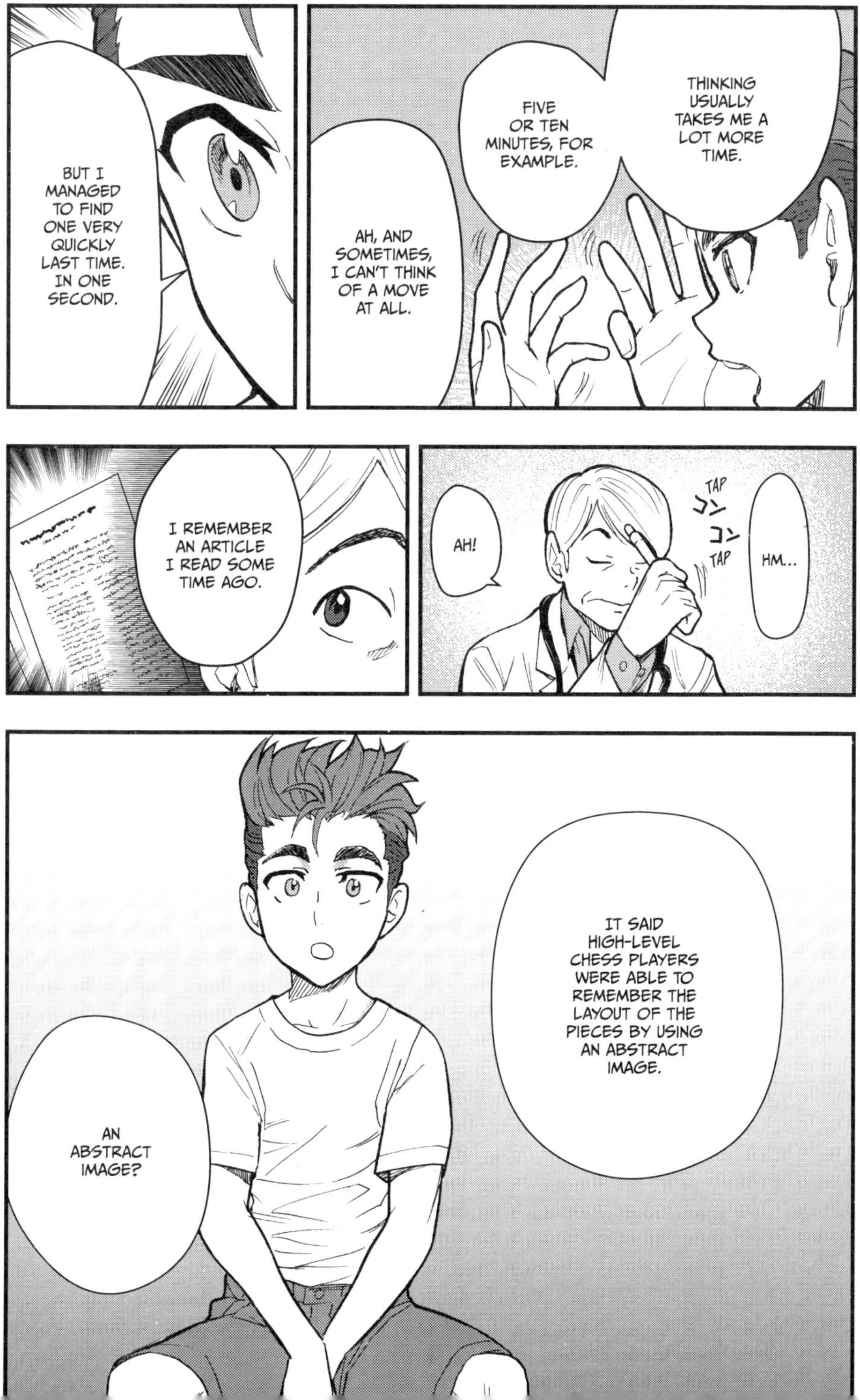
THINKING USUALLY TAKES ME A LOT MORE TIME.
FIVE OR TEN MINUTES, FOR EXAMPLE.
AH, AND SOMETIMES, I CAN'T THINK OF A MOVE AT ALL.
BUT I MANAGED TO FIND ONE VERY QUICKLY LAST TIME. IN ONE SECOND.
HM...
TAP
コン
コン
TAP
AH!
I REMEMBER AN ARTICLE I READ SOME TIME AGO.
IT SAID HIGH-LEVEL CHESS PLAYERS WERE ABLE TO REMEMBER THE LAYOUT OF THE PIECES BY USING AN ABSTRACT IMAGE.
AN ABSTRACT IMAGE?

BEGINNERS NEED TIME TO REMEMBER EACH LAYOUT.

BUT BY USING AN ABSTRACT IMAGE, HIGH-LEVEL CHESS PLAYERS CAN REMEMBER MANY LAYOUTS, WHICH HELPS THEM FIND THE BEST MOVE IN A VERY SHORT TIME.

MAYBE THE SAME THING HAPPENED TO YOU.

HOW CAN I MAKE IT HAPPEN AGAIN?

HM... I THINK YOU NEED TO PRACTICE A LOT.

I ALREADY DO THAT! WHAT ELSE?!

WELL, I'D SAY...

...FOCUS.

LET ME ASK YOU THIS INSTEAD. WHEN CAN YOU FOCUS?

HEY, CALM DOWN.

WHAT CAN I DO TO FOCUS WHENEVER I WANT TO?!

IT'S KINDA COMPLICATED, THOUGH.

IN THAT CASE, GO TO A QUIET PLACE, EAT AND TRY TO STAY CALM BEFORE FOCUSING.

UH... WHEN IT'S QUIET AND I'M NOT HUNGRY, FOR EXAMPLE.

AH, AND ALSO WHEN I'M NOT ANGRY.

WELL, YOU'LL NEED TO SET UP A ROUTINE BEFORE YOU FOCUS.

A ROUTINE?

WOW! THAT'S SO COOL!

BY REPEATING THAT AND MAKING IT INTO A ROUTINE, YOU WOULD MANAGE TO FOCUS ONLY BY HEARING THE SONG OR BY DRINKING WATER.

LIKE: "AFTER I HEAR THIS SONG, I'LL BE CALM".

OR: "I'LL BE MORE RELAXED AFTER DRINKING SOME WATER".

YOU COULD FIND A ROUTINE LIKE THAT FOR WHENEVER YOU NEED TO FOCUS.

THIS IS JUST FROM MY PERSONAL EXPERIENCE.

IT'S THE METHOD I USED TO FOCUS DURING MY STUDIES.

THAT WAS YOUR LAST PATIENT.

AH!

DOCTOR...
DOCTOR!

IF I HADN'T EXPERIENCED THAT MYSELF, I WOULD HAVE SURELY USED MY PRETTY FACE TO BECOME A FAMOUS ACTOR. AND I WOULD BE EVERYWHERE RIGHT NOW, DOING PLAYS AND MOVIES...

BLAH BLAH BLAH

THAT'S WHEN I REALIZED HOW HUGE THE HUMAN BRAIN IS, AND THAT'S WHY I CHOSE TO BE A DOCTOR.

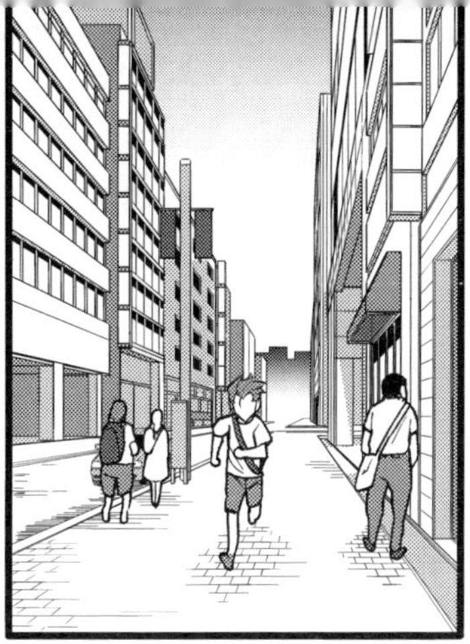

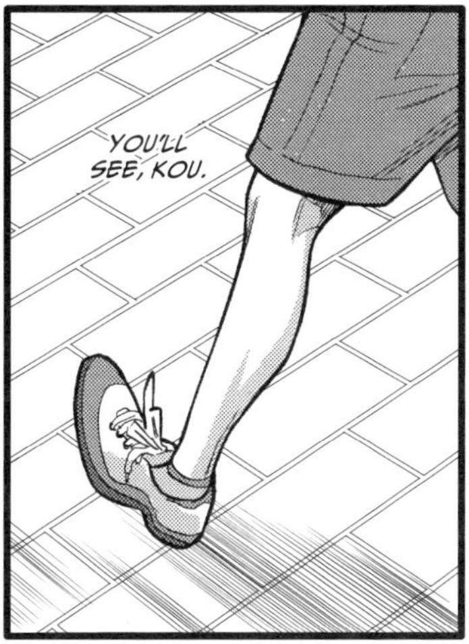
YOU'LL SEE, KOU.

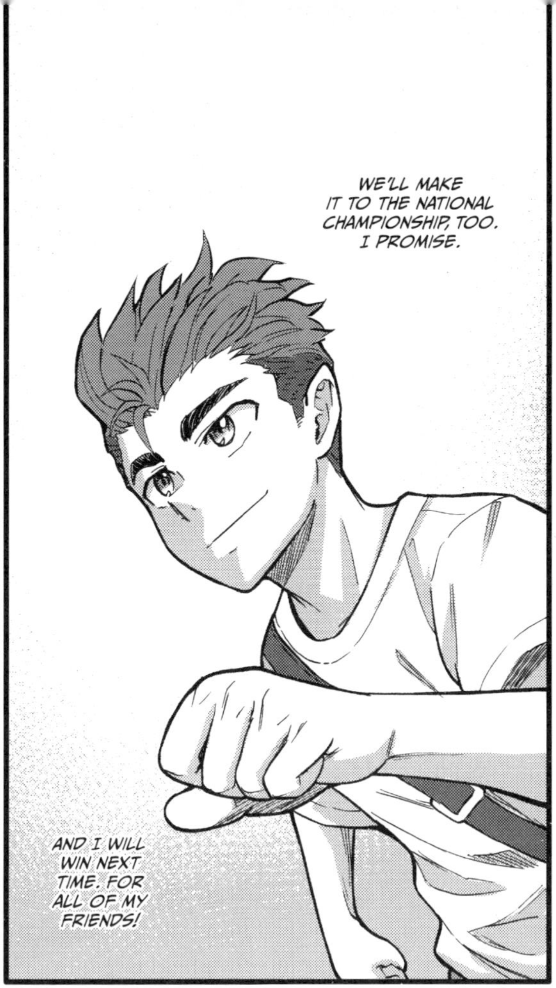
WE'LL MAKE IT TO THE NATIONAL CHAMPIONSHIP, TOO. I PROMISE.
AND I WILL WIN NEXT TIME. FOR ALL OF MY FRIENDS!

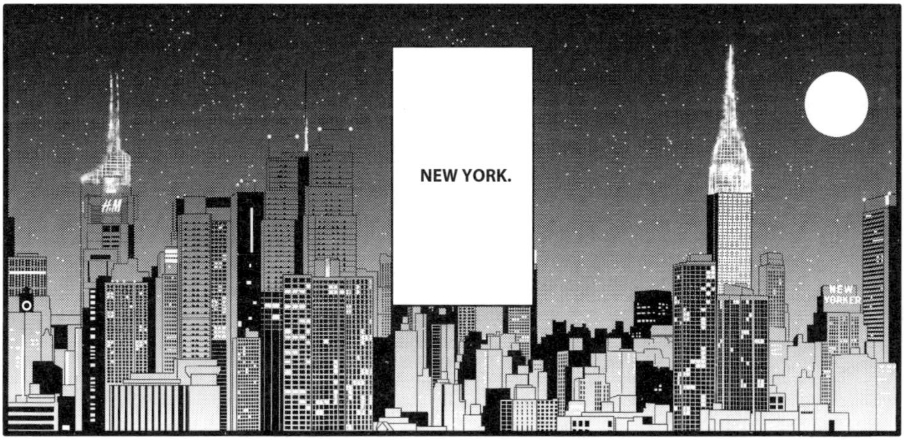
NEW YORK.
NEW YORKER

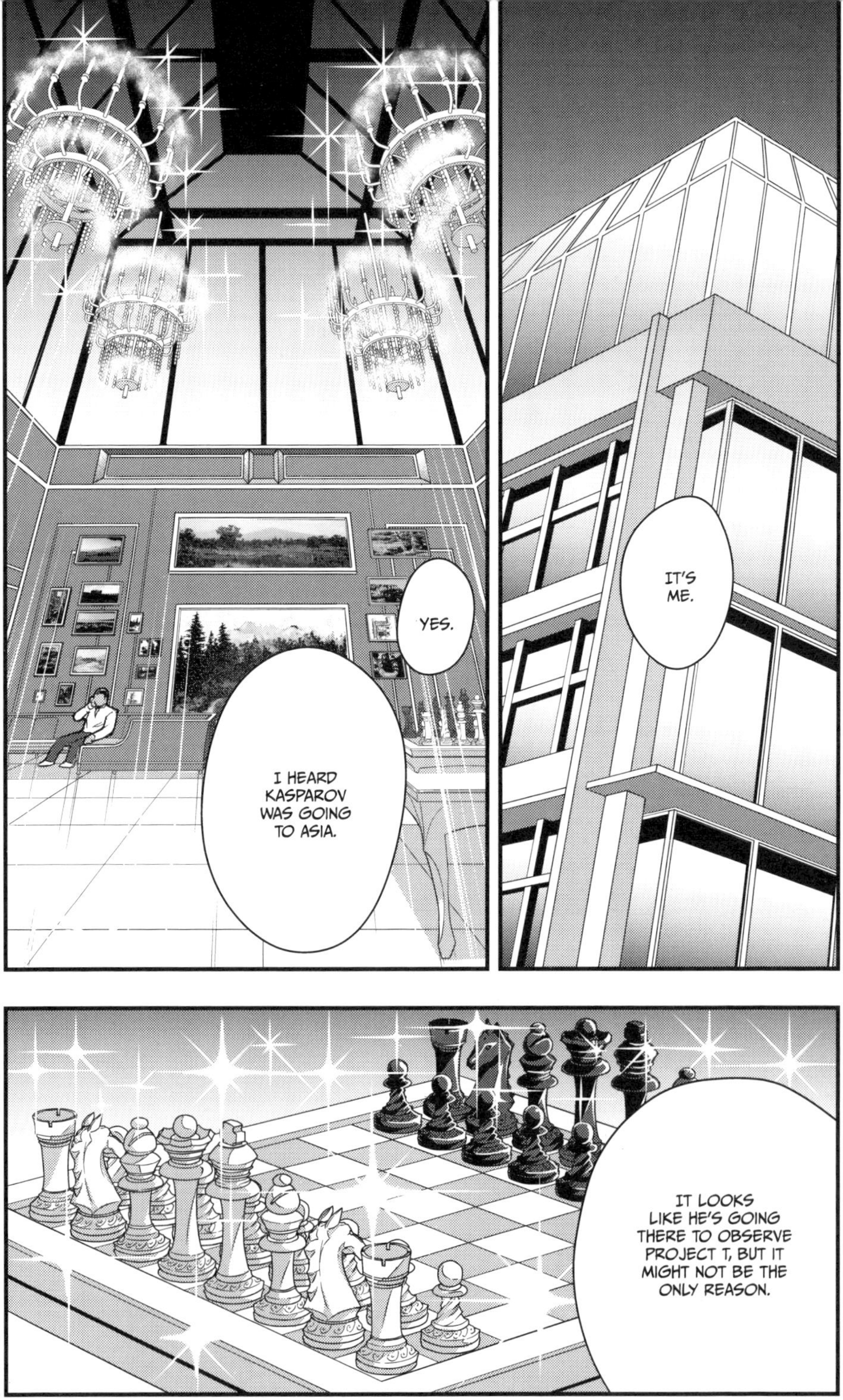
IT'S ME.
YES.
I HEARD KASPAROV WAS GOING TO ASIA.
IT LOOKS LIKE HE'S GOING THERE TO OBSERVE PROJECT T, BUT IT MIGHT NOT BE THE ONLY REASON.

CLINK

TAP

Zzz

YES.

KEEP LOOKING FOR INFORMATION.

ASIA, HUH?

BLITZ

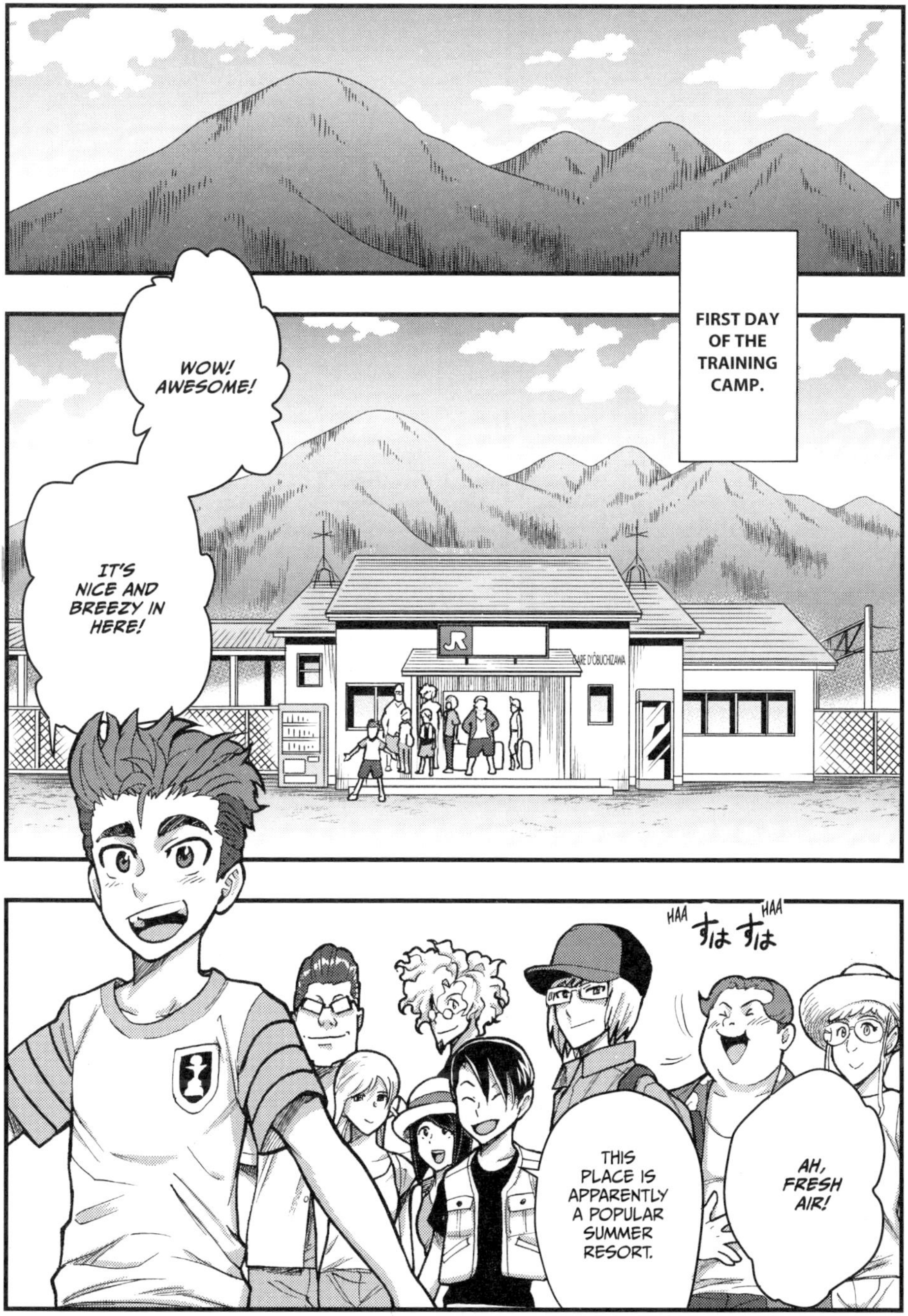
FIRST DAY OF THE TRAINING CAMP.
WOW! AWESOME!
IT'S NICE AND BREEZY IN HERE!
HAA すは すは HAA
AH, FRESH AIR!
THIS PLACE IS APPARENTLY A POPULAR SUMMER RESORT.

Chapter 24: Onwards to the training camp!

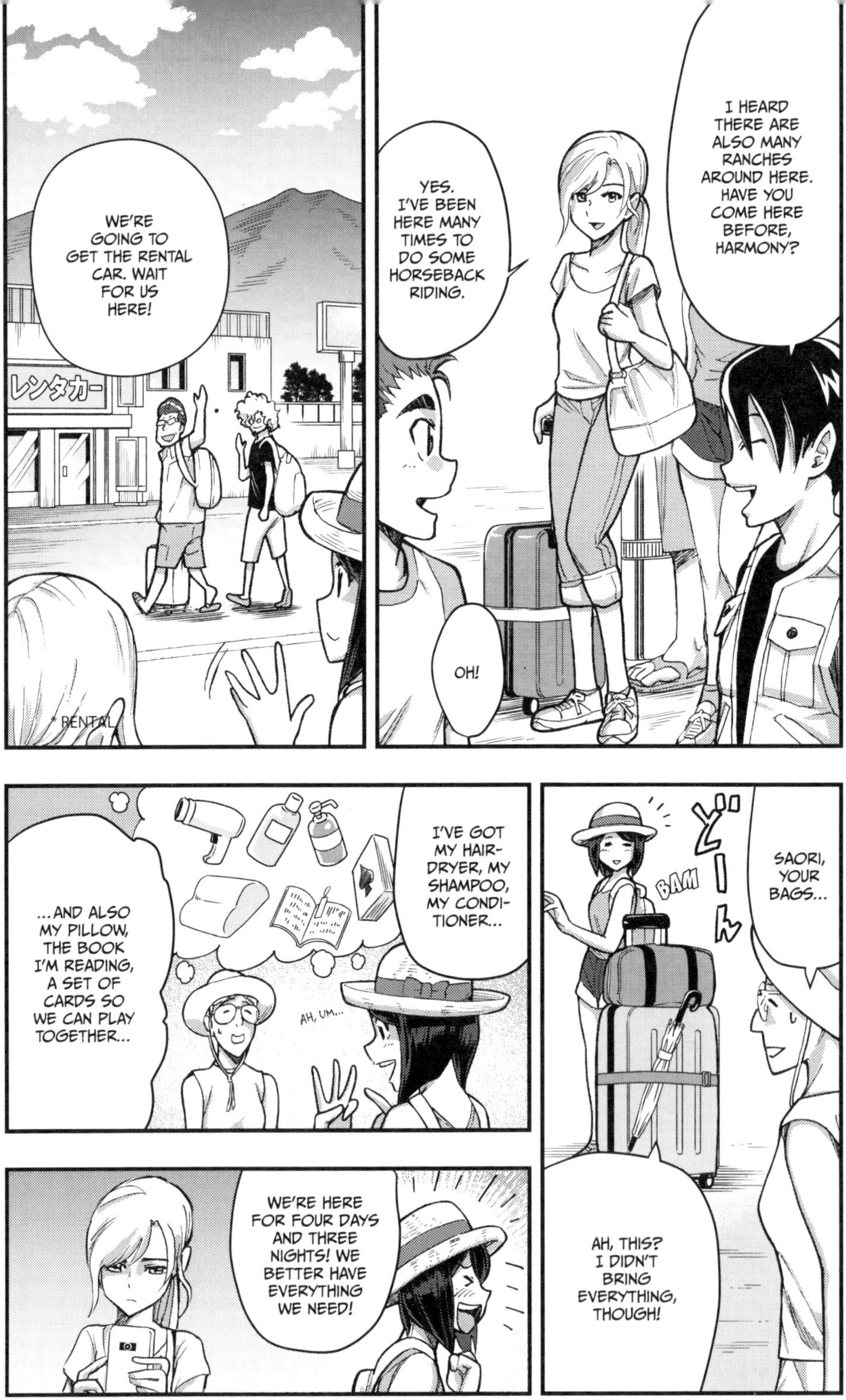
I HEARD THERE ARE ALSO MANY RANCHES AROUND HERE. HAVE YOU COME HERE BEFORE, HARMONY?
YES. I'VE BEEN HERE MANY TIMES TO DO SOME HORSEBACK RIDING.
OH!
WE'RE GOING TO GET THE RENTAL CAR. WAIT FOR US HERE!
レンタカー
* RENTAL
SAORI, YOUR BAGS...
どーん
BAM
AH, THIS? I DIDN'T BRING EVERYTHING, THOUGH!
I'VE GOT MY HAIR-DRYER, MY SHAMPOO, MY CONDI-TIONER...
...AND ALSO MY PILLOW, THE BOOK I'M READING, A SET OF CARDS SO WE CAN PLAY TOGETHER...
AH, UM...
WE'RE HERE FOR FOUR DAYS AND THREE NIGHTS! WE BETTER HAVE EVERYTHING WE NEED!

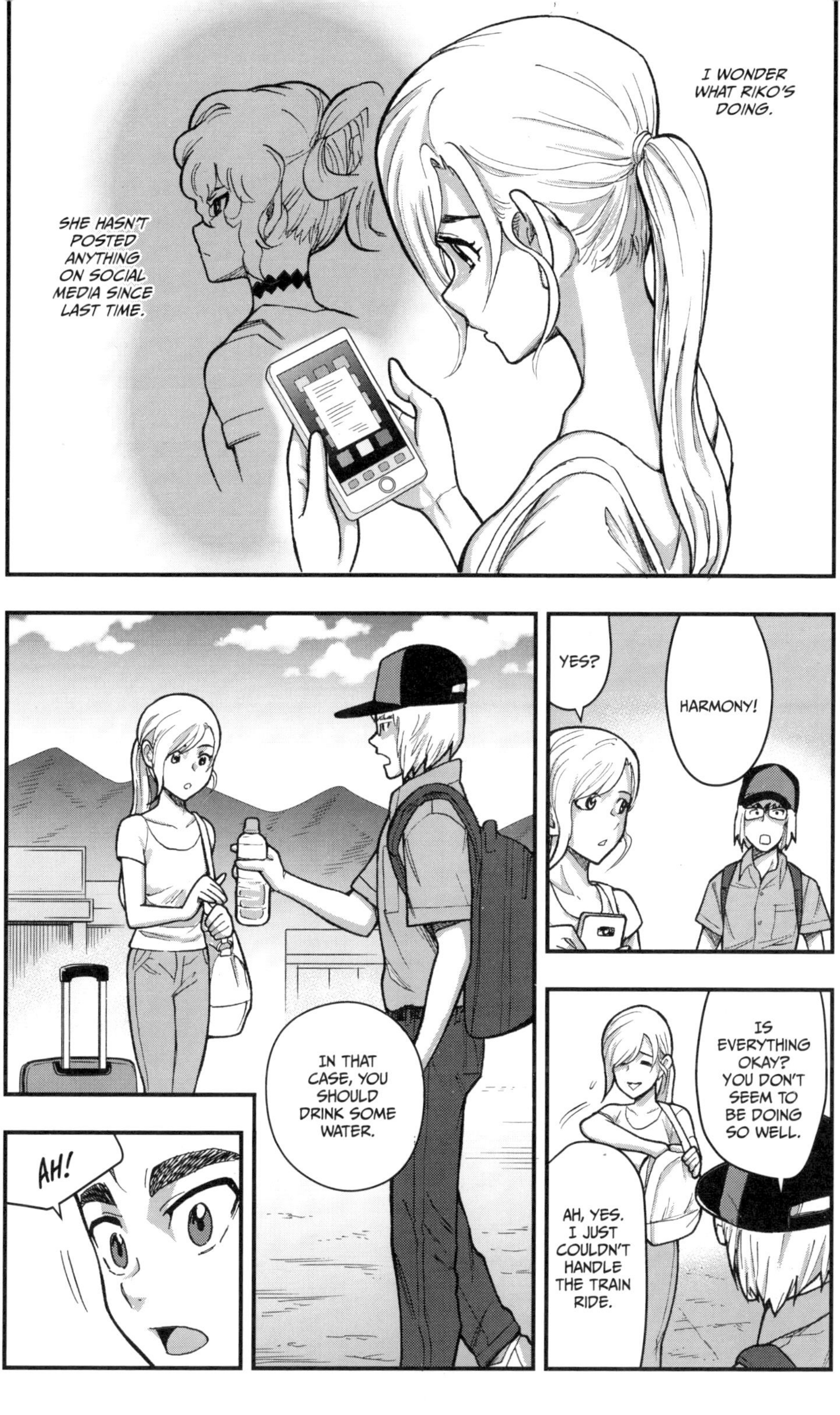
I WONDER WHAT RIKO'S DOING.
SHE HASN'T POSTED ANYTHING ON SOCIAL MEDIA SINCE LAST TIME.
HARMONY!
YES?
IS EVERYTHING OKAY? YOU DON'T SEEM TO BE DOING SO WELL.
AH, YES. I JUST COULDN'T HANDLE THE TRAIN RIDE.
AH!
IN THAT CASE, YOU SHOULD DRINK SOME WATER.

TAP

THANKS!

* SPRING WATER

GRUMBLE

LOOKS LIKE LAURENT'S GETTING AHEAD OF YOU.

HONK HONK

HEY! EVERYBODY INSIDE!

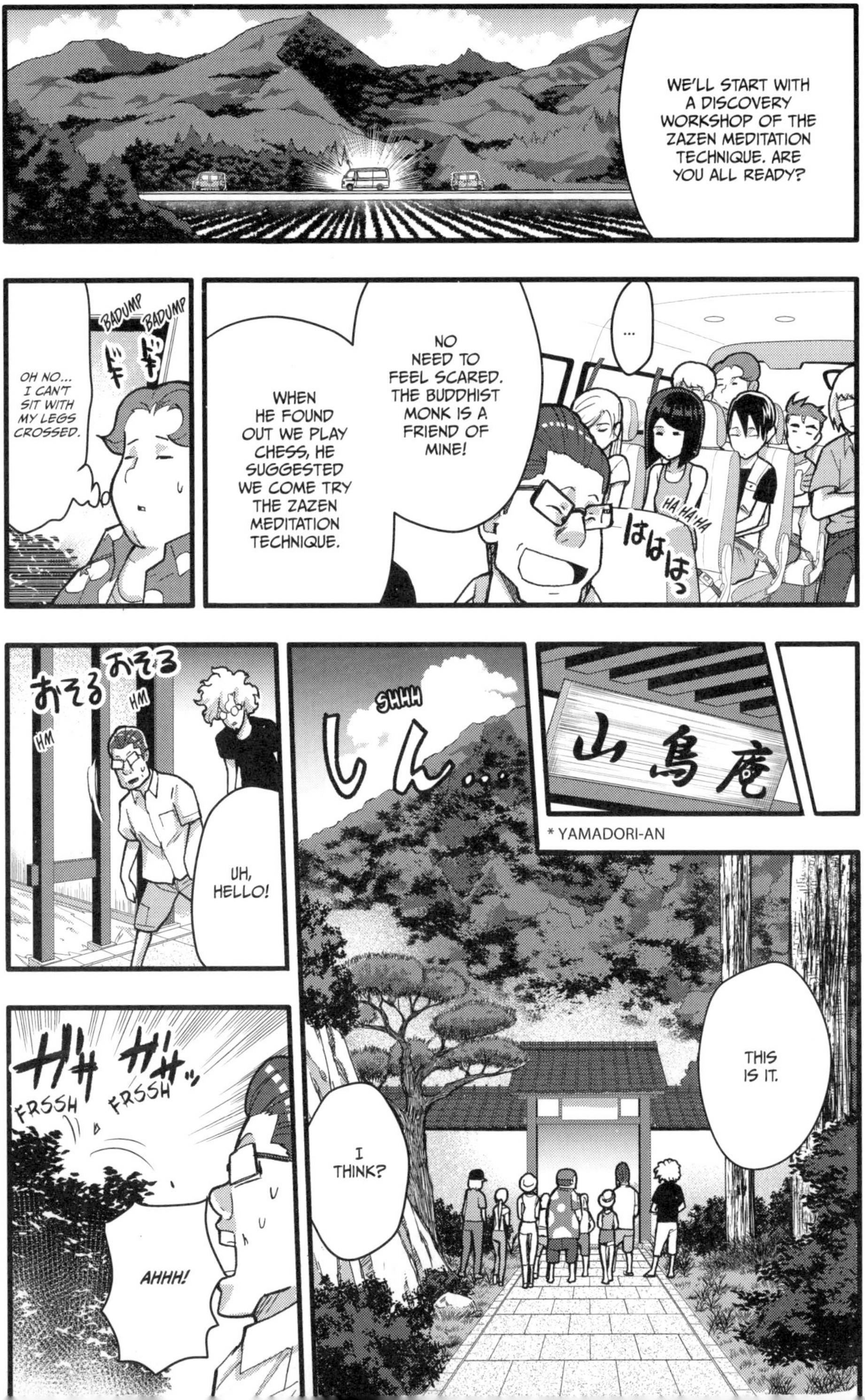
WE'LL START WITH A DISCOVERY WORKSHOP OF THE ZAZEN MEDITATION TECHNIQUE. ARE YOU ALL READY?
...
NO NEED TO FEEL SCARED. THE BUDDHIST MONK IS A FRIEND OF MINE!
はははっ
HA HA HA
WHEN HE FOUND OUT WE PLAY CHESS, HE SUGGESTED WE COME TRY THE ZAZEN MEDITATION TECHNIQUE.
ドキ ドキ
BADUMP BADUMP
OH NO... I CAN'T SIT WITH MY LEGS CROSSED.
山鳥庵
* YAMADORI-AN
しん…
SHHH
THIS IS IT.
I THINK?
おそる おそる
HM HM
UH, HELLO!
ガサ ガサッ
FRSSH FRSSH
AHHH!

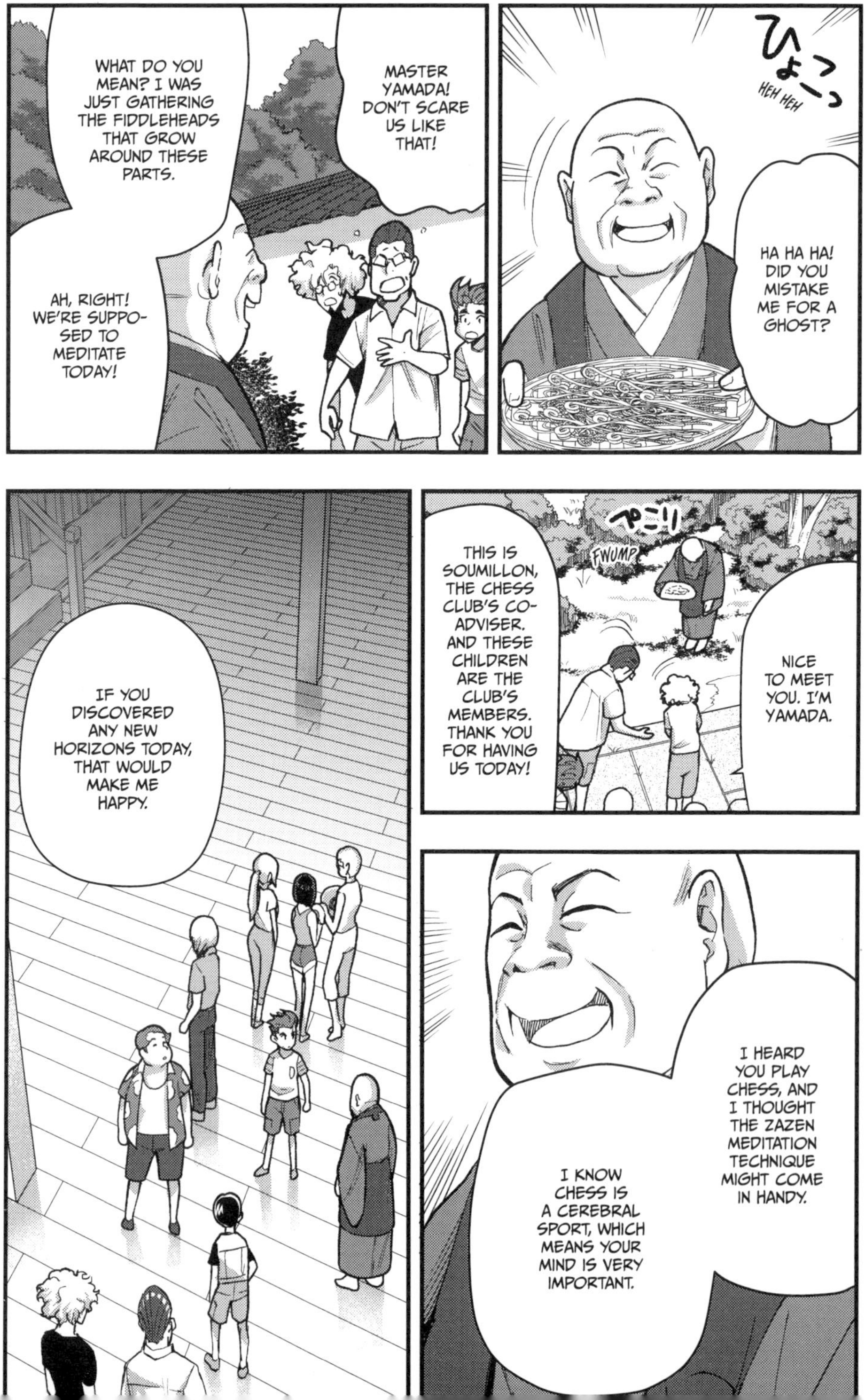
ひょこっ
HEH HEH
HA HA HA! DID YOU MISTAKE ME FOR A GHOST?
MASTER YAMADA! DON'T SCARE US LIKE THAT!
WHAT DO YOU MEAN? I WAS JUST GATHERING THE FIDDLEHEADS THAT GROW AROUND THESE PARTS.
AH, RIGHT! WE'RE SUPPO-SED TO MEDITATE TODAY!
NICE TO MEET YOU. I'M YAMADA.
ぺこ!!
FWUMP
THIS IS SOUMILLON, THE CHESS CLUB'S CO-ADVISER. AND THESE CHILDREN ARE THE CLUB'S MEMBERS. THANK YOU FOR HAVING US TODAY!
I HEARD YOU PLAY CHESS, AND I THOUGHT THE ZAZEN MEDITATION TECHNIQUE MIGHT COME IN HANDY.
I KNOW CHESS IS A CEREBRAL SPORT, WHICH MEANS YOUR MIND IS VERY IMPORTANT.
IF YOU DISCOVERED ANY NEW HORIZONS TODAY, THAT WOULD MAKE ME HAPPY.

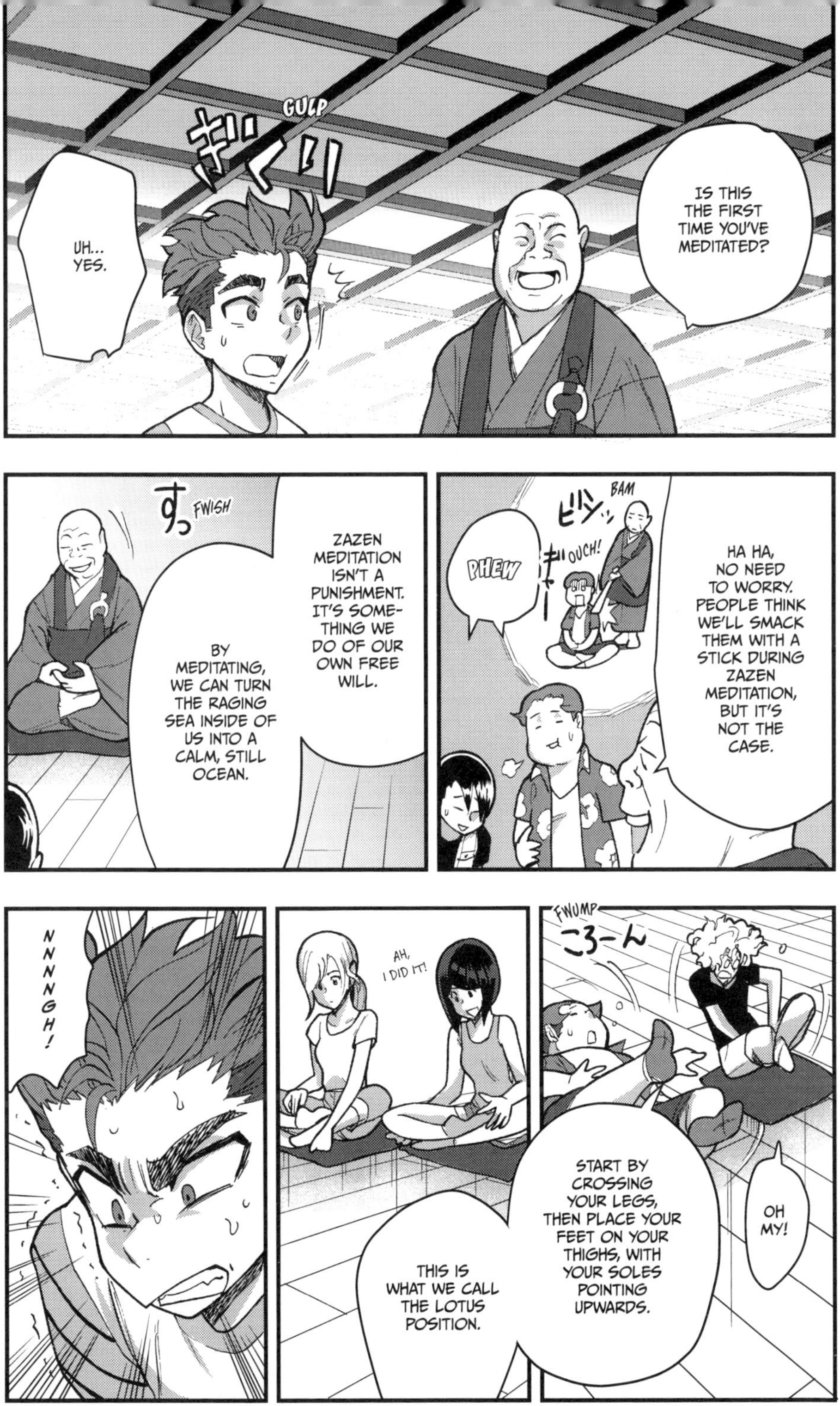
IS THIS THE FIRST TIME YOU'VE MEDITATED?
ぎくっ
GULP
UH... YES.
HA HA, NO NEED TO WORRY. PEOPLE THINK WE'LL SMACK THEM WITH A STICK DURING ZAZEN MEDITATION, BUT IT'S NOT THE CASE.
ビシッ
BAM
ぎゃー
OUCH!
PHEW
すっ
FWISH
ZAZEN MEDITATION ISN'T A PUNISHMENT. IT'S SOME-THING WE DO OF OUR OWN FREE WILL.
BY MEDITATING, WE CAN TURN THE RAGING SEA INSIDE OF US INTO A CALM, STILL OCEAN.
ころーん
FWUMP
OH MY!
START BY CROSSING YOUR LEGS, THEN PLACE YOUR FEET ON YOUR THIGHS, WITH YOUR SOLES POINTING UPWARDS.
THIS IS WHAT WE CALL THE LOTUS POSITION.
AH, I DID IT!
NNNNGH!

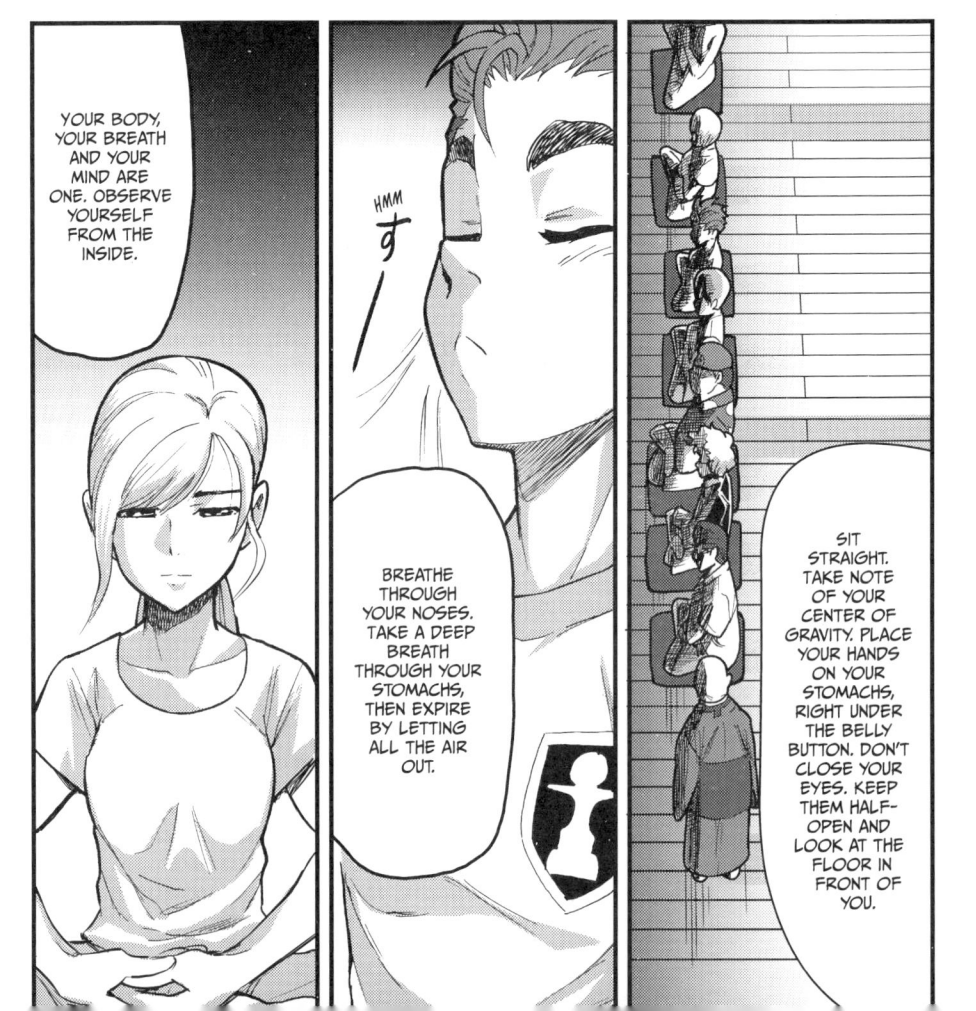

PHEW!

YOU CAN FOLD THE CUSHION BEHIND YOU AND SIT ON IT IF YOU CAN'T DO IT.

NNNGH... THE HALF LOTUS...

YOUR BODY, YOUR BREATH AND YOUR MIND ARE ONE. OBSERVE YOURSELF FROM THE INSIDE.

HMM

BREATHE THROUGH YOUR NOSES. TAKE A DEEP BREATH THROUGH YOUR STOMACHS, THEN EXPIRE BY LETTING ALL THE AIR OUT.

SIT STRAIGHT. TAKE NOTE OF YOUR CENTER OF GRAVITY. PLACE YOUR HANDS ON YOUR STOMACHS, RIGHT UNDER THE BELLY BUTTON. DON'T CLOSE YOUR EYES. KEEP THEM HALF-OPEN AND LOOK AT THE FLOOR IN FRONT OF YOU.

IT'S NICE...

THE TREES SMELL NICE...

FOCUS...

HOW CALM... RE... LAX...

IT LOOKS LIKE YOU MANAGED TO RELAX NICELY. TRY TO FOCUS ON YOURSELF NEXT TIME. THE GOAL ISN'T TO STOP THINKING, BUT TO WATCH THE CLOUDS INSTEAD.

THE CLOUDS?

CONK FWUMP

IT'S ALL RIGHT. ARE YOU OKAY?

HEY! WHAT DO YOU THINK YOU'RE DOING?

HA HA HA

OW!

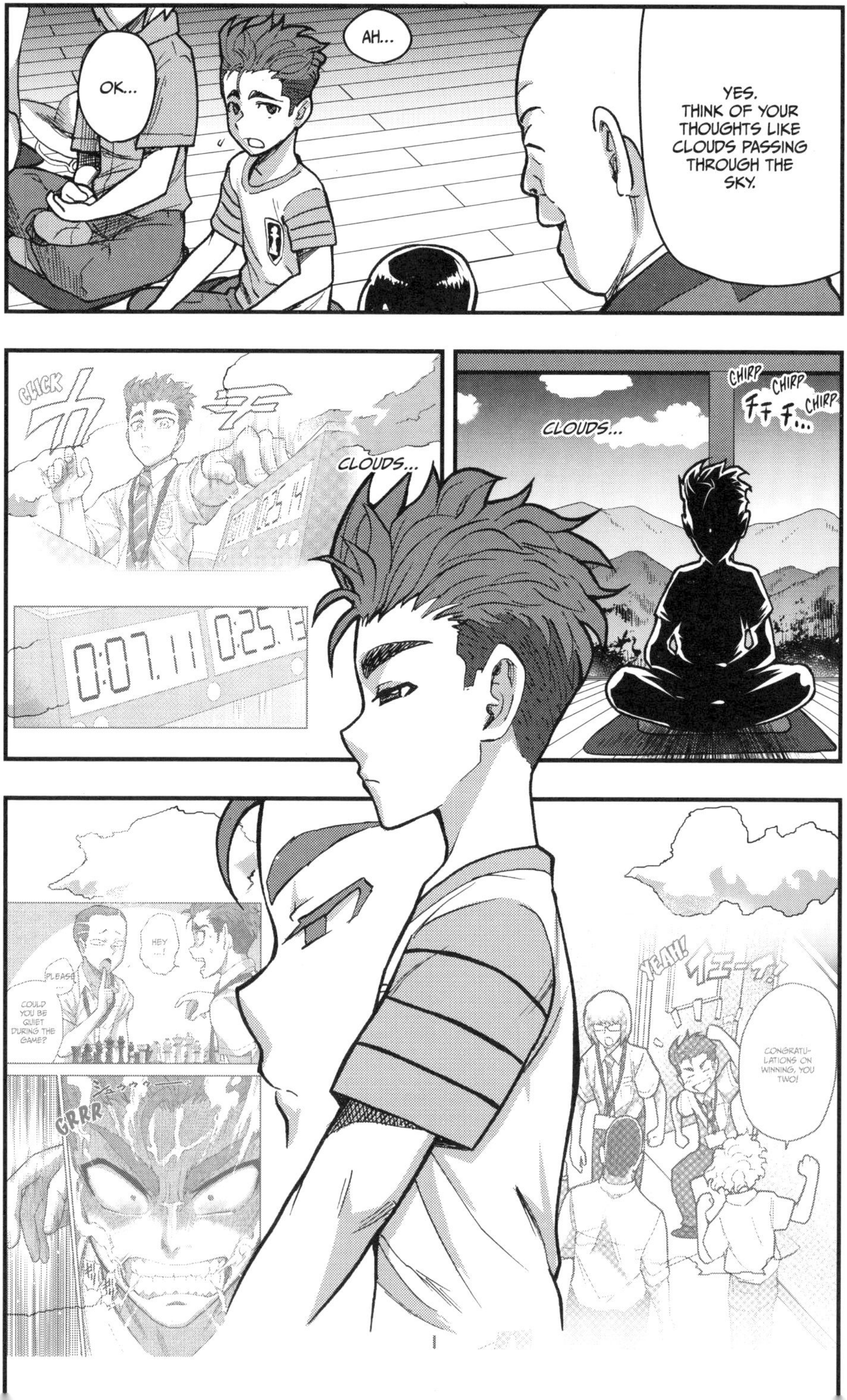
AH...
OK...
YES. THINK OF YOUR THOUGHTS LIKE CLOUDS PASSING THROUGH THE SKY.
CHIRP
CHIRP
CHIRP
CLOUDS...
CLICK
CLOUDS...
0:07.11
0:25.13
HEY ...!
PLEASE ...
COULD YOU BE QUIET DURING THE GAME?
GRRR
YEAH!
CONGRATU-LATIONS ON WINNING, YOU TWO!

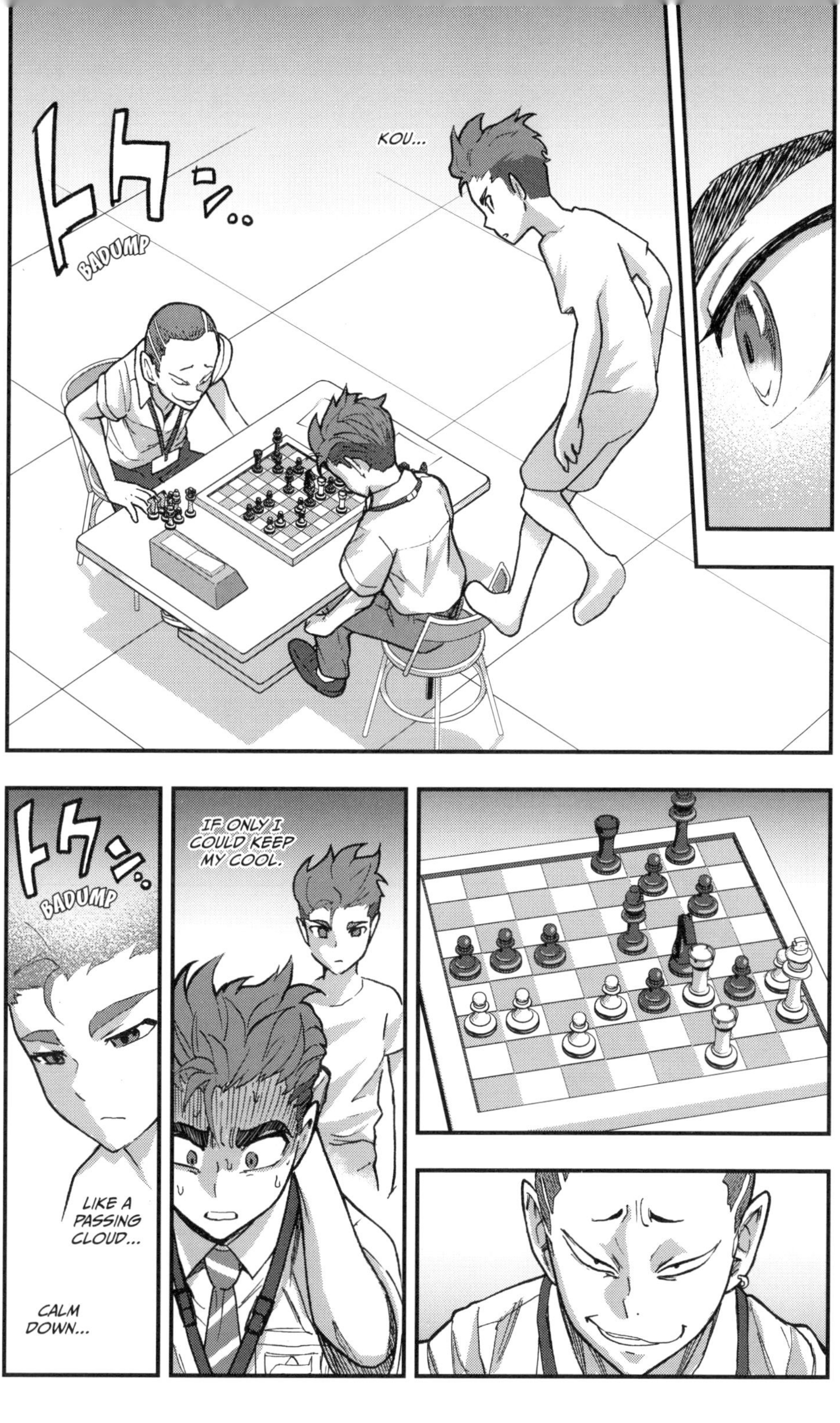

KOU...
トクン...
BADUMP
IF ONLY I COULD KEEP MY COOL.
トクン...
BADUMP
LIKE A PASSING CLOUD...
CALM DOWN...

...YOURSELF. ...OBSERVE... ...YOURSELF. OBSERVE...

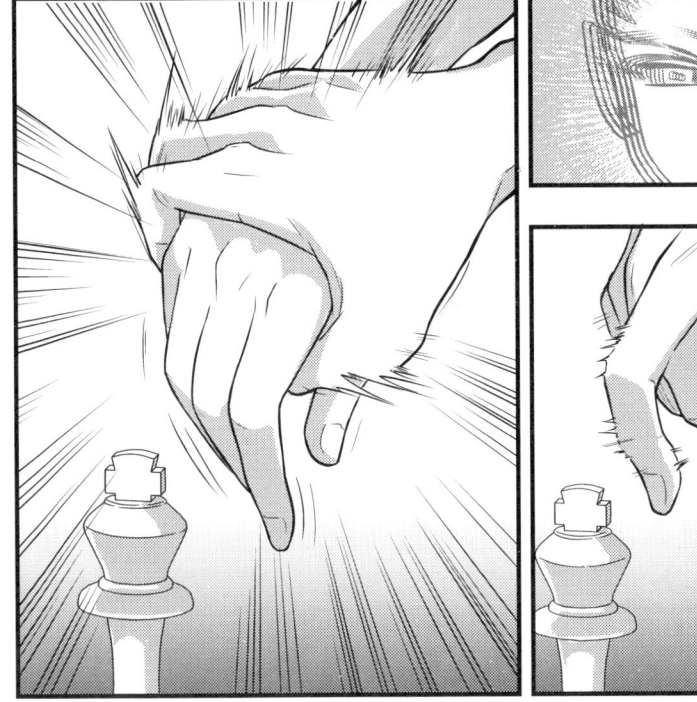

FU!

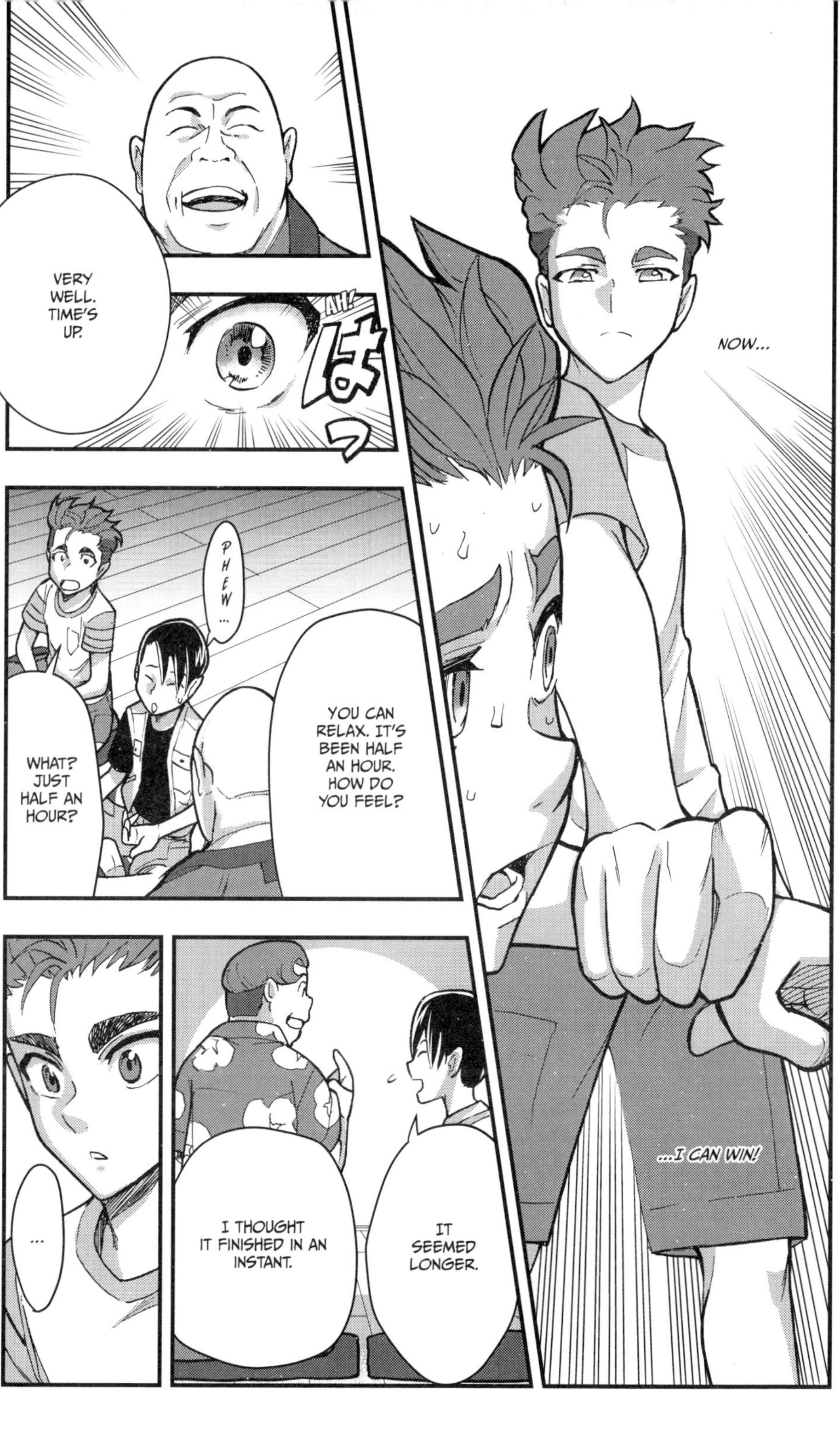
VERY WELL. TIME'S UP.
AH!
ぱっ
PHEW...
YOU CAN RELAX. IT'S BEEN HALF AN HOUR. HOW DO YOU FEEL?
WHAT? JUST HALF AN HOUR?
...
I THOUGHT IT FINISHED IN AN INSTANT.
IT SEEMED LONGER.
NOW...
...I CAN WIN!

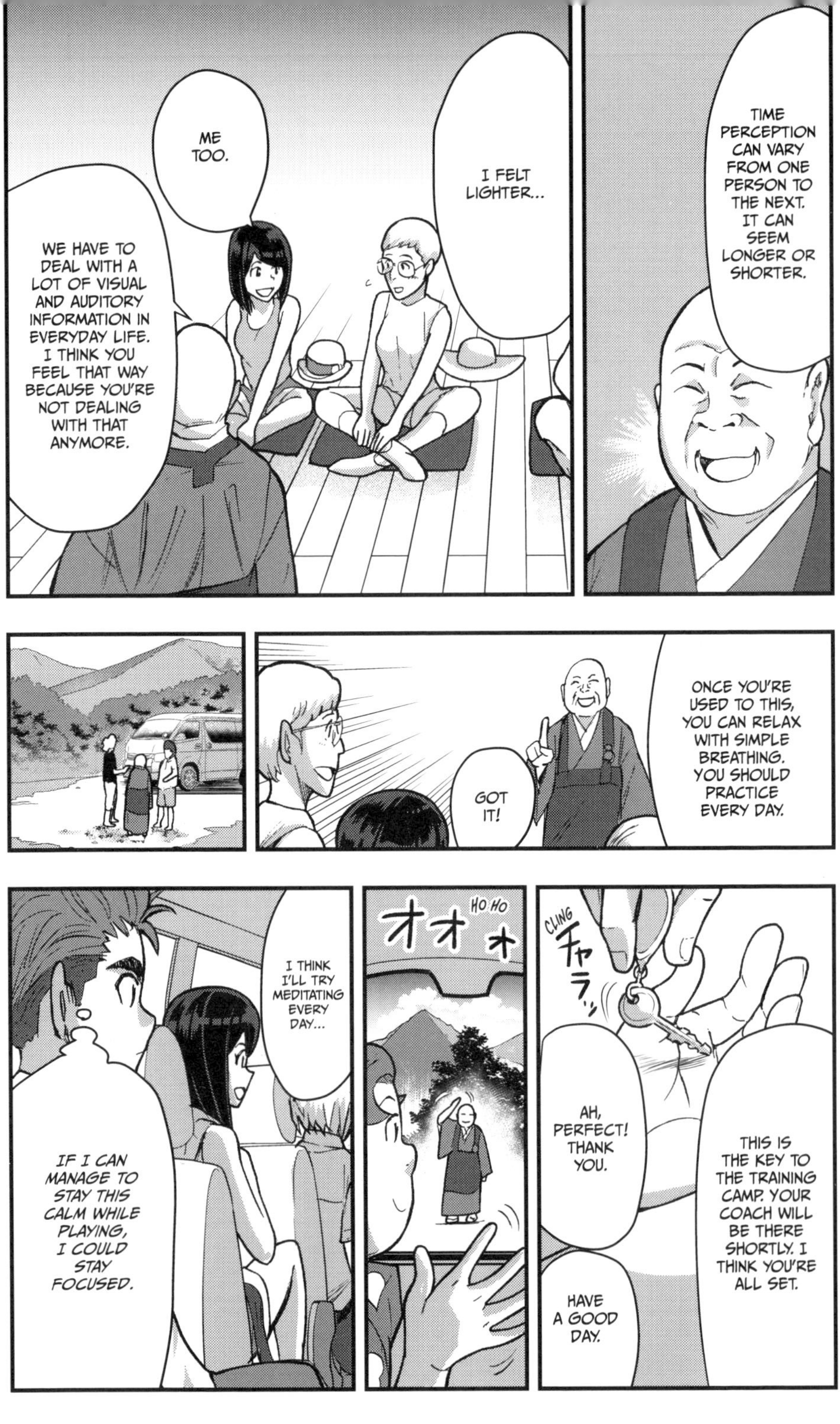
TIME PERCEPTION CAN VARY FROM ONE PERSON TO THE NEXT. IT CAN SEEM LONGER OR SHORTER.
I FELT LIGHTER...
ME TOO.
WE HAVE TO DEAL WITH A LOT OF VISUAL AND AUDITORY INFORMATION IN EVERYDAY LIFE. I THINK YOU FEEL THAT WAY BECAUSE YOU'RE NOT DEALING WITH THAT ANYMORE.
ONCE YOU'RE USED TO THIS, YOU CAN RELAX WITH SIMPLE BREATHING. YOU SHOULD PRACTICE EVERY DAY.
GOT IT!
チャラッ
CLING
THIS IS THE KEY TO THE TRAINING CAMP. YOUR COACH WILL BE THERE SHORTLY. I THINK YOU'RE ALL SET.
AH, PERFECT! THANK YOU.
HAVE A GOOD DAY.
オオォ
HO HO
I THINK I'LL TRY MEDITATING EVERY DAY...
IF I CAN MANAGE TO STAY THIS CALM WHILE PLAYING, I COULD STAY FOCUSED.

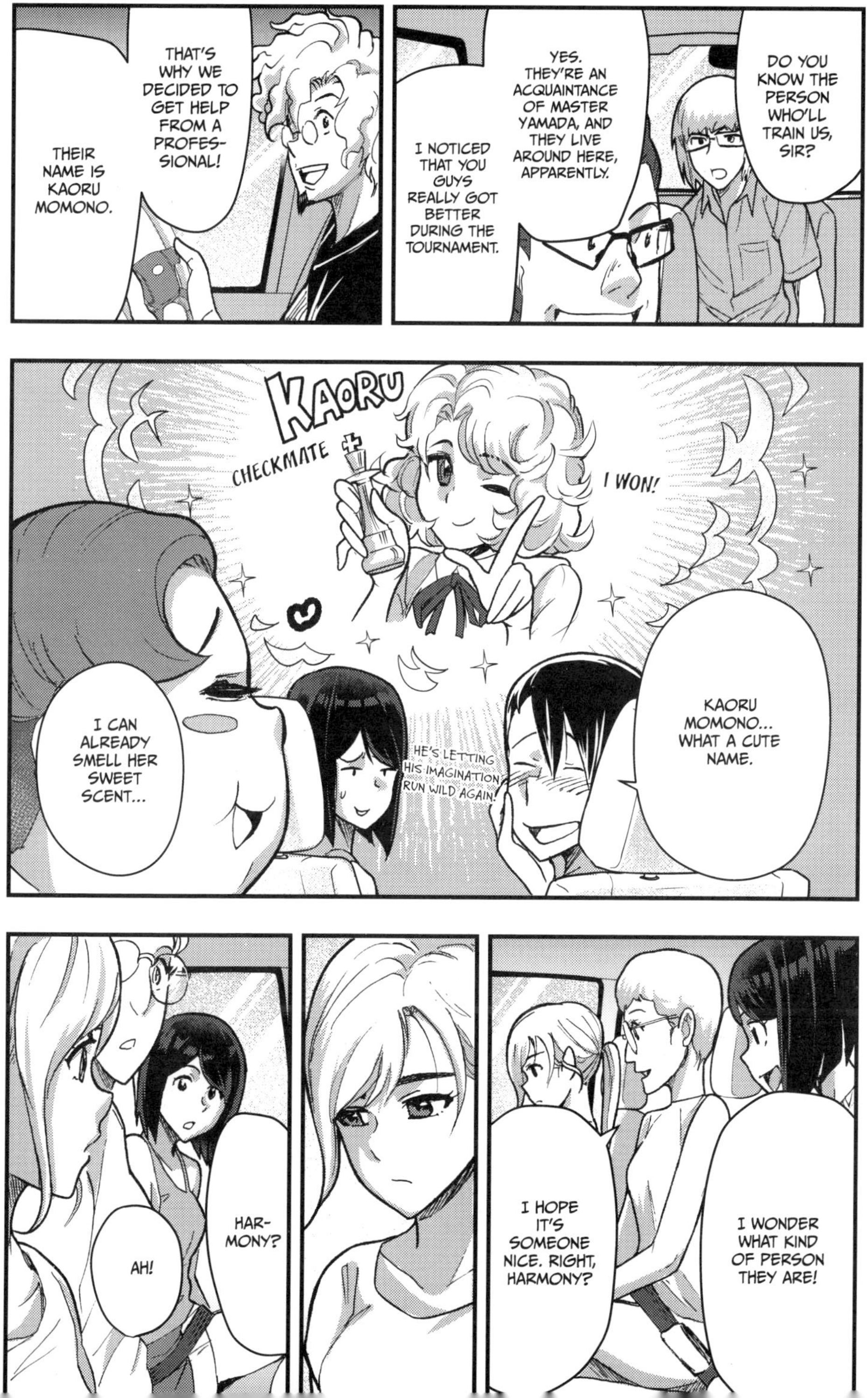
DO YOU KNOW THE PERSON WHO'LL TRAIN US, SIR?
YES. THEY'RE AN ACQUAINTANCE OF MASTER YAMADA, AND THEY LIVE AROUND HERE, APPARENTLY.
I NOTICED THAT YOU GUYS REALLY GOT BETTER DURING THE TOURNAMENT.
THAT'S WHY WE DECIDED TO GET HELP FROM A PROFES-SIONAL!
THEIR NAME IS KAORU MOMONO.
KAORU MOMONO... WHAT A CUTE NAME.
HE'S LETTING HIS IMAGINATION RUN WILD AGAIN!
I CAN ALREADY SMELL HER SWEET SCENT...
KAORU
CHECKMATE
I WON!
I WONDER WHAT KIND OF PERSON THEY ARE!
I HOPE IT'S SOMEONE NICE. RIGHT, HARMONY?
HAR-MONY?
AH!

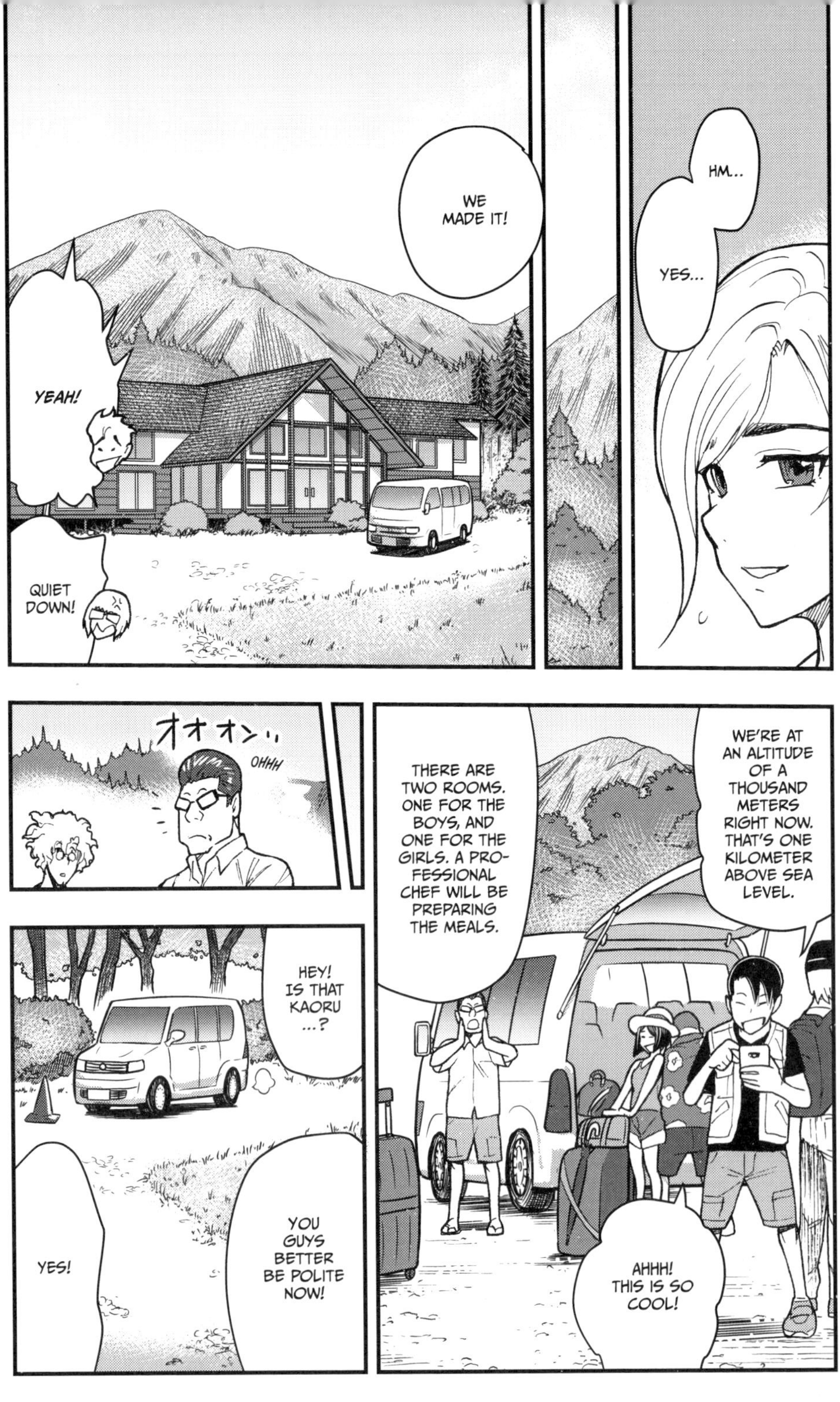
HM...
YES...
WE MADE IT!
YEAH!
QUIET DOWN!
WE'RE AT AN ALTITUDE OF A THOUSAND METERS RIGHT NOW. THAT'S ONE KILOMETER ABOVE SEA LEVEL.
THERE ARE TWO ROOMS. ONE FOR THE BOYS, AND ONE FOR THE GIRLS. A PRO-FESSIONAL CHEF WILL BE PREPARING THE MEALS.
AHHH! THIS IS SO COOL!
オオオンぃ
OHHH
HEY! IS THAT KAORU ...?
YOU GUYS BETTER BE POLITE NOW!
YES!

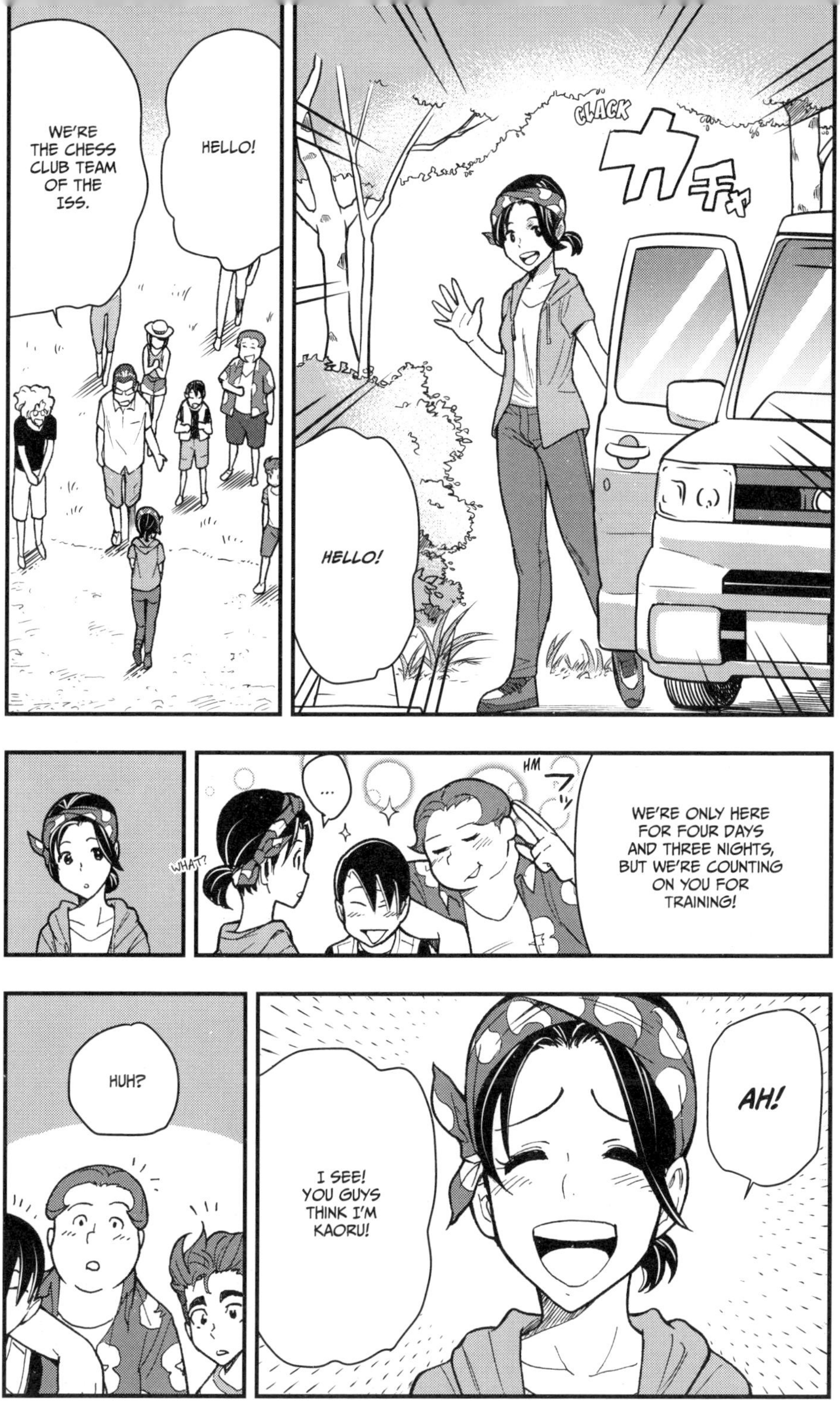

CLACK
カチャ
HELLO!
HELLO!
WE'RE THE CHESS CLUB TEAM OF THE ISS.
WE'RE ONLY HERE FOR FOUR DAYS AND THREE NIGHTS, BUT WE'RE COUNTING ON YOU FOR TRAINING!
HM
フッ
...
WHAT?
AH!
I SEE! YOU GUYS THINK I'M KAORU!
HUH?

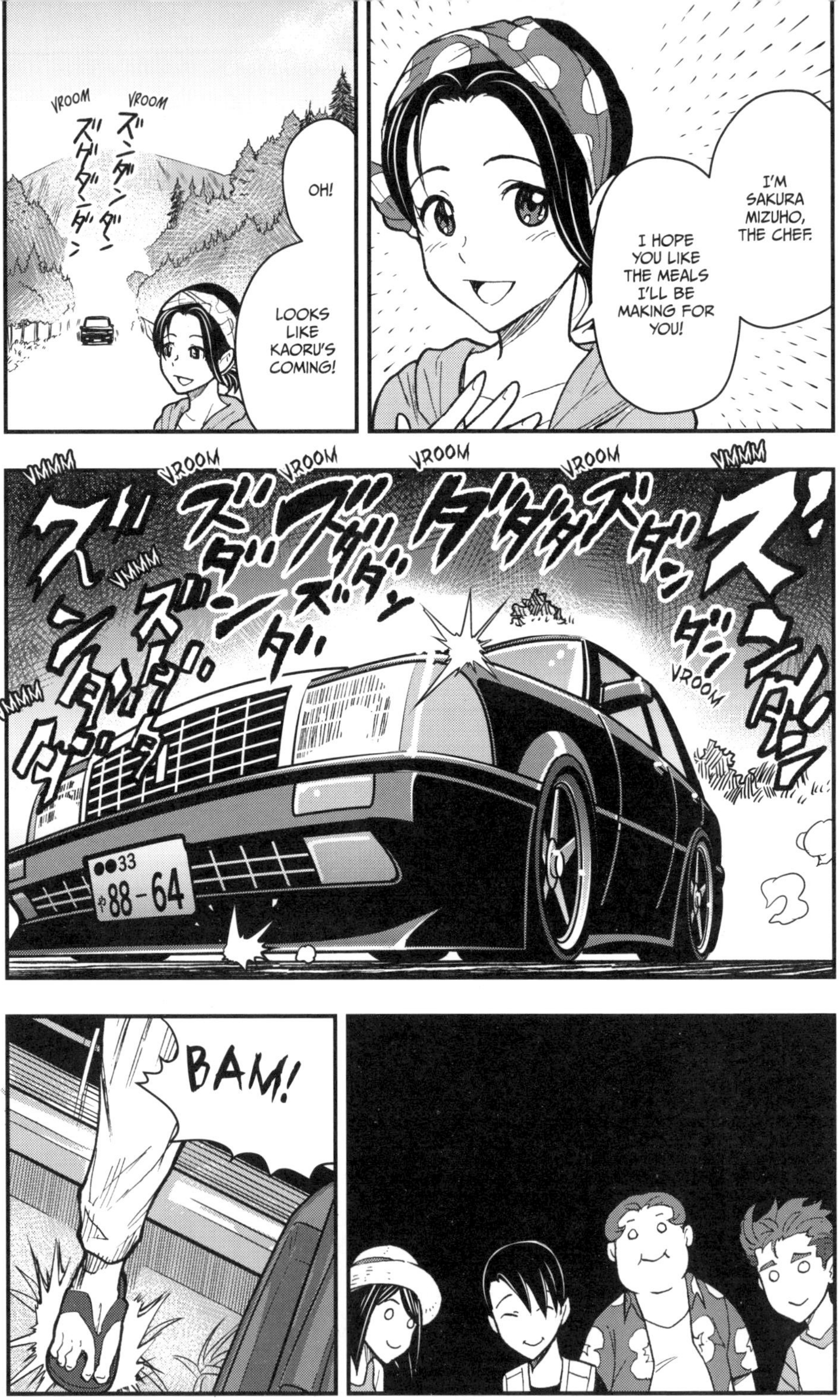
I'M SAKURA MIZUHO, THE CHEF.
I HOPE YOU LIKE THE MEALS I'LL BE MAKING FOR YOU!
VROOM
VROOM
OH!
LOOKS LIKE KAORU'S COMING!
VMMM
VROOM
VMMM
VROOM
VROOM
VROOM
VMMM
VROOM
VMMM
●●33
88-64
BAM!

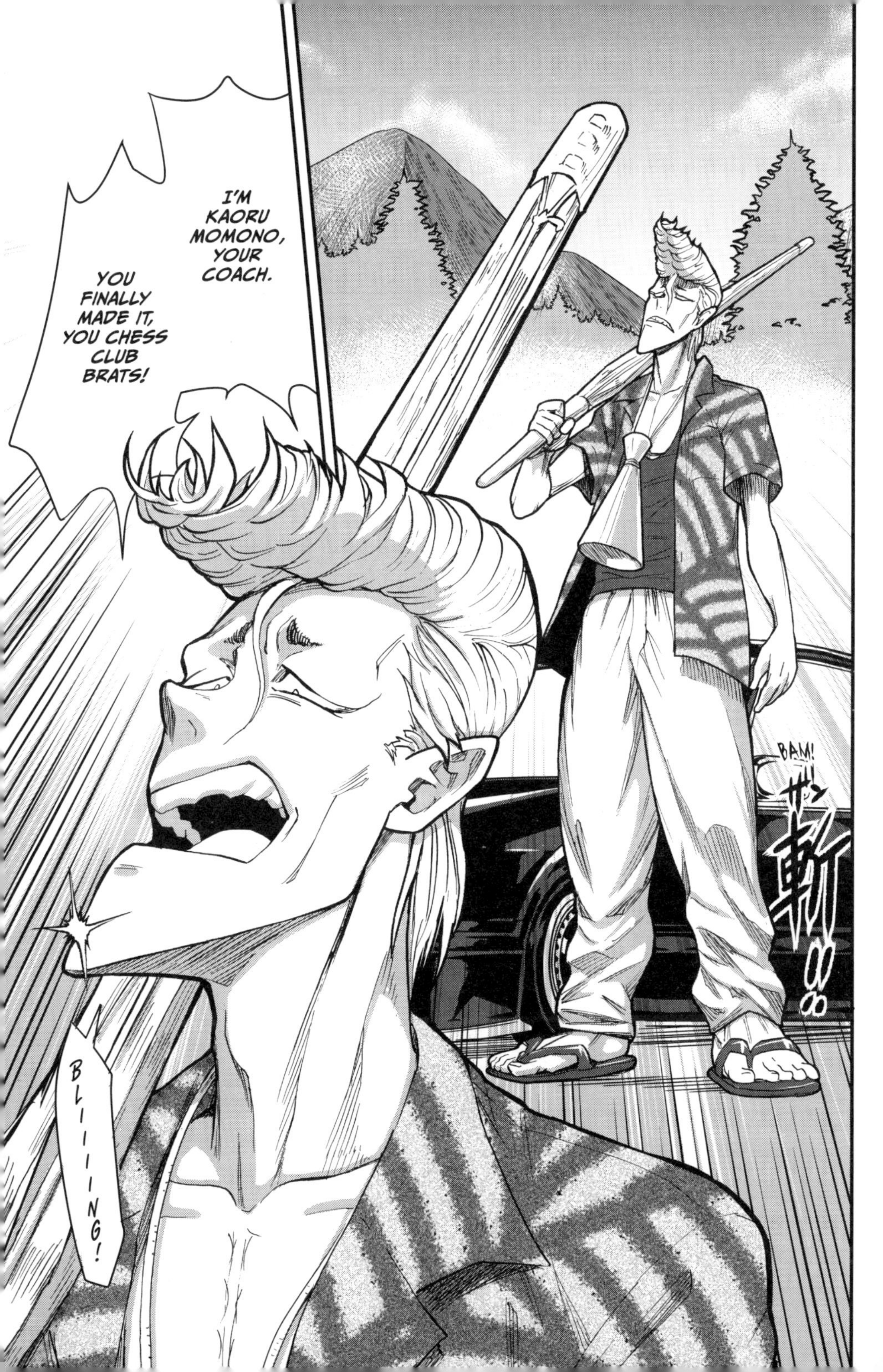
I'M KAORU MOMONO, YOUR COACH.
YOU FINALLY MADE IT, YOU CHESS CLUB BRATS!
BAM!
BLIIIING!

I'M SCARED!

AHHH!

KAORU IS A... MAN?!

STINKS OF CITY BOYS AROUND HERE, HUH?

H-HELLO...

NICE TO MEET YOU...

TACK
TACK
BOOM!

YOU GUYS WILL QUICKLY BECOME GREAT PLAYERS UNDER MY TUTELAGE.

NO WORRIES.

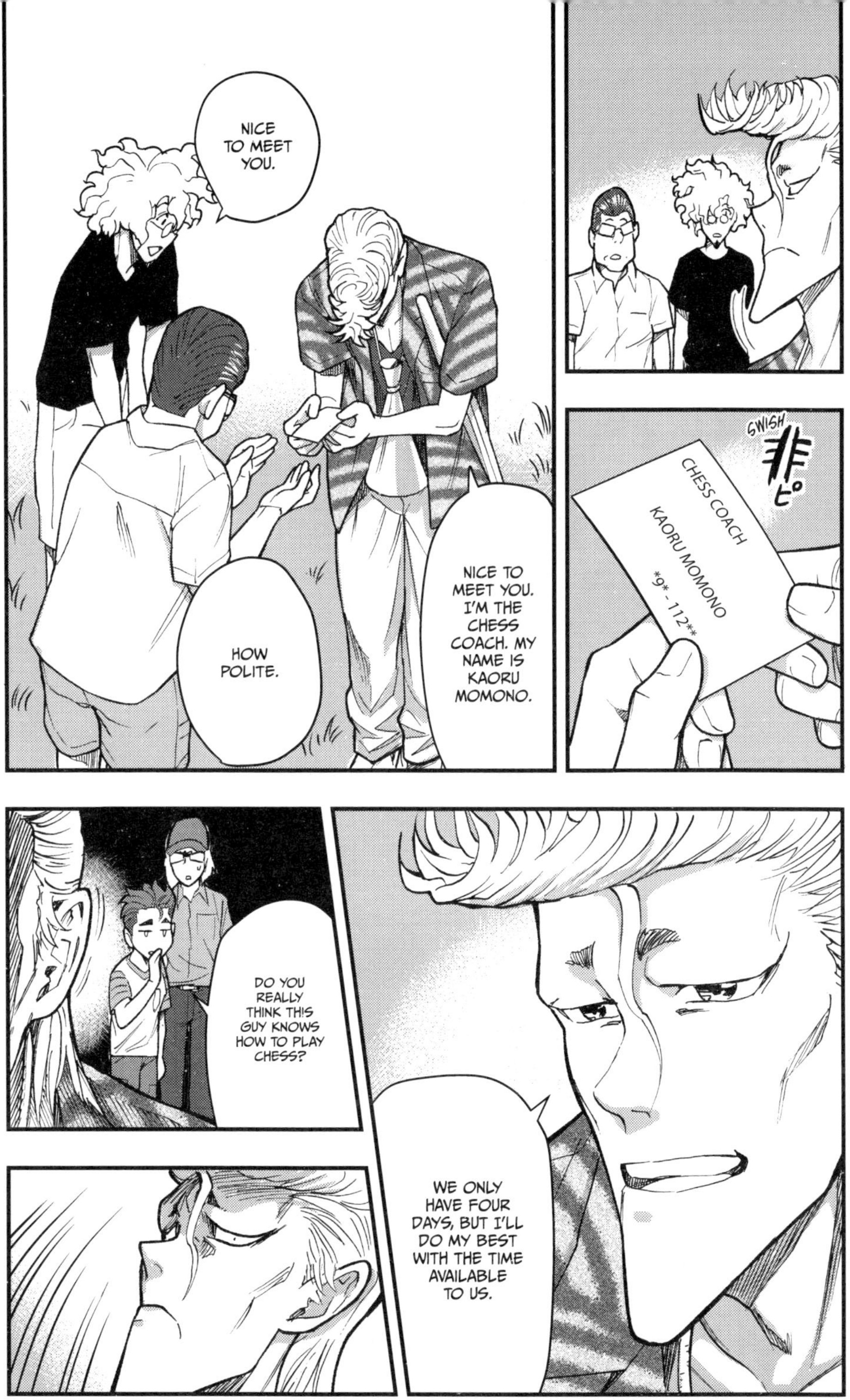
SWISH
CHESS COACH
KAORU MOMONO
9 - 112**
NICE TO MEET YOU. I'M THE CHESS COACH. MY NAME IS KAORU MOMONO.
NICE TO MEET YOU.
HOW POLITE.
WE ONLY HAVE FOUR DAYS, BUT I'LL DO MY BEST WITH THE TIME AVAILABLE TO US.
DO YOU REALLY THINK THIS GUY KNOWS HOW TO PLAY CHESS?

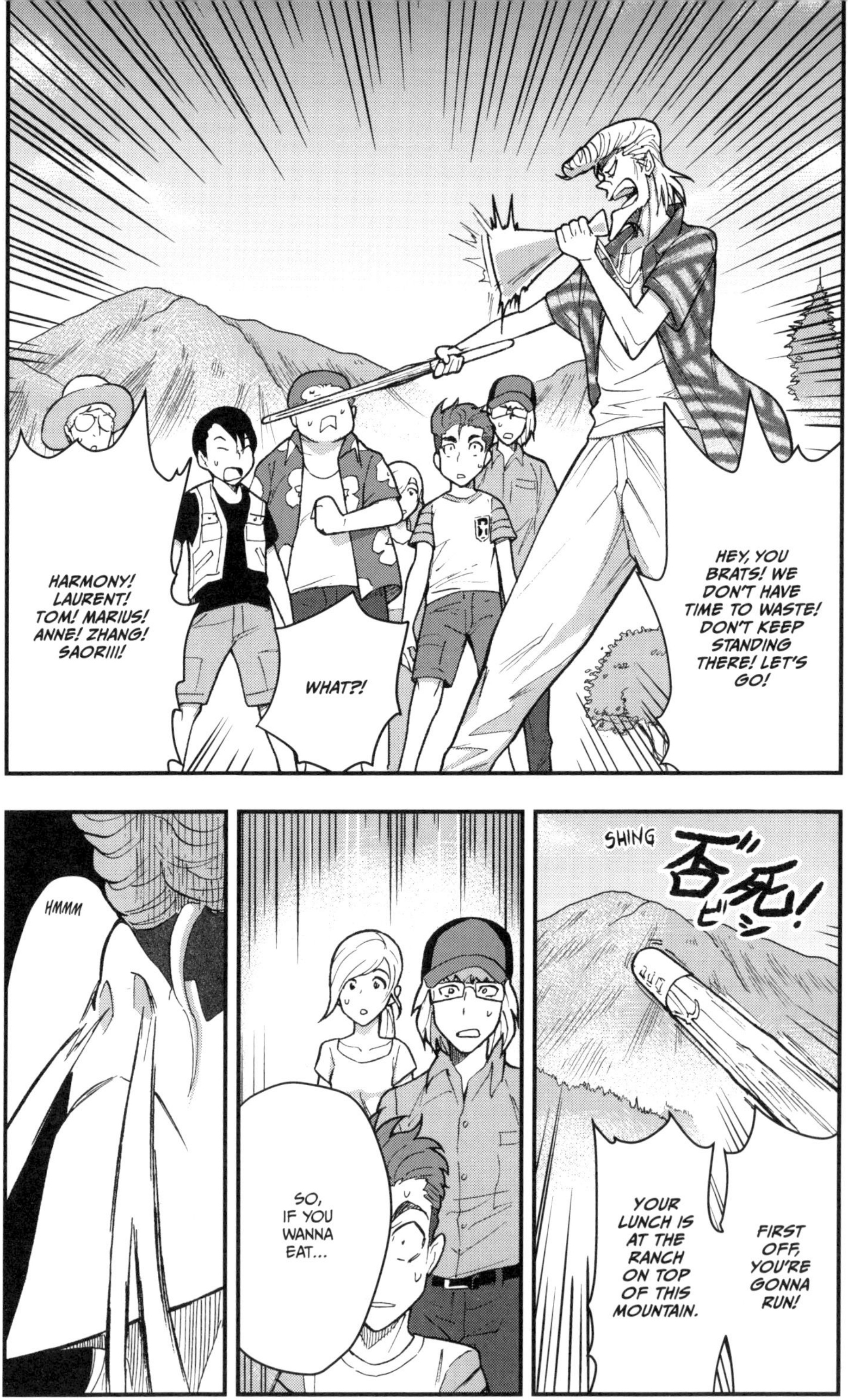
HEY, YOU BRATS! WE DON'T HAVE TIME TO WASTE! DON'T KEEP STANDING THERE! LET'S GO!
WHAT?!
HARMONY! LAURENT! TOM! MARIUS! ANNE! ZHANG! SAORIII!
SHING
否死!
ビシ
FIRST OFF, YOU'RE GONNA RUN!
YOUR LUNCH IS AT THE RANCH ON TOP OF THIS MOUNTAIN.
SO, IF YOU WANNA EAT...
HMMM

WAAAH!

BAM

...THEN RUUUUN!!!

WHAT? | THE RESERVATION FOR LUNCH IS AT 12 O'CLOCK SHARP! IF YOU GET THERE EVEN ONE SECOND LATER, YOU WON'T EAT!

OH MY GOD!

WHAT THE HECK IS THIS?!

WE ONLY HAVE TWENTY MINUTES...

...

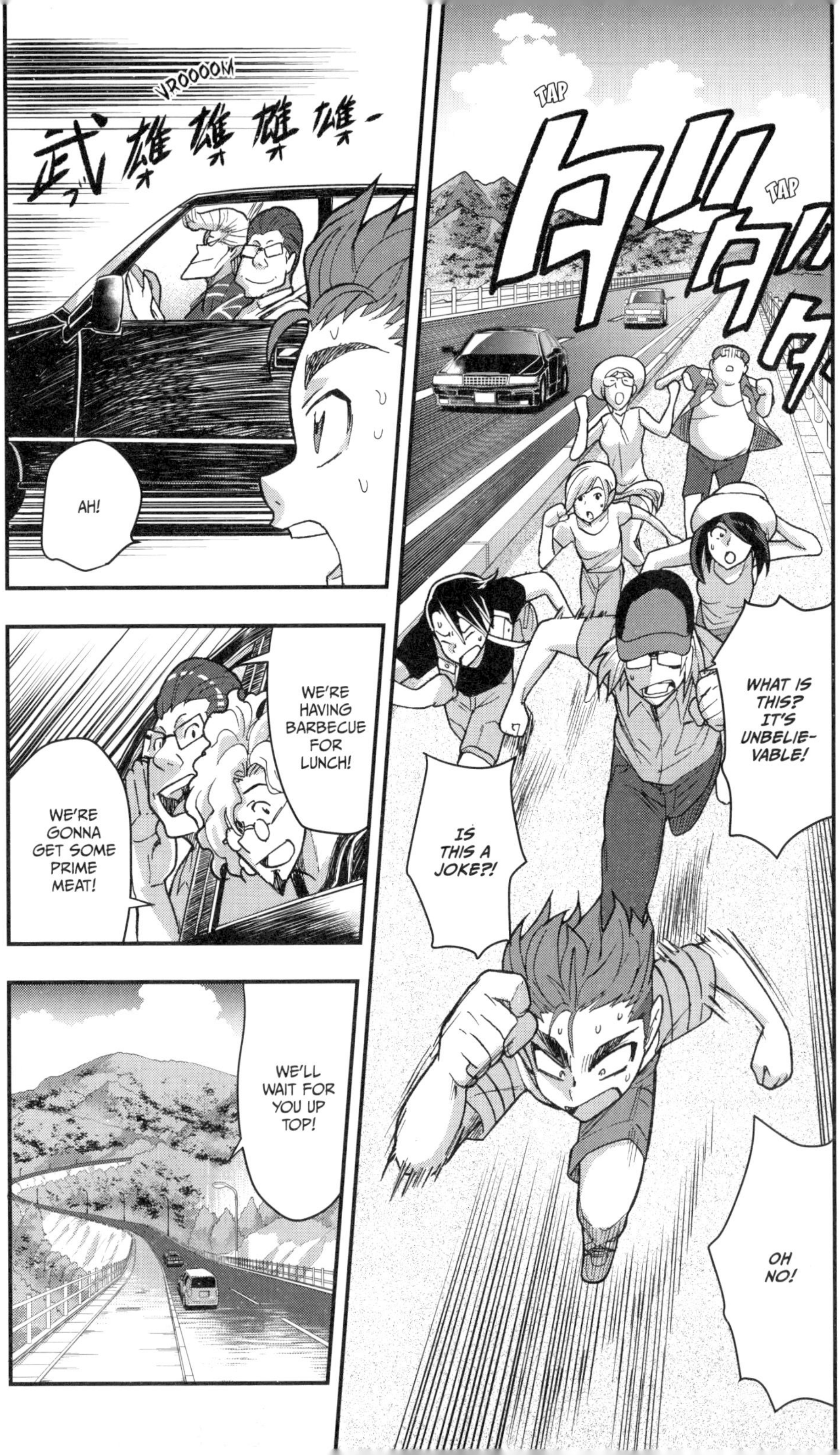
VROOOOM
AH!
WE'RE HAVING BARBECUE FOR LUNCH!
WE'RE GONNA GET SOME PRIME MEAT!
WE'LL WAIT FOR YOU UP TOP!
TAP
TAP
WHAT IS THIS? IT'S UNBELIE-VABLE!
IS THIS A JOKE?!
OH NO!

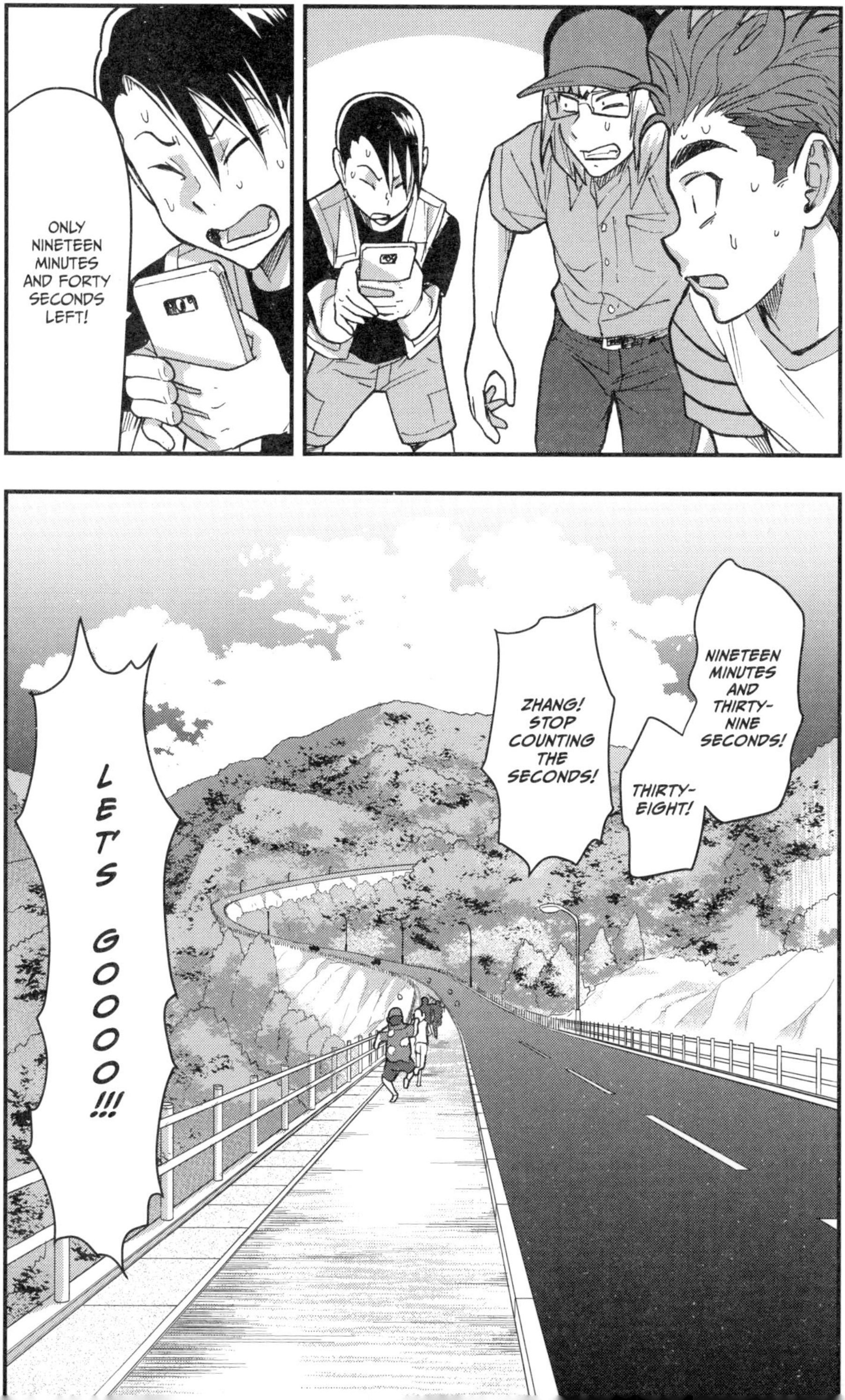
ONLY NINETEEN MINUTES AND FORTY SECONDS LEFT!
NINETEEN MINUTES AND THIRTY-NINE SECONDS!
THIRTY-EIGHT!
ZHANG! STOP COUNTING THE SECONDS!
LET'S GOOOOO!!!

BLITZ

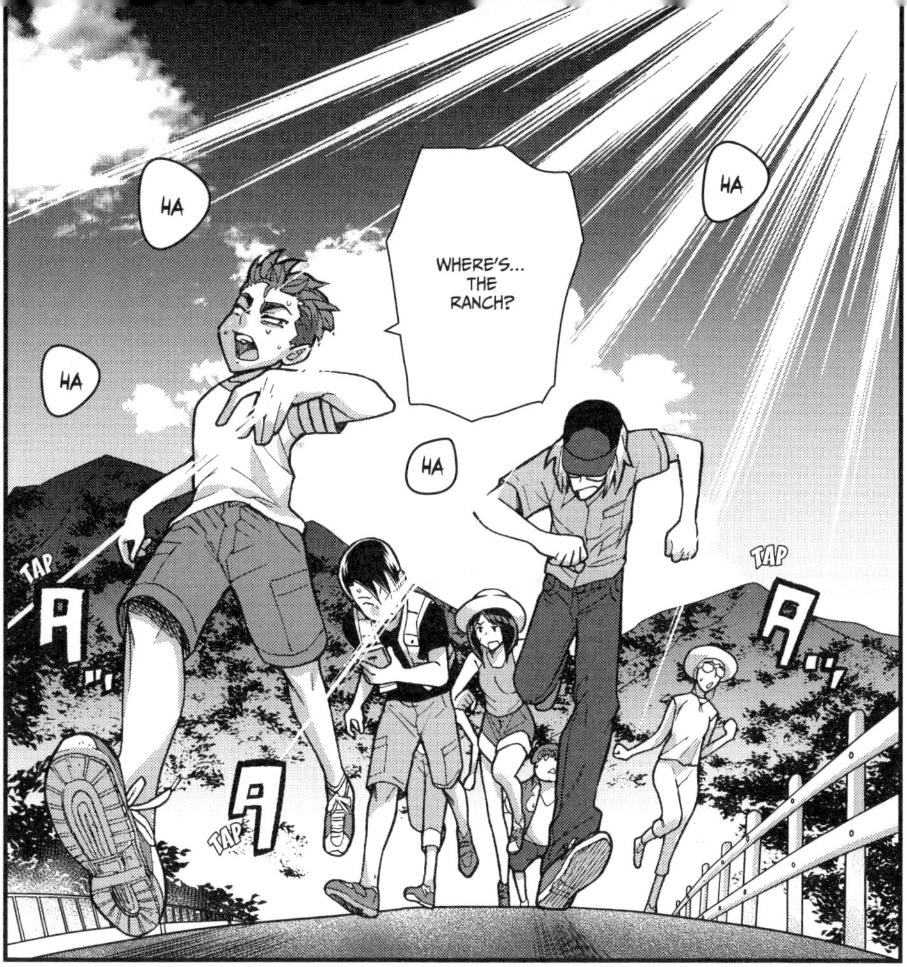
HA
WHERE'S... THE RANCH?
HA
HA
HA
TAP
TAP
TAP

Chapter 25: Tom v. Kaoru

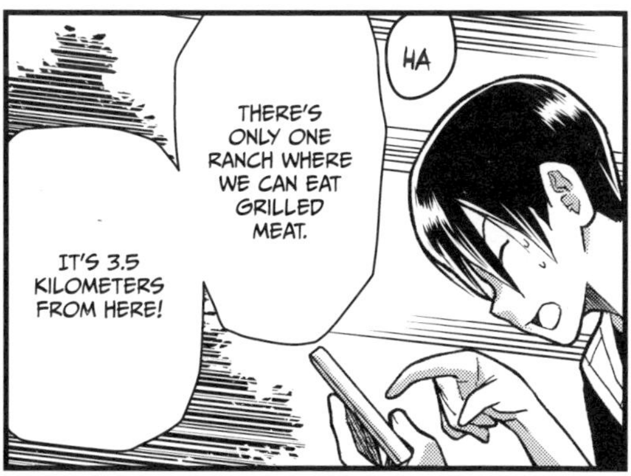
HA
THERE'S ONLY ONE RANCH WHERE WE CAN EAT GRILLED MEAT.
IT'S 3.5 KILOMETERS FROM HERE!

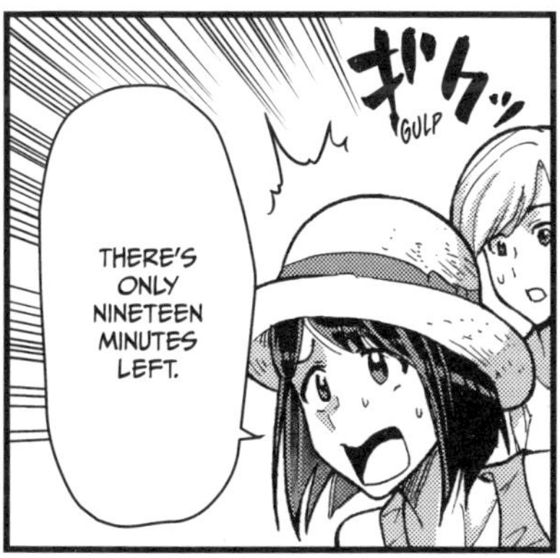
GULP
THERE'S ONLY NINETEEN MINUTES LEFT.

ANNE! MARIUS! HANG IN THERE!

DOES THAT MEAN WE'VE ONLY GOT FIVE MINUTES AND THIRTY SECONDS PER KILOMETER?!

WHAT?! WE'LL NEVER MAKE IT! WE HAVE TO MOVE IT!

NO... IT'S IMPOSSIBLE...

GO ON... DON'T WORRY ABOUT US...

MARIUS!

THANK YOU FOR EVERYTHING...

GUYS... I'LL ALWAYS THINK FONDLY OF THE TIME WE SPENT TOGETHER.

STOP KIDDING AROUND!

WE'RE GONNA EAT BARBECUE TOGETHER!!!

HA

T- TOM!

GWIP

HA

TAP TAP

NINETEEN MINUTES LATER...

YEAH! WE'RE GOING TO BARBECUE HEAVEN TOGETHER!

GWIP

COME ON, ANNE. THIS ISN'T THE TIME TO GIVE UP!

SCRUNCH SCRUNCH

THE MEAT IS WAITING FOR US!!!

OHHH

I'M DOING MY BEST!

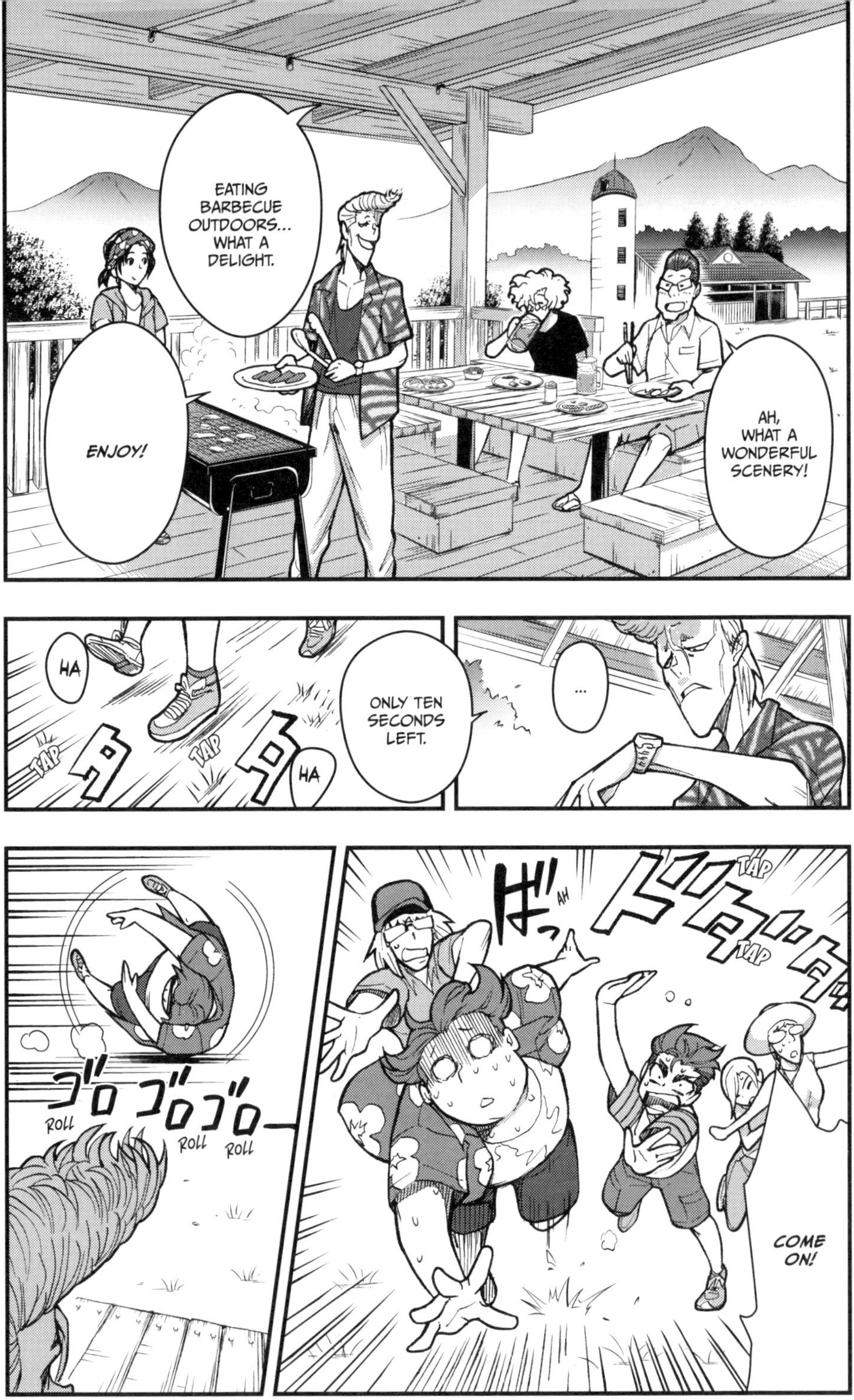
AH, WHAT A WONDERFUL SCENERY!
EATING BARBECUE OUTDOORS... WHAT A DELIGHT.
ENJOY!
...
ONLY TEN SECONDS LEFT.
HA
TAP
TAP
HA
AH
TAP
TAP
COME ON!
ゴロ ゴロゴロー
ROLL
ROLL
ROLL

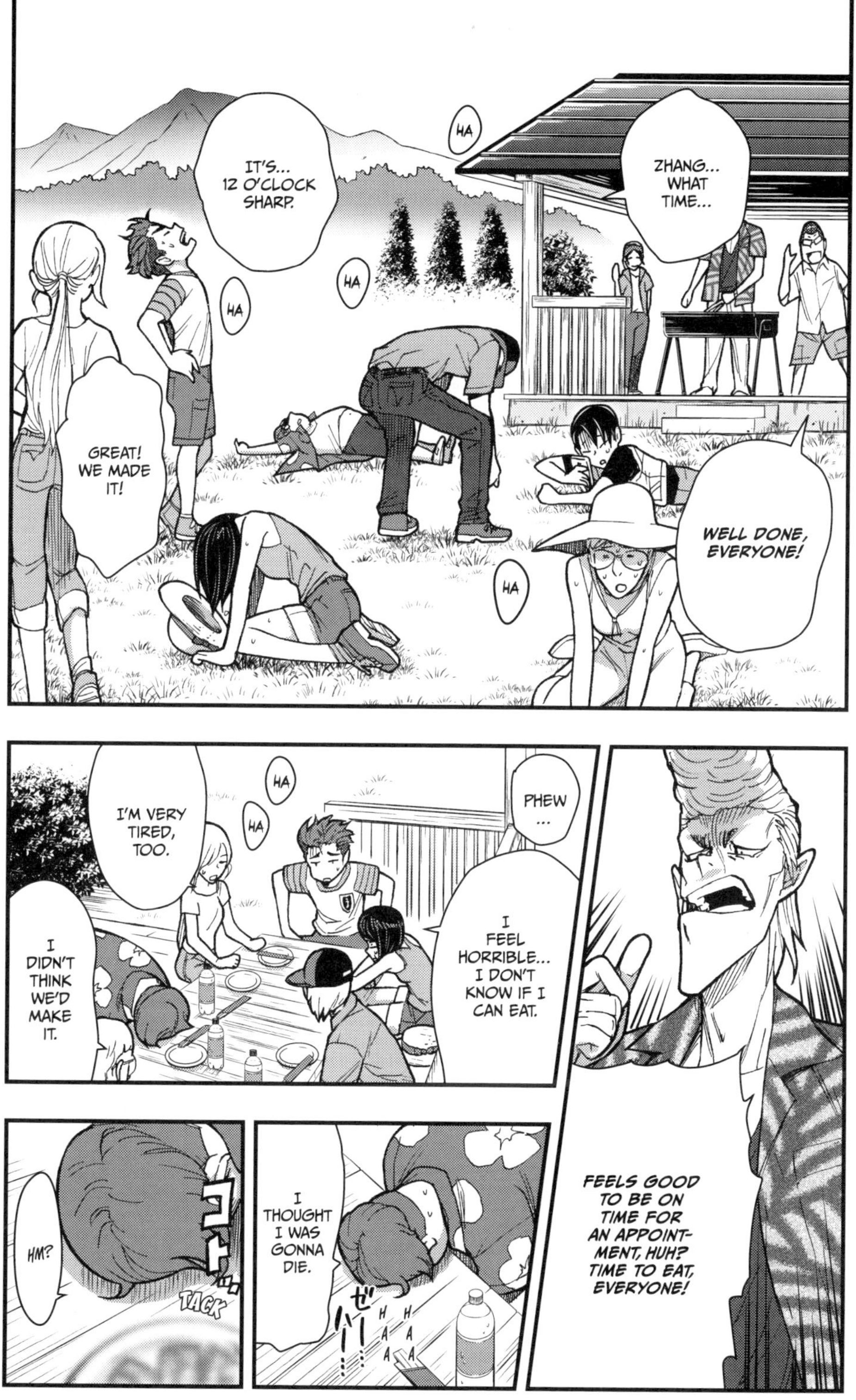
ZHANG... WHAT TIME...
HA
IT'S... 12 O'CLOCK SHARP.
HA
HA
WELL DONE, EVERYONE!
HA
GREAT! WE MADE IT!
PHEW...
HA
HA
I'M VERY TIRED, TOO.
I FEEL HORRIBLE... I DON'T KNOW IF I CAN EAT.
I DIDN'T THINK WE'D MAKE IT.
I THOUGHT I WAS GONNA DIE.
ゼー ハー
HAA
HAA
HM?
コト
TACK
FEELS GOOD TO BE ON TIME FOR AN APPOINTMENT, HUH? TIME TO EAT, EVERYONE!

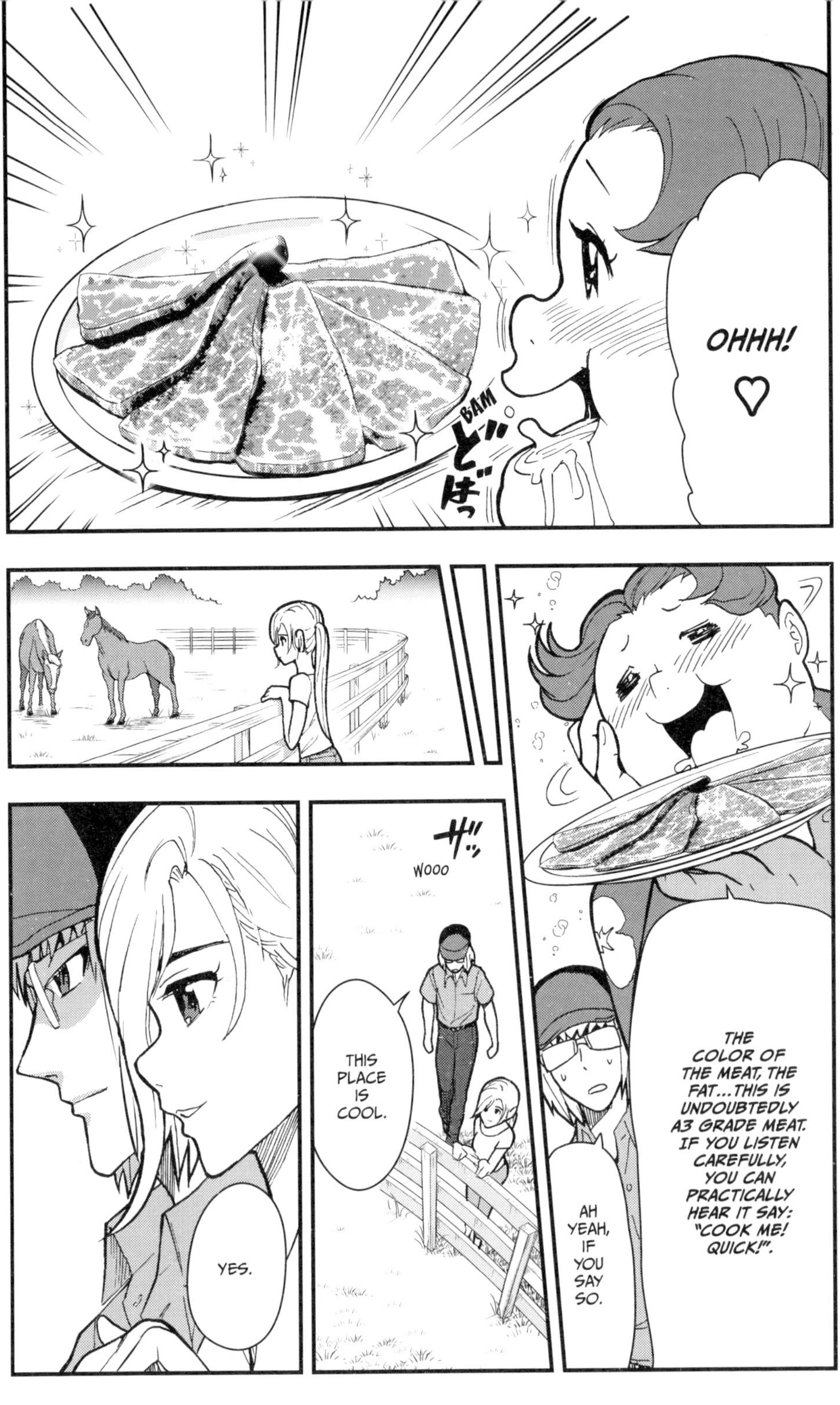
OHHH! ♡
BAM
どどばっ
THE COLOR OF THE MEAT, THE FAT...THIS IS UNDOUBTEDLY A3 GRADE MEAT. IF YOU LISTEN CAREFULLY, YOU CAN PRACTICALLY HEAR IT SAY: "COOK ME! QUICK!".
AH YEAH, IF YOU SAY SO.
ザッ
WOOO
THIS PLACE IS COOL.
YES.

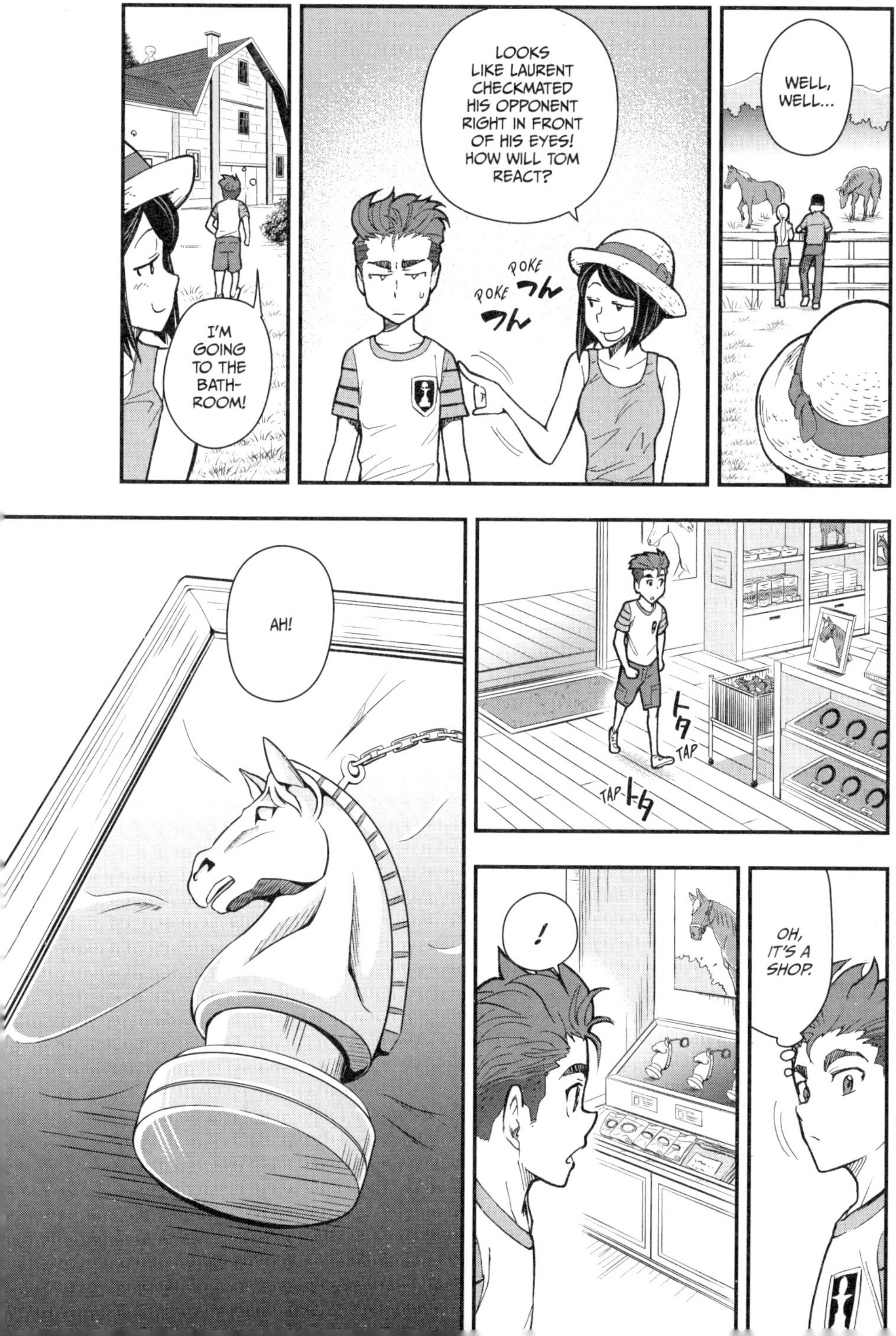
WELL, WELL...
LOOKS LIKE LAURENT CHECKMATED HIS OPPONENT RIGHT IN FRONT OF HIS EYES! HOW WILL TOM REACT?
POKE つん
POKE つん
I'M GOING TO THE BATH-ROOM!
トタ TAP
TAP トタ
OH, IT'S A SHOP.
!
AH!

IT LOOKS LIKE HARMONY'S KNIGHT.

WE'LL PLAY CHESS ONCE WE'RE BACK?

WHAT ARE YOU WAITING FOR? NOW THAT WE'RE DONE EATING, WE'RE GOING BACK! IT'S TIME TO TRAIN.

START RUNNING! AND NO TIME TO WASTE! DRAG YOUR FEET AND THERE'LL BE NO DINNER TONIGHT!

WHAT? WE'RE NOT PLAYING?

CHESS? YOU'VE GOT SOMETHING MORE IMPORTANT TO DO BEFORE THAT!

HEY, ISN'T HE PULLING OUR LEG HERE?

YOU MEAN YOU'VE GOT DOUBTS ABOUT MR. KAORU'S COACHING?

IF YOU THINK ABOUT IT, MAYBE HE DOESN'T EVEN KNOW HOW TO PLAY CHESS!

WELL... WHAT ARE WE GONNA DO IF WE WON'T PLAY CHESS?

TOTALLY.

MASTER YAMADA CHOSE MR. KAORU AS OUR COACH, THOUGH. HE MUST HAVE A PLAN.

HEY, GUYS. DOESN'T IT FEEL WEIRD NOT TO HAVE CHESS PRACTICE?

DOESN'T IT BOTHER YOU THAT WE'RE NOT PLAYING CHESS AT ALL? WE'LL NEVER MAKE IT TO THE NATIONAL CHAMPIONSHIP AT THIS RATE!

WELL...

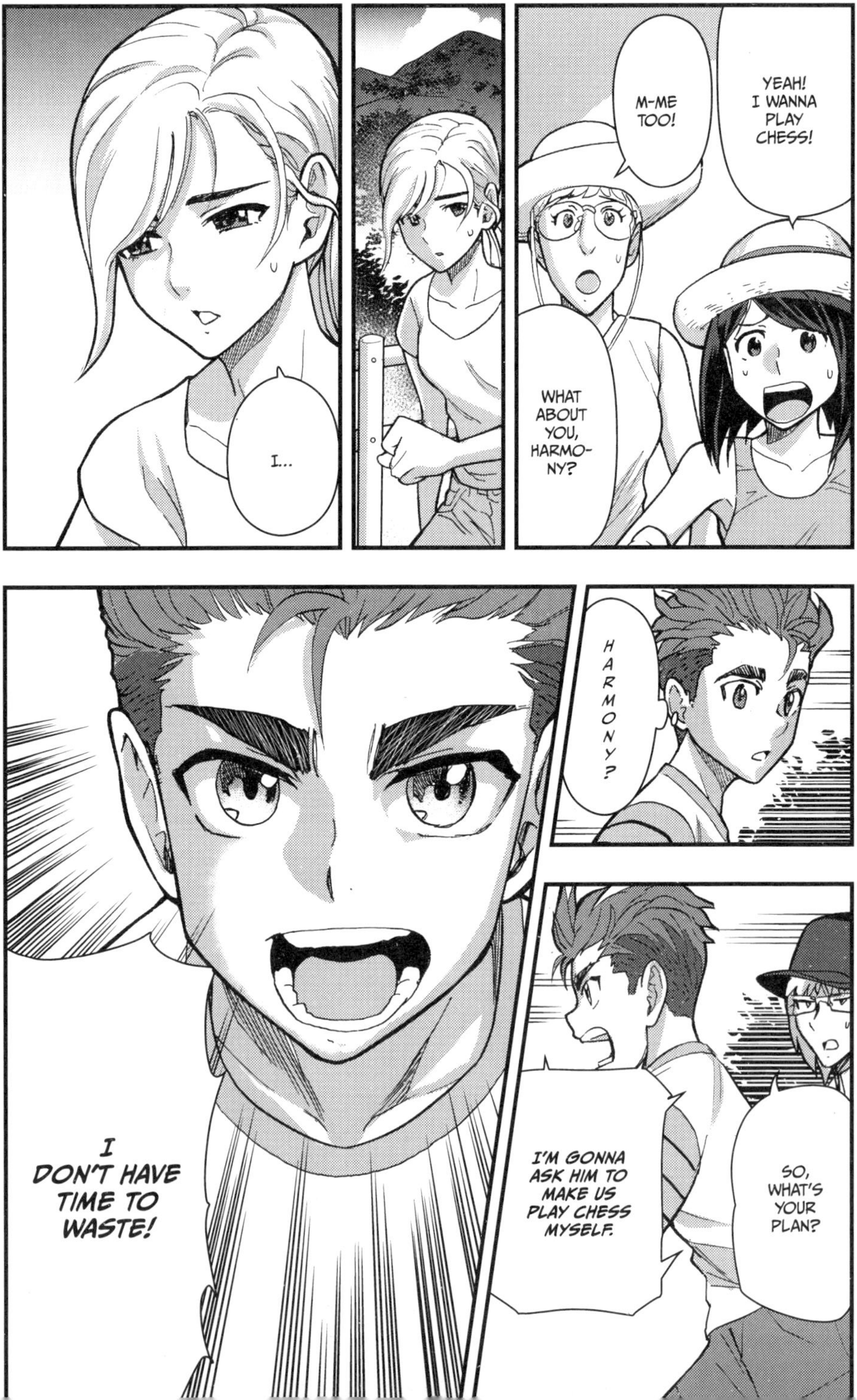
YEAH! I WANNA PLAY CHESS!
M-ME TOO!
WHAT ABOUT YOU, HARMONY?
I...
HARMONY?
SO, WHAT'S YOUR PLAN?
I'M GONNA ASK HIM TO MAKE US PLAY CHESS MYSELF.
I DON'T HAVE TIME TO WASTE!

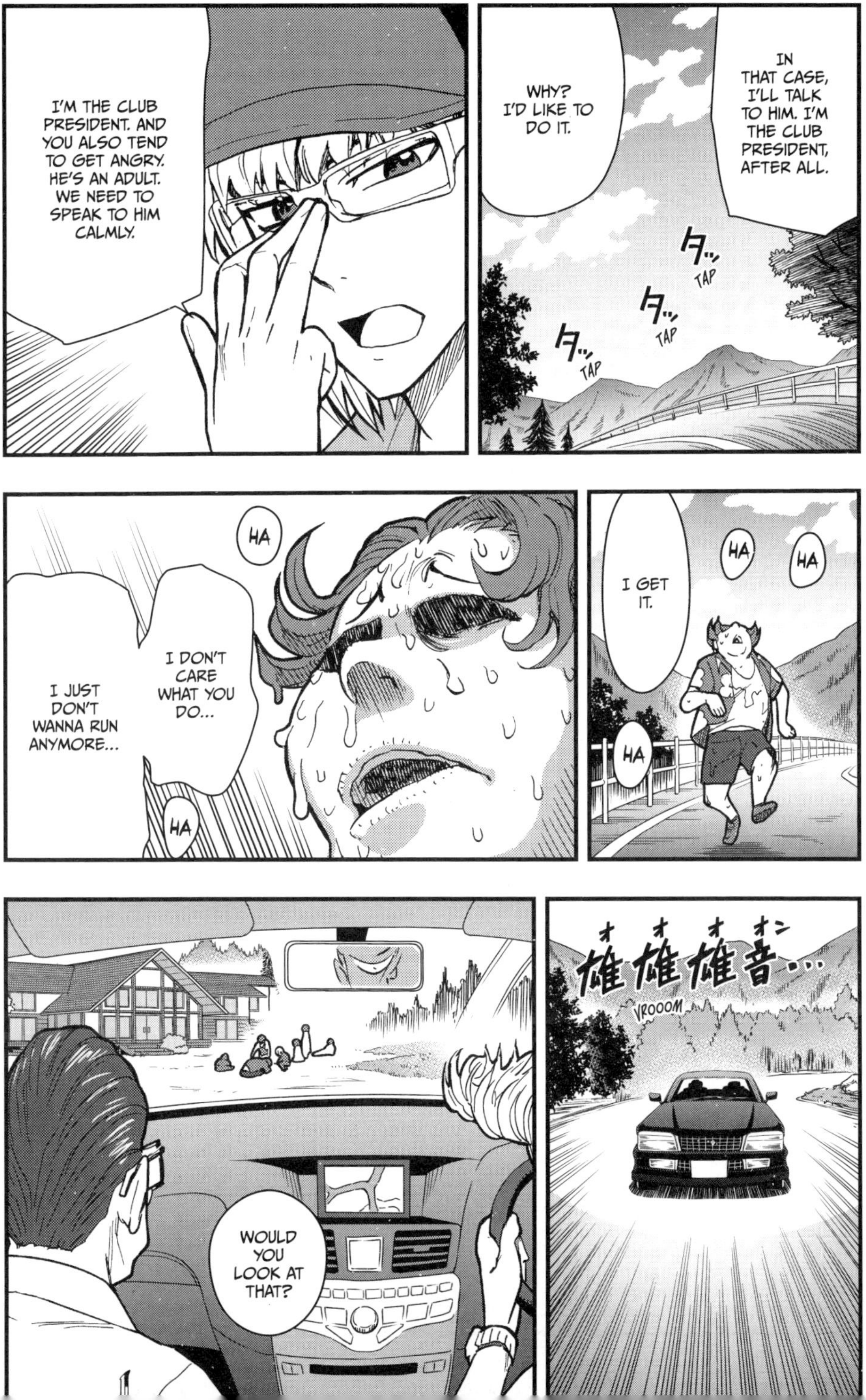

IN THAT CASE, I'LL TALK TO HIM. I'M THE CLUB PRESIDENT, AFTER ALL.
WHY? I'D LIKE TO DO IT.
タッ
TAP
タッ
TAP
タッ
TAP
I'M THE CLUB PRESIDENT. AND YOU ALSO TEND TO GET ANGRY. HE'S AN ADULT. WE NEED TO SPEAK TO HIM CALMLY.
HA
HA
I GET IT.
HA
HA
I DON'T CARE WHAT YOU DO...
I JUST DON'T WANNA RUN ANYMORE...
HA
雄雄雄音...
VROOOM
WOULD YOU LOOK AT THAT?

GREAT! IT LOOKS LIKE YOU MADE IT BACK WITHOUT A HITCH!

UH...

DO YOU WANT TO TAKE A BATH? THERE'S A HOT SPRING, AND IT'S VERY NICE.

AH, WONDERFUL!

WHAT A GREAT IDEA! LET'S GO!

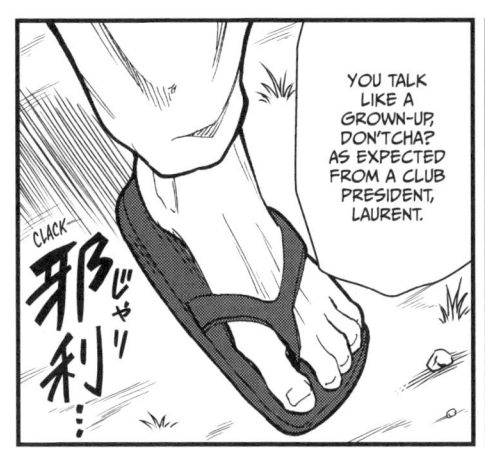

WE'RE HERE TO PLAY CHESS, SO WE CAN PARTICIPATE IN THE NATIONAL CHAMPIONSHIP.	WE'RE... AH? HMPH	SWISH MISTER KAORU. I'D LIKE TO SPEAK WITH YOU.

CLACK

YOU TALK LIKE A GROWN-UP, DON'TCHA? AS EXPECTED FROM A CLUB PRESIDENT, LAURENT.

HMMM... PLEASE, TRAIN US IN CHESS!

GULP

BUT I FEEL LIKE THIS WASN'T YOUR IDEA.

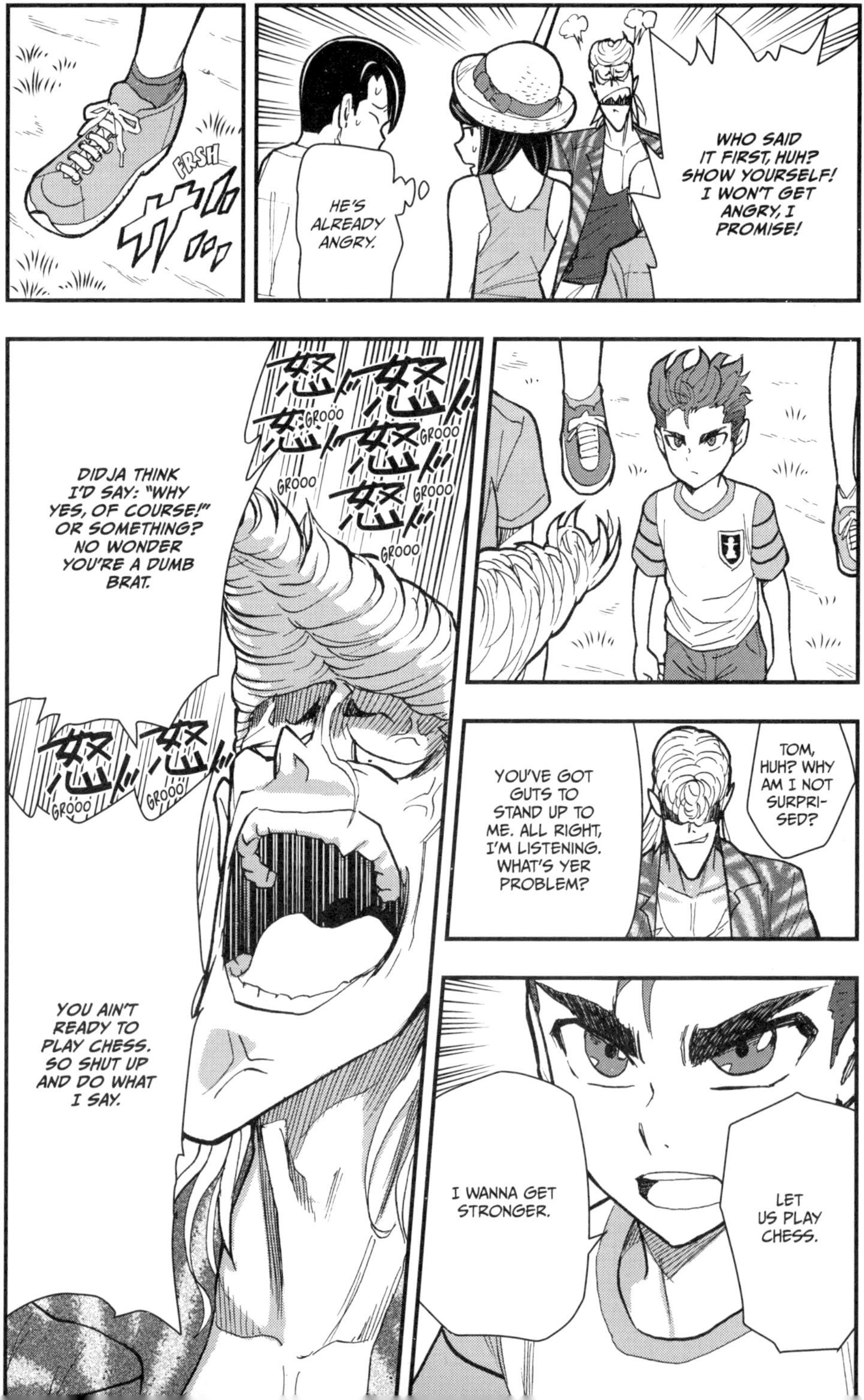
WHO SAID IT FIRST, HUH? SHOW YOURSELF! I WON'T GET ANGRY, I PROMISE!
HE'S ALREADY ANGRY.
FRSH
TOM, HUH? WHY AM I NOT SURPRI-SED?
YOU'VE GOT GUTS TO STAND UP TO ME. ALL RIGHT, I'M LISTENING. WHAT'S YER PROBLEM?
LET US PLAY CHESS.
I WANNA GET STRONGER.
GROOO GROOO GROOO GROOO GROOO
DIDJA THINK I'D SAY: "WHY YES, OF COURSE!" OR SOMETHING? NO WONDER YOU'RE A DUMB BRAT.
GROOO GROOO
YOU AIN'T READY TO PLAY CHESS. SO SHUT UP AND DO WHAT I SAY.

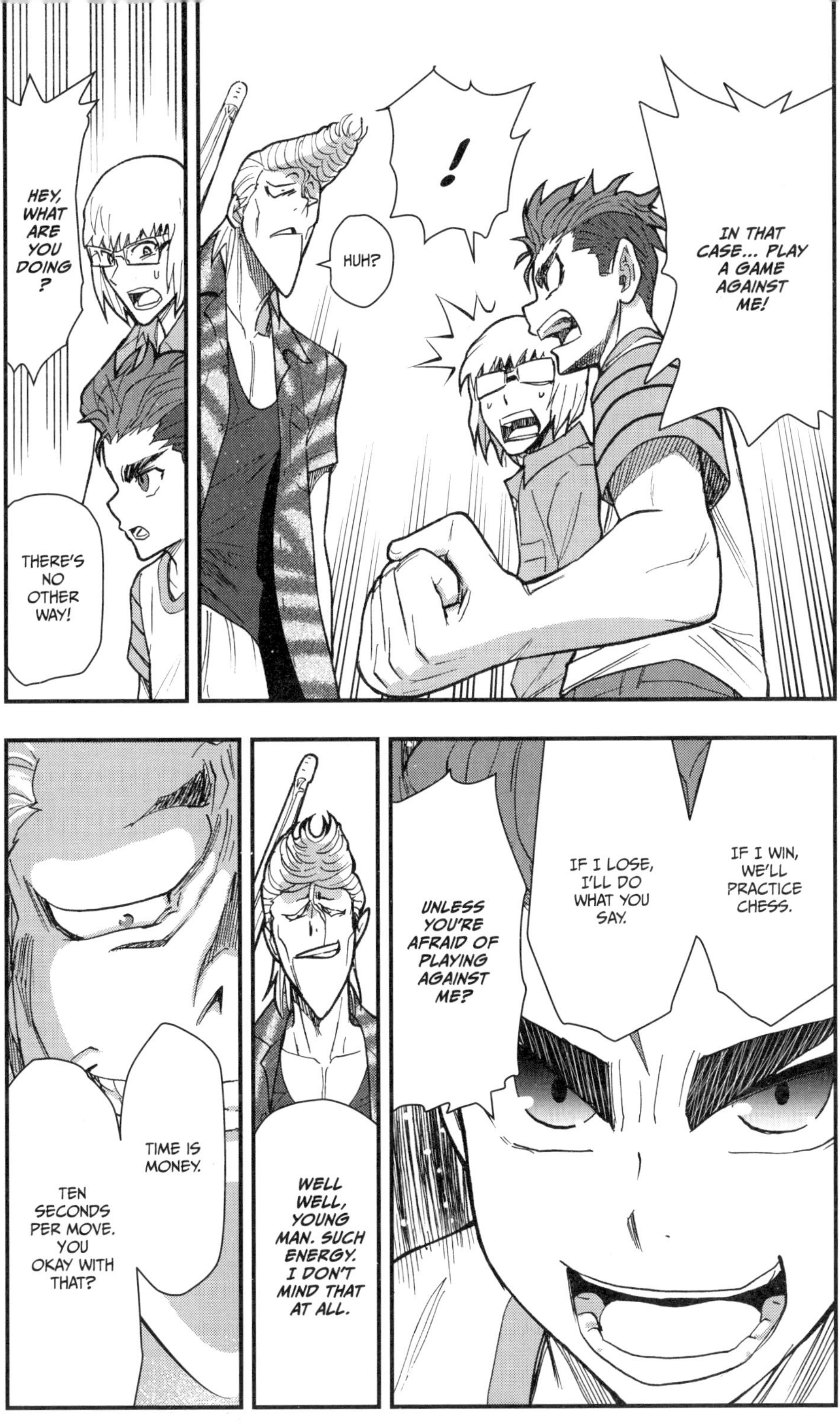
!
IN THAT CASE... PLAY A GAME AGAINST ME!
HUH?
HEY, WHAT ARE YOU DOING?
THERE'S NO OTHER WAY!
IF I WIN, WE'LL PRACTICE CHESS.
IF I LOSE, I'LL DO WHAT YOU SAY.
UNLESS YOU'RE AFRAID OF PLAYING AGAINST ME?
WELL WELL, YOUNG MAN. SUCH ENERGY. I DON'T MIND THAT AT ALL.
TIME IS MONEY.
TEN SECONDS PER MOVE. YOU OKAY WITH THAT?

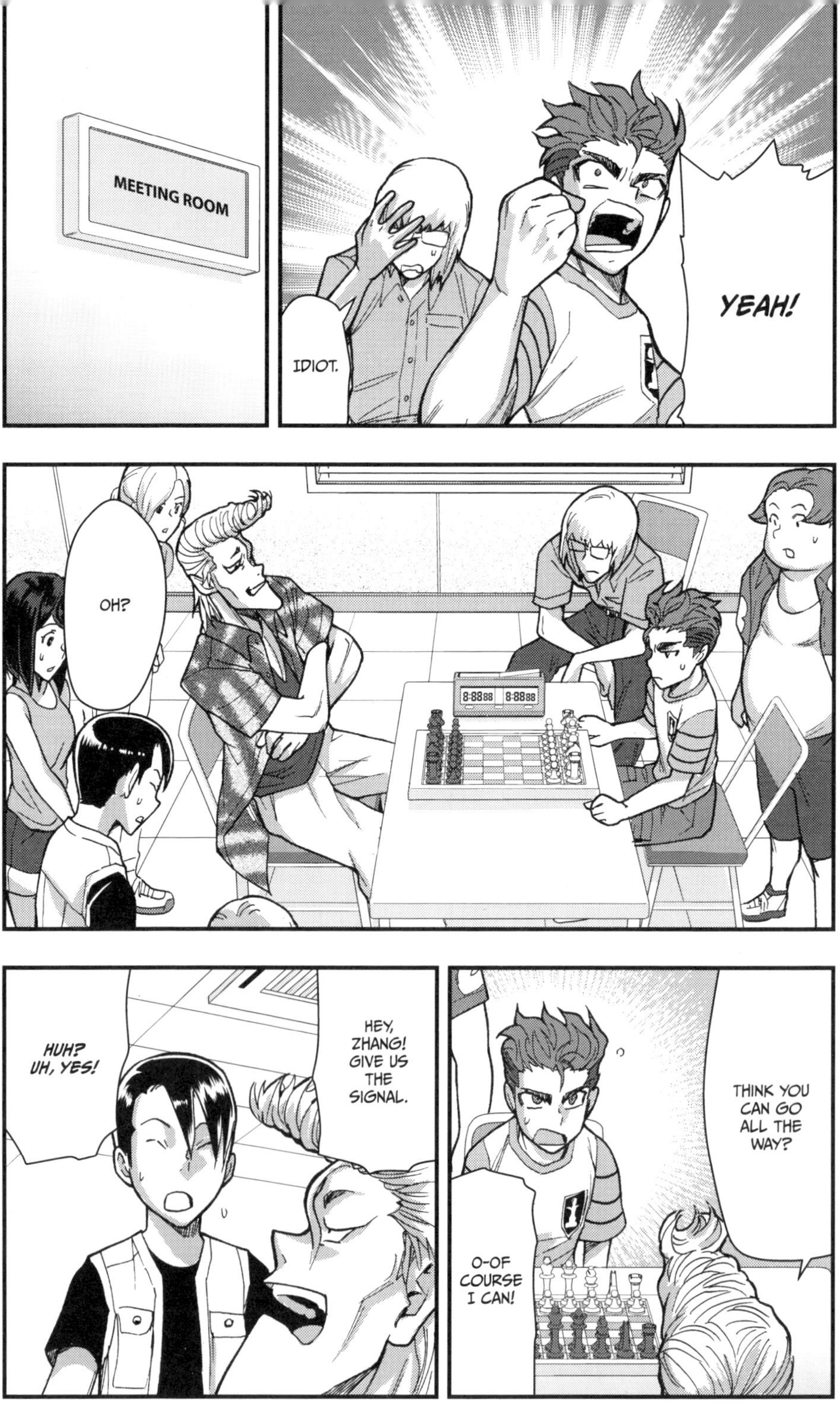
MEETING ROOM
YEAH!
IDIOT.
OH?
HEY, ZHANG! GIVE US THE SIGNAL.
HUH? UH, YES!
THINK YOU CAN GO ALL THE WAY?
O-OF COURSE I CAN!

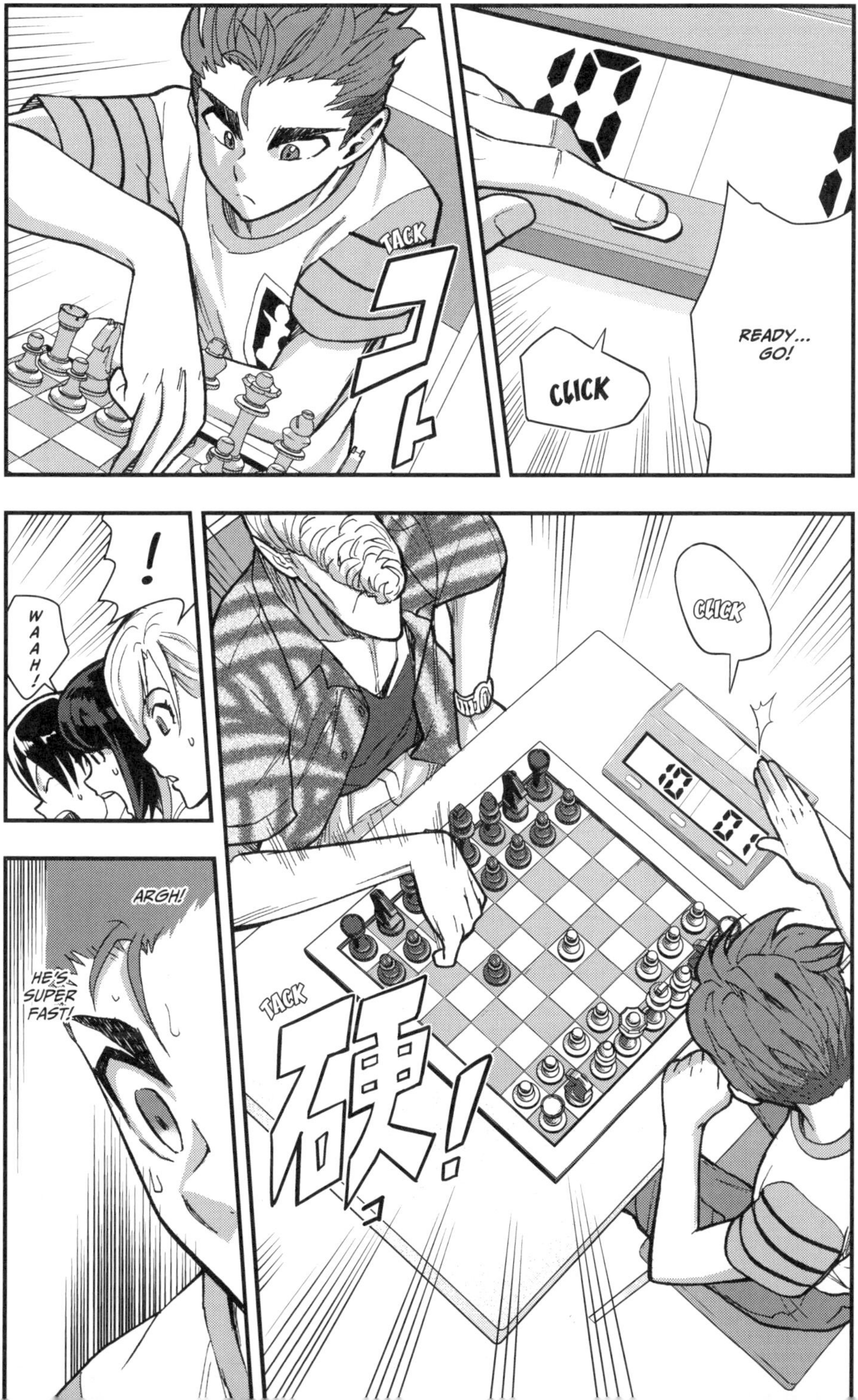
TACK
READY... GO!
CLICK
WAAAH!
!
CLICK
ARGH!
HE'S SUPER FAST!
TACK

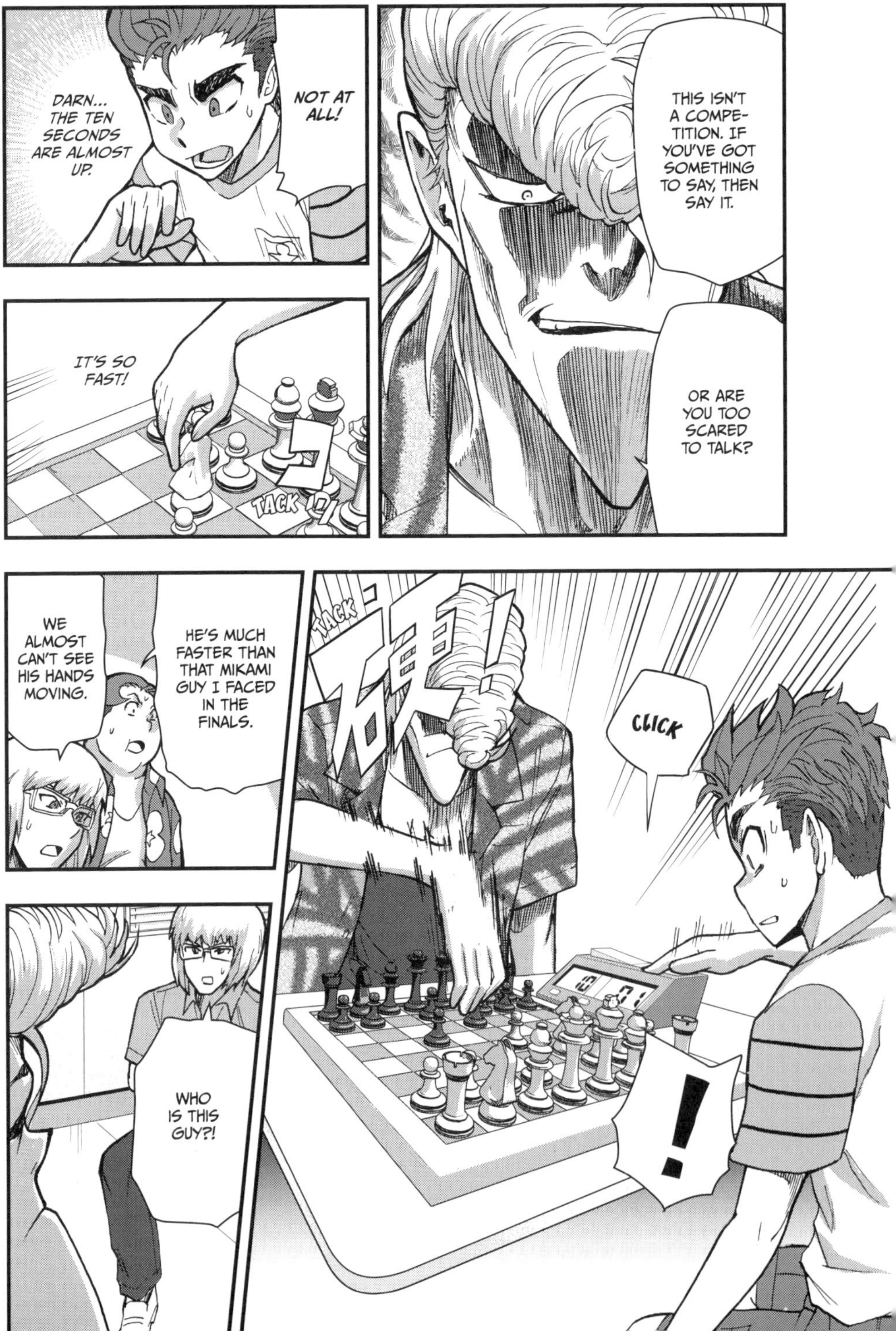
THIS ISN'T A COMPETITION. IF YOU'VE GOT SOMETHING TO SAY, THEN SAY IT.
OR ARE YOU TOO SCARED TO TALK?
NOT AT ALL!
DARN... THE TEN SECONDS ARE ALMOST UP.
IT'S SO FAST!
TACK
TACK
CLICK
!
HE'S MUCH FASTER THAN THAT MIKAMI GUY I FACED IN THE FINALS.
WE ALMOST CAN'T SEE HIS HANDS MOVING.
WHO IS THIS GUY?!

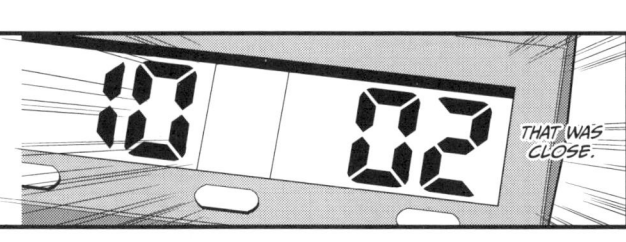

I NEED TO CALM DOWN. I HAVE TO CHANGE MY WAY OF THINKING.

PHEW

THERE ARE TEN LONG SECONDS LEFT.

I'LL THINK FIRST, THEN I'LL WIN!

THAT WAS CLOSE.

GO, TOM!

AMAZING! HE'S KEEPING HIS COOL!

TAKE THAT!

TACK

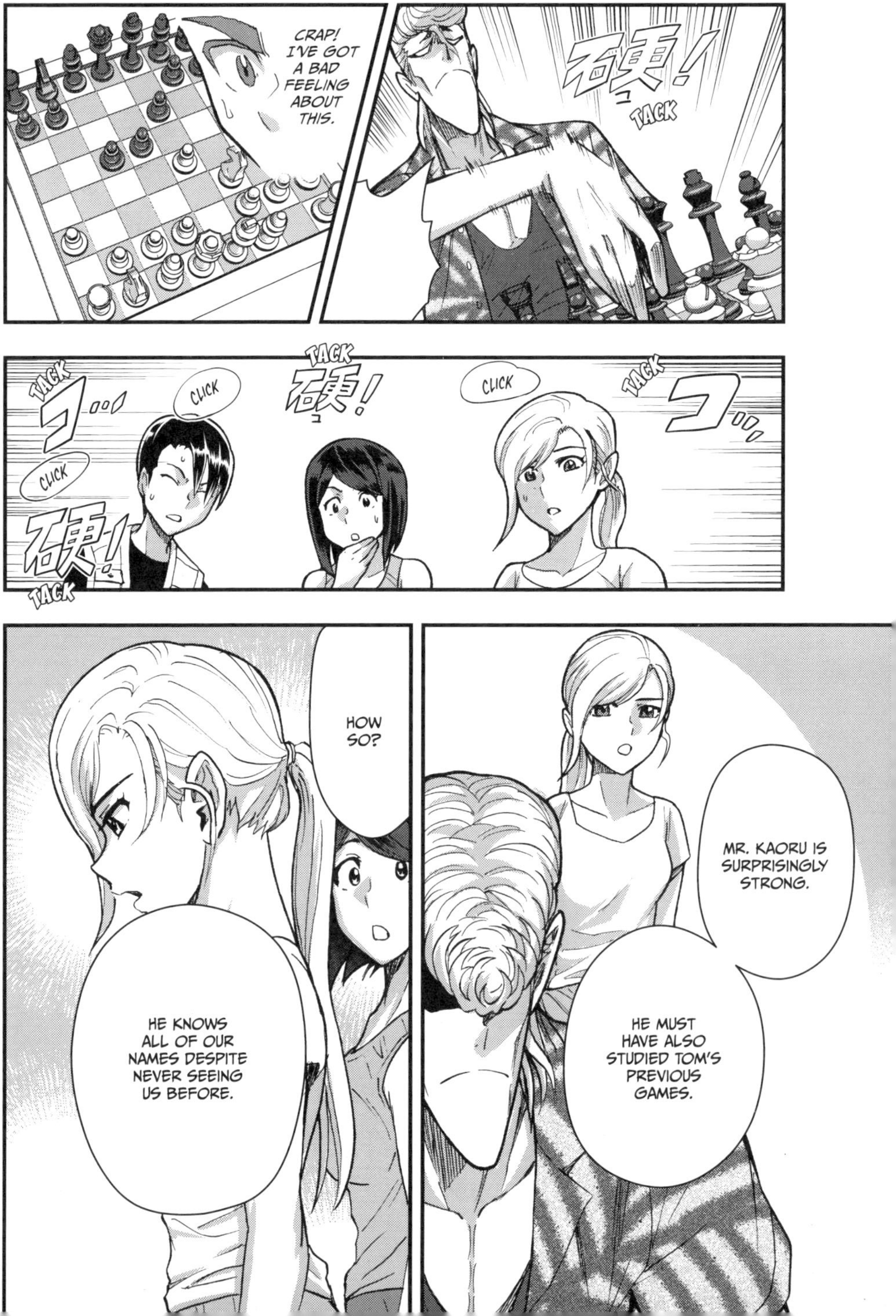
TACK
CRAP! I'VE GOT A BAD FEELING ABOUT THIS.
TACK
CLICK
TACK
CLICK
CLICK
TACK
MR. KAORU IS SURPRISINGLY STRONG.
HE MUST HAVE ALSO STUDIED TOM'S PREVIOUS GAMES.
HOW SO?
HE KNOWS ALL OF OUR NAMES DESPITE NEVER SEEING US BEFORE.

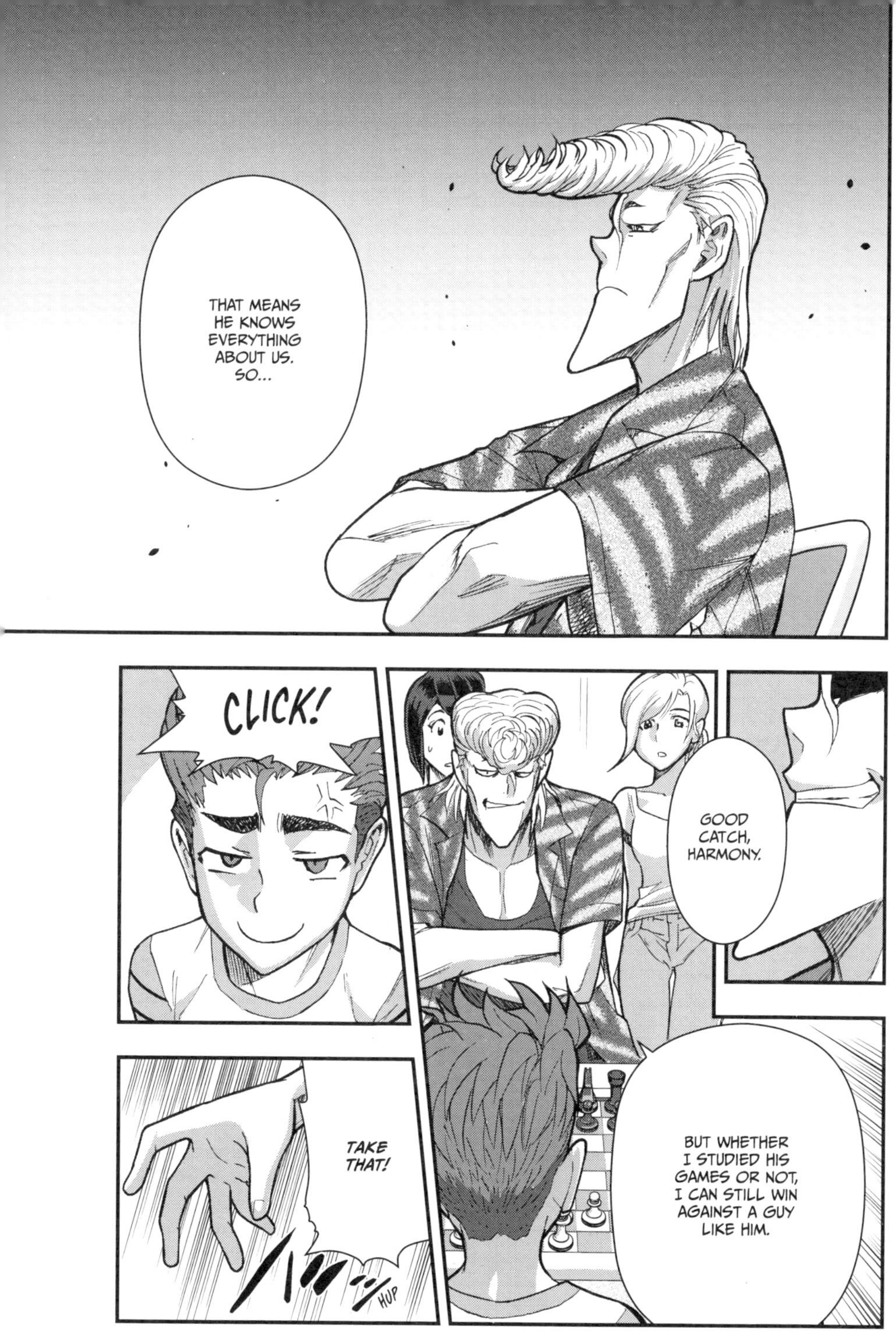
THAT MEANS HE KNOWS EVERYTHING ABOUT US. SO...
GOOD CATCH, HARMONY.
BUT WHETHER I STUDIED HIS GAMES OR NOT, I CAN STILL WIN AGAINST A GUY LIKE HIM.
CLICK!
TAKE THAT!
HUP

TACK

OH!

GOOD JOB, KIDDO!

I'M NOT A KID!

HEH HEH. NOW WHAT?!

AMAZING!

WELL DONE!

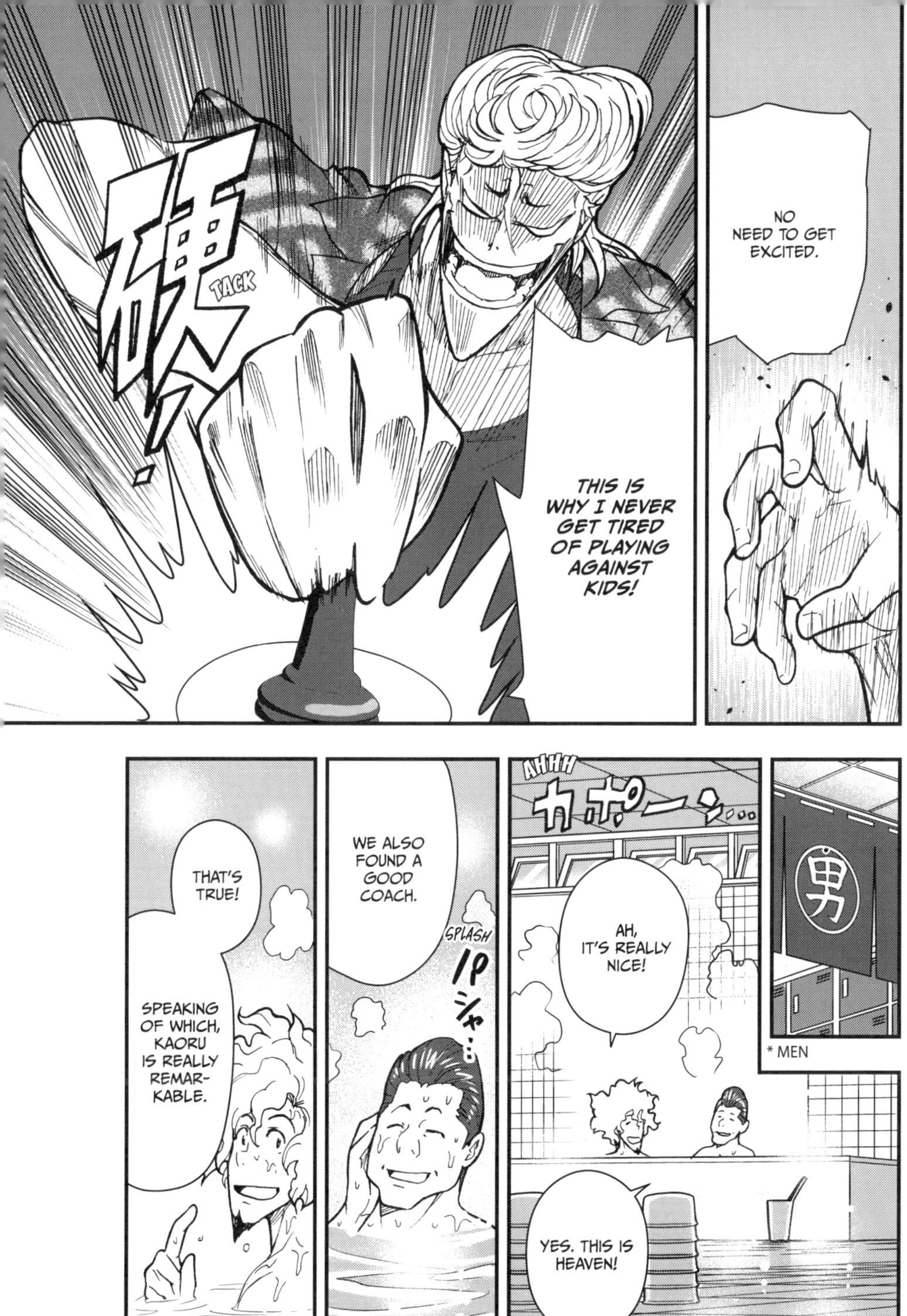
NO NEED TO GET EXCITED.
硬
TACK
THIS IS WHY I NEVER GET TIRED OF PLAYING AGAINST KIDS!
男
* MEN
AHHH
カポーン
AH, IT'S REALLY NICE!
YES. THIS IS HEAVEN!
WE ALSO FOUND A GOOD COACH.
SPLASH
パシャ
THAT'S TRUE!
SPEAKING OF WHICH, KAORU IS REALLY REMARKABLE.

HE DID A CHESS PILGRIMAGE AROUND THE WORLD!

YES, IT'S UNBELIEVABLE.

ちゃぽん…
SPLASH

WE CAN COUNT ON HIM!

AH...

I ALSO HEARD THE SCHOOL HE COACHED WON THE NATIONAL CHAMPIONSHIP BEFORE!

WHAT IS IT, KIDDO?

COME ON... RELAX.

HM...

AH...

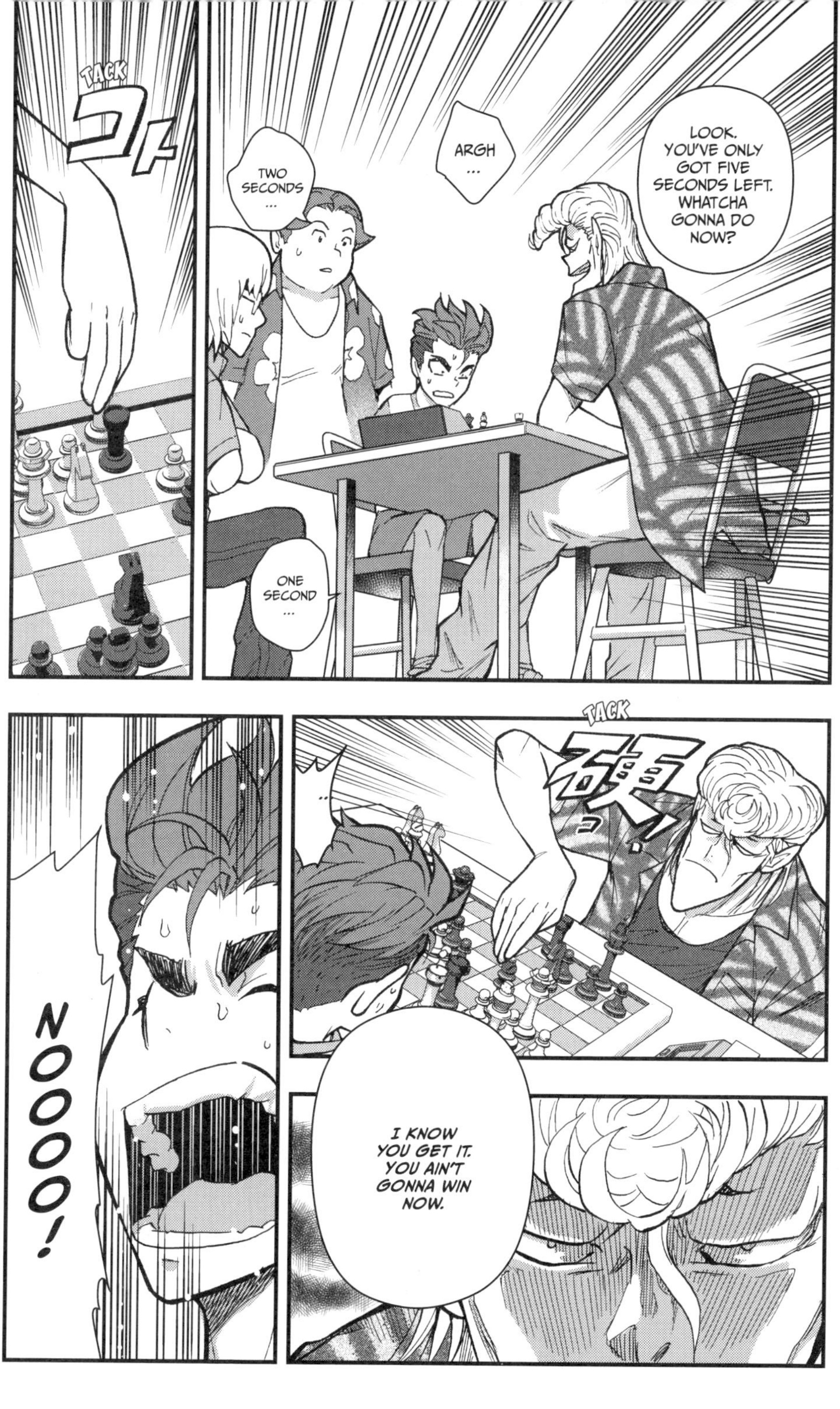
LOOK. YOU'VE ONLY GOT FIVE SECONDS LEFT. WHATCHA GONNA DO NOW?
ARGH ...
TWO SECONDS ...
TACK
コト
ONE SECOND ...
TACK
硬
...
I KNOW YOU GET IT. YOU AIN'T GONNA WIN NOW.
NOOOOO!

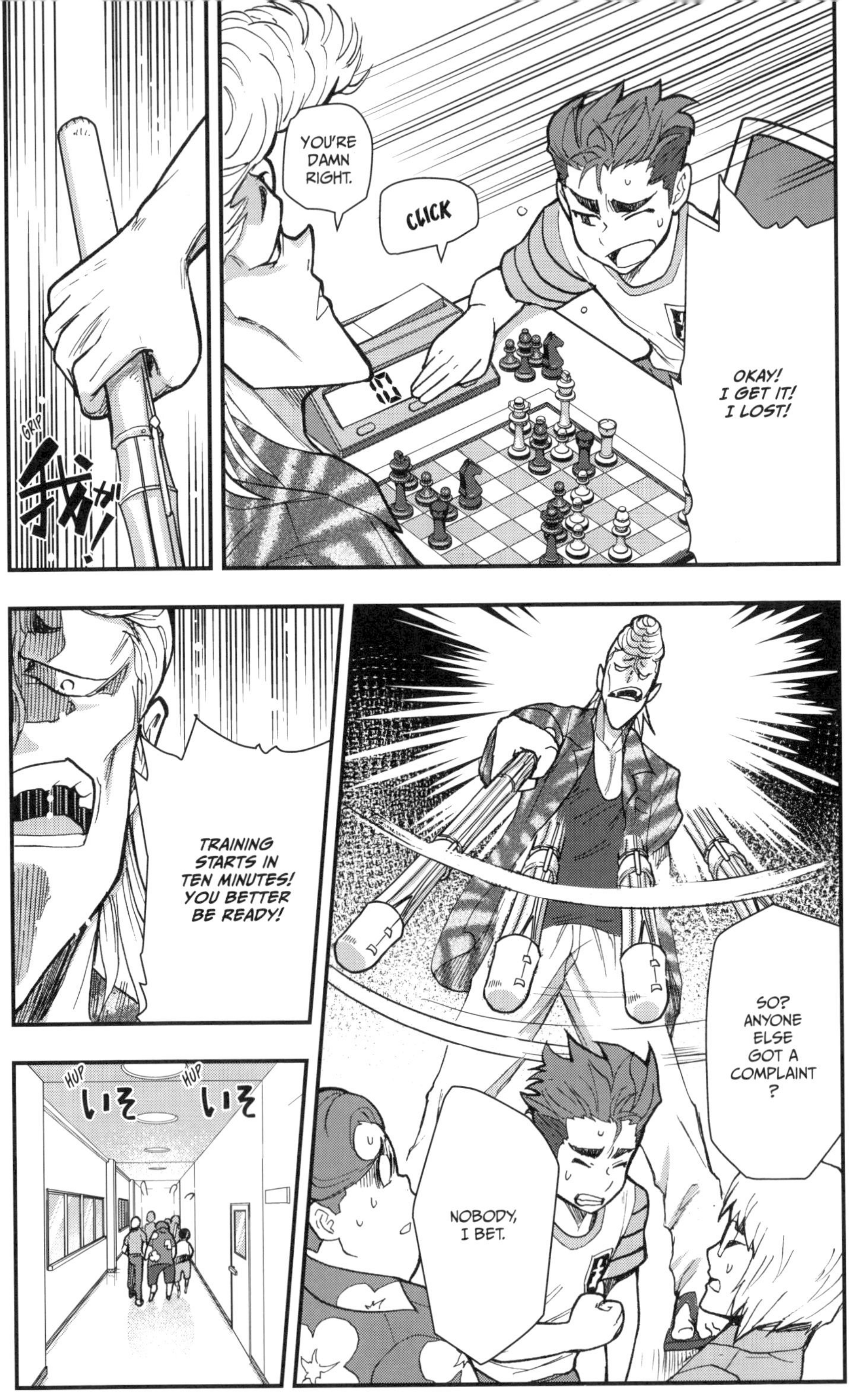
YOU'RE DAMN RIGHT.
CLICK
GRIP
我ガ!
OKAY! I GET IT! I LOST!
TRAINING STARTS IN TEN MINUTES! YOU BETTER BE READY!
SO? ANYONE ELSE GOT A COMPLAINT?
NOBODY, I BET.
HUP
いそ
HUP
いそ

THINGS ARE GONNA GET SERIOUS NOW.

HEH HEH...

SHLACK

...

HE'S A COACH. YOU SHOULD HAVE KNOWN YOU'D HAVE NO WAY TO WIN.

YOU'RE NOT ON THE SAME LEVEL AT ALL.

GIMME A BREAK.

DON'T WORRY ABOUT IT.

THINGS ARE GONNA GET SERIOUS NOW.

YEAH.

YES?

HELLO!

IT DOESN'T HURT TO TRY, RIGHT?

HUH? FOR US?

I HAVE A DELIVERY FOR THE ISS MEMBERS.

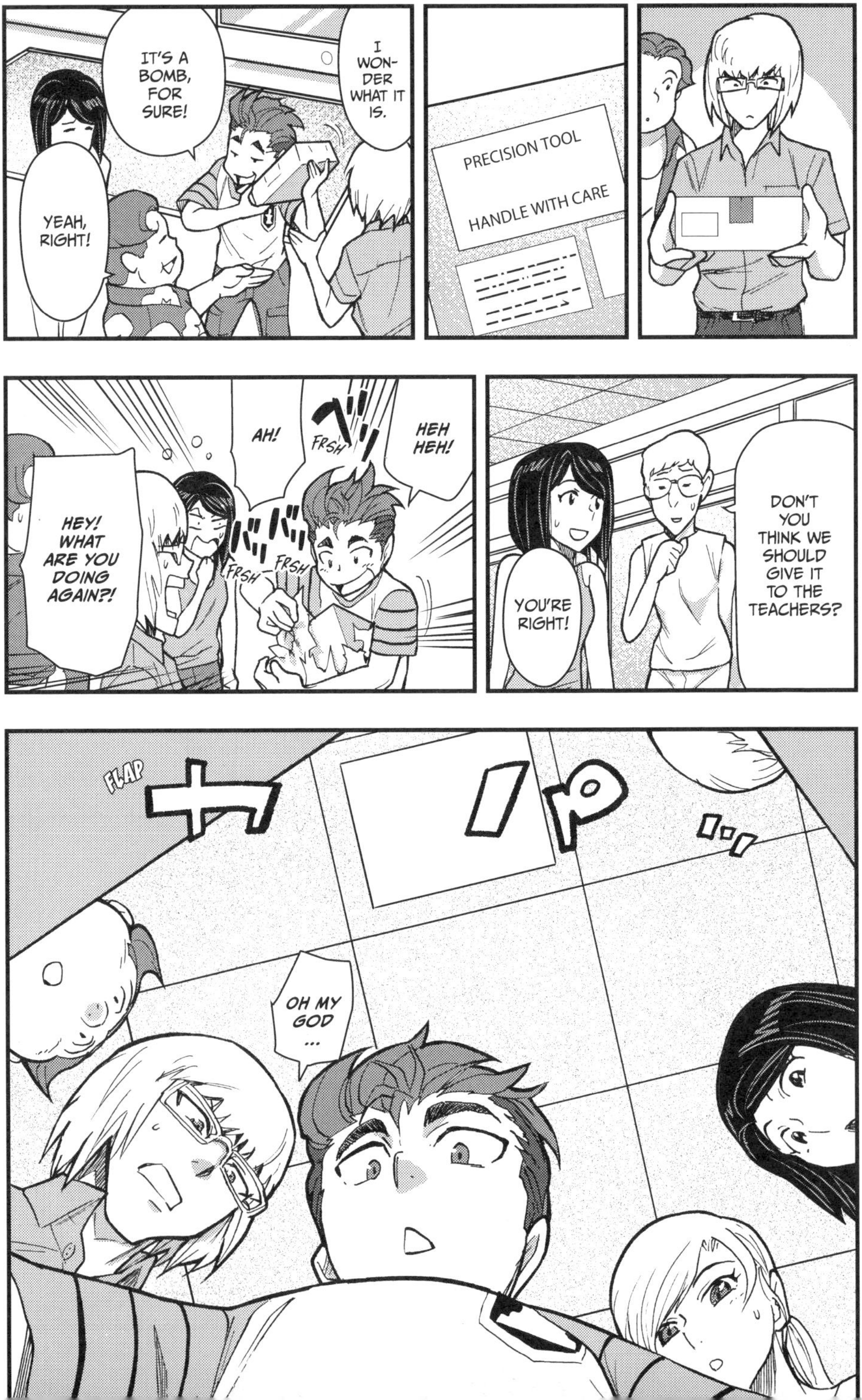
PRECISION TOOL
HANDLE WITH CARE
I WONDER WHAT IT IS.
IT'S A BOMB, FOR SURE!
YEAH, RIGHT!
DON'T YOU THINK WE SHOULD GIVE IT TO THE TEACHERS?
YOU'RE RIGHT!
HEH HEH!
FRSH
AH!
FRSH
FRSH
HEY! WHAT ARE YOU DOING AGAIN?!
FLAP
OH MY GOD ...

WHAT...

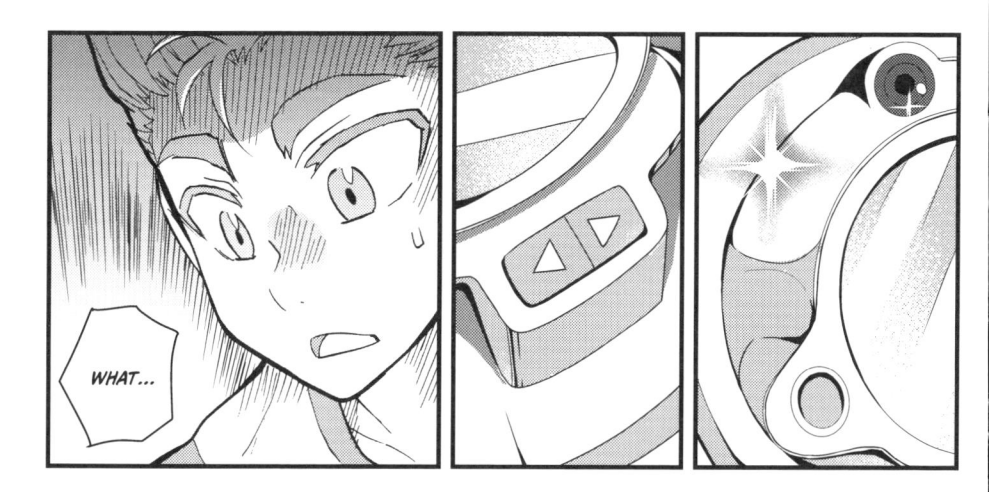

DOOM

...THE HECK IS THIS?

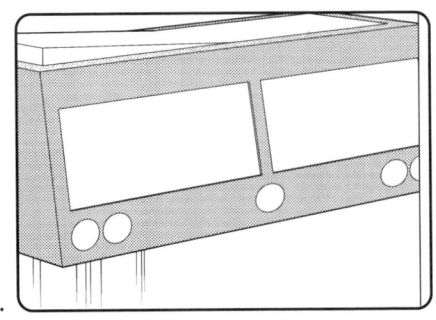

THE GAME WILL CONTINUE...

Written by Cédric Biscay and drawn by manga artist Daitaro Nishihara, Blitz is overseen and sponsored by none other than Garry Kasparov!

"I have always devoted myself to democratizing chess by any means possible. This is a unique opportunity to do so, especially in Japan, where the game is not as popular as Shogi. If you wish to communicate efficiently, you have to use the target audience's language. In a way, manga is the mother tongue of many young people. That is why Cédric's invitation seemed to be the perfect opportunity to promote chess towards a new public, by using a media that is both visual and dynamic."

Garry Kasparov

AFTERWORD
INTUITION

Tom is now sure of it. A particular phenomenon took place within him. He made a move in a single second! However, will he be able to replicate such a mental state? Is it even possible to play like that on a regular basis? How can he remember it? How can he recapture the magic of that amazing chess-related moment?

Following the finals game against Kou the cheater, Tom knows he has to calm himself first. He has to be as serene as humanly possible, no matter what, just like Harmony was calm against Riko. Tom actually explains that to his neurologist. He is able to play well when he is in a quiet place, and also when he is not hungry and angry.

The doctor then gives him precious advice. Tom will have to prepare a routine, which he can go through before each game. He could listen to a song that calms him, for example. Tom could make a habit of it, so he can concentrate only by listening to said song.

IN THAT CASE, YOU SHOULD PREPARE A ROUTINE YOU COULD USE TO FOCUS.
A ROUTINE?

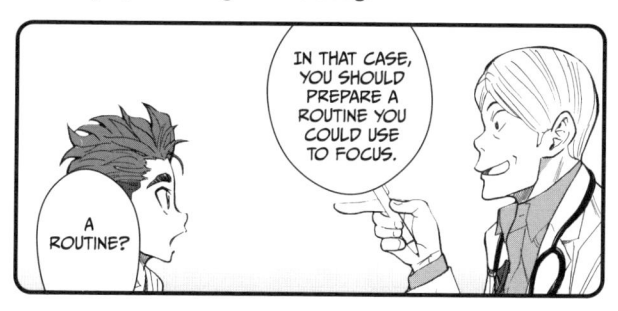

The process explained by the neurologist is the concept of "anchoring". It is a simple and natural process in which you combine an internal state (in this case, calmness) to a stimulus or an external situation (in this case, the song). Triggering the stimulus again is enough to make the mind experience the same state associated to the trigger.

LIKE: "IF I LISTEN TO THIS SONG, I'LL BE CALM".
OR: "I'LL BE RELAXED AFTER DRINKING SOME WATER."
YOU COULD FIND A ROUTINE LIKE THAT FOR WHEN-EVER YOU NEED TO FOCUS.

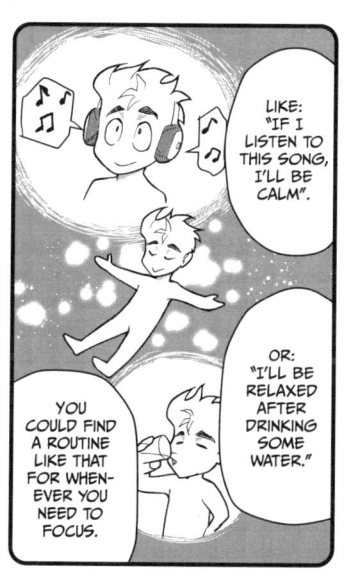

"Anchors" can be auditory, visual, kinesthetic, olfactory or gustatory. You know anchoring too, and you even use it without being particularly aware of it. Did you used to breathe in the scent of your comforter or hug it to soothe yourself? Do you use a particular move to boost your confidence at the moment?

You can create an anchor any time you need a certain resource. To feel more determined, you could anchor that emotion to the feeling of your fingers on a coarse yet soft page of this manga. That page could be showing Tom winning a game, for example.

And if you wanted to feel more serene, you could touch the soft cover of the second volume, which showcases Harmony.

Our brain and body communicate to help us in any possible situation.

FWISH
ZAZEN MEDITATION ISN'T A PUNISHMENT. IT'S SOMETHING WE DO OF OUR OWN FREE WILL.
BY MEDITATING, YOU CAN TRANSFORM THE RAGING SEA INSIDE YOU INTO A CALM, STILL OCEAN.

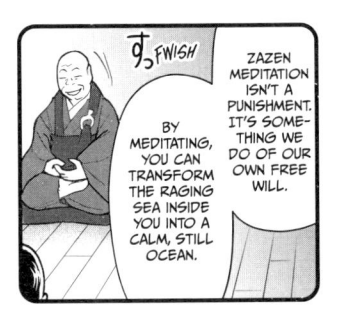

Teachers Doyle and Soumillon are both aware of this. Preparation isn't solely reliant on playing chess. It is also reliant on a healthy lifestyle. And meditation is one of its tools. One of the best, even.

Meditation is a way to help us be, feel and live things through ourselves. It is also a behavior. The word meditation is derived from the Latin word meditatio, which means focusing one's attention on something of one's choice: a task to complete, something happening inside oneself, etc. The objective is to focus that attention back when other thoughts, emotions and feelings try to interrupt it.

Meditation is at the heart of many spiritual practices, like Zen Buddhism, as well as other, more recent forms. One of those forms is full consciousness meditation. It is the focus of many therapies in the West.

Here is the simplest form of meditation that you can use any time you want to center yourself: breathing through the nose, inhale and then exhale naturally, without changing your breathing. Observe your breathing. The way the air enters and exists through your nostrils. Observe yourself.

The monk Yamada is absolutely right. The goal of meditation is not to stop thinking, but to watch the clouds pass by instead.

Developing intuition is another powerful effect of meditation. The two are closely tied to each other. Remember, intuition means to observe carefully, with intent. To grasp immediately and contemplate.

Since the 1960s, numerous scientific studies demonstrated the benefits of meditation and its close ties to intuition. Many studies proved that meditation experts achieve great results in intuition tests. By using electroencephalography and magnetic resonance imaging, it has been shown that meditative and intuitive states generate similar brain functionality. These two states particularly influence the intensity of alpha waves, reminiscent of peaceful conscious state. They also increase the synchronization of brain waves between parts of the brain that are very far from each other. Meditation and intuition push our brain to function fully and broadly, as a whole!

Moreover, studies have recently been conducted on high-level chess players in Japan, and they prove that last point exactly.

By playing a game intensely, or by meditating through it fully, for lack of a better word, Tom has spontaneously experienced the intuitive phenomenon. He only needs to replicate it whenever he wants, with the help of meditation. And it most certainly looks like the tool he just got will help him too.

Intuition and practice are only just beginning!

Alexis Champion

Alexis Champion

Alexis Champion has a doctorate in computer science, with a specialization in artificial intelligence. Over a dozen years, he has been a researcher, then a computer projects director in public and private laboratories, as well as in service companies.

Alexis is also the founder and direction of iRiS Intuition. It is a company dedicated to the use, the development and the scientific research of intuition. Since 2008, iRiS has been active in various fields, such as manufacturing, banking and finance, archaeology and history, energy, law, management and even the arts. The purpose of iRiS is to study decision-making in uncertain or urgent situations, creativity and innovation.

The areas that Alex focuses on are mainly the cooperative use of reasoning and intuition, research on perception and consciousness, the differences between humans and machines and their collaboration, as well as the perfection of psychological and cognitive abilities of human beings.

Garry Kasparov

Born in 1963 in Baku, in Azerbaijan, Garry Kasparov first became champion of the U18 chess tournament of the USSR at the age of twelve.

At 17, he won the title of the U20 world championship. In 1985, at 22, he became known worldwide as the youngest chess champion in history.

He defended his title five times, in a legendary game series against his greatest rival, Anatoly Karpov.

Kasparov broke Bobby Fischer's record in 1990, and his record was unbeaten until 2013.

His famous games against IBM's Deep Blue supercomputer in 1996-97 have played a major role in the introduction of artificial intelligence in the world of chess.

How to practice Zen meditation

Sit down in Zazen position (for Zen meditation) to regulate your body, your breathing and your mind. (Warning: do not use this position if it hurts your knees).

1. Prepare your meditation cushions.

2. Place your right foot on your left thigh.

3. Place your left foot on your right thigh.

4. Align your legs properly.

Tip #1:

Place a large and thick cushion on the floor. Take another cushion, with the same size and thickness as a regular one, then fold it in two and place on the back end of the larger cushion. Sit on the smaller cushion by letting your knees rest on the larger one.

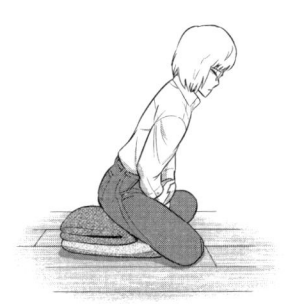

Tip #2:

Once your legs are crossed, center your back by slightly swinging left and right to reduce curvature. You can then lean forward from your hips by keeping your back straight. Raise your chest in a vertical position with your waist leaning forward and the small of your back slightly rounded.

5. Lean forward, then straighten yourself and push your waist forward (by keeping your back as straight as possible).

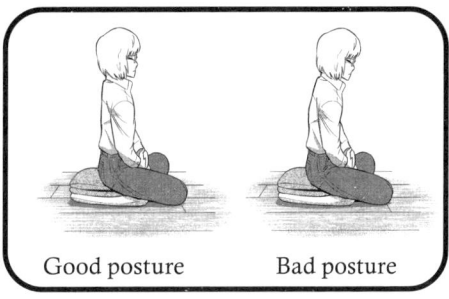

Good posture   Bad posture

Place your hands in the cosmic mudra position (with your left hand on your right palm, and your thumbs touching slightly).

Tip #3:

To achieve the full lotus position, place your right foot on your left thigh, then your left foot on your right thigh (or vice-versa). Push your feet towards your chest as much as possible. For the half lotus position, either place your right foot on your left thigh, or your left foot on your right thigh.

Tip #4:
Keep your eyes open when practicing Zazen meditation.

Keep your eyes open when practicing Zazen meditation.

Keep your head fully straight by tucking in your chin. Fix your gaze on the floor, a couple of meters ahead of you. By doing that, your eyes will naturally assume the half-open meditation position of bodhisattva. Do not close your eyes completely. It encourages passiveness and your mind will wander. Once you are seated properly, breathe through your nose slowly and gently. Count from one to ten between every exhalation, and then start over. This will help you achieve peace of mind.

6. Sit in the full lotus position.

Variants

Half lotus position

Zazan meditation on a chair

For people who have issues with the full lotus position, it is possible to sit in half louts position (one foot on the opposing thigh) or on a chair.

We would like to specifically thank the Institute For Zen Studies (https://www.zenbunka.or.jp), for allowing us to use its documentation on how to practice Zen meditation in the best conditions.

Special thanks to the great master Soushou Yamada, who agreed to make an appearance in volume 3 of Blitz as himself. This means a lot to us.

Sôshô Yamada

He is a Japanese Zen Buddhist monk, and the superior of the Shinju-an. He conducts the religious services of the Daitoku-ji school of the Rinzai branch, one of the three branches of Japanese Zen Buddhism.

Born in 1954 in the prefecture of Fukui, Sôshô Yamada became a monk in 1966 under the supervision of Soubin Yamada, the former superior of Shinju-an.

After getting his degree from the University of Hanazono in 1976, he joined the specialized dojo of Daitoku-ji, where he will study for ten years.

Back in Shinju-an, he will become its 27th superior, and he will direct the religious services of the Daitoku-ji school of the Rinzai branch.

He is currently working on a painting project for the sliding doors (fusuma) of the Shinju-an, which is a historic undertaking. It is actually the first time that the sliding doors will be repainted since their creation, many centuries ago. To accomplish this revolutionary task, Master Soushou Yamada engaged the help of manga artists, anime producers and video game art directors for illustrating the fusuma of his temple, thus putting the spotlight on his project.

Master Yamada hopes this fusuma illustration project will convince more people to visit the temple.

THE MONTE-CARLO CASINO

© IWA / Shibuya Productions

As the first European casino, the Monte-Carlo Casino was founded by François Blanc, with the presence of Prince Charles III and his son Albert, in May 1858.

This casino is one of the prime examples of Belle Époque architecture, which is inseparable from the reign of Emperor Napoleon III.

The idea originated from Prince Charles III.

Playing in the Monte-Carlo Casino is an art! As an essential destination to all the biggest high rollers on the planet, the Monte-Carlo Casino offers a remarkable experience centered on the ultimate gambling luxury. This experience combines thrill of the game, shows, food and shopping.

The Casino Atrium is the entrance to the unique Gambling universe, à la Monte-Carlo. It hosts shows and spectacular artistic installations open to all people of all ages, while also giving them the chance to relax at Café de la Rotonde.

The Renaissance room and its slots are available freely and during the whole day on the itinerary. It is the perfect opportunity to succumb to the gambling experience of the legendary Monte-Carlo Casino.

The Europe and Amérique rooms offer various game tables, like the famous French roulette, slot machines, two restaurants known as Le Train Bleu and Le Salon Rose, a bar lounge and shows for a royal experience befitting of 007. The players can take a break in the comfort of the adjoining terrace and its Belle Époque charm.

Originally crafted as a literary salon, La Salle Blanche and its mosaic-studded bar is reserved to members of My Monte-Carlo, starting from the Gold status. These hardened high rollers can enjoy the game tables of Punto Banco, Black Jack, Roulettes and Poker Texas Hold 'em Ultimate. Smokers can also enjoy a spectacular view of the Mediterranean on a terrace equipped with game tables.

As a true jewel inherited from the Belle Époque, the Monte-Carlo Casino is the perfect place where dreams, pleasure and beauty reign supreme for over 150 years.

It is impossible to talk about the Casino without mentioning the most famous of spies, agent 007, AKA James Bond. Two movies of the series were shot at the casino: Never Say Never Again in 1983, and Goldeneye in 1995. In these movies, James Bond, played respectively by Sean Connery and Pierce Brosnan, goes through the Médecin room to sit at his game table.

However, the Casino has served as a setting for other movies, ever since 1936!

Here are some of the more famous ones. First off, there was *Bay of Angels*, produced in 1964 with Jeanne Moreau as the leading actress. In 2004, things got livelier with the talented robbers George Clooney and Brad Pitt in *Ocean's Twelve*. Laughter was abound in the comedy *Coco*, produced in 2008 with Gad Elmaleh, followed by the animated movie *Madagascar 3* in 2009, and *Turf* in 2011, with Alain Chabat.

CHESS GLOSSARY

Adjusting
This rule allows a player to adjust a piece on the board without playing it. By saying "J'adoube" (meaning "I adjust" in French), the player avoids any misunderstanding with the touch-move rule.

Blitz
A fast-paced game played with a clock, where each player has less than ten minutes. If increments are used, each player has less than three minutes and two seconds to make a move. If increments are not used, each player has less than five minutes to make a move. "Blitz" means "lightning" in German.

Check
A situation where a player threatens the opposing king with a piece (by implying to capture it with the next move). Players cannot check their own king. To deal with a check, the player can move the king, put a piece between the king and the attacker, or capture the attacking piece.

Checkmate
A situation where the opposing king is in danger but cannot avoid capture. This ends the game.

Chessboard
A square board consisting of 64 squares and used to play chess. "On the board" indicates games played in a classic tournament conditions, as opposed to correspondence chess, online chess and analysis.

Deep Blue
A supercomputer created by IBM and specialized in chess. It managed to beat Garry Kasparov in 1997, after losing to him in 1996.

Defense
An opening selected by Black at the start of the game. It also describes a move used to parry an attack.

Deflection
A tactic that forces an opposing piece out of its defensive position.

Diagonal
A straight line composed of squares of the same color. The squares are linked by their angles. For example, the "great diagonal" a1-h8 (or a8-h1).

Diagram
A sketch that represents a position on the board at a given time. That position is usually important or decisive.

Doubled pawns
Two pawns of the same color on the same column.

Draw
A situation where neither player is able to get the better of the other one. The score point is divided between the two: 0.5 point for each.

Major piece
The Rook or the Queen. Also called "heavy piece".

Mate
Abbreviation of "checkmate".

Minor piece
The Knight or the Bishop. Also called "light piece".

Piece
Every battle unit is a piece: the pawns and the bigger pieces (the King, the Queen, the Rook, the Bishop and the Knight).

Pinned piece
A piece that cannot move without putting a bigger piece in danger.

Resigning
A player can resign. The game is then over and it will of course count as a loss for the resigning player. Games often end with a player resigning because it is impossible to continue playing in a hopeless situation.

Round
A set in a chess tournament. In regular tournaments with a classic rhythm, there is one round per day. In blitz, numerous rounds can happen in one day, since blitz tournaments only last for that amount of time

Stalemate
A situation where the player who is supposed to make a move is unable to make a legal one, while they are also not in check. The game ends in a draw.

Touch-move rule
A rule which states that a player has to move a piece if they touch it (if possible). The move is considered complete if the player puts a piece on a square and releases it. If the player touches the opponent's piece, they have to take it.

BASIC ANNOTATIONS FOR A CHESS GAME

+ check

++ double check

checkmate

! good move

!! brilliant move

!? interesting move

?! dubious move

? bad move

?? blunder

+- decisive advantage for White

+/- clear plus for White

+= slight plus for White

= even position

=+ slight plus for Black

-/+ clear plus for Black

-+ decisive advantage for Black

GAME ANALYSIS: RIKO V. HARMONY, CHAPTERS 19-20

(*All of the moves are shown, but only the important ones are analyzed.)

Black starts the clock and White starts the game.

1. d4 d6

2. c4 e5

3. Nf3 Qe7 : A very interesting move that allows the Queen exchange via dxe5 dxe5.

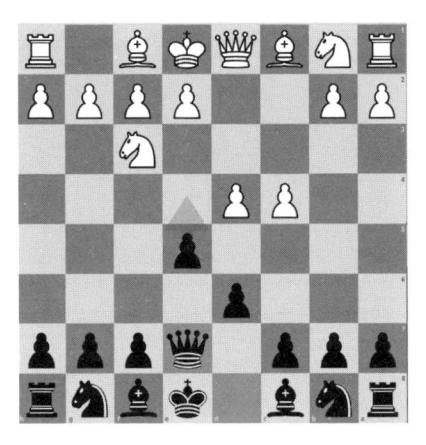

4. Nc3 Nf6

5. Bg5 c6

6. c5 exd4 : After c5, White is much more aggressive and is ready to duke it out!

7. cxd6 Qxd6

8. Qxd4 Qxd4

9. Nxd4 Be7

10. e4 h6

11. Bf4 Bb4

12. f3 0-0

13. 0-0-0 Na6? : We usually say: "A Knight on the rim is dim" to teach children never to put their pieces on the sides. There is a little trick here: Black allows themselves to get eaten by the Bishop on f1 to open columns B and C, which opens the path to attack the White king.

14. Bxa6 bxa6

15. Nxc6 Bxc3

16. bxc3 Be6 : After this move, Black has accomplished their objective: opening columns B and C to attack the White king.

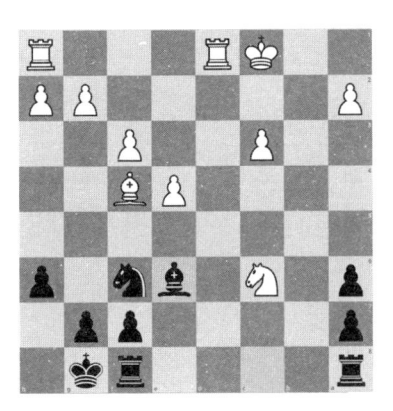

17. Kb2 Kh7 : A necessary move. If Rfc8 had been played instead, White could have made Ne7+, allowing them to do a fork and capturing our Rook on c8.

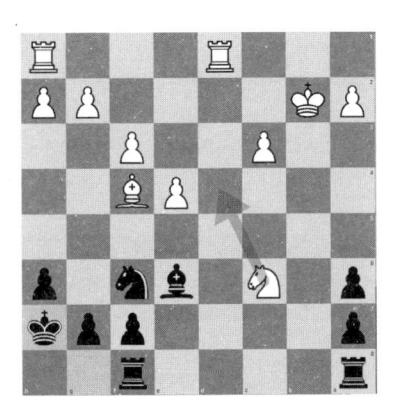

18. Ka3 Rfc8 (after Ka3): A first mistake from White, which leaves the pawn on c3 defenseless.

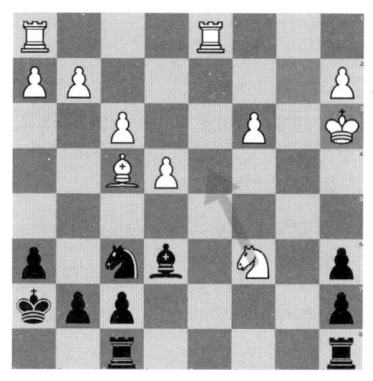

19. Nd4 Rxc3+

20. Kb2 Rc5 : In this position, White has four pawns against three on one side, and one pawn against two doubled pawns on the other. Doubled pawns are usually a weakness because they are hard to move and defend. In this example, Black has doubled pawns, but they compensate that weakness by having columns B and C open, which would allow them to attack the White king.

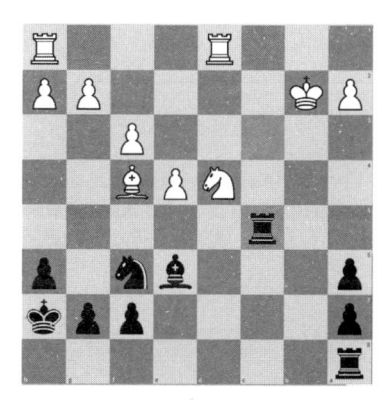

21. Rd2 Rac8

22. Nxe6 fxe6

23. Rhd1 g5

24. Be3 R5c7

25. Bd4 Kg6

26. Be5 Rc5

27. Bd4 R5c7

28. Be5 Rb7+ : After repeating two moves (Rc5 and Rc7), Black refuses to repeat a third one (which would mean a draw) and attempts to turn things in their favor.

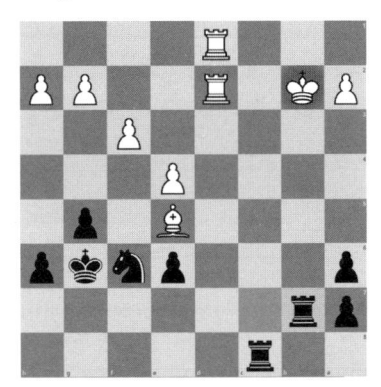

29. Ka1 Rb5

30. Bd4 e5

31. Bb2 a5

32. Rd6 Rc2 Rd6 : This was a blunder after Harmony's move (Rc2). Black takes initiative and starts a lot of counterplay by attacking the bishop on b2, but also the White pawns on g2 and h2.

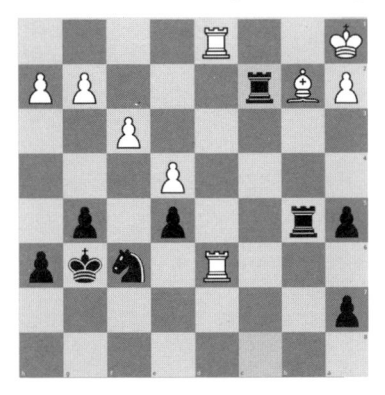

33. Rb1 Rxg2

34. Re6 a4 : Harmony makes a blunder by letting her opponent play Bxe5, which allows them to take the pinned knight on f6!

35. Rxe5 Rxe5 : Now under pressure, Riko does not find an opening and prefers to exchange pieces. The tides turn in favor of Harmony who has much more active pieces.

36. Bxe5 Nd7

37. Bg3 Nc5

38. Rb5 Nd3

39. a3 h5

40. Ra5 h4

41. Bc7 Rc2

42. Rxa7 Nc5

43. Bd6 Nb3+

44. Kb1 Rd2

45. e5 Rxh2

46. e6 Re2

47. e7 Nd2+

48. Kc1 Nc4

49. Bc5 h3

50. Ra8 h2

51. Rh8 Kf7

52. Rf8+ Kg7

53. Bd4+ Kg6

54. Rg8+ Kf7 : With their position still compromised, White makes their last mistake of the game by letting Black take the e pawn and leading the h2 pawn to a promotion.

55. Rg7+ Ke8

56. Bc5 h1= Q+ : The mate will be inevitable after Bg1 and Qxg1#.

Game references for Blitz, volume 3

Chapters 19-20
Riko v. Harmony game
Pytou v. Nikame (lichess.org 2020)

Chapters 21-22-23
Tom v. Kou game
Noelajoyce1512 v. Tygs (lichess.org 2020)

Chapter 22
Harmony v. Shindo game
JM Rapaire v. Pinocchio55 (lichess.org 2020)

Marius v. Mikami game
Timking v. FM ChickenElephant (lichess.org 2020)

Anne v. Tanosaki game
Agnalap 509 v. JM Rapaire (lichess.org 2020)

Laurent v. Tamachi game
Mikhail Tal v. Alexander Koblents (chessgames.com Riga 1961)

Chapter 25
Tom v. Kaoru game
JM Rapaire v. Hakimovf (lichess.org 2020)

Barely a year since the release of volume 1 and we are already on volume 3. It's crazy! These last few months have been very special for everyone. Let's all have fun in what we do. Good reading!

Cédric Biscay
@CédricBiscay

Special thanks to :
Garry Kasparov
Kosta Yanev
Dasha
Mariana
Yuma Shinano
Toru Nakayama
Alexis Champion
Dolly Sananes Bascou
Marie Ducruet
Master Sôshô Yamada
Monte-Carlo Société des Bains de Mer

DOWNLOAD THE GAME FOR FREE!

BLITZ

All rights of translation, adaptation and reproduction are reserved for all countries.
© IWA / Shibuya Productions
www.shibuya-productions.com

original idea: CÉDRIC BISCAY
illustrator: DAITARO NISHIHARA
written by: CÉDRIC BISCAY & TSUKASA MORI
editorial direction: YASUHARU SADAIE

coordination: DOMINIQUE LANGEVIN
translation and lettering: STUDIO MAKMA

cover illustration: DAITARO NISHIHARA
colorization: HERVÉ TROUILLET
counsel: JEAN-MICHEL RAPAIRE, STÉPHANE BRESSAC

FOR ABLAZE
managing editor RICH YOUNG
editor KEVIN KETNER
assistant editor AMY JACKSON
designers RODOLFO MURAGUCHI
& JULIA STEZOVSKY

BLITZ VOL 3. Published by Ablaze Publishing, 11222 SE Main St. #22906 Portland, OR 97269. BLITZ © IWA / Shibuya Productions. All rights reserved. Ablaze and its logo TM & © 2023 Ablaze, LLC. All Rights Reserved. All names, characters, events, and locales in this publication are entirely fictional. Any resemblance to actual persons (living or dead), events or places, without satiric intent is coincidental. No portion of this book may be reproduced by any means (digital or print) without the written permission of Ablaze Publishing except for review purposes. Printed in China. This book may be purchased for educational, business, or promotional use in bulk.
For sales information, advertising opportunities and licensing email: info@ablazepublishing.com

10 9 8 7 6 5 4 3 2 1

Publisher's Cataloging-in-Publication data

Names: Biscay, Cédric, author. | Mori, Tsukasa, author. |
Nishihara, Daitaro, artist. | Kasparov, G. K. (Garri Kimovich), contributor.
Title: Blitz, vol. 3 / writers: Cedric Biscay & Tsukasa Mori; artist:
Daitaro Nishihara; featuring Garry Kasparov.
Description: Portland, OR: Ablaze, LLC., 2023.
Identifiers: ISBN: 978-1-68497-185-5
Subjects: LCSH Chess—Comic books, strips, etc. | Kasparov, G. K. (Garri Kimovich)—
Comic books, strips, etc. | Graphic novels. | BISAC COMICS & GRAPHIC NOVELS / Manga / General
Classification: LCC PN6790.B43 .B57 v. 1 2022 | DDC 741.5—dc23

/ablazepub @AblazePub @AblazePub

www.ablaze.net
To find a comics shop in your area go to:
www.comicshoplocator.com

STOP!

THIS IS THE BACK OF THE BOOK!

This manga collection is translated into English, but arranged in right-to-left reading format to maintain the artwork's visual orientation as originally drawn and published in Japan. Start in the upper right-hand corner and read each word balloon and panel right-to-left.